THE
MINERS
STRIKE
BACK

For the miners

THE MINERS STRIKE BACK

KEVIN DICKS

y Lolfa

Cover image: Olwen Fowler/iStock
Cover design: Olwen Fowler

ISBN: 978 1 80099 432 4

Published and printed in Wales
on paper from well-maintained forests by
Y Lolfa Cyf., Talybont, Ceredigion SY24 5HE
e-mail ylolfa@ylolfa.com
website www.ylolfa.com
tel 01970 832 304

Coed Mawr Allotments

* Coed Mawr (English – Big Wood)
Coed pronounced as 'coyd', and Mawr rhymes with 'hour'.

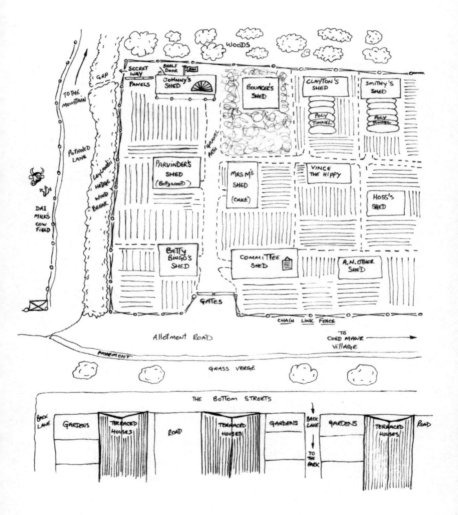

ONE

THE REDISCOVERY OF COAL

Johnny the Cutter

'Perhaps it's the lad who burned his house down,' said Mrs M over a tightly clutched clipboard while surveying the vandalised corner of Betty Bingo's plot.

Johnny squatted like a frontier scout and prodded Reebok tracks in the soil. 'It could be.'

'He sleeps rough in the park and carries a dirty sleeping bag around with him,' continued Mrs M. 'Practically wears the filthy thing.'

'The park,' said Johnny, as if uttering the word and sciatica were one and the same thing.

'Or it could be a malicious thug out to ruin our chances of winning a third consecutive allotment championship? Yes, that's it, sabotage.'

With a twinge of back pain Johnny stood up. 'No, it's a kid. I can tell by the trainers, the fu ... flipping waster.'

Mrs M righted an overturned compost bin. 'It's the second time this week we've had a visit from the vandals. Betty will be upset. She's worked hard to make her plot one of our best.'

Johnny scanned the west perimeter fence but found no

evidence of damage. Outside the chain links, a lush leylandii hedge windbreak at three metres high and two metres deep provided ample cover for potential intruders. 'The waster must know a way through our windbreak and jumps the fence in the early hours. Either that, or he's mastered the art of teleportation.'

Mrs M, Coed Mawr Allotment Association's officious secretary, had interrupted Johnny with news of the break-in while he was contemplating the particulars of his shed extension. Eager to return to his work-in-progress, he marched off Betty Bingo's plot and onto the gravel path. 'Someone will have to catch the waster in the act.'

Mrs M followed in his wake. 'The last time I rang the police they said we should be more vigilant with our own crime prevention. They didn't take it seriously. You'd think by having former police officers on the committee we'd get a better response.'

'Today's police are happy for us do their job for them. Where's that bobby on the beat who'd appear from nowhere to kick my backside up to my shoulder blades whenever I went off the rails as a kid?'

'We must do something or the effort we've put in this year will be for nothing. We'll have no chance of winning.'

'There's always razor wire, machine-gun towers, and regular patrols with snarling dogs.'

'It's an allotment not a prisoner of war camp.'

'It'll deter a sleeping bag carrying arsonist before he gravitates to torching our sheds.'

'My thoughts are along the lines of CCTV.'

'Committee meetings will drag on for months with that one.'

'Talking of things dragging on,' said Mrs M as they neared the WWI shell hole of Johnny's work-in-progress, 'when do you expect to finish your shed extension? It's been weeks.'

'I dug down but couldn't find a clay bottom for the posts, then my back played up and whatever.'

'I hope it's finished soon.'

'It'll be a Rolls-Royce of a shed in no time. Retirement beckons and I'll have more time to get on with it.'

'I don't know if retirement will suit you, Johnny. You like work far too much for your own good.'

'I'm practically retired now. One last day to go after I've used up my leave – and no more packed trains to Cardiff, no more rude policy holders, and no more Clanger Insurance. It's hard to believe I started there when they closed the colliery. I thought I'd give it a go for a couple of months and for my sins it's been twenty-five years.'

'Where does the time go? It seems only yesterday you were a regular at the timekeeper's window, black with coal dust, arguing about your overtime, or was it just to see Julie?'

'Always an excuse to see Julie, but they were happy days in a real job where you could argue face-to-face with a human being about your pay. And fair play, Mrs M, you always put up a good argument.'

The earth under Mrs M's foot collapsed into the hole and she skipped back like a girl playing hopscotch. 'You know if someone fell in this hole during the allotment championship ...'

'... we'll have no chance of winning. I'll get on with it today, if I don't have any more interruptions.'

They were interrupted by a squabble down at the allotment gates. Johnny's daughter and Coed Mawr's only legit mobile hairdresser, Joanne, manhandled her son Jayden out from her decaled 'Joanne the Cutter' Fiat 500 and yanked him by the hoodie up the allotment path.

'Dad!'

Jayden resisted in a tangle of hairdryer flex and curling tongs. 'Let me go!'

Joanne dragged the teenager like a sack of spuds, 'Dad!'

'What?'

'It's Jayden.'

'I can see that. What about him?'

'The swine's been doing that self-harming again.'

'Owww,' cried Jayden as Joanne grabbed his arm.

Johnny's self-restraint eroded the closer they got to him. 'You lazy, good-for-nothing article.'

Faced directly with his nutter of a grandad, Jayden quickly changed pose from rebellious teenager to one of a little boy hiding behind his mum.

Joanne held back the tears. 'I can't handle it any more. He's cut himself down both arms and there's blood splatter all over the bathroom like a crime scene. He's been out all night and reeks of drink and I don't know what.'

'You little bas …' Johnny remembered Mrs M who had turned away from the palaver. 'Mrs M, don't let us keep you. I'm sure there are other tenants to visit with the championship looming on the horizon.'

A relieved Mrs M happily accepted the exit from the Morgan family to-do. 'Three o'clock for a cuppa in the committee shed?'

'Perfect. I'll bring a packet of Welsh cakes.'

After exchanging polite salutations with Joanne and Jayden, Mrs M made her way down the gravel path.

'Go on,' said Johnny when Mrs M got out of earshot.

'I had to drag him to the surgery to get his arms stitched.'

Jayden peeped around his mum. 'It was full of zombies.'

Johnny rolled up a sleeve and pounced at his cowering grandson. 'I'll give you some more.'

'Woah, it's not his fault.' Joanne held them apart. 'I blame his father. If I ever see him again I'll …'

'Let's not talk about his father or you will wind me up. Now what's this got to do with me?'

'I'm worried he'll do it again. Can you keep an eye on him?'

'Babysitting, at his age?'

'Mum, don't set Grandad on me. Everyone in the village knows he's barking mad.'

Johnny swung for Jayden and he hid behind his mum. 'Like I'm the one slicing myself up.'

'Dad, watch your blood pressure and stop getting so angry all the time. Please try to be more sensitive.'

'I can do sensitive.' Johnny picked up a bunch of marigolds from his porch bench. 'I was going to put fresh flowers on your mother's grave later this morning.'

'Dad, I've got appointments all day. Mrs Thomas wants her rinse and I'm already late for half-a-dozen old dears at the rest home. Perhaps you can talk some sense into him because right now he needs a man's hand.' She wiped away a tear. 'I'm sure Mum won't mind if Jayden comes along with you.'

Johnny picked imaginary bugs from the marigolds knowing he was beaten. 'Go on then. Get going. Someone's got to work to keep this waste of brain space in cider and laughing gas.'

Joanne gave him a peck on the cheek. 'Thanks, Dad.'

Johnny scowled at his grandson. 'After we visit your grandmother you can help me with my shed extension.'

'Now, be good for Grandad.' She gave her son a big kiss.

'Gerroff, stop treating me like a little kid.'

'Stop behaving like one then!' screeched Joanne. She left Jayden cowering on the gravel and hurried down the path, retrieving a wayward hairdryer along the way.

'Good on you, my girl.' Johnny thrust the bunch of marigolds onto his grandson and led off to his van. 'Let's go ... waster.'

Jayden the Cutter

The hillside churchyard commanded an impressive view of the small Coed Mawr valley. At the graveside Johnny and Jayden looked down at a vase of fresh orange and yellow marigolds on the plain grave.

Johnny removed his cap. 'It's not much of a headstone for someone who raised thousands of pounds and kept this valley fed and watered all through the worst of the Miners' Strike is it? I've been trying to think of something more elaborate to help people remember what a remarkable woman Julie was. In all our years together I never heard her say a bad word about anyone. She always saw the good in people. Not like me, calling an arsehole an arsehole. We were opposites there. That's why we got on so well.'

Jayden nodded vacantly.

'Your grandmother was as brave as a lioness. She never once complained in those months she soldiered on in pain with the big C. Even at the end when she had all the tubes sticking out of her to keep her alive. I couldn't do it, especially now I've witnessed where it leads to. I'd have to find a way to end it all before it got to that stage. I could never be as brave as she was.'

Johnny tilted his head to the wind as it picked up and put a hand on Jayden's shoulder. 'Hear that?'

Jayden looked around and listened. 'Hear what?'

Johnny smacked him across the face with his cap. 'The sound of your grandmother turning in her grave.'

Jayden ducked from the blows. 'Owww, what's that for? Owww, chill Grandad, Mum said to watch your blood pressure.'

He pulled Jayden face-to-face. 'If you carry on with this nonsense I'll batter you senseless from here to Christmas and you won't ever think of self-harming again.'

'You don't understand.'

'*You* don't understand. Man up. And wise up.'

He released Jayden and the relieved teenager sat down on the path. Johnny had not finished. He picked up a wire bin and emptied the putrid contents over his grandson.

'Have some rotten flowers, wimp.'

'Ugh! They're minging. I'm going to be sick.'

Johnny raised the bin high and bounced it off Jayden's back.

'That fucking hurt then.'

'It was supposed to.'

Jayden crawled away. 'People are looking. Help! Help! He's trying to kill me.'

His cries attracted the attention of several visitors dotted around the gravestones, who although intrigued by the performance, wisely minded their own business.

Johnny retrieved the bin and raised it above his head to strike again. Jayden shrank at the expected blow but it did not arrive as Johnny went rigid with a spasm of back pain. He dropped the bin behind him.

Jayden got to his feet. 'What's the trouble, Grandad?'

'Kids ... kids are the trouble. You can't slap 'em any more when it should be an Olympic sport.'

The Nolan Sisters and the Rediscovery of Coal

Johnny exited his allotment shed with a shovel and put it in Jayden's hands. He stared at the implement.

'You don't even know which end is which.'

'Course I do.'

'Get on with it then. The hole's down there.'

Johnny adopted a supervisory stance as Jayden sulked his way into the hole and clumsily stuck the shovel into the loose earth.

'Get your knee behind it. I want this extension up by the end of the week.'

'A week, I thought you only wanted help today?'

'That was before you aggravated my back.'

'You did it yourself when you hit me with the bin.'

'I'll pay labourers' rates. You'll kiss my flowery backside at the end of the week when you've got cash in your hand.'

'I'm not used to this.'

'Pretend it's a wicked new Xbox game called "Hard Work Never Hurt Any Fucker".'

'It's hurting me.'

'It'll be alright, mun. A young man like you needs proper work, and a few shifts on the shovel will do you the world of good.'

Jayden put the shovel aside, removed his hoodie and threw

it onto the porch rail. Small bloody stitches ran down both arms like the tracks of a Hornby model railway.

The sight of Jayden's self-harming left Johnny speechless for a short while as conflicting emotions bubbled up within him.

Jayden resumed work on the shovel.

Johnny tried to make light of it. 'I bet the nurse wished she'd booked the day off when she set eyes on you this morning.'

His quip met silence.

'Why do you do it?'

'Do what?'

'Cut yourself like that?'

Jayden ignored the question and struggled on with the shovel.

'C'mon, you're not on a shrink's couch, you're in a hole in the ground, in an allotment, with barking-mad Grandad.'

Jayden gave more of the silent treatment.

'I can get philosophical about it if you want. We are nothing more than pubic hairs stuck on the urinal of life, and sooner or later we all get pissed off.'

Jayden pretended not to hear and kept shovelling.

'Is it because your father ran off to Australia with a lap-dancing barmaid all those years ago?'

Jayden intensified his shovelling and Johnny thought he may have hit the mark. He squatted down for a closer word in his ear. 'You're not the only one who wants to kick his head in. Mind you, a lot of his generation left the valley when they shut the collieries. You can't blame them when there's no work up here.'

Jayden kept shovelling.

'Is it because he gave you a girl's name?'

Jayden threw down the shovel. 'It's my girlfriend!'

Johnny stood and nursed another back twinge. 'I knew it.'

'Ex-girlfriend, she dumped me because I'm always rinsed out.'

'It happens when you're short of a few bob.'

Jayden circled his toe in the dirt. 'I introduced her to a mate of mine with a car. She got in, they drove off, and I haven't seen her since, apart from dissing me on Instagram.'

'Some mate. A local boy?'

'Not really a mate, from Trewatkins.'

'Says it all; and cutting yourself will bring her back?'

'It's my way of dealing with it.'

'It doesn't look like "dealing with it" to me.'

'Grandad.'

'Stop worrying, it won't be the first time or the last, at your age girlfriends and boyfriends come and go like buses, so don't go worrying about things like that. We all make mistakes in our relationships. Learn from it, move on and don't look back.'

Jayden circled his toe in the dirt. 'It's doing my head in. Can't get her out of my mind.'

'We've all been there, mun. Before I met your grandmother I was engaged to a girl from Bargoed. We were both stupid kids about your age and it was over before it started. Like you, well not quite like you, I got all cut up when I found out she was still playing the field. Many a time I wished I hadn't met her in that disco in the Seventies. I've often thought I should've stayed at home, watched TV and had a wank over the Nolan Sisters.'

'The Nolan Sisters?'

'As for mates, the best friend a man can ever have is the pound in his pocket. You remember that. And the next time you see your mate's car, give it a good keying down the side. Better his car than your arms, isn't it?'

'Yeah,' said Jayden as if it had only just dawned upon him.

'But don't tell your mum I said, and don't let anyone see you.'

They share a smiling moment until Johnny realised Jayden had stopped work. 'C'mon, nobody told you to stop working.'

Jayden kicked at the dirt. 'It'd be easier without all this lumpy black shiny stuff.'

'What lumpy black shiny stuff?'

'I'll get you a lump.' Jayden picked up a lump of black shiny stuff, 'Catch.'

Johnny caught it, blew away the loose dirt, wiped it down his jeans and held it at eye level. 'Fuck me hooray.'

'What is it, Grandad?'

Johnny felt faint with disbelief. '*What is it, Grandad?* Don't you know coal when you see it?'

'Coal?' said none-the-wiser Jayden.

'That is sad. We've regressed so much in this digital age our own grandchildren can't recognise a piece of coal when they see it.' He buffed a shine to the coal with a sleeve. 'Any more down there?'

'It's everywhere.'

He sprang into the hole like a gymnast, snatched the shovel and dug. 'Let the dog see the rabbit.'

Jayden stood back, impressed by the volume of coal his grandad quickly shifted. 'I thought you had a bad back?'

Johnny stopped shovelling and crouched down. He ran his fingers along a line of coal. 'Look at this.'

'Look at what?'

'This coal seam under the shed, it's incredible. Who'd have thought it? I wonder how deep it goes and where it goes?'

Johnny jumped out of the hole as if from a trampette. 'North-Eye needs to look at this.'

'North-Eye?'

'Don't let anyone see this coal. Bag it up in the potato sacks in my shed.' He hurried onto the gravel path. 'I'm getting North-Eye.'

'Who's North-Eye when he's about?'

'He's our old mining surveyor.'

'Why do you call him North-Eye?'

Johnny broke into a jog and did not want to waste time explaining. 'He's got eyes like Marty Feldman.'

'Who's Marty Feldman when he's about?' said Jayden, but Johnny was running down the gravel path. He watched him run out of the allotment gates and jump into his battered white Ford Transit Courier. The van started with a splutter but took off like a rocket.

'There's nothing wrong with his back,' Jayden muttered as he took his hoodie from the porch rail and sat down on the shed bench. Bagging the coal could wait. He produced a small hunchback spliff from a pocket, sparked it up and Googled on his phone.

'Marty Feld ... whoa!'

North-Eye

North-Eye sat in a shed bursting with mining memorabilia like a bug inside a gigantic industrial orchid. Underground plans, colliery signs, and photographs covered the roof while neat rows of lamp chargers, oil lamps, cap lamps, and vintage black leather helmets lined the side panels. A tripod-mounted theodolite stood sentinel before a framed collection of brass lamp checks in pride of place on the far shed panel.

It appeared to Johnny the old surveyor had grown a large eye since their last meeting as North-Eye squinted through a pair of thick glasses into a hands-free magnifying glass at a small brass disc on his work bench.

'After all those years you spent driving a cutter through the face, district after district, Johnny the Cutter, you of all people should know there were more ways to get maimed or killed working underground than in any other occupation.'

Johnny examined the CCTV warnings and Neighbourhood Watch stickers plastered over the shed door. 'You're making mining sound like a bad thing.'

Moving the magnifying glass aside, North-Eye positioned a number punch onto the brass disc, picked up a hammer and took aim. A pink tongue of concentration crept out of the corner of his mouth.

'I know you have a reputation for being a bit of a nutcase but if you think you can open a coal level, and in a busy allotment of all places, without the tenants, the Coal Authority, the Local Authority, the police and any climate conscious do-gooder or banner-waving eco-activist getting to hear of it, you're completely off your bastard head.'

'Not a coal level. I was thinking more along the lines of a proper colliery with a shaft and some form of winding gear and ...'

North-Eye missed the punch and clouted his thumb with the hammer. 'Owww, you *are* off your bastard head!'

As he shook his throbbing thumb, Johnny picked up and examined the brass disc. 'At least I haven't stooped so low as to forge lamp checks.'

'It's not what you think.'

'There are a lot of gullible collectors out in boot sale land who couldn't tell a tidy lamp check from a dodgy one.'

North-Eye snatched the disc from his hand. 'I'm cleaning a few checks for a mining exhibition in the library.'

'With a hammer and a number punch, that's a funny way of cleaning lamp checks? But you've always had funny ways.' Johnny dug into a pocket and tossed a lump of coal onto the bench. 'It must be fun playing at being a miner out here in your shed but there might be a way for you to be the real deal again.'

North-Eye set the magnifying glass over the coal and gave it a brief examination. 'This is high grade anthracite.'

'You still know what it looks like, then?'

North-Eye opened a drawer and got out a Moleskine notebook. He took a helmet from the rack. 'Let's go see what you've found.'

Taking a Section of Coal

Potato sacks of coal covered the shed porch. Jayden and Johnny looked down into the hole where a helmeted head bobbed about below them. Scoops of debris sporadically flew up as if from a dog burrowing for a long-lost bone. Through a swirl of dust they heard a tap of a rock hammer, the opening and retraction of a tape measure, and the twang of an elastic band against a Moleskine notebook.

'What's he doing?' said Jayden.

Johnny paced around like an expectant father. 'He's taking a section of coal. But don't worry about him, you just keep a look-out for anyone nosing around.'

Jayden shrugged, none the wiser, and kept look-out.

North-Eye stood up, squinted through his thick glasses and showed Johnny his notebook. 'You've got eleven inches of coal; eighth of an inch of shale; two feet of coal; two inches of mudstone ...'

'Mudstone?' said Jayden.

Johnny screwed up his face, 'Muck.'

Jayden shrugged, none the wiser, and kept look-out.

'... thirty-three inches of coal and two inches of shale as a bottom, that's roughly a six-foot seam of good quality.'

'I knew it.' Johnny gave clueless Jayden a celebratory back slap.

North-Eye rubbed his chin in thought. 'It looks like the seam runs under the allotment to the south and into the hillside to the north. Your guess is as good as mine east or west.'

'So if I extend the shed over the hole and shore up the sides, put in a trapdoor and a ladder ...'

'You're not still thinking of working this?'

'It's a Godsend. What's stopping me?'

North-Eye twanged the elastic band on his notebook. 'For one thing, it's against the law.'

'You don't think I'd apply for a licence and all that bollocks.'

'Even if you did you wouldn't get it. The Welsh Government banned all new coal mining operations in Wales.'

'Fuck me hooray, who'd have thought it? Mining banned in Wales by those tinpot AMs in the Senedd. What do they know? The very ground they park their lard arses on in Cardiff Bay was built on coal. Anyway, we won't tell them. We'll keep it quiet.'

'If you work this seam it'll be irresponsible of me not to report you to the Coal Authority. They'll jump all over you anyway if they found out further down the line, and you being you, someone is bound to drop you in it. Their grassing-up phone line is open twenty-four seven.'

An uncomfortable silence descended as the old miners faced off. Johnny put a hand on Jayden's shoulder. 'Jayden, go and put the kettle on. A big cup of tea sorts just about everything.'

Jayden slunk off into the shed.

Johnny picked up and studied a lump of coal. 'I wonder what stance Trading Standards take on forged mining memorabilia, not to mention the police.'

'You wouldn't?'

'Wouldn't I? Then the inevitable questions will arise regarding how you came by your collection in the first place.'

'You wouldn't do that.'

'A lot of stuff got nicked when they shut the colliery. They'll need someone to identify which bits were pinched to build a case.'

'Now hang about, Johnny.'

'The police are keen on historical crimes lately. It's an easy nick. They'd confiscate the lot first mind, everything in your shed including that old theodolite, and your prized check collection only for it all to disappear in a bent copper's car boot to be sold on eBay.'

At the thought of losing his beloved collection, North-Eye clutched his heart. 'OK, you've trumped me, but you don't know what's behind that exposed seam. Drive in ten or twenty feet and you could hit water in old workings, the pressure would go off like a champagne cork, and we'd find you in Dai Milk's cow field impaled on a fence post, like a sausage on a stick, with a big look of *I'm so bastard stupid* on your face.'

'Or it could pinch out.'

'I think it's a pillar of coal holding back flooded old workings. It's highly dangerous and shouldn't be disturbed in any way.'

'I can see where you're coming from,' said Johnny with a laugh. 'We don't want another sinkhole crisis like when the posh houses all but disappeared into old workings.'

North-Eye lived on the far side of Coed Mawr village on Summer View estate, although everyone knew it as the posh houses. At one time it really meant something to the valley inhabitants to live on the Summer View estate. Everyone wanted to live in the posh houses.

That was until the 1980s when sinkholes appeared in the roads and gardens. Old mine workings riddled the estate and it took years to stabilise the properties with countless tons of concrete pumped into the cavities. Pumps, compressors and drilling rigs went up and house values went down. No one wanted to live in the posh houses.

North-Eye kept a stone face. 'It wasn't funny when it happened. People awoke to the sound of their houses splitting in half. They watched their gardens slip into big holes in the ground. I opened my kitchen door and the kitchen wasn't there. The back of the house and garden had gone, cooker, fridge, gnomes, the bastard lot.'

The surveyor's sense of humour failure forced Johnny to change tack. 'Isn't there a map or plan or something?'

'No one knew there were workings under our estate so don't get your hopes up. A hundred and fifty years ago these outcrops of coal were easy to get at and were quickly worked out. No one took care to survey them properly, but I'll have a look anyway.'

'Yes, you will. It's the most exciting thing that's happened to you in years. What if I work the seam the other way, under the allotment?'

'You could still have no end of problems.'

'There'll be less chance of it going off like a champagne cork and getting a fence post up my arse.'

Jayden cheerfully bounced out of the shed and clanked a couple of mugs together. 'How do you like your tea?'

'Milk no sugar for me and a cup for you Jayden. Unfortunately North-Eye can't hang around. He has to visit the library, and who knows where else, to search through drawers of dusty old plans.'

'In that case,' said North-Eye, 'I'll see you when something turns up. In the meantime try and not get yourself or your grandson killed.'

They watched North-Eye stride down the gravel path.

'And North-Eye, keep it quiet.'

With a wave of his notebook North-Eye kept on his way.

'The same goes for you Jayden. Keep it quiet.'

'No worries, but what are we going to do with this coal?'

'We'll store it in the shed for now then sell it at boot sales and around the streets from the van. There are still a few houses with coal fires and multi-fuel burners, and fire pits and chimineas are popular. I'll take a little for expenses but everything else we make is yours.'

'Mine?'

'You're going to be digging it out.'

'I am?'

'I can't, with my back playing up. We'll need more help further along but we'll think about that when we get there.'

The work moved quickly in the next few days. To be free from prying eyes they erected the skin of the shed extension around the hole, allowing them to shore up the sides of the mine shaft unseen. They secured a ladder to the shaft timbers, fashioned a bespoke trapdoor in the floorboards and knitted the roof to the existing shed.

As a finishing touch and without any black paint handy, Johnny chose a navy and yellow paint job like the NCB colliery colours of old. He stood back to admire the handiwork and took time to pride himself on having the best-looking shed at the best-possible location in the top-west corner of the allotment. Not only did his location give him clear sight of the comings and goings down the gravel path at the allotment gates, but also it enjoyed the most delightful views down the Coed Mawr valley.

The last job on the list involved cutting and modifying the fence at the corner concrete post so the links drew like a curtain. Johnny called it his 'secret way' and it led through a hidden gap in the leylandii hedge, out to a potholed lane running between the allotment, and Dai Milk's cow field, a field famed locally for the potency and annual yield of magic mushrooms. The alternative access proved handy when smuggling bags of coal out to Johnny's van parked in the lane before an audience of Dai Milk's curious cud-chewing cows.

Johnny did indeed know of a few houses with coal fires and he and Jayden knocked doors, made sales and took orders. They flogged the remaining bags at a midweek boot sale near Merthyr.

The sales delighted Johnny and he let Jayden know on the drive home. 'That's not bad going for a midweek boot sale and a spin around the village. When we increase our production and get a regular table at Dai Milk's Friday boot sale we'll be flying. Fair play, you've worked hard. What are you going to spend your money on come pay day, skunk and a few Babychams?'

'I want a new trackie and trainers.'

'I'm going to Cardiff at the end of the week. I'll give you a lift down and you can have a man-shop.'

'As long as you pretend you're not with me and …'

'… walk ten paces behind you. Don't worry, I've a few things to do myself.'

'Grandad, there's a couple of bags left in the back of the van.'

'That's the muck left over from the coal. It doesn't burn. No one's going to buy it.'

'Why's it in the van if we can't sell it?'

'You'll find out tomorrow.'

Dances with Pixies

The Coed Mawr Crew were coming down from a banging night in the park completely off their tits on magic mushrooms. Gangly Spider puffed a spliff, unbuttoned his flies and urinated against the colliery monument, a rusty sheave set into graffiti-stained concrete, known as the Old Wheel.

'Pixies!' screamed Slouch leaping out of his filthy sleeping bag.

Spider jumped with fright and pissed on his trainers.

Slouch danced a thigh-slapping Schuhplattler around the Old Wheel in grubby underpants. 'The pixies are biting my legs!'

Spider glared down at his piss-soaked Reeboks. 'Chill, or I'll knock you out.'

Slouch whirled and slapped his way around the rusty

sheave. 'They're crawling up my legs and biting me, get 'em off, Charlie.'

Charlie, wrapped in a hoodie, scarf and with a pair of bug-like mirrored sunglasses and dangling from a wheel spoke like a Goth terrorist, recorded the spittle-laden psychotic episode on a phone.

With another puff, Spider buttoned up. 'Lippo, give Slouch a shake before my head goes and I bang his fucking lights out.'

'I'm on it, bro.' Lippo, a smaller weasel-like clone of Spider jumped to attention and joined Slouch in orbit around the sheave. 'Come here headshot.' Lippo caught Slouch by the scruff and kicked his rump. 'You scoffed all our magics.'

Breaking free from Lippo's hold, Slouch commenced a screeching trouser-less Irish jig.

'What the fuck have you done? I said give him a shake, not kick him up the arse.'

Jayden lay on his back in the damp grass, moping over his ex-girlfriend Chloe. Propping himself up onto an elbow, he watched as Lippo gave Slouch a shake. No good came from it and the screaming spectacle continued. Knackered from working on the shed extension and digging coal, he wished he had spent a night tucked up in bed instead of a night fucked up with the Crew, and now because the noise did his head in, he felt stupid for filling Slouch's sleeping bag with stinging nettles.

Jayden knew what Spider planned next and did not want any part in it. Crawling away on the dewy grass, he got out of sight behind a stand of knotweed. He stood up, wiped his hands down his trackies and peeked back at the Old Wheel where Spider, Lippo and Charlie menacingly closed in on the screaming lunatic. Tall and sinewy, Spider put a gangly

bow leg in Slouch's path and with a straight jab chinned him
sparko. Slouch dropped unconscious onto a pile of pizza boxes
and chip papers. The screaming stopped, the pixies had gone,
and so had Jayden.

Spider blew on his knuckles. 'Thank fuck for that. When he
comes to, we'll raid the allotment and keep him happy with a
bag of spuds.' He looked around as if he had lost something.
'Where's Jayden?'

Riverdance

Shh-wing ... the sound of an arsehole vaulting over a chain-link
fence shivered across the allotments. Lippo uprooted potatoes
in Parvinder Singh's plot as if born to it and threw them over
the fence to the Crew. While Slouch, wrapped in his beloved
sleeping bag, bent over to gather up the spuds, Spider dumped
a handful of Maris Pipers, dirt and all, into his hoodie. 'Don't
say I don't give you anything.'

Slouch, no stranger to a spot of dirt from sleeping rough in
the park for months, twizzled around and examined the mess.
'Lippo, can you bring a carrier bag next time, butt?'

'You knows I'm not walking around all day with a carrier
bag sticking out of my arse pocket,' said Lippo with a spud
in each hand. 'You shouldn't have torched your house, you
headshot donut.'

'I didn't torch my house.'

'You got spiced, left the chip pan on the gas and burnt
the fucking house down. You knows it, I knows it, everyone
knows it.'

Slouch shouldered his sleeping bag. 'It didn't all burn
down, and I'm not headshot.' Thinking no one had heard
him, he said it again. 'I'm not headshot.' He asked Charlie

who surfed on the phone. 'I'm not headshot, am I, Charlie?'

Charlie looked at him through bug-like mirrored shades and Slouch had no idea what was going on behind them. Charlie held up the phone and played a film of Slouch's screaming trouser-less psychotic episode in the park.

'Pixies! The pixies are biting my legs! They're crawling up my legs and biting me, get 'em off, Charlie.'

Slouch shivered. 'I've still got marks where they fucking bit me.'

'They were stinging nettles, headshot, not pixies,' said Spider. 'Jayden put stingies in your sleeping bag before he fucked off.'

'They were crawling up my legs and biting me.'

Spider raised an eyebrow at Charlie. 'Is that shot-to-bits headshot or what?'

Without answering, Charlie tucked away the phone.

Slouch picked up a potato. 'I'm not headshot. Jayden's the one who's headshot, slicing his arms all the time.'

Lippo demonstrated rubbish juggling skills with three spuds. 'You all knows I should be in a circus.'

'Yeah … as a fucking clown,' said Spider, back-slapping a laugh out of Slouch.

Lippo played keepy-uppy with a spud and Spider lost patience. 'Leg it, clown. I'm not hanging about to get nicked.'

Lippo tossed a potato into the air and put his laces through it when it came down. The tuber flew up and over the cap of a fast-approaching angry old man wielding a shovel like a battle-axe.

Spider grabbed the fence. 'Leg it!'

Johnny the Cutter moved quickly for a man in his sixties

and soon had the terrified teenager ducking and diving from the scything shovel. 'Get out of the allotment, you waster.'

'Bro,' squealed Lippo, 'he's trying to off me.'

Lippo Riverdanced from the shovel blade and his cries for help sent the Crew into hysterics.

'Come here, you waster.'

Johnny swung the shovel and Lippo fell backwards through a row of bamboo bean sticks.

'He's a nutter. Spider, help me, bro.'

Johnny hacked away the bamboo and Lippo crawled through the collapsing debris. 'Keep out of the allotment.'

Climbing the chain links with gangly bowlegs, Spider sat on a post and dangled a leg either side of the fence. 'I told you to leg it and now look. You've a senile old Shovel Man on your arse.'

Slouch strutted like a superhero. 'It's Shovel Man.'

'He's gonna kill me! Do something, bro.'

'He's a hundred years old, you melon.'

Lippo dodged behind a water butt. 'Give him a slap, Spider.'

Johnny turned his attention on Spider and advanced to the fence. 'Yes, give the hundred-year-old man a slap, Spider. I'll pull your spindly legs off.'

'Bring it on, Shovel Man.' Spider flashed a grin at Slouch and Charlie. 'I can't give him a slap, it'll break his colostomy bag.'

As Johnny reached for a spindly leg, Spider sprang from the post and gave the Crew a good laugh.

Johnny caught his breath. 'If you know what's good for you, you'll keep out of this allotment.'

Lippo saw his chance and with a running jump the asshole sprang up and over the fence with a *shh-wing*.

Spider lit up and puffed smoke rings through the links at Johnny. 'Oops, the waster got away.'

'Don't let me catch you wasters in this allotment again. Now I know who you are, I'll know where to find you.'

Safely behind Spider, Lippo launched into a St Vitas Dance-like exhibition of street gestures, creative bad language, and a rapid incomprehensible tirade of sexist, gay, and ageist taunts.

While trying to decipher the insults, Johnny noticed multi-piercings, ear plugs and a black nose ring hanging from Lippo's nostril like a bogey. He concluded the lad to be off his face on a white powder concoction of ant killer cut with a small amount of amphetamine. 'Your boyfriend needs a speed awareness course.'

Spider exhaled smoke through his teeth. 'You take a shovel to Lippo, you have to take the meltdown.'

Johnny shouldered the shovel like a rifle. 'You wasters don't seem to be getting the message so I'm coming around. If you've got any sense you'll get going.'

'Happy days,' wheezed Spider, holding in another puff.

Johnny walked away.

Lippo jumped onto the fence like a macaque and gave it a good shake. 'You knows we'll be giving out slaps if you come around here. We don't care you're an oldie.'

Johnny disappeared behind a shed.

'Hey look, the oldie's going the wrong way,' said Lippo. 'The way out is down the front, stupio.'

Spider pulled Lippo from the fence and booted him in the backside. 'Whatever. We're getting the fuck anyway.'

Johnny entered his shed and snatched the van keys from a cup hook on the main wall. Either side of the cup hook hung a framed photograph: one of Coed Mawr Colliery in its prime, the other of Julie and him, taken in their younger hippyish days in the Seventies.

He paused while trying to remember a joyous technicolour dream he had in the armchair before waking to the sound of an arsehole vaulting over a chain-link fence, something about Julie, hippies, marigolds and canaries. He kissed a finger and held it to her image. 'Thanks for keeping me company all night. I'm nipping out for a short while.'

Julie's voice sang in his mind like his conscience. *'Johnny, now don't you go doing anything stupid.'*

'Me, do anything stupid?'

He locked the doors, put the shed key under a pot on the porch bench and took the opportunity to lean on his shovel and scan the vicinity. Not a waster in sight and the plots calm after the storm. The quiet barked at him down at the allotment gates, out on the allotment road and on the grass verge leading to the village bottom streets. The bottom streets faded and abruptly vanished into a ghostly mist clinging to the valley floor.

Gazing down the valley, his thoughts wandered back to the days when three colliery headgears stood above the mist as if perched on a cloud. He saw them in his mind's eye and heard the hum of winding ropes and the song of coal from spinning wheels. It seemed only yesterday the collieries were alive and in full production; now all that remained of those great giants lay hidden in the mist, three namesake villages moulded and created from their essence, Coed Mawr, Trewatkins and Abercwmcoedmawr, still loyally orbiting around their long dead and departed hosts.

Johnny smiled and grew a couple of inches taller at the memory of the coal-producing days of his youth when the villages were vibrant and full of life. At the thought of how it had all changed with the closures in the wake of the Miners' Strike, Johnny spat, and deflated with a sigh.

Satisfied with the all-clear, he went out the secret way through the leylandii windbreak and stepped into the potholed lane. A lone cow in Dai Milk's cow field viewed him with suspicion as he jumped into his old Ford Transit Courier and wedged the shovel on the passenger side. Johnny knew where to find the wasters – down in the park hanging around the colliery monument they called the Old Wheel.

'Game on.'

The little white van started with a splutter but took off like a rocket.

The Phantom Colliery

The van screeched to a halt at the park cycle gate. Before getting out, Johnny thought of back-up to his trusty shovel. He searched under the seat, found what he was looking for, and tucked it in his jacket. A wayward potato pointed the way as he strode through the cycle gate and into Parc Coed Mawr, the parkland regenerated on the industrial footprint of the three collieries that once dominated the valley. Johnny scowled the further he walked into this bugbear of his. Evidence of anti-social behaviour surrounded him as the park had become a magnet for the troublesome, where drinking, solvent abuse, and petty drug deals were the norm. Sexual assaults and violence were commonplace, and dog walkers were likely to get Fido chewed up by a dealer's pitbull cross. Compared to the festering sore Parc Coed Mawr had become, the dirty old collieries gleamed like the Taj Mahal. He swung his shovel and sent a plastic bottle into a mound of fly-tipped rubbish besieging a vandalised bin.

'If this is regeneration I'll eat my cock.'

Johnny stopped in his tracks and leaned on the shovel as he tried to get a bearing on where the colliery buildings once stood. Surprised at the height and lushness of the trees, he felt like a stranger in his own community. He gazed at an overgrown hazel where a large NCB sign, now long gone, had once denoted the colliery entrance. He saw the sign as clear as day.

COED MAWR COLLIERY, SOUTH WALES AREA

In some places, where the park grass had been worn thin by cycle tyres, the spoil peeped through like black memories of time long past. He thought of the many times he had travelled on this colliery road, which was either ankle-deep with black slurry in the winter, or caked like liquorice in the summer.

Johnny marched on and, as he reminisced, the colliery materialised from the greenery. Flashbacks, memories, smells, voices and all manner of sensations bombarded his psyche as the dead colliery lived again before him.

Ghostly whisperings of gossip and a clatter of tableware came from the canteen.

An acrid odour of cigar smoke assaulted the senses near the NUM lodge with echoes of wily old lodge secretary Clever Trevor's gravelly voice: *'All those in favour raise their hands … motion carried.'*

A wall of clammy boiler heat hit him when the cycle path went through the pit head baths. He heard laughter and the slam of lockers, while singing echoed throughout the showers.

Pausing at a bend in the cycle track, Johnny used the shovel to point out, and get right in his mind, the stores, the blacksmith's, the fitting shop, electric shop and the lamp room.

Johnny strolled between rows of lamp chargers in the lamp room and followed a team of ghostly miners joking and laughing on their way to the pit head until they disappeared into a mist still lingering on the valley floor.

A tall ash tree occupied the position of the colliery office block.

Green leaves gave way to a dirty but beautiful Victorian façade of locally quarried stone. Nearby, the undergrowth offered glimpses of more structures built with the very fabric of the valley; the twin winding houses, the fan house and the powder magazine.

The phantom colliery melted back into the greenery at the sound of the medical attendant's gurney metallically rattling on the way to meet stretcher-bearers coming up from the pit with an accident victim.

Johnny shuddered as if someone had jitterbugged over his grave.

The old industry was ingrained in him more than he thought. 'Too many ghosts and not enough sleep.'

He walked on, but unable to shake away thoughts of the colliery. 'It doesn't make sense. The key to regeneration is jobs not cycle paths and flowerbeds. Why didn't they convert the offices into flats and the workshops into units? They could've packed miles of underground roadways with landfill and plastics, used the mine water as green energy to provide heating for homes and public buildings. Look at the jobs it would have created and the good it would have done for the environment. Where's the foresight? They couldn't wait to get shot of it all and that's the problem. When you're quick to bury the past, your future gets buried with it.'

Johnny made a beeline for the place where every quoin, every key stone, flagstone, brick, bath house tile and every crafted piece of stone now lay. Demolishing the village heritage moved so quickly after closure, the local vandals had little time to smash the windows or half-inch the slates as the powers-that-be bulldozed the buildings to fill in the shafts. The Old Wheel was the headstone of a colliery grave over half a mile deep.

The Old Wheel

Spider sat on the Old Wheel bench knocking up a joint. Lippo admired the master at work and smoked a toothpick spliff so small it looked as if his fingers were on fire.

Slouch compared phone footage with Charlie. 'That's sick.'

'Come here, you waster.'

Slouch showed it to Spider and they roared laughing at Lippo Riverdancing away from the shovel blade.

'He's a nutter. Spider, help me. Come on, bro.'

'Lippo,' laughed Spider, 'should be on Strictly Come Fucked Up.'

'You knows the nutter tried to off me with a shovel. You knows it, bro, you knows it.'

Spider resumed his joint-making skills. 'Send it to Jayden. He'll be gutted, he snuck off and missed Lippo fill his pants.'

Using a potato as a microphone, Slouch delivered a spoof news item to the Crew. Charlie, in shades like a Gothic bug-eyed insect, exhaled a genie of vape while filming Slouch in action.

'Police are looking for a one-hundred-year-old Shovel Man who swung his shovel in the allotments until Lippo filled his pants.'

'You knows I'll fuck you up, Slouch.'

Spider kicked Lippo up the backside. 'Shut it down, melon.'

Slouch stood akimbo like a superhero, using his sleeping bag as a cape. 'Wherever you find a waster yapping like Lippo, Shovel Man will appear and swing his shovel in the name of colostomy bags, spuds and bad drugs. Is it a bird? Is it a plane? Is it fuck, it's ...'

'Shovel man ... Owww!' Lippo burnt a finger on his tiny spliff as he pointed at a ghostly figure appearing out of the mist.

Lippo hid behind Spider, Charlie jumped up onto the concrete base and dangled like a mantis from a wheel spoke.

'Bang out of order that is, walking around our park like he's marmalade,' said Spider, grabbing Lippo by an earplug and leading him forward. 'Crew, stand your ground.'

'But bro, he's like a Terminator, you knows it.'

'I told you I was coming around.'

Spider stepped forwards with his gangly legs and low waistband jeans. 'Don't make me stop you, Shovel Man.'

'You couldn't stop a pig in a passage. Have you had an accident in those jeans?'

'Hey oldie, bring it on, you can't be hard if you need a shovel to take a pop at us.'

Johnny leaned the shovel against a tree. 'I've no shovel now.'

Lippo crept back behind Spider. 'This is our turf, so get the fuck.'

Johnny looked up at the Old Wheel where Charlie dangled

menacingly above him. 'This is your turf? You have no idea.'

'Go on,' said Slouch, as if shooing a little dog away. 'You heard what they said, now you go back to your allotment.'

'I'll say it again in case you're all as stupid as you fucking look, don't let me catch you in the allotment again because I'll know where to find you.' Skinning a powder fire extinguisher from his jacket, he sprayed Spider and Lippo.

Spider punched blindly into the powder and smacked Lippo in the mouth. They jumped from the spray and made off down the path towards Trewatkins. Slouch ran after them in a burst of white powder.

Johnny sprayed Goth Charlie from the spokes. 'And you, Jihadi John.'

'We'll be back,' shouted Spider.

'Yeah, and we'll bring a big Merthyr girl to squash you with her giant arse,' said Lippo. 'We knows a few, don't we, bro?'

'You really are funny little fuckers.'

'And you're a senile old zombie,' said Lippo.

'Don't get ageist with me. I got to see thirty, you won't.'

Spider dusted himself down. 'We'll sort you out.'

'You knows we'll sort you out,' said Lippo.

'What you lot? The Special Needs Coed Mawr Crew, average mental age of four, will sort me out? You can't even sort your fucking selves out. You all need care in the community.'

To his surprise, the Crew appeared wounded by his taunt, and as they dusted themselves down and made their way along the path, Julie's voice sang in his mind like his conscience. *'Call yourself a socialist? In so many ways that was an awful thing to say, you should be thoroughly ashamed of yourself.'*

'Yeah, I am,' he muttered as Lippo gave a V-sign parting shot before vanishing into the mist.

Using the shovel, Johnny filled a rusty shopping trolley with litter from around the Old Wheel. He shovelled a slew of nitrous oxide canisters into a pizza box and gingerly picked up a home-made bong. 'How green was my valley ... no one cares.'

When finished, he placed the shovel on top of the tightly-packed trolley, removed his jacket and draped it over the handle. He gave the Old Wheel a swift John Wayne salute in farewell and set off with the trolley up the cycle path.

A few moments later a pack of kamikaze cyclists zoomed up behind him and Johnny jumped for his life.

'Out of the way you vagrant.'

'Get a job, you homeless sponger.'

'Get off the cycle path.'

Johnny swung his shovel at the veering cyclists as they zipped past. 'Tax-dodging, drug-taking cheats. I hope you chafe your numb nuts raw.' He caught his breath and looked back at the Old Wheel. 'This is not a cycle path. This is Coed Mawr Colliery.'

Clayton and Smithy

Jayden looked rough and capable of sleeping on a clothesline when Johnny picked him up from Joanne's for a day's work in the allotment. The morning warmed up and lifted the mist from the valley by the time Johnny parked the van in the potholed lane. With a bag of muck to collect from the shed, he left Jayden snoozing in the passenger seat and went in through the secret way.

Rounding the corner of his shed, Johnny nearly bumped into Allotment Association chairperson Clayton, deep in discussion with his sidekick and Association treasurer Smithy.

They stepped away from his porch and walked across Bouncer Williams' plot. Top of the grassing-up list, they were the last people Johnny wanted to see snooping around his fledgling coal mine.

Ex-miner Johnny and retired police officer Clayton had little time for each other. Everything had to be done Clayton's way or not at all. Suffering from a lateral lisp, a smug half-smile appeared stapled to the corner of Clayton's mouth, giving the impression he held a high opinion of himself, which of course he did.

The rotund rugby-mad CMAA treasurer Smithy also had a policing background and he and Clayton were as thick as thieves, backing each other up on trivial allotment business and opposing Johnny at every turn. Committee meetings were a joy with Clayton and Smithy always taking one side, Johnny and Parvinder the other, neutral Mrs M stuck in the middle, and no other tenant bothering to turn up other than this split quorum of five. It was a minor miracle the CMAA had won two consecutive championships and were now in the hunt for a third.

In a little ritual to announce his residency, Johnny hoisted the Welsh flag on the shed flagpole and gave it a swift John Wayne salute.

Mrs M made her way up the gravel path. 'We've had a visit from the vandal again. He's made quite a mess of Parvinder's plot.'

'I caught the waster in the act this morning. It wasn't the lad who burned his house down but he was there with others.'

'Good Lord, you must've been up early?'

'I spent the night keeping watch from my shed. It was the only way to catch them at it.'

'That's very considerate and terribly brave,' said Mrs M, full of admiration.

'Our ex-coppers Clayton and Smithy weren't going to sort it out, were they?'

'Did you have any trouble?'

'They were just gobby kids. I followed them down to the park and had a quiet civilised word. Then they ran off.'

'Do you think they'll be back?'

'Who knows with kids, but at least I know what they look like and where to find them. Does Parvinder know about the damage yet?'

Parvinder Singh and Johnny enjoyed a friendly rivalry vying for the best plot accolade in the championships and often had a beer or three on the porch at the end of the day to watch the setting sun. Parvinder roped in his entire family, Team Singh, into weeding, turning the earth, planting, and precision measuring every neat vegetable row. Team Singh had a peculiar habit of materialising as if from the ethers, with Parvinder orchestrating the work by clipboard. With the plot flawless, Team Singh vanished back to Singh's corner shop as quickly as they had appeared.

'No, he doesn't know yet. I've only had time to telephone the police. They still didn't take it seriously.'

'There you are. I did the right thing by having a quiet word with the wasters.'

Mrs M admired the shed extension. 'At last, you've finished. But I'm not sure about the colours.'

'I thought it would make a change.'

Something caught Mrs M's eye on his raised bed. She whipped out a tape and measured the distance between two spring onions. 'You're half an inch short on your onions.'

Johnny could not resist the open goal. 'They tell me size isn't everything.'

Mrs M retracted the tape with a snap. 'It is with the valley allotment championship looming on the horizon.'

'I'm sure we'll survive the hideous experience.'

'Best move this row of spring onions before Clayton sees them.'

Johnny thought back to Clayton and Smithy snooping around his shed and got the feeling it had nothing to do with his spring onions. 'I'll move them today. I don't want to give him any bullets.'

A Surreal Trip to the Tip

Coed Mawr was the last mining village in a closed-end valley, nothing more than a small offshoot of the larger Rhymney Valley. This abrupt end to civilisation led the village to be widely referred to as 'the end of the world', but in less polite circles, particularly in the neighbouring villages of Trewatkins and Abercwmcoedmawr and because of its run-down nature in the wake of the pit closures, Coed Mawr was known as 'the arsehole of the world'.

Johnny drove the van up the potholed lane and joined the mountain road above the top terraced streets. The road hair-pinned its way up steep slopes to Coed Mawr Mountain – a wilderness of rocky outcrops, bracken, wild ponies and sheep. It had been a while since Johnny had driven across the mountain and the further they travelled, swerving to avoid dead sheep and potholes, the more the roadside became punctuated by building rubble, mattresses and burnt-out cars.

When they neared a rotating wind turbine, Johnny slowed the van for a good look. 'How long's that thing been there?'

'It's always been there, hasn't it?' said Jayden without looking up from his phone.

Johnny veered off the road onto a dirt track leading to the colliery tip. Mounds resembling gigantic breasts pointed at the sky and led the way up to a plateau of coal spoil, greened and reclaimed by Mother Nature, the length of three football pitches.

'This tip is proof we miners were once a powerful group of people. All the great civilisations of the world have raised huge mounds, monuments and pyramids, like the Incas, Aztecs, and the Egyptians. Those ancients would appreciate we built ours with materials from deep in the dark earth and raised them on top of mountains as if to honour and worship the sun.'

Mention of ancient civilisations rendered Jayden slack-jawed.

Once on top of the tip, Johnny walked to the tip edge to admire the scenery. 'Look at the view. Down there you can see right across the Bristol Channel into Eng-er-land, and up the other way, you can see the Brecon Beacons and into the heart of Wales.'

Jayden took a selfie. 'Awesome.'

Johnny drew in a deep breath of mountain air. 'Thank God they can't mess up the view.'

Voices fluttered up from the tip base. Johnny looked down at Dai Milk in his tractor cab supervising several workmen floating a raft of concrete. 'Although Dai Milk is doing his best to mess it up with wind turbines, and it looks like he's got another one on the way.'

He stormed back to the van and emptied out the bags, creating a small pyramid of spoil.

'Isn't this fly-tipping?' said Jayden as Johnny shook the dust from the last paper sack.

'Are you soft in the head? This is a coal tip. Its only *reason to be* is to have coal muck tipped onto it.'

He got in the van on the passenger side and threw the sacks over his shoulder into the back.

'Grandad, what are you doing?'

'Get in.'

Jayden got in and sat behind the wheel.

'This is a good place to give you a driving lesson.'

'Awesome,' said Jayden, and he kept repeating the word with a huge beaming smile all through the next twenty minutes as Johnny put him through the rudiments of driving. He learned fast, growing in confidence as he drove up and down the length of the tip. They were having a great time, quality time. Until Jayden's phone rang.

'Sappinin, butt?' answered Jayden.

Johnny grabbed the wheel. 'Get off the phone, dickhead!'

'*Sappinin? Trewatkins Zulus are playing up, that's sappinin, where've you been?*' said Spider.

'Can't talk, I'm having a driving lesson, tar-rah butt.'

'Why'd you answer it then?' shouted Johnny. Jayden dropped his phone, panicked and lost control of the van. It went over the tip edge and hurtled down the slope. Dai Milk's workmen looked up from the wet concrete of the turbine base as the fast-approaching van bounced, swerved and sped erratically down towards them. They scattered with trowels in hand. Dai Milk watched dumbfounded as the van, using a badger mound as a ramp, jumped his tractor and landed with a splat in the shining pristine concrete.

Dai Milk dismounted his tractor, hitched up the rope belt of his trousers and waded through the remaining concrete in his wellies. He tapped on the driver side window. Jayden wound it down.

'Did you do that on purpose?' said Dai Milk while pushing his jam-jar glasses higher up his nose.

'Of course he didn't do it on purpose,' shouted Johnny, 'what do you think he is … a fucking stunt man?'

Dai Milk, Minge Jenkins and Spanners

Dai Milk hauled the van out of the concrete and towed it to Spanners' garage. Throughout the journey, the tractor cab reeked of bullshit in more ways than one as the myopic farmer waxed lyrical about wind turbines and clean renewable energy.

Johnny knew if ever there was a man who did not give a wet fart about saving the planet, it was Dai Milk. Renowned for wanting something for nothing, the farmer only cared about money. Back in the day it was a common sight to see him drive onto the colliery coal stocks with a horsebox and help himself to a couple of ton. Dai Milk made full use of his farm assets in his pursuit of coin. He operated Dai Milk's farm produce shop on a daily basis from a shed in a field and sold plots there on Fridays for a weekly boot sale. His barn held the annual riotous Coed Mawr barn dance, and an old quarry on his land supported Dai Milk's skip hire where he allowed tradesmen to dump rubble and groundwork for a fee, selling any top soil back to the community via his landscaping business. His north woodland contained Dai's paintballing and zipline interests, while he also rented out holiday cottages a little too close to his cowshed. Dai Milk had fingers in more pies than an alcoholic baker with the DTs.

Dai blew his trumpet about how fortuitous it was he happened to be there with his tractor to pull them out of the concrete and suggested Johnny was financially beholden to him.

45

'With all this clean energy and your concern for saving the planet, you won't be interested in any free house coal then, Dai?'

Dai pushed his jam-jar glasses higher up the bridge of his nose, 'Free house coal?'

Johnny had hooked the farmer with the first cast of the fly, 'High grade Welsh anthracite. You've still got an old coal boiler?'

'I get my coal from Minge Jenkins of Trewatkins. I've always got my coal from … Minge … Jenkins.'

Dai delivered his response slowly to get a reaction from the old miner.

'Minge Jenkins, there's a name I haven't heard for a while,' said Johnny after a brief reverie. 'The big ginger fuck is still going then?'

'He's struggling, but he's building houses on the side.'

'Yet another cowboy builder.'

Minge Jenkins was the last family coal merchant in the valley and Dai Milk knew Johnny had history with the Trewatkins nutcase. In the Seventies they had a legendary fight from one end of Trewatkins to the other – from the Trewatkins Hotel, through the terraces, all the way to the gates of Trewatkins Colliery. Johnny rarely acknowledged the fight, but if pressed regarding the duration of the encounter he'd reply, 'We kept hitting each other in all the wrong places'.

Perhaps Johnny could get one over on his old nemesis. 'I'll tell you what I'll do, Dai. I'll give you a dozen bags for your trouble today, see how it goes, then if you spread the word around the farms perhaps I'll let you have coal at a discounted price.'

Johnny gazed through the Perspex at the passing Welsh

scenery as Dai's mind ticked over. Some good might come from Jayden's stunt-driving after all. Jayden buried himself into his phone after the bump, and when they got to the garage he snuck off without a word.

Spanners, a sweaty, no-neck rugby prop of a mechanic, cursed as they arrived on his forecourt and moaned all through the diagnosis.

Spanners wiped his brow. 'Why don't you get a new van?'

'I'm happy with this one.'

'You might as well, once you've coughed up for repairs.'

'It's got sentimental value. I bought this van brand-new over twenty-five years ago with my Coal Board redundancy money.'

'There's a little place in Bargoed selling vans. Good ones.'

'I don't want a new van.'

'Tell them I sent you. They'll give you a good price.'

'Will it take long to repair?'

'I can give them a ring and tell them you're coming.'

'Spanners, do you want the work or what?'

'I'm up to my neck,' said the sweaty, no-neck mechanic.

'Cash in hand, no taxman, and I'll even throw in a couple of bags of coal. Got a wood burner that takes coal?'

'Looks like a couple of shock absorbers and the labour. You'll have it back next week.'

On his way home from the garage, Johnny checked his muted phone and found a shedload of texts and missed calls from Mrs M. At short notice, Clayton had called an extraordinary meeting of the CMAA. Already late, he headed for the allotment wondering what it could be all about.

A Shed Too Far

Johnny walked through the allotment front gates and, surprisingly, found the committee shed deserted. He noticed a crowd of tenants standing around his shed and a scattering of cowboy hats gave them a lynch mob appearance.

Parvinder ran down the gravel path. 'Glad you're here. Clayton and Smithy, they're going to make you rebuild and repaint your shed. They've rounded everyone up for a vote.'

'Where's Mrs M?'

'She's stalling them as best she can.'

They made their way up the path to the edge of the crowd where Smithy held a clipboard and smugly smiled his way. 'Did it cost much to paint and extend your shed?'

'None of your business,' said Johnny as he pushed past.

'It's going to cost you a lot more to put it right. That's why you'll never find,' scoffed Smithy in a false plummy English accent, 'a coal mine in the Home Counties.'

The plump ex-copper found amusement in making persistent snide remarks at the ex-miner, but it did not make any sense to Johnny and he always ignored them.

He pushed his way through the crowd and discovered Clayton bent over and squinting through his shed window.

'Clayton, what the fuck are you doing on my porch?'

Although initially startled, Clayton regained his composure, stood his full height and sneered down his nose at the miner.

'Committee business, Mr Morgan, and this is a committee meeting,' said Clayton through the half-smile of his lateral lisp as Smithy officiously stepped onto the porch in support.

'Is that right, Madam Secretary? Is this an official meeting?'

Mrs M looked up from her clipboard. 'Yes, Mr Morgan, we

opened the meeting at the committee shed and moved to your plot at the behest of Chairperson Mr Clayton.'

'I'd rather see cat shit in my onions than a pair of conniving coppers on my porch, so fuck off!'

'There's no need for that sort of shocking language, Mr Morgan,' sneered Clayton. 'There are ladies and children present.'

'My apologies to all offended, but I suffer from coal miners' Tourette's when I'm stressed to high bollocks.'

'No offence taken, Mr Morgan,' said Mrs M as the younger Team Singh children held hands to their ears. 'I'll omit it from the minutes.'

'But I'd like it minuted,' said Johnny as he shoved the ex-coppers off his porch and onto the gravel path. 'It's *only* Chairperson Mr Clayton and Treasurer Mr Smithy that I want to fuck off.'

His feathers ruffled, Clayton pointed a scrawny finger at the shed and went on an all-out lateral lisp, spittle-laden, offensive.

'This monstrosity has ruined our chances of winning a third consecutive allotment championship. Not only is it six centimetres longer than our agreed specifications ...'

'Six centimetres too long, no problem,' interrupted Johnny going to the end post of his porch. 'I'll move this post six centimetres inside my porch and job done, anything else?'

'The paint job is disgusting and wholly inappropriate for our allotment. Our rules regarding shed painting and colours have been breached and it's you, Mr Morgan, who has breached them. Isn't that correct, Mr Smithy?'

'Absolutely Chairperson Mr Clayton,' said Smithy obsequiously. 'Our rules regarding shed colours are quite clear.'

'What rules?'

Clayton turned his back on Johnny and put his nose in the air as if unconcerned. 'Read it, Mr Smithy.'

'Coed Mawr Allotment Association, minutes of meeting dated first of July 1969.'

'1969,' laughed Johnny, 'the Beatles were still together in 1969.'

'To preserve the horticultural ambience, all sheds are to be of one colour,' read Smithy, 'black, brown or forest green.'

Clayton thumbed his gilet lapels and strutted around like a prosecution barrister. 'But this shed is navy blue and yellow. Mr Smithy, please check again, is navy blue and yellow on the list?'

'No,' Smithy smirked, 'only black, brown or forest green.'

'There we have it. You have seven days to repaint your shed.'

'Seven days? You haven't put it to a vote.'

'It doesn't need a vote. I'm upholding our constitution as Chairman of the association.'

'Chairperson,' said Mrs M under her breath.

'Your duties are to chair the meetings, not dictate to us tenants like the big dick ... tator you are. And where did seven days come from? You're making it all up.'

'Is this why you've dragged us here, Chairperson Mr Clayton,' said Parvinder. 'A few centimetres of shed and what colour it's painted?'

'It would be an unwelcome precedent, Mr Singh.'

'There are more important things going on here. Where were you when those vandals were tearing up my plot? I'll tell you where Johnny Morgan was, he was chasing them off with a shovel. You can see for yourselves, it's all on YouTube. I think

Johnny's shed looks magnificent and as far as I'm concerned it can stay as it is.'

'It's a stupid rule written ages ago,' said broad-shouldered Hoss from under his cowboy hat. 'Most of the Beatles are dead.'

'Those are dull colours, mind,' said Betty Bingo in a shrill voice. 'I'd like to see something more vibrant.'

'Mine could do with a lick of paint too,' added Parvinder.

'It'd brighten up the place,' said Vince the Hippy, a grey pony-tailed tenant smoking a suspicious-looking rollie. 'I could put up wind chimes, dream catchers and disco lights, it'd be far out.'

'This is an allotment,' raged Clayton. 'I won't stand here and watch you turn it into Bollywood or Glastonbury festival.'

Clayton's examples had the reverse effect on the tenants and, as they raised eyebrows and murmured, Johnny went for it.

'Madam Secretary, as this is an official committee meeting and I am a committee member, I'd like to make a proposal. I propose we can paint and decorate our sheds in any manner we like.'

'Wait a s-s-second, this isn't why we're assembled here,' stuttered Clayton.

'It's exactly why we're assembled here, Chairperson Clayton, and it's thanks to you that we have full attendance at a committee meeting for a change, so let's have every tenant take a vote on it now. Have you minuted my proposal, Madam Secretary?'

'Mr Morgan has proposed we can paint and decorate our sheds in any manner we like. Is there a seconder to the proposal?'

'As a committee member,' said Parvinder, 'I second the proposal.'

'No, this is anarchy,' argued Clayton, 'it's not on the agenda.'

Mrs M smiled wryly. 'All tenants in favour raise their hands.'

'If this vote goes against me, I'll resign,' threatened Clayton as every hand shot up apart from his, Smithy's and neutral Mrs M.

'Wait a minute, Mr Singh, only one vote per plot,' said Smithy pointing out that the whole of Team Singh held up their hands.

'It doesn't affect the outcome,' smiled Parvinder.

'Carried,' said Mrs M recording the minutes. 'Is there any other business? No? Meeting closed.'

The tenants happily dispersed whilst discussing the nuances of shed decor. Clayton played the martyr to the full, hand to brow, and muttering to Smithy all the way to his shed.

Johnny celebrated by hoisting the Welsh flag and giving it a swift John Wayne salute.

'What have you done? No one else wants the chair,' said Mrs M. 'I'll have to grovel and talk him back into it.'

'He'll be back sooner or later, Mrs M. He enjoys wielding power too much, no matter how small and trivial it may be.'

Brad Pit

Johnny kept his word to take Jayden on a man-shop to Cardiff despite an invisible barrier between them regarding the stunt driving incident. Joanne drove them to Abercwmcoedmawr train station in her decaled 'Joanne the Cutter' Fiat 500. Johnny sat in a nest of hairdressing equipment in the back of the car as

Joanne happily chirped away about the change in Jayden since his allotment work. Blissfully ignorant of the tip incident, other than Johnny's lame excuse, 'the van's off the road,' Joanne enthused about grandfather and grandson spending so much time together and she beamed loving smiles at Jayden in the passenger seat who sat face-in-phone.

'The happy pills have kicked in then,' he said without looking up.

Johnny did not have the heart to tell Joanne the real reason for this Cardiff trip. He only offered to take Jayden shopping because it coincided with his last day in Clanger Insurance and he needed to finish up with HR. Twenty-five years of working in the insurance industry about to end. With the discovery of coal in the allotment, he had hardly given his final day a thought and did not know what to expect, but he knew one thing, by the time they arrived at the train station he knew his daughter could talk for Wales.

He disentangled himself from a set of curling tongs and got out of the car. 'You won Joanne.'

'Won what?'

'The talking competition, we hardly got a word in all the way from Coed Mawr.'

'Oh Dad,' she gave his arm a playful thump and pounced on Jayden to give him a big kiss.

'Gerroff.'

'Oh, don't be silly, and come by,' she put lick and spit on to a handkerchief, pulled him to and scrubbed away. 'You could grow potatoes behind that ear.'

Jayden fought her off. 'You're making me look a right tit.'

'No one can see,' she said as the train pulled into the station and passengers gawked at them through the carriage windows.

Johnny set off for the platform. 'C'mon, right tit, here's the train.'

Joanne waved, blew kisses and sang her way back into the car.

Johnny stared out the train window worrying about North-Eye's radio silence on the plan search. The discovery of coal had flicked a switch marked 'Mining' from off to on within his psyche and the switch could not be turned back to off. He thought mining every minute of the day and long-forgotten aspects of the industry simmered and bubbled up into his consciousness. He realised that he and others like him possessed knowledge soon to be lost for good, and as sturdy as his generation of miners once were, they and their skills would shortly slip away, leaving nothing more of the industry than a page or two in the local history books.

Throughout the journey, he stared at the industrial scars left in the passing valley landscape. His trained eye identified trackways leading to old hillside levels and he saw slopes punctuated by subsidence and sinkholes. Tints of reclaimed green subdued the menace of coal tips looming along the skyline. Terraced streets fanned out from long-gone collieries and he visualised where pit headgears once stood proud. Aware only he in the carriage could see these things, he laughed aloud at the thought of being some kind of invisible tour guide on a mining ghost tour of the valley.

'Grandad?' said Jayden, looking up from his phone.

Johnny came down to earth with a bump. 'What?'

'Sorry about the van.'

'Apology accepted. We'll resume lessons as soon as the van's back on the road but if your phone rings again when you're driving I'll make you eat it.'

The train slowed near Llanbradach, known locally as 'the Brad', allowing Johnny to take in the remaining colliery buildings of Llanbradach Colliery, or 'Brad Pit' as he liked to call it.

The carriage began to fill and by the time they rolled into Caerphilly it resembled an overcrowded cattle truck.

'Welcome to the morning commute. Too claustrophobic for you?'

'It's doing my head in,' mumbled Jayden as he watched an empty train travelling in the opposite direction pull into the station. 'Why is this train packed and there's no one on that one over there?'

'You really are a right tit. There are no jobs up the valley, they are down in the city. Come five o'clock, it will be reversed, the trains will be empty coming down and full going up. You see, they keep putting jobs in the wrong place, but if they put the jobs in the right place, closer to where people actually live, there'd be no problem.'

The sardine-packed passengers lurched to one side as the train jolted and left the station.

'And despite the fact the first train in the world ran in the south Wales valleys from Merthyr to Abercynon in 1804,' said Johnny a little louder to his captive audience, 'when it comes to providing a decent service they still can't get it right.'

He received a couple of laughs and a ripple of confined-space applause. A minute later, the train hurtled around a tight bend towards the Caerphilly tunnel and to the best part of Johnny's daily train journey as it reminded him of his time spent underground.

As if some higher intelligence knew it to be the ex-miner's last commute, instead of the same-old-same-old ride through the mile-long tunnel, the carriage lights were out of order. The train roared into the tunnel blackout and the old miner laughed quietly at the initial gasps of panic from the startled passengers in the pitch-black carriage.

'Fuck,' said Jayden.

Along the dark carriage random phone torches lit up and shone like the cap lamps of miners working in an underground roadway. A minute later, the ordeal ended and the train re-emerged into daylight.

The Caerphilly tunnel marked the demarcation point between the Rhymney Valley and the city suburbs, and once on the Cardiff side Johnny found no further evidence of mining with the exception of the railway line they travelled upon and Cardiff itself, the capital city built on coal.

'Anything Goes' in Clanger Insurance

Johnny followed ten paces behind Jayden as he wandered the city centre on a hunt for new trainers and trackie. After an hour or so of indecision from his fussy grandson, Johnny headed towards the Clanger Insurance building.

'They don't sell trainers in there, do they?'

'We'll take a break from the shopping, or lack of shopping. I've got to call in here for five.'

'What for?'

'I work here.'

Jayden gaped in confusion.

'In Clanger Insurance, for the last twenty-five years, after I finished working in the mining industry.'

'Oh,' said Jayden. It was news to him.

Johnny looked up at the ten-storey building. 'I used to work underground but now I work up there. Impressive, isn't it?

But the shaft of our Coed Mawr Colliery could take twelve Clanger buildings stacked up on top of each other. The Old Wheel marks where the shaft was. Remember that when you next take a piss against it.'

Dizzy from looking up, Jayden staggered behind his grandad to the entrance.

'When I started there were thirty of us in a decrepit eyesore up a city side street but now we've a state-of-the-art building and thousands of Clanger employees all over the world. Pity they didn't put any Clanger up our way, it would've done a lot of good. Perhaps it's because they think of us in the valleys as a bunch of hillbillies.'

Once Johnny had signed Jayden in at Clanger reception, they stepped into a high-speed elevator. When it accelerated up, Jayden threw himself against a side panel in terror. On the tenth floor, Jayden followed his grandad out of the elevator with trembling knees.

'Man up, if you'd been in a mining cage every day up and down the shaft, you'd know that was only the speed of a dressmaker's fart.'

They entered the Chill room where an intense doubles game of table tennis was underway. A group of employees sat on a pool table having a natter, another excited group played a game of FIFA on PlayStation, while others lounged about on comfy seats, face to phone. A microwave pinged in the kitchen area and Jayden smelled toast.

'This is our Chill room. It's got all the facilities you'd ever need to keep you comfortable at work. It's a million miles from my old pit canteen.' Johnny became suspicious. 'Something must be up. It's usually empty this time of day.'

He led Jayden to the floor area and paused at the door. 'No messing about and be on your best behaviour. You're going to learn something today and it's going to be a good lesson for you. This is what it's like to work in a professional call centre environment.'

A ball of paper bounced off Johnny's head as they entered into a hailstorm of paper throwing. A game of touch rugby thundered down the aisle to a cacophony of music as chaos raged across the floor. Johnny kicked a wayward ball of paper. 'I knew something was up. The phones are down.'

They made their way through the melee to the two work pods containing Johnny's boisterous team. 'Oh, I forgot about that.'

'Forgot about what?'

'There's a team saying, "Anything goes", and the conversation rarely goes above the waist.'

Horner, a biracial, multi-tattooed and multi-pierced Sammy Davies Jr lookalike, knelt over his chair simulating gay sex and banging his head against the pod partition. 'My head was banging the headboard all fucking night. He destroyed me. No wonder I couldn't walk this morning, I'm ruined.'

The gym monkeys in the next pod were more interested in flexing their muscles at an audience of young women, who looked school age, sat on the desks dangling legs clad in spray-painted leggings.

Horner banged his head harder against the partition to get more attention. 'I'm telling you, Mohammed, it takes a real man to take it up the chuffer.'

'Who's that?' said Jayden.

'That's Horner, my work colleague.'

'Is he ...?'

'As ninepence, his claim-to-fame is he's had more pricks than KerPlunk.'

Horner fell off his chair. 'Johnny, where've you been?'

Johnny went to his desk. 'Hiding from you lot of prurient perverts.'

'Johnny,' shouted the muscle-bound Mohammed from the gym monkey pod, 'how are they hanging?'

Lucy, a fifty-five-year-old prune of a woman trying to look twenty-five, grinned and waved from Mohammed's lap.

'Not as sweaty as yours with Lucy spot-welded to your groin.'

'The phones are down and we're hoping to get sent home,' said Lucy wrapping her arms in ownership around Mohammed. 'It's a manager shit storm for the IT guys.'

Johnny noticed a cluster of managers panicking around the IT team in a far corner of the floor. 'It's about time those lazy know-alls did some work instead of playing games and surfing the internet.'

A collage of newspaper cuttings depicting prominent Tories was plastered over Johnny's screen. Margaret Thatcher occupied pride of place. He ripped the offending material to shreds. 'Who put this M-word picture on my monitor?'

'You mean Margaret Thatcher?' said Joel effeminately while showing phone porn to a colleague. 'Not me.'

'Oh yeah, Joel, you're so innocent.'

'Been up to any granny shagging lately, Johnny?'

Lucy gasped and put a hand over her mouth in shock as the mood deflated throughout the team.

'Do you want to say that again without any teeth?'

Joel rolled his eyes. 'Don't be Mr Moany, you know anything goes on this team.'

'It's only anything goes if you're a fairy in Tinkerbell central.'

'You can't call me that,' said Joel.

'Can't call you what?'

'A fairy, it's offensive.'

'Propagating an anything goes culture in the workplace means anything goes. You can't play the homophobic card when you get offended if you're making offensive, ageist, sexual remarks, leaving politically offensive material on desks and showing workmates gay porn on your phone. Read the HR manual about workplace conduct.'

'You've always been such a prude,' said Joel. 'Get with it and move with the times.'

'Ah, the times,' mused Johnny. 'It's times like this I get nostalgic for the old days. I mean, whatever happened to the quaint British pastime of queer bashing?'

'Legend,' said Mohammed, as laughter burst from the team.

'You can't say that,' said Joel.

Johnny bounced a ball of paper off Joel's head, 'Anything goes.'

'And who's this fine-looking young man with you?' said Horner, sniffing around a terrified Jayden.

'You're right, Horner, he is a beaut,' purred Joel.

'I know I would,' said Horner.

'So would I,' agreed Joel.

Johnny searched through his desk drawer. 'Behave yourselves, stop sexually harassing my grandson.'

'I thought he'd joined the club and gone Greek,' Horner said to Jayden. 'Any more where you come from, gorgeous?'

Jayden instinctively drew his phone and showed him a pic of Lippo.

'He's fit, and he's got earplugs like mine, looks like he

might like a train in the tunnel. What do you think, Joel?'

'You'll bring him out.'

Johnny smiled as he found a photograph in his desk. He showed it to Jayden. It was of a woman and child with a banner supporting the miners. 'This was taken before you were born. The little girl is your mum, and that's your grandmother when she had a BBC news interview during the Miners' Strike.' Johnny put the photograph in his pocket. 'I'll send you a copy.'

'When are we having a few beers, Johnny?' said a gym monkey in the next pod.

'End of the month.'

'We're all up for it,' said the gym monkey.

'Crucial,' said Mohammed.

A tall figure emerged from the manager shit storm around IT in the corner of the floor and approached the team.

'What's that?' said Jayden.

'That's Marilyn,' reassured Johnny, 'my manager.'

Marilyn, a six-foot seven-inch transgender woman with a shock of orangey-purple hair, thumped along the floor towards the team in Doc Martens boots. The manager paused to hitch up a tight purple skirt over her black leggings. 'C'mon, get back on the phones. There are calls coming through.'

The team collectively groaned and dispersed back to their workstations. 'Savage,' said Mohammed as Lucy slid from his lap.

Marilyn looked inquiringly at Jayden as he gaped at the giant manager's multiple piercings and tattoos.

Johnny smoothed his grandson's lack of manners. 'Marilyn, this is my grandson Jayden. Will it be OK if he listens in for a while with one of these perverted heathens?'

'Your grandson can sit in with Lucy. I've got your file here. Shall we go into the Chill to finish up?'

'No worries,' said Johnny as he reached for his chair.

'I got it,' said Horner, wheeling Johnny's chair to Lucy's desk and positioning Jayden upon it.

'A word of advice,' said Horner to Jayden. 'Don't fall for Lucy's seductive charms, unless you *want* to stick it in a cave.'

Lucy swung a slap but Horner pirouetted away. 'Every hole's a go, isn't it, Lucy?'

'Fuck off, faggot,' said Lucy as a call came through on her headset. 'Hello, you're through to Lucy at Clanger Insurance, can I take your policy number please.' She flashed Horner the finger and received a blown kiss in return.

Marilyn stomped towards the Chill room and Johnny lagged behind to have a quick dig at the gym monkeys before they took calls.

'No offence to you young women,' he said with a wink.

'No problemo,' said one of the girls as they giggled, intuitively knowing a wind-up was on its way.

He picked up and examined a tub of muscle building supplement. 'Guys, how does it feel to know you're doing a little girl's job? Not only can these girls do your job but they do it better.'

'Yes,' agreed the girls to a few high fives.

'If you did a proper man's job like I did in the mining industry, you wouldn't need to spend time and money going to the gym.'

'Back in the day,' Mohammed yawned to the others.

'Back in the day, no miner worth his salt had gym membership. We were too bollocksed doing a man's job all day to fanny about in a gym. Enjoy your expensive supplements and steroids.'

As Johnny turned away from the team, a bird wing fluttered at the side of his cheek, stopping him in his tracks.

Moses, a sleek Afro-Caribbean kick boxer, had delivered a reverse roundhouse kick, his foot so close to Johnny's face he smelled his ankle sock. 'I could've knocked you out then, Johnny.'

Moses retracted his foot and danced around in a whirl of punches and kicks to the laughter of the team.

'Slamming,' laughed Mohammed.

Johnny calmly walked away to meet Marilyn in the Chill. 'Moses, you'll do yourself a mischief with those high kicks.'

A Chat in the Chill

The Chill room emptied as everyone got back on the phones. Marilyn sat at a wall-to-floor window overlooking the city traffic on what appeared to be a child's chair but as Johnny neared he saw it was an adult's chair and Marilyn's sheer bulk had created an illusion.

Marilyn offered a pen, pointed to the dotted lines and he signed away. 'You know we've got a great culture here and we keep in touch with all our valued former employees and help them keep in touch with each other. I'll forward the group details to your home email.'

He returned the pen and looked out of the window at the traffic ten floors down. 'No need, I'll be fine. Once I'm gone, I'm gone.'

'You'll be such a loss. I've always prided myself on having the most diverse team in the company.'

'I prefer to think it was because I've worked at Clanger since virtually the beginning, in just about every department and my twenty-five years' experience will be sorely missed, not

63

because you have to find another oldie to redress the diversity balance. C'mon Marilyn, I remember your first day at Clanger when you didn't know whether to wear cami-knickers or budgie smugglers.'

The chair creaked as Marilyn ejected a bellowing laugh. 'I suppose you won't know what to do with yourself. I know I wouldn't.'

'I used to say I'd rather have a wasp up my arse than retire, but now I don't think there'll be enough hours in the day.'

'You've something lined up?'

Johnny took time replying, mesmerised by the amount of eye make-up Marilyn wore, as it looked as if her black eyelids were bench pressing. 'I've found a seam of coal under my allotment shed so I'm opening a small colliery.'

Marilyn paused to compute and it appeared to Johnny as if a passing train in the distance drove into her ear and out of the other. 'As you do … Is it … a valleys thing?'

'You could say that.'

'Hmm … you qualify for a long-service award and …'

'I don't want any more bits of glass telling me how great I am.'

'And the team would like to say their goodbyes.'

'I've told them I'll be out for a drink at the end of the month. Marilyn, I don't want any fuss. A few hours legless on the razz, we say our goodbyes, then they can all go clubbing, or to sex dungeons, or whatnot, I'll get the train home and job done.'

'They think a lot of you. Half of them would've been sacked years ago if it wasn't for you.'

'Because Clanger has no union representation and with my NUM background I could see some employees were being treated unfairly by bullying managers. The lack of a union has irritated me but I will say this; you in particular and all concerned at Clanger were exemplary when Julie died. I won't ever forget that, Marilyn.'

Tears welled in Marilyn's eyes and Johnny soon found himself on the receiving end of an uncomfortable bear hug from his manager.

'Anyway, if we're done here I'd better get back to my grandson. Horner frightens him to death.'

A ball of paper bounced off Johnny's head as they entered the floor into a chaotic hailstorm of paper throwing as the phones had gone down again. Marilyn thumped off to IT muttering obscenities.

Lucy had reattached herself to Mohammed's lap and squeezed his bulging bicep. Joel sat on Jayden's lap while Horner gave the frightened teenager a manicure. Johnny slapped a hand on Joel's shoulder and separated him from his grandson while Horner pirouetted away to safety.

'You suffer from toxic masculinity,' trumpeted Joel.

'And Mr Anything Goes suffers from toxic homosexuality, so shut the fuck up or you're on HR's shit list for sexually harassing a visitor.'

Joel sat down in a sulk, 'You are so Mr Moany.'

Johnny spied Moses showing off and stroking his six-pack in front of the girls. He crept behind him unawares and delivered a body punch to the ribs. Doubled-up and winded, Moses tried to speak but no words came as his mouth opened and closed like a guppy. Ever the gentleman, Johnny helped the breathless young man to a seat among his equally speechless gym monkey colleagues.

'I could've knocked you out then, Moses.'

'Sweet,' said Mohammed.

Marilyn appeared in the pod. 'What's wrong with Moses?'

'He's done himself a mischief with those high kicks,' said Johnny as he grabbed Jayden. 'C'mon, let's get out of this madhouse.'

As they left, Horner donned a bowler hat, straddled a chair and went into a rendition of 'Cabaret' in a storm of paper throwing.

While waiting for the lift Jayden picked up a text. 'Grandad, have you got any duck tape?'

Johnny smelled a rat. 'What do you want duck tape for?'

'Er, my Xbox stand is falling apart and I want to tape it up.'

Johnny didn't believe a word. 'I've got some in my shed.'

'Thanks.'

'Remember where you found it.'

Bollywood Comes to Coed Mawr

Bhangra blared across the allotment as Team Singh decorated Parvinder's shed in a pink, orange and gold Bollywood style. The older Singh children reached precariously from stepladders as they attached lanterns, throws and beads to the eaves. while their younger siblings painted the lower slats to the rhythm of the music. Parvinder enjoyed a relaxing beer with Johnny on his porch bench. Coal burned like a dream in the chiminea, and Johnny looked into the glow as if meeting an old friend he had not seen in a while.

The tenants raced to finish decorating before dark, with the Bollywood groove enhancing many a brush stroke. When Mrs M added strawberry and cream stripes to bright yellow panels, her shed took on the appearance of a huge, delicious sponge cake. A cascade of brightly-coloured bingo balls decorated Betty Bingo's shed, while Hoss built a hitching post and fixed louvred batwing doors to his Wild West saloon shed. Vince the Hippy used a remote to test the flashing function of his new disco lights in between his wind chimes.

'Far out.'

Johnny's NCB colours neatly fitted in with the others and any mining activity had a chance of hiding in plain sight of snooping ex-coppers. Clayton's wobbly about the paint job was a stroke of luck.

'They're up to something,' said Parvinder, 'perhaps they're pulling the bugs out of each other's backsides.'

Clayton and Smithy had attached polytunnels to their sheds and they wandered behind the opaque polythene as if conducting all manner of weird experiments. Their work resembled an old black-and-white horror film of Dr Frankenstein and Igor stalking around and cutting bits off corpses on a mortuary slab.

'Sticking more bugs up there is more likely.'

'How come they got polytunnels? Only three months ago Clayton pushed a vote against new polytunnels.'

'He's got the hump because he lost the shed painting vote,' said Johnny swigging a Cobra beer courtesy of Singh's Corner Shop, 'but as long as they're out of our face.'

Parvinder poked the coal with a bamboo stick. 'Where are you getting this coal from? Minge Jenkins?'

'Boot sale in Merthyr,' Johnny fibbed with a burp.

'Don't let the emissions police catch you burning coal, they'll throw away the key.'

'I'm yet to see a coal detector van in the village.'

'I'm sure coal detector vans are only a matter of time.' Parvinder looked down the valley. 'It must've been some sight to see when the three collieries were working all those years ago.'

'It was a sight to see and kept us all in work; nothing here now.'

'We talk a lot about the collieries in the Historical Society,' smiled Parvinder. 'One of our members found a fascinating 1861 newspaper account about the start of deep mining in Coed Mawr and an older enterprise known as Mountain Road Works. Why don't you come along to our next meeting?'

'Is there any committee or organisation in Coed Mawr you don't belong to, Parvinder?'

'There's the Coed Mawr Women's Carpet Bowls Club. I was black-balled.' He took a drink. 'Or had black balls or something.'

They shared a laugh.

'It sounds a tad racist and sexist of them.'

'Talking of racists, there's been kids stealing from my shop. One of them kept calling us Pakis. So we shot him.'

Johnny spat out his beer. 'Shooting racist shoplifters might make a great game show but it won't get you re-elected to the Community Council.'

'I didn't shoot him. My eldest son Gaganjit shot him. Only with an airgun but he still jumped ten feet in the air. Little mouthy boy with staples in his ears.'

'He's the one I chased with the shovel from your plot. Didn't you recognise him from the YouTube footage?'

'The little ... well, he won't be jumping over fences for a week.'

'What did he pinch?' asked Johnny, as with cameras, mirrors, peep-holes and members of the Singh family following customers around the aisles, shoplifters had more chance of robbing Fort Knox than shoplifting in Singh's Corner Shop.

'That's a funny thing. He stole a pack of minced beef. Can

you believe it? Why didn't he steal the cider? They always try to steal the cider. Next to chocolate, it's number one on the stealing list. Now I'll have to move a camera over the fucking fridge.'

Joanne made her way up the allotment path.

'Here's your Joanne.' Parvinder downed his beer. 'I'd better get Team Singh back to the shop before the shelves are emptied.'

Parvinder passed Joanne on the path and they both got into the music groove with a little Bollywood dance-off.

'Dad, what's happening?' said Joanne with a twirl, 'the dreary old place is bumping.'

'Amazing what a lick of paint can do, isn't it?'

'I've called in to say I've put a dinner up for you.'

'Thanks, I am getting a bit Hank Marvin come to think of it, but take the weight off for five and have a look at this coal fire.'

'So that's what it's all about?' she said as she sat on the bench.

'What's what all about?'

'Jayden said you are opening a little coal mine under the shed.'

'For fu ... I told him to keep it quiet.'

'He hardly speaks to me then suddenly he's excited and telling me all about it.'

'I hope you can keep it quiet.'

'Who am I going to tell?'

'A mobile hairdresser with a Master's in gossip?'

She crossed her heart. 'I won't say a word. Mum wouldn't.'

'She wouldn't. I'd have to fight her off from joining in and taking over. She always said she wanted to work underground.'

He poked the fire.

'A coal fire, there's nothing like it. They shut the pits but people still want the warmth and glow of coal so they made artificial fires with artificial coal with artificial flames. It's like vegan food imitating meat, plastic grass, decaf coffee, or worse … alcohol-free beer. The hypocritical insanity of the world never ceases to amaze me.'

'Reminds me of when I was little and we had a coal fire. There was a little shovel, tongs, a poker and I loved the little brush.'

'A companion set.'

'I'd play with the brush in the fireplace sweeping up all the bits onto the shovel and I'd throw it on the fire. Sometimes you'd let me use the tongs to turn the coal over, or sprinkle a shovel of small coal from the bucket to make the fire stay in.'

'Kids playing by the fire? The 'elf and safety jobsworths would have a fit. I'll dig out that old companion set. There's a place for it again. Anyway, how's Jayden shaping up?'

'What have you done? He's a changed boy. He comes home from helping you in the allotment, has a shower, has his tea and collapses in a heap.'

'He's found out in his own way the benefit of hard work. All he needed was a few shifts on the shovel, a little belief and money in his pocket. With every bag of coal he digs out, he can see the worth in what he does. There are not as many physical jobs around as there used to be, where a young man learns the value of work, and how the work makes him feel worthwhile. Men need that, even if we need a nudge to help us along.'

'I can't believe the change in him.'

'But is he doing that self-harming?'

'Not as far as I know.'

'See, he only needed to be shown the shovel. He won't do that nonsense again.'

'Before I came out I looked in on him. He was fast asleep like a baby, on top of the bed with shopping bags everywhere.'

'He's had a long week. What dinner have you put up for me?'

'Chops, mash, peas and onion gravy, like Mum used to make.'

'It'll take a lot to get me away from this coal fire,' he said getting to his feet, 'but chops, mash, peas and onion gravy does it for me and there's only one person on the whole planet who can make a dinner as good as your mother.'

Joanne held back a tear and burst into a smile.

Johnny locked the shed, hid the key under a pot and lowered the flag to a swift John Wayne salute.

'What about the fire, Dad?'

'It'll be alright, mun. It'll burn down slow. It's coal.'

They walked down the gravel path.

'Those who do hard physical work are too cream-crackered to get up to any mischief. Now Jayden knows the benefit of hard work he won't be doing any of that antisocial behaviour.'

The Trewatkins Zulus

Uttering a prolonged burp, Jayden urinated against the Old Wheel and over his new trainers.

'You can get twelve Clanger Insurance buildings stacked on top of each other under the Old Wheel. Did you know that? Walk carefully because it's half a fucking mile down from here.' He tip-toed away from the Old Wheel with a large damp patch on the front of his tracksuit bottoms.

'See, he's the one that's headshot,' said Slouch.

Lippo pointed an index finger at his backside. 'It hurts where that Paki shot me in the arse.'

'You mustn't say that,' said Slouch. 'It's not nice.'

Slouch did the shoplifting from Singh's Corner Shop. The Trewatkins Zulus were playing up and only minced beef could halt their advance. Slouch ran into the shop, snatched the minced beef, ran back out, and down the street. He hid in the chippy doorway while Lippo bought a carton of chips at the counter. Team Singh gathered in the street and Gaganjit zipped air pellets at Slouch.

Lippo stepped out of the chippy with chips in hand. 'You're not scared of the Pakis? They can't hit fuck all from …'

A pellet took Lippo in the buttock. Chips scattered over a wide area of tarmac as the Welsh high jump record shattered. Lippo rubbed his backside with one hand and shook a fist at Team Singh with the other. 'You cock-eyed Paki bastards.'

With no reason for confrontation other than over 150 years of fighting tradition between the neighbouring villages, the Coed Mawr Crew and Trewatkins Zulus faced-off in the park.

'C'mon, start then,' shouted Jayden, 'wankers.'

Car headlamps were on full beam way back at the Trewatkins cycle gate and a posse of Zulu silhouettes mustered within fifty yards of the Crew. Jayden necked back the last dregs of a cider bottle and threw it down the cycle path. The bottle smashed to smithereens and sent a small sparkling wave swashing against Zulu trainers.

Spider grabbed Jayden by the scruff and pulled him to. 'Did you get the duck tape?' Jayden ceremoniously produced the tape from a pocket. Spider took the tape, strolled further down the path and halted near a tree. 'Coed Mawr Crew, stand your ground, they're all little girls in Trewatkins.'

'Where's Charlie?' said Slouch nervously, sinking deeper into his sleeping bag. He tried counting the Zulus but kept losing track as they ducked from a cave troll of a lad by the name of Pea-Brain who casually swung a baseball bat around his head. 'Twenty?' said Slouch to no one in particular.

'Twenty-two,' corrected Lippo, 'without the dog.'

'Where's Charlie?' said Slouch, pondering the odds. He draped his sleeping bag over a branch and shivered, as vulnerable as a snail out of its shell.

At the edge of the cycle path Spider stood cocksure, leaning his hand against a birch tree. 'Lippo, work your magic.'

Lippo launched into a St Vitus Dance-like exhibition of street gestures, creative bad language, and a rapid, incomprehensible tirade of taunts. The Zulus got the gist of it from his masturbation mime and advanced. Lippo hid behind Spider while Slouch and Jayden stood firm at his side.

'Here they come,' said Spider.

Pulled by his one-eyed albino pitbull cross Rocky, Minja Jenkins marched out in front of the Zulus. Square-headed and with sticking-up ginger hair as if fresh from a scary séance, Minja stared crazily at the Crew. He unleashed the dog to the dancing glee of the Zulus.

'Rocky … kill!'

'Slouch,' said Spider as the snarling dog flew at them.

Slouch ripped open the packet of mince and held it out. 'Who's a nice dog then? Come on, Rocky. Nice dog, good boy, good boy.' Slouch had a way with dogs and Rocky was all over him and sniffing the beef. He put the mince down and, as Rocky ate, he clipped on a leash secured to a tree.

'Fuck you, Rocky.' Minja drew a twenty-inch Sabatier knife and waved it around. 'This is a small knife where we come from.'

Spider stepped away from the tree with a large screwdriver duck taped to his hand. 'And this is the sharpest screwdriver in Coed Mawr. Bring it on, you twisted up piece of ginger shit.' With fancy footwork, Spider danced and jabbed the screwdriver at Minja's face. 'It'll look better sticking out of your … white … lard… arse.'

Minja's eyes doubled in size at the failure of his plan. The Coed Mawr Crew were supposed to run away.

Charlie, wielding a cricket bat, ran out of the woods into the flank of the Zulus and cracked Pea-Brain's head. The Zulu dropped the baseball bat, stiffened and fell like a plank of wood. Panic set in and the Zulus were legging it back to Trewatkins before Charlie could swing a second time.

Minja dropped the knife and ran like Usain Bolt through the retreating Trewatkins Zulus with Spider right behind him. With a valleys yell, Slouch, Jayden and Lippo charged after them. Minja had forgotten an age-old truth about the south Wales valleys, the further you travel up them, the crazier are the inhabitants. With Spider closing in, Minja ran straight past his Volkswagen Golf parked at the cycle gate. Jayden stopped at Minja's car as the others kept up the chase. A group of excited girls sat on a nearby bench and Chloe, his ex-girlfriend, sat among them. After a brief glance Chloe's way, Jayden took out his house key and keyed a line down the side of Minja's Golf. Johnny the Cutter would be proud of him.

An Epiphany Moment

With the van off the road, Johnny had a pleasant morning walk from his terraced house in the top streets, downhill into the village and along the allotment road. Making his way up the gravel path, he observed early bird Clayton's blurred outline mysteriously creeping around inside his polytunnel. At the shed, he noticed the coal had burned to ashes in his chiminea. The Welsh flag went up to a quick John Wayne salute but when he looked under the pot the key was missing. A chorus of snores came from the slightly ajar shed doors. Johnny opened a door, stepped onto the floorboards and stumbled on a line of trainers sticking out from a makeshift blanket of weed membrane. Jayden slept with three other lumps curled next to him and, further away, a lump in a grubby sleeping bag gave off a bit of a whiff. Cider bottles and spliff ends covered the floorboards. Before Johnny's blood boiled, his phone rang and he stepped outside to answer.

'Joanne?'

'Dad, Jayden wasn't in his room this morning. His bed hasn't been slept in. I think he's been out all night.'

'It's OK, he's with me.'

'With you?'

'He's asleep in the shed.'

'In the shed, how'd he ...?'

'Look, he's alright.'

'But why's he sleeping in your shed?'

'Don't worry he's with his grandad.'

'Is he alright?'

'You know he's alright, mun.'

'Well, look after him. You know he's had a rough time.'

'I'll look after him, don't you worry about that, tar-rah.' He hung up. 'Once I've given him a good shake.'

He stepped into the shed and gave Jayden a good shake.

'Oh, my head,' said Jayden coming around, 'Grandad?'

'What's going on here?'

Jayden held up the duck tape. 'I've brought back the duck tape.'

'Fuck the duck tape!' Johnny removed the membrane from the sleeping teenagers. 'It's those gobby wasters who ripped up Parvinder's plot.'

'I knows you, you're the senile old Shovel Man,' said Lippo.

'You obviously didn't learn your lesson. Where's my shovel?'

'I told you, bro,' said Lippo. 'He's gonna start.'

'I'm hanging,' yawned Spider, 'come back after and hit Lippo with the shovel, we're all in bits by here, mun.'

Johnny went for his shovel. 'You soon will be.'

Jayden pulled him back. 'They're with me, Grandad.'

'What have I told you? You hang around ...'

'Yeah, yeah, you hang around with wasters and you become a waster. I know.'

'All you wasters can get out right now. And that goes for you too, Jayden.' He sniffed the stench wafting through his shed. 'What's that horrible smell?'

As the Crew pointed at the lump in the grubby sleeping bag, it squeaked a prolonged high-pitched fart. Slouch unzipped and popped out his head. 'I think I followed through.'

'Right, that's it,' shouted Johnny, 'everyone out.'

'Grandad.'

'I said everyone out, now.'

'Listen to what they've got to say?'

'What have they got to say I'd be interested in?'

'It's about the coal.'

'You've told them about the coal?' Johnny looked as if would explode. 'I told you to keep it quiet.'

'You said we needed help because of your bad back.'

'We do, but I didn't mean these wasters. I meant North-Eye and maybe some of the old guys from the colliery.'

'Old guys, is right. They're all zombies haunting the doctor's surgery. C'mon, give them a chance.'

'What would they know about it?'

'It's not their fault they know nothing about it.'

'I don't need you to tell me it's not their fault. I know it's not their fault. I'm the one who went through the Miners' Strike. I fought for this community, fought for the colliery, fought for jobs and spent time in police cells so there'd be a future in Coed Mawr ...' Johnny faltered as he caught sight of Julie's photograph and heard her voice in his mind.

'That's why I raise funds, to preserve these jobs not just for the here and now but for our children and grandchildren so they can have an economic future in their own community.'

With his mind racing, Johnny stormed out of the shed and paced around on the porch. Noise filled his head like an empty panzer chain conveyor clanking along a coalface. He stood on the gravel path and looked up for inspiration at the Welsh flag fluttering in the breeze. Casting his eye around the allotment, he spotted a plastic flowerpot on the edge of Bouncer's plot. The pot leant back at an angle on a small mound of earth like a rugby ball begging for a good kick. Unable to resist, he adopted a kicking stance. When fully focused he ran and kicked the pot over the middle of Bouncer's shed. Three points, and the cheers from the imaginary crowd were deafening.

The pot landed on Clayton's polytunnel and rolled off. As quick as a funnel-web spider, the ex-copper was out suspiciously scanning the allotment for the perpetrator. Safely obscured from view behind Bouncer's shed, Johnny milked the adoration of his imaginary crowd. Full of Zen, the panzer chain conveyor glided along the coalface muffled with freshly-cut coal.

A Big Cup of Tea

Johnny stepped into the shed. 'I don't know about you boys, but I could do with a big cup of tea. Jayden you and Sunglasses get the kettle on. A cup of tea sorts out everything, even cider and whacky-baccy hangovers.'

Jayden gave a sigh of relief. 'It's not Sunglasses. It's Charlie.'

Charlie's menacing shades went Johnny's way. 'Charlie, please help Jayden with the tea.'

Johnny turned to the others. 'The drug dealing and raiding allotments market has dried up, the life plan isn't working and now you want to be coal miners?'

'I'm rinsed out,' said Spider. 'We all need the cash. Jayden's got new clothes, and paid for our weed and cider all night. He's minted.'

'Why don't you knuckle down and get yourselves proper jobs?'

'Who's going to give us a job?' shrugged Spider. 'Even the scrappy won't have us.'

'I can't argue with you by there.'

'You knows there are no jobs in Coed Mawr,' said Lippo.

Johnny nudged the lump in the sleeping bag with his foot. 'What about this smelly article? What do you think?'

Within seconds, Slouch got out of the bag, out of the doors and went behind the shed to vomit.

'Don't let anyone see you.' Johnny kicked the sleeping bag outside and wafted his hand. 'Jayden, open the sink window or we'll be out there chucking with him.'

Jayden opened the window as Charlie arranged the tea mugs.

'At least you had a job back in the day,' grumbled Spider.

'And it was just down the road, where the park is now. Coed Mawr Colliery and I worked there for twenty-five years as a cutter driver on the coalface until it closed in '93.' He removed the colliery photograph from the wall and looked at it with affection. He handed it to Spider. 'You wouldn't know there'd been a colliery there but for the sheave.'

'Sheave?' said Jayden as the kettle started to boil.

'You boys know what I'm talking about, the Old Wheel where you wasters light fires, drink cheap cider and smoke the weed.'

Spider passed Lippo the photograph. 'It's somewhere to go.'

'It's the only place to go,' said Jayden, 'they move us on from the village with dispersal orders.'

'Lippo's got a criminal behaviour order to stop him going to the centre of the village,' said Spider. 'Haven't you, Lippo?'

'You knows it doesn't stop me, bro,' bragged Lippo. 'I goes anywheres I wants. I was in the chippy yesterday.'

'Until you got shot in the arse,' laughed Jayden.

'Shut up, headshot, cutting all the time.' Lippo rubbed his wounded backside at the reminder.

'Slouch can't go within a half-mile of his house,' said Spider. 'His dad put an injunction on him because he nearly burned the place down one night when he fell asleep and left the chip pan on the gas.'

Johnny sat in his armchair. 'A chip pan? I thought they went out with video recorders.'

Lippo passed the photo to Charlie. 'They always move us on.'

'Moving a problem doesn't sort it out. It ticks a box for the police but it only creates a problem elsewhere. The Old Wheel you wasters piss on meant something once. It wound up the coal and without it there'd be nothing here. No village, no streets, no school, no corner shops or allotments to rob. There'd be nothing here.'

'There's nothing here now,' shouted Spider.

'And don't I know it. There were a few thousand employed in the valley's heyday. Of course, it's long gone, grassed over and wooded, in the name of regeneration. But it didn't regenerate into the same thing with a different face like Doctor Who. They regenerated thousands of jobs into a safe haven for drug-taking, anti-social behaviour, and somewhere to take the dog for a dump.'

Jayden took the colliery photograph from Charlie and passed it back to his grandfather, 'Why, Grandad?'

'We were too militant. Miners brought down the 1974 Heath Government and I'm proud to say not one NUM member in the three collieries of this valley broke the '84–'85 Miners' Strike. You won't find a monument to that statistic in the park, unless it's the park itself and the lack of jobs. I believe there was a hidden agenda not to regenerate this valley economically, so we ended up with a park. In the last twenty or so years, call centre jobs have boomed in Wales but you won't find any on old colliery sites where they are most needed.'

Spider put his head in his hands. 'I hated school so I don't want the history lesson or the sad story. I just want the money.'

'I haven't decided yet if you're up to it.'

'We knows there's fuck all to it, don't we bro?'

Johnny took hold of Lippo's hands and looked them over. 'It's hard work for girly little hands like yours.'

Lippo pulled his hands away. 'I haven't got girly little hands. You show us what to do and you knows we'll do it.'

Johnny sank back into his armchair. 'Knowing how to make a bong won't help you underground.'

'Look,' sighed Spider, 'we neeeeed the ackers.'

'Fair comment, it was the pay packet at the end of the week that kept us all going.'

'C'mon, Grandad, we can't do it on our own. You've got a bad back and the boys can help us out.'

Johnny got up and replaced the colliery photograph on the wall. He admired it for a moment and left the wasters awaiting his decision.

Lippo twiddled his nose ring, 'We needs to know.'

'Is that tea ready yet?' said Johnny without taking his eyes from the photograph. 'It'll be stewed to high bollocks.'

Jayden poured the tea and Charlie stirred a spoonful of milk power into each cup.

After righting the photograph on the wall, Johnny announced his decision. 'OK, you're in.'

The Crew cheered as if scoring a goal in the Cup final but Johnny held up a hand like a linesman catching them offside. 'But you all have to get trained.'

'Shut up,' said Spider as if in his death throes. 'Jayden dug loads out, easy like.'

Johnny took his tea from Charlie and had a sip. 'That was only a hole in the ground. We'll be driving into the seam, opening a face, shoring up the sides, supporting the roof, transporting materials, ventilating, keeping safe and you'll have to learn how to lift heavy objects without dangling your testicles around your ankles.'

'I hate learning stuff,' said Spider from behind his hands.

'If you want money that's the way it is but if any of you want to go back to pissing up against the Old Wheel, the door's by there.'

Slouch appeared at the door wiping away spittle with a sleeve. 'There's someone coming.'

The Battle Cry of the Strike

They peered through the windows at the bespectacled figure striding up the gravel path with a cardboard tube under his arm.

'It's North-Eye with news about the coal seam. Best you boys keep your heads down.'

Johnny stepped out onto the porch. 'North-Eye, how did it go?'

North-Eye removed a plan from the cardboard tube. 'My library and online searches drew a blank but I found this in the Glamorgan Record Office.' He unrolled the plan and they had a good nose at it. 'I don't know how accurate this is but it appears there are old workings a hundred yards or so off in the woods behind your shed but nothing under this allotment.'

'Looks good to me.'

North-Eye admired the shed. 'Nice paint job.'

Johnny rolled up the plan. 'Not everyone thinks so but it has started a trend.'

Spider threw Lippo with a wrestling throw, thumping him flat on the floorboards. North-Eye looked through the shed window and saw the wasters bouncing around kicking each other's backsides.

'All I need now is a surveyor, a ventilation officer, a safety officer and a mining inspector. You fit the bill for all those duties.'

North-Eye was not quite listening. 'There's a load of idiots having an arse-kicking competition in your shed.'

'But my immediate need is for a training officer.'

'Training officer? You're not thinking of working this seam with these kids?'

'I was sixteen when I started in the industry. These are older.'

'We're not social workers, or drug and alcohol counsellors. They've got a baths locker full of problems.'

'We've all got a social responsibility, even you, or you wouldn't be in the Neighbourhood Watch.'

'They won't last a bastard week.'

'They will if you tell them mining is highly unpopular, highly dangerous and highly against the law. They're well up for that.'

To a chorus of laughter inside the shed, Lippo burst backwards out through the double doors and landed flat on his back. He looked up at North-Eye before getting to his feet and staggering back into the shed, closing the doors behind him.

North-Eye retrieved the rolled-up plan from Johnny. 'I'm not up for it. It's like the bastard Wild West.'

'It's an opportunity to get back underground.'

North-Eye put the plan into the tube. 'You're out of your mind.'

'Remember what the fight was about in '84?'

'Don't you go starting on about The Strike or we'll be talking bollocks all day. We fought, we lost, the war's over.'

'It's never been over.'

'It's been over for more than thirty years. If that's not over, Johnny, I don't know what bastard is.'

The wasters stopped messing about and gathered at the shed window to listen and record the arguing miners on their phones.

'We fought for this community and for our future generations so they could have an economic future on their doorstep. That was the battle cry of the strike.'

'Thirty years?' said North-Eye with an attack of conscience. 'I can't believe I just said that, seems like yesterday, or last weekend.'

'And it'll soon be forty years. Those kids in there are the future generation we fought for and they've got nothing.'

North-Eye felt a little uncomfortable. 'It's not my fault they've turned out the way they have. We all did our bit and more.'

'Hostilities may have ended in '85 but the battle still rages in every mining community in the country because they never replaced the jobs. Forty years on, our grandchildren are fighting the Miners' Strike and they don't even know it.'

'I hear they were vandalising the allotment last week.'

'They show willing and I need help training them up.'

North-Eye peered through the shed window. 'You won't get a tune out of them. They're so skinny they'd have to run around in a baths cubicle to get wet.'

'No one thought they'd get a tune out of us but we did

alright for ourselves. Come on North-Eye, I can't remember all the technicalities. All I know is how to drive a cutter.'

'You'll get one of these kids killed or perhaps all of them killed and your stupid self with them. I'm off.'

'To hide in your shed while waiting for a wooden overcoat, is that the next time you want to go underground?'

'Working underground wasn't as romantic as you make it out to be, particularly at the end. Some couldn't wait to finish, they were counting down the days.'

'And many would go back tomorrow if they had the chance.'

'If anything goes wrong with these wasters it'll be on my conscience for the rest of my life.'

'I'm still driving a heading and opening a face.'

'You open a face?' laughed North-Eye. 'You haven't a hope. You couldn't keep the cutter to the line of the bastard coal. I had to double back every week to survey a line through the face for you.'

'And not one word of thanks for the regular overtime.'

'In every district you worked, the line of the coal face was as straight as a dog's hind leg.'

'You see, I needed your surveying expertise back then, like I do now. I don't want to start out in Coed Mawr allotments and end up in fucking New Zealand.'

'It's still no.'

'Another thing to think of, if anything does go wrong with these wasters, it'll be on your conscience for the rest of your life because you didn't muck in when asked to.'

'I can't,' said North-Eye storming off.

'When our generation goes, it's not just the skills and mining knowledge going out with us, it'll all go – the laughs, the characters and all the old stories. There'll be no one left to put us in a glass case or a collection. We'll be grassed over and forgotten like the collieries we worked in.'

North-Eye stopped and looked down at his boots for a short while. 'It'll do you no good trying to resurrect the past. The world has moved on without you.'

Johnny watched as North-Eye made his way down the gravel path. He went back into the shed expecting to find it in bits but was amazed to find the place in one piece and the wasters sitting quietly.

'From now on you are not wasters. From now on you are trainees, and training starts immediately.'

'North-Eye not joining us?' said Jayden innocently.

Spider gave him a push. 'C'mon stupid, we all heard.'

Johnny offered an explanation. 'North-Eye has a few hobbies to be going on with.'

Lippo grinned. 'You knows oldies got to keep their minds active.'

Johnny opened a trunk under the sink and took out a miner's oil lamp. He held it up for all to see. 'This is a safety lamp. It's used for ... used for ... testing for gas.'

'Testing for what gas?' asked Lippo.

'You know, er, the gas underground.'

Johnny was inept in front of a class. He knew it. They knew it.

'What's it called?' said Spider, to give Johnny a roast.

'It's called, um, it's called ...'

'This is wicked. He's having an old git moment,' said Lippo. 'We'd be better off asking Slouch.'

Johnny decided to take a different tack. He put the lamp on the sink. 'Let's talk money. All the money will be weekly sales based and cash in hand.'

Spider relaxed back in his chair. 'What about cash for training?'

'Don't worry, I'll sort something out and besides, we'll have on-the-job training so there'll be coal to sell as we go along. There's one big rule you should all know about and that is, keep it quiet.'

Lippo decided to be awkward. 'What's this gas underground?'

'What about it?'

'What's it called again?'

'It's on the tip of my tongue.'

North-Eye entered the shed, 'Firedamp.'

'Firedamp,' Johnny sighed with relief, 'that's it.'

'Firedamp, also known as methane, but you'll also find other gases underground like blackdamp, afterdamp and stink-damp.'

'What's stink-damp?' said Jayden.

'Stink-damp smells of rotten eggs,' North-Eye wafted a hand, 'like it does in here.'

'That's Slouch,' said Lippo.

Slouch sniffed himself. 'I don't smell.'

'If firedamp gets into the main body of air between five and fifteen per cent it forms an explosive mixture with oxygen and, bang, you can kiss your arse goodbye.'

Spider was gobsmacked. 'Shut up.'

'This is your training officer, North-Eye,' said Johnny.

'Trainees, any mining activity we carry out here will be highly unpopular, highly dangerous and highly against the law.' It hit the right note with the trainees and drew an approving nod from Johnny. 'So there'll be a written test at the end of your training.'

'I hate learning stuff,' whined Spider as the mood nosedived.

'You'll learn stuff if you want cash in hand,' said Johnny rummaging in his trunk under the sink. He resurfaced wearing an old leather mining helmet. 'And by the way, North-Eye said you won't last a bastard week.'

TWO

JULIE'S COLLIERY

What Goes Around Comes Around

The trainees sat attentively in the shed kitted out in new white overalls and old black leather helmets like *Clockwork Orange* cosplayers. They disliked the new white shiny helmets from the DIY superstore and insisted on black leather helmets like Johnny's. Luckily Johnny remembered a rack of them in North-Eye's memorabilia collection and, after prolonged nagging, the surveyor reluctantly agreed to loan his antiques to the trainees.

When Spider refused to wear 'dickhead orange hi-vis', a fussy Trinny and Susannah nightmare ensued over the workwear. When the trainees had settled for white plasterer overalls, they were ready for basic classroom instruction.

North-Eye held up a head torch. 'We'll wear head torches until I connect up the lamp charger and cap lamps from my collection.'

Johnny held up a pair of steel toecap boots. 'Trainers are out. Steel toecaps are in. Don't get any ideas about wearing them to any scuffles with the Trewatkins Zulus.'

'This is a toolbar,' said North-Eye holding up a looped metal bar with a padlock. 'Used for storing tools, and you put the tool on the bar like this.' He slipped the end of the bar through a small hole in a shovel blade and locked the padlock. 'Hence the saying "The tools are on the bar", meaning the end of the shift.'

Lippo threw his knee pads at the wall. 'These oldies are doing my head in. We'll be as old as you pair before we fucking start.'

Spider slapped Lippo across the ear. 'Shut it, melon.'

'There's no sense rushing,' said North-Eye. 'The coal has waited millions of years for you boys to come along and dig it out. It can wait a little longer until we train you up and get it right.'

'What Lippo is trying to say is,' said Spider standing and turning out his pockets, 'we're all busted. If I don't get a wad soon I'll go back to dealing.'

'Right,' said Johnny, 'I'll nip down to the cashpoint and sub you all a ton today, everyone happy?'

Not only were they happy, they had already spent it, as pound signs flickered across their grinning eyes. North-Eye could hardly believe his ears. 'That's very generous of you, Johnny?'

'I trust them to work it back.'

'Kitted out in new gear,' said North-Eye, 'and a hundred pounds cash in hand, that's not bad for one day.'

'They still have to listen to everything us old mining dogs say,' added Johnny, 'because if they don't they'll be out the door.'

Mrs M knocked the window. She popped her head around the door, mystified at the strangers in white overalls. 'Sorry to disturb you, Johnny. I called to see if you wanted a cuppa and didn't know you had visitors. There are no names in the visitors' book.'

'Um, er, visitors' book, I knew there was something.'

Mrs M grew suspicious. It was as if she had wandered into a lodge meeting of a strange cult. 'White uniforms?'

'The secret is out,' said North-Eye. 'It's time to own up.'

Johnny sighed gloomily. 'I suppose it is.'

North-Eye opened his wallet and flashed his Neighbourhood Watch ID. 'These young people are my Neighbourhood Watch volunteers.'

'Volunteers?' said Mrs M.

'Fu ... volunteers?' said Johnny.

North-Eye patted Lippo's helmet. 'That's right, you're my volunteers, aren't you boys?'

A cautious affirmative nod came from the trainees.

'And you wanted to keep it a surprise, Johnny,' said North-Eye.

Johnny clicked on. 'A Neighbourhood Watch ground force to clean up the allotment before the championship.'

Mrs M was delighted. 'That's so thoughtful of you. And I've spoiled the surprise, how silly of me.' She patted Lippo's helmet. 'Helmets in an allotment, Johnny?'

''Elf and Safety gone stark raving mad, when do you want the volunteers to start?'

'I can find plenty for them to do right away. Mr Williams' plot in particular has fallen into neglect since his stroke and needs a little TLC. I hope they like tea and cake.'

'Anything for nothing,' Johnny patted Lippo's helmet much to the teenager's irritation. 'Isn't that right, boys?'

'I'll have to nip out for extra Welsh cakes.'

'They'll turn over the allotment and Dai Milk's cow field for extra Welsh cakes,' said Johnny. 'OK, you Neighbourhood Watch volunteers, let's get to work.'

The trainees got busy grafting in the allotment and their white overalls and black helmet appearance caused a stir as Hoss, Vince the Hippy, Betty Bingo and other tenants curiously looked on. Spider and Lippo erected fence panels in front of the secret way, while Jayden, Charlie and Slouch weeded and turned over Bouncer Williams' plot. Johnny and North-Eye supervised.

'That was sharp thinking on your part,' said Johnny.

'Our Neighbourhood Watch volunteers don't look too happy about it.'

'A bit of "what goes around comes around" won't hurt them. A few days ago they were vandalising the allotment and now they're tidying it up. More importantly, they've put up fence panels to screen our movements through my secret way.'

Mrs M supplied them with tea and Welsh cakes from a large serving tray. 'Thank you, Mrs M,' said Jayden as he passed cups to Charlie and Slouch and took one for himself.

'He's such a nice polite young man is your grandson,' said Mrs M as Johnny and North-Eye each liberated a cup from the tray.

'It helps he's a big fan of Welsh cakes like his grandad, it brings out the best in him.'

Like a magician's prestige, Team Singh materialised around the Bollywood shed and Parvinder strode up the path.

'What's all this? A Team Johnny to rival Team Singh?'

'I can't give up the best plot award without a bit of a fight.'

'Tea and Welsh cakes for Team Johnny, Mrs M?' said Parvinder eyeing the empty cups and a plate of crumbs on the tray. 'You're spoiling them.'

Mrs M made her way gracefully down the path. 'I'll get the

kettle on. There's plenty to go around, Parvinder. I got a few extra packets from your shop.'

'If I'd have known I would've given you a good discount.' Parvinder suspiciously eyeballed Lippo as he and Spider passed by with a fence panel.

'There's no Team Johnny,' said Johnny with a mouthful of cake and stepping in Parvinder's line of sight.

'They're my Neighbourhood Watch volunteers,' said North-Eye. 'You may see them around now and again doing odds and ends in the allotment.'

'Ah,' said Parvinder.

'Just ignore them if you see them about,' Johnny said quietly. 'They are not anywhere near as efficient as Team Singh.'

Happy to hear it, Parvinder scanned the allotment at the work until he saw Clayton. 'You've been spotted on Clayton's radar.'

Clayton fastened a CCTV camera to his shed apex while atop a step ladder held steady by Smithy. From his high vantage point he suspiciously observed the busy strangers in white overalls. He climbed down and gave instructions to Smithy. Clayton had ceased speaking terms with the ex-miner after his shed painting humiliation and he instructed Smithy to find out what was going on.

Smithy marched across the newly-turned neat furrows of Bouncer's plot to the exasperation of Jayden, Charlie and Slouch. Johnny gestured them to calm down and they made do with a synchronised show of two-finger salutes behind Smithy's back.

'Mr Morgan, is this costing us anything?' said Smithy with an air of arrogance.

'Is what costing us anything, Mr Smithy?'

Smithy waved a condescending hand at the trainees. 'This work going on, with these strangers, is it costing the CMAA?'

'Volunteers cost nothing,' said Parvinder.

'You'd know all about that, Mr Singh. It's nothing short of forced child labour on your plot.'

North-Eye and Johnny held back Parvinder from the ex-copper.

'They are my Neighbourhood Watch volunteers,' said North-Eye, getting fed up with saying it.

Smithy nodded in the direction of Lippo and Spider. 'Those fence panels must have cost something Mr Morgan?'

'They did, but as they are my fence panels and I paid for them, it's none of your business.'

'The committee should be informed of any fence erection before work starts in the form of a written proposal.'

'The committee should be informed of any polytunnel erection before work starts in the form of a written proposal because the committee recently voted to limit the number of polytunnels. I know these things. I'm on the committee.'

'I know these things too,' said Parvinder, still vexed by the ex-copper's insult. 'I'm also on the committee, unlike you Mr Smithy, who has recently resigned.'

Smithy blanked Parvinder, pointed at the trainees and belly-laughed. 'How stupid do they look? Are they miners' hats?'

Slouch took off his helmet, examined it all over but could not find anything wrong with it.

'Helmets,' corrected North-Eye.

That was enough for Johnny and he ushered Smithy away. 'Don't let us keep you from reporting back to Mr Clayton.'

Smithy snorted a laugh. 'That's why you'll never find,' he

scoffed in a false plummy English accent,' a coal mine in the Home Counties.'

His shoulders heaved with laughter as he ploughed another trail across the neat furrows of Bouncer's plot.

'Wait a minute,' said North-Eye, 'what about ...'

Johnny kicked North-Eye's shin. 'Now's not the time.'

North-Eye rubbed his shin. 'What's it supposed to mean?'

'It's a wind-up he's said to me for years. I like to leave him basking in ignorance.'

'They're up to no good I tell you,' said Parvinder as Gaganjit cranked up the Bhangra and Team Singh threw shapes while they worked.

Johnny noticed the trainees were poking around Bouncer's shed. They appeared interested in the security features, trying the locked door and peering through the bolted windows. Johnny got in among them. 'What are you wasters up to over by here now?'

'Never mind us,' said Spider, 'who's the blimpy bumping his gums?'

'The blimpy bumping his gums and the other one, who looks like Dracula without the charisma, are ex-coppers with an over-inflated sense of their own importance.'

Spider's eyes widened, 'Filth?'

Johnny removed Lippo's hand from the door handle. 'Leave worrying about the filth to me. What are you up to? Mrs M said to turn over Bouncer's plot, not turn over his shed.'

'We were only having a look, Grandad.'

'Why isn't he doing his own work?' said Lippo.

'Bouncer Williams had a stroke. He's too ill to work his plot but it's got to look perfect for the allotment championship.'

'Bouncer,' said Spider oozing with approval. 'Sounds like

he's a big hard bastard working the doors and giving out slaps.'

'No, he's a little guy. We call him Bouncer because he was a colliery winder. He drove the winding engine to wind up the cage and was renowned for the best porno mag collection in the colliery. You've got instant access to phone porn now but back in the day it was porno magazines.'

'The times that maniac Bouncer had us bouncing up and down the shaft like a yo-yo,' said North-Eye joining them. 'Coal speed, man-riding speed, and emergency stops, it was all the same to him as he'd put his foot down whatever he was winding. We'd stagger out of the cage with enough G-forces to qualify as NASA astronauts.'

Johnny shepherded the trainees away from the shed. 'We always said when Bouncer was winding he was jacking off with his other hand, and considering the extent of his magazine collection, he probably was.'

Action Xtinction

Minge Jenkins yawned as he descended the stairs of Coal Yard House in his dressing gown and slippers. The sixty-eight-year-old Trewatkins coal merchant had hardly slept a wink after a night tossing and turning with worry. The future looked bleak for one of the last family coal merchants still trading in the valleys. Clean air legislation soon meant the end of coal and customers were already dropping like flies as more converted to cleaner energy.

Adding to his angst, Dai Milk and Spanners were cagey and non-committal about their coal orders over a drink in the Trewatkins Hotel the night before. He could not get to the bottom of it even after buying a couple of rounds and the veiled threat of violence. Minge suspected it had something to do with a rumour he had heard of coal being sold from the back of a van in the valley. He resolved to scour the boot sales for the moonlighting grabbing bastard.

When a trickle of coal coming up the valley replaced the torrent of coal going down the valley, Minge adapted and branched out into house renovations, extensions and new builds despite having no building qualifications. With his current project, gutting a terraced house in Abercwmcoedmawr brimmed with damp problems, he figured it would cost a lot more than he had estimated to renovate.

Minge cheered up at the smell of bacon and eggs wafting into the lounge from the kitchen where his wife Rose cooked a full breakfast.

He took a comforting look at his collection of coal merchant memorabilia where his grandfather's leather hood and shoulder flaps took pride of place on a bust in a glass case. His grandfather had founded Jenkins & Son Coal Merchants over a hundred years ago to supply house coal to the valley, and Minge stubbornly refused to submit to the inevitable end of the family tradition as the coal fire went out without so much as a whimper.

In front of the bust, a Corgi coal lorry parked at an angle next to a tiny pile of coal. Miniature coalmen humped the bags from the lorry and emptied the coal into the pile. Smiling at the little figures, Minge opened the glass case and picked up the toy. 'Jenkins & Son Coal Merchants,' he read proudly from the side of the lorry. He thought of the days when coal merchants were a common sight in the Valleys and large black mounds of coal dotted the streets as if the terraces were infested by giant moles.

'Now it's superstores selling smokeless fuel made from renewable or recycled materials with low CO2 emissions,' said Minge to the lorry. 'Genuine Welsh anthracite, the clean burning steam coal that built this country, and fuelled an empire, is a thing of the past. Any coal you can get your hands on now is imported rubbish.'

'Breakfast is ready,' trilled Rose from the kitchen.

'I'll be there now in a minute, Rose love.' He replaced the toy lorry in the glass case and made his way to the kitchen.

'I still can't find my Sabatier knife,' said Rose while putting two plates of bacon, eggs and mushrooms on the table.

'I'll ask that half-wit grandson of ours if he's seen it.'

'I'm lost without it. I used a steak knife to slice the mushrooms.'

Minge rolled his eyes and tucked into his breakfast.

'It's the serrated edge, it doesn't cut right. I'm fed up of looking and I've looked everywhere.'

'Have you looked behind the orchid pot on the windowsill?'

'No, I haven't, I'll look now.'

'It'll still be there after breakfast,' said Minge tetchily, downing his knife and fork.

As Rose lifted the orchard pot, a grinning skull gurned at her through the window. Minge almost hit the ceiling when Rose dropped the pot in the sink and screamed.

Minge Jenkins raced through the back door into the coal yard and grabbed the skull-faced mime artist by the cravat. Before he could stick one on him, he looked around the coal yard not believing his eyes. The Jenkins & Son Coal Merchant wrought iron gates swung open into the yard decorated by half-a-dozen women in pink overalls chained to the railings.

Through a swirl of pink smoke, flags depicting 'Action Xtinction' and 'AX' fluttered in the breeze. Protesters waved placards – COAL IS DEAD, DEATH TO COAL and FOSSIL FUEL IS OVER.

Wearing his gorilla onesie pyjamas, Minja held Rocky on a short leash to worry a group of Bip the clown mimes, stilt-walkers, and jugglers.

'Mr Jenkins,' shouted Trudi Anderson in a Norwegian accent from her chained position high on the gates, 'my name is Trudi Anderson and I am the founder of Action Xtinction. Our peaceful protest today is necessary for the protection of our planet and part of a wider movement of non-violent civil disobedience. Our aim is to reduce the UK CO2 emissions that are overheating our planet and to totally eradicate the archaic practice of coal burning, a practice that you exacerbate from this property and are therefore personally responsible. We are here today to hold you to account for your heinous crimes against our climate.'

Minge released the choking mime artist. He stepped over the chained lines of students and pensioners sitting in his yard and snatched a banner reading PLANET NOT PROFIT from an inflatable plastic dinosaur. He tore it to bits.

'What fucking profit? I'm practically bankrupt.'

'I remind you Mr Jenkins,' shouted Trudi, 'this is a peaceful protest and we are filming you on our phones.'

'We're not in the EU any more so why you foreigners keep thinking you can tell us what to do is beyond me. We're too soft in this country. Where are all those coppers who were about during the Miners' Strike to give you lot a good kicking?'

'Our concern,' continued Trudi as the gate swung on its

hinges requiring her to crane her head sideways, 'is the United Kingdom continually lies about climate change at a time when we face an extinction threat far greater than that of the dinosaurs.'

'Well, Trudi fucking Anderson, founder of Action Xtinction, you may have fooled this bunch of clowns into believing you know your shit but you're so clever you can't even spell extinction.'

A pantomime French accent came from the flapping jaw of the inflatable dinosaur. 'Zee meessing "E" eez seem-bol-eek of zee ree-al-eety of zee dees-er-peer-ance of zee planet Earth, zo we do not een-clude eet in zee word exteen-ction.'

Minge punched the dinosaur into a chained nest of startled students, 'More fucking foreigners.'

'I remind you again, Mr Jenkins,' shouted Trudi, 'this is a peaceful protest and any harm that may befall us and any attempt to remove us by force will be dealt with by the authorities.'

'That's what you think,' shouted Minge, 'you are all trespassers and I'll exercise all reasonable force to remove every single one of you tree shaggers from my property. Minja, get the hosepipe.'

Minja's eyes lit up obediently. 'Awesome.'

Minge pointed at the skull-faced mime. 'Make sure Rocky takes a chunk out of Mr Pasty Face's arse for scaring your grandmother.'

Minja's day was getting better, 'Super awesome.'

Minge muttered to himself as he picked his way through the protesters. He got out his phone and dialled. 'Masters of the industrial world we once were. Now we can't burn a piece of coal in this country without climate Nazis jumping out from behind the trees they've been shagging and telling us we're killing the planet.'

'Owww,' squealed a pensioner protester as Minge inadvertently stepped on his hand, 'you're on my hand.'

'Fuck, off,' shouted Minge as his call connected. 'Hello, Dai Milk? I need a favour. I'll make it worth your while.'

Minja happily hosed down the protesters with the coal yard's powerful industrial hosepipe and, like a water cannon, it rolled the activists this way and that. Rocky chased the skull-faced mime up a lamp post after taking a chunk out of the seat of his tights. Rocky then playfully jumped through the water spray snarling and scaring the shit out of the climate protesters as Trudi's pleas for non-violence were drowned out by shrieks of terror. When the protesters were drenched and demoralised, Minge called Minja and Rocky into the house.

The Jenkins family watched from the upstairs windows as Dai Milk drove his tractor up the street to the coal yard. He carefully reversed his manure tank to the gates and opened up the putrid spray.

After bravely enduring an industrial hosepipe and a mad pitbull cross, what little resolve remained evaporated when it came to a head-to-foot plastering in manure and the protesters could not get out of the yard quick enough. Trudi and the activists on the gates received the worst of the muck spreading, as they took an inordinate amount of time searching for their padlock keys, unlocking and unchaining.

'My contribution to a cleaner planet,' said Dai Milk, pushing his jam-jar glasses higher up his nose as Trudi and her defeated Action Xtinction die-hards filed past his tractor with barely a trace of pink left visible. Nosey neighbours slammed doors on the rank smell as AX activists oozed their way down the terraced street.

Contraband and the Pit

To give the trainees the bigger picture, the two miners decided to take them in the van on a pit visit to Deep Mine Museum.

Before they set off, Johnny searched them for contraband – smoking material or anything capable of igniting an explosion underground. Like Ali Bongo performing magic tricks on innocent members of the audience, Johnny found cigarettes, cigarette papers, matches, a cannabis leaf rollie tin, loose spliffs, a silver Zippo, two cheap plastic lighters, two tubes of glue, a vaping kit and vape liquids, several suspicious foil-wrapped substances, half a dozen nitrous oxide canisters and a glass bong.

The offending items filled a shoe box held by North-Eye, and throughout the journey he sat in the passenger seat with a lap full of smoking and drug paraphernalia.

'There are enough drugs in there to sedate a herd of elephants.'

Johnny reached over and fondled the silver Zippo. 'I'm away with the fairies looking at it.'

'I could never see the point. It always made me feel funny and gave me a headache,' said North-Eye. 'I could get that from a couple of pints of rough cider in the Dog and Ferret.'

'With this lot on your lap, pray we don't get stopped by the law because *you'll* have a lot of explaining to do.'

The thought tickled Johnny and he guffawed. Contemplating that possible scenario, North-Eye gulped.

Throughout the drive along the Heads of the Valleys road, Johnny insisted North-Eye held Slouch's smelly sleeping bag out of the passenger window for a good airing. This North-Eye managed with some difficulty due to the shoe box of drugs on his lap. They passed a parked police car monitoring the traffic flow. Johnny gave it a wave and bellowed laughing at the terrified look on North-Eye's face. The surveyor sighed with relief when the headgear of Deep Mine Museum came into view.

Two mining guides, Geronimo and Billy Donkey, sat on a dry stone wall outside the museum entrance enjoying a sly smoke and a chew of tobacco. Geronimo, a tall lank of a man with long grey hair and an aquiline nose, who looked as if he would be at home in an Apache wickiup, spat a globule of tobacco juice into a litter bin as the van pulled up in the car park. Billy Donkey, a medium-sized spritely man with dark eyes sparkling like anthracite, lit a rollie he retrieved from a hiding place within the dry stones. They thought nothing of the van's arrival until Johnny opened the back doors and unleashed the dazzling trainees in white overalls.

'Shunt my drams ... mining trainees?' said Billy Donkey in disbelief. 'We were just talking about them.'

'With a deputy and training officer?' said Geronimo.

Johnny had commandeered a deputy's stick from North-Eye's memorabilia collection and he used it to manoeuvre the trainees to the entrance while North-Eye followed at the rear.

'Now there's a pair of ghosts of collieries past,' said Geronimo, 'Johnny the Cutter and North-Eye the surveyor.'

'Fuck me hooray, it's Geronimo and Billy Donkey,' enthused Johnny. 'This makes a change from seeing you at funerals. How long have you pair been working here then?'

'We've been here for years, mun,' said Billy Donkey, 'place would fall in without us.'

Johnny leaned on his stick. 'You kept that quiet. You must be onto a good thing.'

'Not for much longer, butt,' said Geronimo. 'They've put us on part-time and there's no one coming on behind us. We are the last genuine miners and once we're gone there's only museum curators left to tell the story. And what do they know?'

'Dick shit,' said the four old miners.

'The end of an era,' said Billy Donkey looking over the trainees. 'What've you got by here then? They look like what we need – mining trainees. We were just talking about mining trainees over by here now and as if by magic here they are. Unbelievable isn't it, Geronimo?'

'Just this second, over by here now, we were saying it,' Geronimo agreed. 'What this place needs is mining trainees to carry on the knowledge before it goes out for good.'

'No, they are not mining trainees. They are ...' Johnny looked to North-Eye for an answer.

'Students,' lied North-Eye, 'from the University of Glamorgan researching the economic impact on valleys communities and changes in the employment sector in the last thirty years, since the demise of the Welsh mining industry, to bullet-point how employment has adapted to what we see in the present day, track that metamorphosis, and evaluate any lessons to be learned. It's about finding answers.'

'Shut up,' said Geronimo with a spit of tobacco and a broad smile betraying the fact he did not believe a word.

'Students?' said Billy Donkey smoking his rollie and eyeing them with a suspicious eye. 'Is that why they're wearing white overalls?'

Lippo tugged at Billy's sleeve. 'It's because we didn't want to look like dickheads in orange overalls.'

Geronimo and Billy Donkey gave their orange overalls a once-over and laughed.

'Right then boys,' said Geronimo, 'introduce yourselves and tell us where you are from and what you're studying, like they do on *University Challenge*.'

'It's not what they are studying,' said Billy Donkey, 'it's what they are reading.'

'I stand corrected,' said Geronimo with a spit of tobacco.

'Look,' said Johnny abruptly, 'they're studying or reading what North-Eye said, with shagging and beer drinking, like all students.'

'In that case,' said Billy Donkey, getting up and stamping on his rollie, 'c'mon you dickheads in white overalls who are studying or reading what North-Eye said, with shagging and beer drinking. It's this way.'

'He hasn't changed, still running around like a blue-arsed fly,' said Johnny. 'C'mon train … students.'

'You should try working with him,' said Geronimo. 'The visitors are down, around and back up the shaft before they can spit.' He spat tobacco and took Johnny aside. 'What are you up to, Johnny the Cutter? Students, my arse!'

'Honest to God, Geronimo, they are students like North-Eye said.'

'And when did you start strutting around like a colliery manager and pointing a stick?' Geronimo took the stick and examined it. 'This is the real thing. What's going on?'

All through the underground visit Geronimo and Billy Donkey did their best to wheedle information out of Johnny and North-Eye but they stuck to the story and the 'students' kept it quiet. They went through the visit like a dose of Andrews liver salts and it was a big relief for Johnny and North-Eye to be back in the van.

The two mining guides watched from the car park as the van spluttered and took off like a rocket.

Billy Donkey lit a rollie he plucked from a crack in the wall. 'That was a quick visit even for me. Students! They couldn't spell their own tattoos.'

'I've met cleverer sheep,' agreed Geronimo with a spit of tobacco juice. 'And once we started asking questions they couldn't get away fast enough.'

The Climate of Fear

Geronimo was right. Johnny could not get away from Deep Mine Museum fast enough as he put the van through the gears and bombed up the road. They did not speak until the van turned off onto the mountain road above the Coed Mawr valley.

'For a pit visit and for the speed of it, I thought it went well, all things considered,' said North-Eye clutching the shoe box of contraband. 'The museum will give our trainees an idea of what it was like underground. Course, it's not like the real thing.'

'They're onto us,' worried Johnny. 'Geronimo found a million different ways to stick his nose in. And Billy Donkey asked at every turn. They didn't believe a word of our student alibi.'

'What harm could they do?' said North-Eye hanging on to the contraband shoebox as the van bounced in a pothole. 'They wouldn't grass us up. They're on our side.'

'They'd want to get involved.'

'Is that such a bad thing? The more experience the better.'

'The less people in the know the better.'

They drove up a sheep-covered rise and as they reached the crest North-Eye squinted into the distance. 'The drugs must be leaking out of this bastard box.'

Johnny slowed the van, 'Have a look at this, boys, it's a sight you won't see every day.'

A crowd of dishevelled manure-covered stilt walkers, dinosaurs and mimes trudged alongside the road like refugees. Trudi Anderson led the remnants of Action Xtinction home to the tent village outside the gates of the Merthyr-Bargoed-Dare open-cast mine. The bus driver for the coal merchant day of action had refused to let the filthy protesters onto his gleaming coach.

Johnny wound down the window for a gawk while the trainees roared with laughter and fought for film space in the back windows. 'Funny place for a fancy dress?' said Johnny to Trudi as she glared through him like a Gorgon. 'Phew, what a whiff.' He quickly wound up the window and sped away.

'What a happy-looking bitch.'

'That's Trudi Anderson and her climate activists, Action Xtinction.'

'X-stink-shun?' said Johnny laughing at his own pun. 'Because they stink like they've rolled around in Dai Milk's cow field?'

'They're always up to something or another and pulling publicity stunts. The Action Xtinction climate camp is outside the gates of the open-cast mine.'

'And that's making a difference to the climate?'

'I can't see logic in it either with the phasing out of coal.'

'They are gutless gloaters jumping on the bandwagon and

rejoicing at the end of the coal age, an end they played no part in bringing about. You won't find these climate cowards out in the real battlegrounds like Brazil or Borneo where they destroy the rainforests because they know they'll end up in shallow graves. Open-cast is not proper coal mining as I understand it but I'm yet to hear of any orangutans dying up there. In fact, we miners are a fellow endangered species alongside the orangutans.'

North-Eye smirked at Johnny going further off his head.

'I don't deny there's a problem with the climate but where have those Seventies scientists gone to, who told us the next Ice Age was coming? Where's the next Ice Age gone to? The only climate scientists are interested in is a climate of fear. Why people believe the blaggers is beyond me. I'd rather believe Mystic Meg. They told us we'd end world famine by growing giant vegetables by the year 2000 and we'd be living on the moon wearing shiny suits, but not one of them predicted the mobile phone or the joy of PPI cold callers.'

'You watched too many episodes of *Tomorrow's World* and paid far too much attention to what you read in the *Beano*.'

'Ask two scientists the same question and you'll get two different answers. They are nothing but blaggers.'

'I don't know about that,' said North-Eye just to wind him up and watch him go, 'but I can see you've put serious thought into this.'

'Scientists in the Seventies told us the oil was going to run out by the Millennium and because we had over 800 years of coal reserves left in this country the future of deep mining was secure. We'd have a job for life in the coal industry because there'd always be a need for coal. When it comes to predictions they get far more wrong than they get right, so why should we listen to the blaggers about the climate emergency?'

'Interesting, but your take on the big picture may need tweaking.'

Trudi Anderson watched the white van disappear into the distance towards the Coed Mawr valley. She vowed never to be caught napping again by these inbred valleys retards.

The Miniature Coal Mine

With each passing day Johnny's shed evolved into a whimsical, fully-functioning miniature colliery and North-Eye's memorabilia added an unintentional steampunk character. Johnny's winding engine inside the shed consisted of a racing bicycle attached to a system of wheels and pulleys, while a large flywheel on the roof took the strain and spun inside a timber headgear. Moving the flagpole from porch post to headgear completed the visual impact. A vuvuzela warning blast down the shaft signalled his intention to wind, and pedal power wound up a cage fashioned from supermarket trolleys through the trapdoor.

He created a concealed entrance by cutting and hinging the slats near the sink to provide easy access behind the fence panels to the secret way. Johnny camouflaged the entrance as shelving, and superglued paint tins to the shelves to complete the deception.

Suction for the ventilation system came from three vintage canister vacuum cleaners tightly taped together, their intertwined hoses connecting to a wider column of ducting running down the side of the shaft. Near the trapdoor an upright fan with coloured streamers forced air into a funnel leading into the colliery workings.

It bothered Johnny that the trainees were politically incorrect by 'walking the streets like the Black and White Minstrels' as he put it to North-Eye, so when he found a shower unit in a skip he plumbed it into the shed disguising it as a corner tool cupboard. North-Eye added authenticity by donating a Pit Head Baths sign to the door and a colliery soap dish. The trainees used the shower on a rota, with the exception of Charlie who preferred bathing at home. For a good laugh and to improve Slouch's hygiene, the trainees regularly stripped him and threw him in the cupboard, but as soon as he became reunited with his stinking sleeping bag their efforts were of little avail.

Johnny recruited a cage of singing canaries and the little yellow birds became popular team members, the cage resting on top of the rows of dials and cap lamps of North-Eye's lamp charger. The cap lamps charged up overnight on the charger rack and the LED battery head torches went into storage. A check board next to the canary cage recorded the number of miners underground and every black leather helmet had a home on a row of hooks across the wall.

On-the-job training suited the trainees and they enjoyed the on-a-jolly visits to mining museums and heritage centres in south Wales. Heads drooped in shed classroom lessons as they stifled yawns and played on their phones to any talk of mine gases and safety. Without any training films, they made do with mining DVDs. They dozed through black and white screenings of *The Brave Don't Cry* and *Proud Valley*, but films in colour helped as they took interest in *Still the Enemy Within* and had a good laugh at *Pride*.

Far easier than feared, North-Eye's dreaded written test had multiple choice answers. Johnny thought it appropriate to take them to the Old Wheel to officially pass them out, which they did with a few celebratory cans, and when he bestowed the team captaincy on natural leader Spider, there were no arguments. When they got back to the shed Charlie filmed Spider, Lippo, Jayden and Slouch mooning in celebration at Clayton's CCTV camera.

As the underground workings spread, they scoured the valley terraces for skips and helped themselves to any discarded pallets and timber to use for supports. They reclaimed fireplaces, cast iron drainpipes, pine kitchen units, a set of pastel-coloured doors, and fitted them underground to shore up the sides and roof. The young miners took turns accompanying Johnny to the tip where the pyramid of muck grew bigger and they practised their driving skills. On the return journey they filled the empty bags with fly-tipped plastics, toys and rubble to tightly pack in the voids of the workings.

Johnny got on well with the teenagers but they sniggered behind his back as if they knew something he did not. Even Jayden would not let on what it was.

Johnny was impressed by the brittle quality of the seam – the coal fell easily from the mandrel, making it child's play to shovel into bags for the young miners. The brittle nature bothered North-Eye who advised extra roof vigilance, but Johnny called him a big Julie Andrews for worrying about nothing.

Joanne grew into an important team member in the running of the colliery as she called in daily with bagged sandwiches for the workforce, and did the laundry. She made sure the team started every week with clean, ironed and neatly-folded white overalls. One evening Joanne cheerfully finished a shift on the ironing and carried the folded workwear upstairs to the landing airing cupboard. As she passed Jayden's open bedroom door, she noticed him sitting on the bed with Charlie. They were busy at the PC, unaware she lurked behind them in the doorway, and when Jayden put an arm around Charlie, Joanne's chirpiness vanished. Thunderstruck, she went back down the stairs, put the pile of workwear on the hall table, and got out her phone.

Johnny balanced precariously with one foot on a step-ladder, the other foot on the sink, while nailing a cable grip to the roof. As he raised the hammer, his phone rang on the sink below. 'Fuck me hooray.' He dropped the hammer to the floorboards, where it flipped over on impact and disappeared down the shaft through the trapdoor. 'Double fuck me hooray, if this is a cold caller ... poor bastard.' He got down from the ladder and answered the phone. 'Joanne?'

'Dad?'

'What is it, girl?'

'It's Jayden.'

'What's he up to now? Not doing that self-harming again is he?'

'No it's not that ... it's um ... I don't know.'

'I haven't got all day trying to guess. You've rang when I'm a little bit busy over by here now, mun.'

'You're not still at the shed?'

'You said it was Jayden.'

'But you've got a home to go to and ...'

'Never mind me still at the shed, I'm happy keeping busy instead of moping around an empty house on my own. Now what is it?'

'It's Jayden ...'

'I know, c'mon spit it out.'

'It's Charlie …'

'It's Charlie? You said it was Jayden.'

'It's both of them.'

'What about them?'

'They are um … I don't know … I just saw Jayden … in his bedroom and he put his arm around Charlie … and it looked a bit … you know.'

'And?'

'What do you mean *and*? Isn't that bad enough?'

'Are you trying to tell me you think my grandson is gay?'

'Every evening they're in his bedroom on the internet up to something or another … sending for things … I don't know what.'

'What's wrong with that? He can access all sorts of stuff and send for things easily from his phone if he wants to.'

'He's secretive about deliveries he's had … it's all very worrying.'

'The other day you were worried he was going out till all hours, now you're worried he's in his bedroom. Is there anything the boy can do without you falling to bits?'

'Can you have a word?'

'If he is gay, so what, perhaps he's only trying to double his chances of a date on a Saturday night, and as long as he's happy who cares where he puts it.'

'I don't think Charlie is a good influence on Jayden. He gives me the willies all wrapped up like that and with those sunglasses. I'll have to put my foot down and stop him coming to the house.'

'They've been friends for years and now they're workmates.'

'Yes, I'll stop Charlie coming to the house.'

'Hold your horses. You don't want to set him off again with the cutting nonsense. I'll have a word and find out what's going on.'

'Thanks, Dad.'

'No worries,' he said looking up at the unfinished cable grip. 'I've got to get on, so tar-rah.' He hung up. 'Where'd I put that hammer?'

Julie's Colliery

Johnny spoke to Jayden at the start of a new working week. Delighted at his explanation, he called a team meeting in the shed.

'Jayden and Charlie have been secretly busy,' said Johnny with an eye on Joanne who bit a fingernail in trepidation, 'working on a colliery name and logo.'

Relief registered across Joanne's face.

'Of course,' said North-Eye, 'we've got to have a name. It didn't even cross my mind. How did we bastard miss that?'

'Too busy with our heads up our backsides,' said Johnny. 'Jayden will explain.'

'We sat in the park trying to think of a design for the colliery then Charlie drew the Old Wheel.'

Lippo sniggered. 'We all knows Charlie's artistic.'

Jayden unfurled a nylon flag. 'We had the design custom-made on a flag. We both came up with the name.'

Seething with jealousy, Lippo folded his arms tight across his chest, 'Julie's Colliery? You knows that's girl pants shite.'

Spider gave Lippo a backhander. 'I like it.'

Lippo rubbed his earplug. 'I've got a better name.'

'Let's hear it then,' sighed Johnny.

'Call it Wasters' Colliery, because we're all wasters.'

'All those in favour of calling it Wasters' Colliery, because we're all wasters, raise a hand,' proposed Johnny half-heartedly.

Only Lippo raised a hand.

'We could call it Dog Colliery,' said Slouch, 'because I like dogs.' No one said anything, so thinking no one had heard he said it again. 'We could call it Dog Colliery?'

Johnny draped the flag over the canary cage.

'I want Julie's Colliery with the Old Wheel design embroidered on our overalls, customised on our lamp checks, stamped on our coal bags and on anything else we can think of.'

'Flying from the flagpole?' suggested North-Eye.

'That's a no. It'll literally flag up where the coal is coming from.'

'It'll be a shame if the flag doesn't fly after all Jayden and Charlie's good work,' said Joanne, back to her chirpy self.

'The flag will fly one day but for now we'll keep it in the shed.'

Johnny gathered everyone outside the shed, posing with shovels, lamps, canaries and the flag. He positioned his phone on a water barrel, set the timer and joined the team. 'Everybody say ... testicles.'

The framed result joined the two photographs at pride of place on the wall in Julie's Colliery.

Not so Good Vibrations

When the ventilation system played up and a scorching summer's day made it too hot to work inside the shed, Johnny dismantled a vacuum cleaner canister on the porch bench. He brought the canaries outside for company and suspended the cage from a cup hook.

Voices from the direction of Clayton's shed interrupted his repairs and he downed tools to investigate. He peeked around the side of Bouncer's shed where Clayton, Smithy and Mrs M were having a discussion outside Clayton's polytunnel. Clayton shushed them, and they listened while looking down at a pan of water at their feet. Like a gunfighter fast on the draw, Clayton pointed a finger at the rippling water. The ex-coppers squatted down for a closer look while Mrs M set off Johnny's way.

Johnny jumped for cover behind the shed panels. 'They can hear the boys working underground!'

He ran back across the porch and into his shed, spooking the canaries in a flutter of shit and feathers. Through the window he saw Mrs M fast approaching across Bouncer's plot. With no time to stop the team working, he slammed the trapdoor shut, calmly stepped out onto the porch and fiddled with the vacuum cleaner.

'If you're in a cleaning mood, Johnny, you could give my shed a good hoover when you're done.'

'I've wanted to fix this retro cleaner for years and now I've more time I thought I'd give it a go. I hate chucking stuff out.'

'So I see,' said Mrs M looking into the shed. 'You seem to be collecting a lot of junk.'

'North-Eye's mining memorabilia.' He stepped between Mrs M and the shed doors. 'He's loaned it to me to enhance the mining theme of my shed. I'm hoping the authenticity will catch the eye in the allotment championship.'

'And he was happy to part with his memorabilia? That's unusual for a collector.'

'He's enthusiastic about the theme.'

Mrs M stood on tiptoe to see over his shoulder. 'Is that a bicycle?'

Johnny manoeuvred her to the canary cage. 'A fixing-up job for my grandson. Don't you just love retirement?'

Mrs M took a shine to the canary cage. 'Canaries are so cute.'

'I might breed them. Good fertiliser from the droppings.'

Mrs M got to the point. 'Have you heard anything unusual in the allotment recently?'

'No, can't say I have.'

'Mr Clayton and Mr Smithy claim to have heard noises and felt vibrations.'

'Sounds serious ...'

'Shh, what was that?'

'What was what?' said Johnny, feeling troubled because he also heard it.

'I thought I heard something.'

'I didn't hear anything.'

'Sounded like digging.'

'Digging?'

Mrs M crept around the porch. 'There it is again.'

Johnny spoke up to mask the noise. 'I can't hear anything. Mind you, I did get a loss of hearing payout from British Coal. Not that it means anything, but it helped pay for my conservatory.'

'Quiet please, Johnny.'

They listened but only heard chirping canaries.

'I can't hear anything now.'

'The stress of the looming allotment championship is getting to you. Clayton and Smithy have got you worrying over nothing.'

'No, I heard digging.'

'Come to think of it, I've noticed it myself.' He led Mrs M away to look at the allotment. 'I'm no New Ager like Vince the Hippy but perhaps all the sheds are channelling Feng Shui energy at my shed, or a simple case of acoustics as all the sound carries into this corner from the rest of the allotment. I can hear Hoss turning his compost, Vince and Betty Bingo forking, and Team Singh are quite deafening.'

He saw Clayton and Smithy observing from a distance. 'Perhaps that's what Cagney and Lacey can hear.'

Not convinced, Mrs M returned to his porch and pointed through the window. 'It came from inside your shed. If we are quiet, we may hear it again.'

They listened for a while and Johnny racked his brain for inspiration. He snapped a bamboo stick in half.

'Wouldn't you rather hear my Ringo Starr?' He played a drum solo on pots, buckets, windows and the canary cage.

'I seem to remember back in '65 you were the talk of the school when you saw The Beatles in Cardiff, on the final date of their last ever British tour. Everyone died of jealousy.'

'Beatle-mania, that's so embarrassing.'

'Why?'

'I was a screaming child madly in love with George Harrison.'

'I never saw The Beatles and it turned out to be the last chance anyone around here ever had.' He drummed a cowbell sound out of the chiminea. 'Dave Clark Five?'

'More like Animal from the *Muppet Show*?'

Johnny feigned offence and dropped his sticks. 'You can go off people you know. I didn't even get to my Keith Moon.'

'Thank heavens for small mercies,' she laughed. 'Perhaps I am a little stressed.'

'Stressed, but you know your drummers,' said Johnny as he ushered her away from the shed and off the porch. 'A cup of tea sorts out everything. Three o'clock in the committee shed is good for me.'

'I'll inform Mr Clayton of your theories of Feng Shui energy and acoustics. It's Battenberg today.'

'Battenberg, lovely, and we'll have a good old chinwag about The Beatles, The Monkees, and the Swinging Sixties.'

Later that evening, as Bollywood gave way to country and western classics blaring out of Hoss's batwing doors, all was revealed.

'Leeks,' said Parvinder swigging a Cobra beer on Johnny's porch. 'Clayton and Smithy are growing giant leeks. I got it from Vince the Hippy when he called in for a necklace of Bollywood beads. They went to a horticultural show in the north-east to find out how to grow leeks and came back with a bucket-load of big ideas.'

'It makes sense. Leek growers are notoriously secretive about their tricks of the trade.'

'Clayton and Smithy are worried about their leeks. They're not responding to the expensive feed they bought up north.'

'Sounds like they've been had; my bet is they went to an old pit village in the north-east like ours and they saw straight through them.' Johnny raised his bottle to those unknown comrades.

'They interrogated Vince the Hippy for advice on compost, drainage and growing under artificial light. Of course, he denied any such knowledge but he freaked out when they asked for a wind chime to locate the cause of strange vibrations in Clayton's polytunnel.'

Johnny spat out his beer. 'Sorry, it went down the wrong way.'

'It sounded too ghostly for Vince so he gave Clayton a wind chime to shut him up.'

'I wonder if Clayton's wind chime is tinkling to the vibrations from this country and western.'

'We all know music is good for plants. Oh, and I've some allotment gossip for you. Vince the Hippy and Betty Bingo have got a thing going on.'

'Shut up?'

'I'm surprised you haven't noticed when you can see all the comings and goings from this porch.'

Parvinder nudged Johnny and they spied Vince surreptitiously exiting from Betty Bingo's shed.

Scargill

'Nightmare; Mrs M and the coppers can hear the boys working,' said Johnny when North-Eye called in the following day.

'You've left them working underground unsupervised?'

'They'll be alright, mun.'

'They won't be "alright, mun". You can't leave them down there on their own, they haven't got the experience.'

'I can't be in two places at once. I've got to be up here winding and filling the van. Since I've trusted them I haven't heard a peep.'

'It's like little children, when they're quiet, they're bastard up to something.' North-Eye examined his lamp charger. 'Anyway, is my lamp charger working?'

'Like a dream.'

'How are you paying for the electric?'

'I can't think of a better use for a coal board pension.'

'Every day in every way you're going further off your bastard head.' North-Eye produced a gas detector from his pocket and opened a small portable canary cage. 'Let's take a gas reading.'

'Good.' Johnny reached for a knapsack on the sink. 'Joanne just dropped off the lunches. It's grub time.'

Johnny and North-Eye made their way through the colliery workings shored up with scavenged pallets, kitchen units and pastel-coloured doors. Moving cap lamps illuminated the miners at the coalface. Spider hewed at the seam with a mandrel while Charlie, keeping up a bug-eyed Goth image in safety goggles, shovelled coal into a bag Jayden held. Lippo sat on a coffee table with his hands in his pockets.

Johnny pulled Lippo off the table by the scruff. 'You must want to have an accident sitting under an exposed roof. Get a post up before a piece of minestone squashes you as flat as a witch's tit.'

'If I bend over again I knows I'll grow a fucking hunchback.'

'Hurry up about it. My mother could work quicker than you.'

'That's so super unbelievable.'

'She wasn't sitting down all day playing pocket billiards.'

'Remember your safety training,' said North-Eye as he moved a pile of loose timber littering the floor.

'Spider,' shouted Johnny, 'as team captain, make sure they keep the workplace cleaned up.'

'Stop coming down on us with the shit-fits.'

Jayden put a bag of coal too many into an overloaded shopping trolley and it keeled over.

'Jayden, watch what you are doing. We don't want broken legs.'

'Sorry, Grandad.'

Johnny admired Charlie work the shovel. 'Look at Charlie go.'

'Like a Trojan,' said North-Eye.

'Charlie, that's the hammer.'

Charlie turned the bug-eyed safety goggles at the old miners for an instant before returning to the work.

Johnny sniffed. 'Where's Slouch? I smell him but I can't see him.'

Slouch, wearing his sleeping bag like a cape, drove up behind them on a mobility scooter pulling a line of shopping trolleys. He sounded a horn and the two old miners jumped with fright.

'Frighten us to death, you headshot imbecile.'

'My bad, I didn't think.'

'Because you haven't got anything to think with.' Johnny blew the vuvuzela. 'It's about time you all started to fucking shape up, but meanwhile, grub time.'

North-Eye hooked the canary cage on an iron drainpipe while Johnny opened the knapsack. Slouch put his feet up on the mobility scooter and the team settled down.

Johnny threw out the sandwich bags. 'It's a Welsh cake, corned beef pasty and either a ham or cheese sandwich.'

Slouch got the willies, 'Cheese?'

'What's wrong with cheese?'

'Cheese gives me nightmares.'

'You're scared of cheese nightmares when you consumed enough drugs to have hallucinations about pixies?'

'Headshot can have a ham one,' said Jayden.

'Think yourselves lucky because these corned beef pasties are better than the ones we had in the old pit canteen. They were all pastry, fresh air and fag ash. You'd think you'd won the pools if you found any corned beef.'

'What's the pools?' whispered Slouch to Charlie.

'So what's it like for you boys now you've done a few shifts underground?' said North-Eye.

'Smashing it,' said Spider.

Charlie signalled with thumbs up.

'Scary,' said Slouch before stuffing a whole sandwich in his mouth.

'Awesome,' said Jayden.

'What about you, Lippo?' said Johnny. 'Not hurting your girly little hands, is it?'

'As long as the accas keep coming I don't care. Same for you too isn't it, bro?'

'I don't want to go back dealing,' said Spider.

'Everyone knows it. Bro was the go-to man if you wanted stuff until he got nicked for selling with intent to supply.'

Spider kicked him. 'Melon. *"Selling with intent to supply?"*'

'Perhaps you could get us some morphine,' North-Eye thought out loud. 'For our first aid station,' he added as they trained enquiring cap lamps on him.

Spider bit into a pasty. 'How does it feel to be back underground, North-Eye?'

'I didn't realise how much I missed it. Not the work, I'm quite happy watching you boys do that, but this, sitting here with the lights dimmed at grub time with your workmates, having a chat and a laugh. I forgot how good it felt. You can take the miner out of the mine but you can't take the mine out of the miner.'

Spider nibbled his pasty. 'Johnny?'

'You'll laugh when I say this, but whenever I was underground I always thought of a coal mine as a living thing, as alive as you or I.'

Slouch looked around the workings with a shiver. 'Alive?'

'Very much alive and could destroy me if I forgot to treat it with respect. That's how I feel now, even in this smaller colliery.'

'How can this hole be alive?' said Slouch thinking of the trouble he had with the pixies.

Johnny continued, 'A colliery meets all …'

Lippo bit into a pasty. 'Is this a long story?'

Spider pushed the pasty into Lippo's mouth. 'Shut it.'

'… the definitions of a living organism. Collieries had lungs and breathed in and breathed out. They ate away at the coal and left waste products. They constantly moved with tentacles of underground roadways. They reproduced, as others like them sprang up all around, and they also had a brain in the colliery offices.'

'A brain in the colliery offices,' scoffed North-Eye. 'If there was – no one could ever bastard find it.'

'They had a heart and soul, the miners who worked the coal and kept the colliery alive. Like you boys down here.'

Lippo bit into a Welsh cake. 'Now we all knows it, you're the headshot one.'

'I must be, I even mucked out the canaries today. What do you think I made the Welsh cakes with?'

Lippo spat cake onto a post.

Slouch peered into the canary cage. 'Aww, the canary's dead.'

North-Eye jumped to his feet. 'Dead, what do you mean dead?'

'D-E-D, dead,' said Slouch.

North-Eye held the small cage at eye level and all lights shone on the little star of the show lying feet up on the floor.

'Perhaps it was an old canary and died of natural causes,' said Johnny.

'Or a young healthy canary dying of unnatural causes like carbon monoxide or methane poisoning,' said North-Eye.

As they sadly looked into the cage Johnny took a pencil from North-Eye's overall pocket and gave the canary a few prods in forlorn hope of reviving the poor bird. 'Scargill ... Scargill ... wake up.'

North-Eye took a gas detector reading. 'We've a build-up of gas. Everyone out before the whole bastard place goes up!'

Three Lamp Checks

The old miners had all weekend to remedy the ventilation. North-Eye decided to conduct a thorough, unbiased mining inspection without Johnny in his face on Saturday morning. Johnny reluctantly agreed to keep scarce until lunchtime but come the morning he got fed up kicking his heels alone in an empty house and went to the shed earlier than expected. He caught North-Eye examining the vacuum cleaners.

'These old vacuum cleaners haven't got enough oomph for the workings and your upright fan is quite frankly pathetic.'

'A good morning to you too,' said Johnny. 'The fan blows fresh air down through the funnel and the vacuum cleaners suck up used air through the ducting, creating a continuous flow underground.'

'It's a wonder they haven't all suffocated – and explains the gas in the workings.'

'It'll be alright, mun.'

'It won't be "alright, mun" and it's expensive on the electric.'

'Don't keep worrying about the electric.'

'There's been something I've been meaning to tell you.'

'What else is giving you kittens?'

'We've only one way in and out of the mine. For safety reasons we've got to have a second way out in case we have an incident.'

'It'll be alright, mun.'

'It won't be "alright, mun".'

'It'll have to be, anything else?'

North-Eye picked up an electric cable running through the shed and flicked up a wave in the flex. 'This electric cable is nowhere near safe. It's a cheap extension lead from an overloaded point.'

'It hasn't fucked up yet.'

'By some miracle. One clout with a shovel and you're electrocuted, or it sparks an explosion, or the overloaded point burns the shed down, trapping everyone underground because there's only one way in and out. I told you at the beginning you'll get one of these kids killed or perhaps all of them killed, and your stupid self with them. This is a good way to bastard go about it.'

'I don't remember mining being so complicated.'

'It needn't be.'

'What do you mean?'

'Questions have been asked about where the coal is coming from?' said North-Eye almost apologetically.

'I told you to keep it quiet, what questions and from who?'

'I got to talking to a few of the old boys from the colliery and we …'

Johnny went to the check board. 'What old boys? Fuck me hooray, there's three lamp checks on this board.' He scrambled into his overalls and helmet. 'Who's down there?'

'It's only a little pit visit.'

Johnny took a cap lamp from the charger. 'Who's down there?'

'We can't keep it a secret forever and they can help us out.'

'Yeah, but who?' said Johnny on his way down the ladder. 'Don't tell me, I'll find out for myself.'

Johnny headed towards three light beams trained on the coalface. The lights shone his way as he approached. The miners sat on the floor, each with a wooden board angled against the side of the workings as a back support. The nearest light spoke first.

'It's Johnny the Cutter,' said Geronimo with a spit of tobacco juice.

'Geronimo, don't you work Saturdays in Deep Mine Museum? You spent more time underground than a fucking mole at Coed Mawr.'

'We knew you were up to something – students my arse!'

'Your choice of materials is a little unorthodox,' said Billy Donkey tapping a cast iron drainpipe and admiring the pallets, pine kitchen units and pastel-coloured doors.

'The kitchen units are Scandinavian pine, there's none of your MDF rubbish down here.'

'You remember Banger from the electric shop?' said Geronimo.

'Banger, I haven't seen you in donkey's years. In fact, I haven't seen you since Elvis the Washery's funeral.'

'Elvis the Washery is still going, mun. It's Fast Eddy the Pumpsman you are thinking of,' said Banger with an air of authority.

'I could've sworn it was Elvis's funeral. You go to so many they blend into one.'

'He knows his funerals,' said Billy Donkey. 'We call him Banger Doom and Gloom now.'

'There was a logjam of funerals a few years back but it's thinned out now,' said Geronimo.

'Because there's not many of us left, butt,' said Banger.

'You're the sparky who wired up all your outside Christmas lights from a lamp post,' said Johnny. 'You could see your house for miles down the valley, it was like Blackpool Illuminations.'

'He can do the same trick for us,' said a shining light belonging to North-Eye as he sat down beside them, 'Coed Mawr being the arsehole of the world and last in line for eco-friendly lamp posts.'

'That'll be handy,' said Johnny. 'The nearest lamp post is down at the allotment entrance, you could …'

'I'm all over it,' interrupted Banger, 'and I can put my hands on a few rolls of armoured cable to make it safer for your boys at work.'

'What'll it cost?'

'I'll install it for the crack. It's better than sitting in the house waiting for my own funeral.'

'Tidy. I hope you haven't got shovel-shy in your old age. It's a long way from the lamp post and we'll need a trench.'

'That's where Geronimo and Billy Donkey come in,' laughed Banger.

'Typical of a sparky to need help when it comes to using a shovel,' said Billy Donkey. 'You'd always find a nest of them underground reading newspapers and doing crosswords. Sparkies came up the pit cleaner than when they went down.'

'Billy, there's no need for that,' laughed Banger. 'Don't forget, I can do your job but you can't do mine.'

Geronimo spat tobacco onto a post. 'I wish I had a pound for every time I heard that old chestnut from a fitter or sparky. The truth is the other way around; they couldn't do our job because none of them knew how to use a fucking shovel.'

The old miners spent the rest of the weekend installing electrics. Johnny parked his van next to the lamp post using the open passenger door to shield the work in progress from prying eyes. The hedge and fence panels hid the comings and goings perfectly while the old miners dug a trench for the armoured cable. Late Sunday evening Banger gave the final thumbs-up from the trapdoor and Johnny threw the safety switch. Many Coed Mawr villagers were perturbed by the fizzing and dimming of the streetlights, while at Julie's Colliery pit bottom was illuminated like a palace.

The miners returned on Monday morning to see their handiwork in practice and to view the boys at work. They sat on the floor leaning back against wooden boards, impressed by what they saw.

'From what we've seen by here,' said Geronimo, 'they're a tidy set of hard-working boys.'

'Thank you.' Johnny blew the vuvuzela and startled the old miners. 'We know they're a good team.'

Banger clutched at his heart. 'What the ...'

'Take a whiff,' shouted Johnny. 'Come and see some of the old miners from Coed Mawr Colliery. Geronimo and Billy Donkey you've already met at Deep Mine Museum, but this is Banger, he installed the electric on the weekend.'

The team sat on the floor around the old miners.

'We wondered who was shining lights in our eyes,' said Spider.

'How are your studies going in the University of Glamorgan,' said Billy Donkey to Lippo.

'Still wearing dickhead orange then, butt?'

Billy Donkey and Lippo had a staring competition and Lippo blinked first. 'Why do they call him Billy Donkey?'

The old miners shared a good laugh.

'Don't sit too close to Billy,' said Johnny, 'he might whip it out of his overalls and put it in your ear when you're not looking.'

Lippo edged safely behind Spider as Billy Donkey gave him a wink.

'Johnny,' said Banger, 'why don't you bring your team along to our next Coed Mawr Colliery reunion?'

'Looks like we already have.'

'Serious, we're having one next week at the Trewatkins Hotel.'

'I haven't been in the Trewatkins Hotel since the Seventies.'

'We've held our reunions there ever since they demolished the Workmen's Hall and the Miners' Welfare Club.'

'It was criminal how those buildings went,' said Billy Donkey, and the old miners grumbled in agreement.

'When the Miners' Welfare got demolished it kicked the teeth out of the village,' added North-Eye. 'There's still a gap in the street thriving with knotweed and buddleia where it used to be.'

Geronimo cleared his nose. 'Aye, after the Strike, clubs for working men fell like dominos.'

'That's the way it is,' said Billy Donkey.

'You don't know what you've got until it's gone,' said Banger. 'These youngsters don't know any different.'

'Buzzing, happy old fuckers, aren't you?' said Lippo.

Johnny returned to the subject. 'Reunions are not my thing.'

'He'll be there,' said North-Eye. 'Besides, you wouldn't want to upset Banger when he can put his hands on a box Tannoy system.'

'A Tannoy?'

'It's only four boxes,' said Banger. 'It's all I could fit in my car boot when the colliery closed.'

'What the fuck are they talking about now, bro?' said Lippo.

'Fuck knows,' said Spider.

'It's a box speaker phone system you talk into by pressing buttons,' explained North-Eye. 'We had them underground.'

'And I'll install it for you,' said Banger enthusiastically. 'It's been on a shelf gathering dust in my garage since the colliery closed. At the time I didn't know why I took it home, but I do now.'

Geronimo nudged Billy Donkey. 'You'll need our help.'

'Banger, you can't install a complicated box Tannoy speaker phone system that you talk into by pressing buttons all on your own,' said Billy Donkey.

'That'd be good,' said Johnny. 'I wouldn't have to shout down the shaft.'

'So what do you say, Johnny?' said Banger. 'Turn up to the reunion and you can chuck that Venezuela thing away.'

'I'll think about it.'

'Only a handful turns up anyway,' assured Banger.

'Too many know already and I want to keep it quiet.'

'Now who are we going to tell?' said Geronimo.

Behind the Green Door

Long after the end of the shift, Johnny and North-Eye returned to Julie's Colliery to take a gas reading and to scout for likely positions for the Tannoy boxes. On their way to the coalface, they heard and felt the thumping of a deep bass.

North-Eye leaned on a post. 'Team Singh are ripping it up tonight.'

'That's too much bass for Bollywood.' Johnny pointed at coal dust pulsating on a green door shoring up the side of the workings. 'Look, it's jumping to the bass.'

Johnny turned the handle and to their surprise the door opened. The music grew louder as they walked along a roughly-hewn passageway leading to a pallet ladder. Climbing the pallets, they opened a trapdoor an inch and looked up into a shed of shining black polythene, strip lighting and cannabis plants. Through thick smoke they made out the rear ends of Spider, Lippo and Charlie as they spied through a blacked-out window.

'Go Jayden,' said Spider.

Unbeknown to Johnny and North-Eye, Jayden was creeping around the allotment on a mission to spike Clayton's teapot with acid. The team had bribed Vince the Hippy with a bag of weed to lure Clayton and Smithy away from the polytunnel to look at his wind chimes. To avoid CCTV detection, Jayden hid under an upturned water barrel and manoeuvred his way across Clayton's plot until he entered the polytunnel. He got in, did the teapot deed, and got out before Clayton heard the first tinkle of Vince's wind chimes.

'He's out,' said Spider, passing a spliff to Lippo in celebration. 'And he's on his way back.'

Slouch sat on a cardboard box thumbing through a battered

glossy magazine. 'These women have got hairy fannies.' No one said anything so he said it again. 'These women have got hairy fannies.'

Charlie looked at Slouch but he could not tell what was going on behind the scarf and shades. 'Boxes full of them.'

'Sorted,' said Jayden as he entered to whoops of jubilation. He snatched the spliff from Lippo as a reward.

Johnny slammed open the trapdoor and climbed up into the shed with North-Eye. The surprise element coupled with weed paranoia made the team look as if they could shit all the way to China.

'Once a waster, always a waster, this is why you were always hanging around outside Bouncer's shed and sniggering behind my back,' he said stepping up onto the pot-laden floorboards. 'What the fuck are you playing at, Jayden?'

'Sorry, Grandad.'

The shock subsided and cosmic sniggering filled the shed.

Spider purred like a cat. 'This skunk, very more-ish, isn't it?'

'And you didn't want to go back to dealing.'

'No need to go throwing dustbins. I knows what you're thinking but it's not a commercial thing.'

Lippo blew a smoke ring. 'We're not dealing we're chilling.'

'It doesn't look like it from here.'

'It's for our own personal use. It was a pity to waste an empty shed with all these pots, compost and gardening stuff, so we brought a few plants in. That's what an allotment is for isn't it, growing things?'

'It keeps us off the streets,' said Jayden.

'And away from the Old Wheel,' said Slouch trying to open a magazine. 'These pages are stuck together.'

'What about the two ex-coppers next door?'

'They knows shit,' said Lippo, 'and besides tonight we've …'

Spider cut him off with an elbow to the ribs.

'We've been in here ages,' said Spider. 'We tunnelled up using the skills you taught us and copied your trapdoor design.'

'Aren't you the clever fuckers?'

'You should be proud of us, Grandad.'

'You have to admire their enterprise,' said North-Eye examining the strip lighting. 'They are bright lads.'

'All this is going,' said Johnny grabbing a pot. 'I want this place empty. We'll load the van and take it up the mountain even if it takes all night. What you do with it from there is your own business.'

'Dump our skunk up the mountain?' said Spider. 'Dream on.'

'That's fly-tipping, bro.'

'You can make a big bonfire. It'll be seen for miles and you can dance around it like trouser-less gypsies all night.'

'Let's not make any rash decisions,' said North-Eye. 'Why don't we let them keep their weed factory for now?'

'You're having a giraffe?'

'They've sorted the problem of one way in and out of the mine. This will be our second way out. And they've solved the ventilation. We'll set up an air circuit in from your shed and out through this one.'

'We knows all that,' said Lippo cockily.

'Did we bollocks,' said Jayden.

'North-Eye, you want our upcast shaft to be a weed factory?'

'Skunk house,' corrected Spider.

Johnny and North-Eye were getting stoned the longer they stood in the shed, and when Vince the Hippy put his head around the door, wearing an Elvis quiff wig, a dinner jacket and bow tie, it did not appear unusual to the two old miners.

'Guys, the filth are chilling in the polytunnel.' His eyes lit upon Jayden's spliff. 'Give us a pull, I've got a date and I'm in a hurry.' Jayden passed the joint and before having a pull Vince gave North-Eye the thumbs-up. 'Your Neighbourhood Watch guys are sound.'

Johnny tapped North-Eye and went back to the trapdoor. 'If we don't get out of here soon, we'll be as fucked up as they are.'

Pigs

A little later Johnny and North-Eye glowed orange against the twilight as they sat before the chiminea. Spellbound by the burning coal, it was as if the miners had lost all power of speech. Johnny snapped out of it and poked the fire with a bamboo stick. 'Fuck me hooray, I don't know if I want a shit or a haircut.'

'The stuff is stronger than in our day. It's giving the kids serious psychotic episodes and mental illness.'

'As if kids don't get enough of that.'

'In our day it was long hair, Afghan coats, cheesecloth shirts, patchouli oil and trying to figure out the meaning of Genesis lyrics.' North-Eye removed his glasses and gave them a wipe, 'Now it's screwed up with social problems and I don't know what.'

'We knew where to draw the line then. We had jobs to go to.'

'Disappointed with the team?'

'We knew what they were like. I'm concerned about Clayton. When I asked about the coppers, Spider gave Lippo a dig in the ribs to shut him up. What's that about?'

'No idea. Go and ask Clayton, he's hovering behind his polythene.'

'Smug fucker won't speak to me since I won the shed painting vote. All the police who went through the Strike are smug fuckers. If you talk to one now they still brag about how they spent the overtime money. Holidays, cars and house extensions – to them it wasn't about communities or the destruction of a way of life, it was all about the money and they couldn't get their snouts deep enough into the trough. Pigs has never been a more apt description.' He spat into the fire.

'Don't you go starting on about the Strike,' said North-Eye. 'We'll be talking bollocks all night.'

Half an hour after a cup of tea in Clayton's shed, Smithy agreed to close his operation and bring his most promising leek specimens into Clayton's polytunnel where they could double their efforts to get the best results.

Smithy felt light-headed, decided on an early night and left Clayton checking his CCTV footage. To Clayton's horror he found a line of bare backsides mooning at him. 'Neighbourhood Watch hooligans,' he lisped. He made a mental note to move his camera from the shed apex to the corner of the polytunnel to get a clearer view of Johnny's plot. 'I'll get Mr Morgan and the lot of you nicked.'

Clayton then found astonishing footage of a water barrel moving across his plot. He replayed and examined the clip so many times it seemed as if reality itself warped and echoed into eternity while his leeks smiled and grew to enormous size in the polytunnel. His focus shifted to the wind chime as it rhythmically tinkled to vibrations of distant deep bass. While studying the hypnotic crystals, he travelled light years into crystalline essence where the secrets of the universe resided but lay tantalisingly out of reach. Clayton re-emerged into the polytunnel via his thumbnail with the realisation that if he acquired more crystals, he would be party to the grand sum of all God's knowledge.

The former police officer felt funny floating his way down a purple velvet pathway to Vince the Hippy's shed. He lived in a cartoon and knew he had travelled this path a million times in a million different lifetimes. Built at the beginning of time, Vince's shed loomed like a cathedral in the twilight. Clayton marvelled at the incense burners, dream catchers, and wind chimes tinkling in rhythm with the cosmos.

The shed shook with lovemaking as Vince and Betty Bingo rutted away on a creaking potting table. Vince's Elvis quiff wig had strayed across his head and he spoke into a bingo microphone wired to his dinner jacket lapel. 'Kelly's Eye, number … one.'

'House … house,' shouted Betty in the throes of passion.

Clayton, completely off his face and beaming a gormless smile, glided in through the door behind Vince, and when Betty clocked him she screamed, shattering a row of jam-jar tea lights.

'Steady on,' said Vince in the belief his skills had hit the mark.

'Clayton,' screeched Betty.

'Clayton?' Vince turned in mid-stroke to follow her gaze. 'Hey, far out man, you've got eyes like piss-holes in the snow.'

They rolled off the potting table and composed themselves. Vince adjusted his Elvis quiff wig. 'Where's Smithy?'

Smithy sat stark naked on a trig point on the mountain common.

Clutching a rugby ball with his knees, he slipped a pair of skid-marked budgie smugglers over his head as a scrum cap. His brain resonated with classic Seventies Welsh rugby matches and he thought he was Gareth Edwards. Jumping down from the trig point, Smithy punted the rugby ball high, gave chase, and when the ball splashed into a muddy puddle, he dived in. An astonished courting couple viewed the bizarre spectacle from a parked car.

Smithy as Gareth Edwards played for Wales against Scotland at Cardiff Arms Park in 1972. He kicked the ball high and ran splashing after it as Bill McLaren's commentary cosmically echoed in his mind.

Mervyn Davies takes the tap-down from Peter Brown ...

It's beautifully laid back for Gareth Edwards ...

Edwards, over the Welsh ten-yard line ...

... over halfway ...

... the kick ahead by Edwards, can he score?

It will be a miracle if he could ...

... he may well get there ... and he has!

Smithy belly-flopped into a puddle and came up with the ball and a faceful of mud.

You can't get anything better than that in international rugby.

*

Early next morning Dai Milk halted his tractor when spotting Smithy tickling trout in the mountain brook. Opting for a paintball gun over his 12-bore shotgun, the farmer dismounted his tractor, hitched up the rope belt of his trousers and stalked through the ferns. Alerted to the farmer's presence, Smithy listened out for a short while before splashing upstream at full pelt. Dai Milk brought the ex-copper down with half-a-dozen multicoloured paintballs to the rump. He took Smithy home to the posh houses, and it caused quite a stir in the street when he jumped from the tractor trailer naked but for a scrum cap of budgie smugglers and girdled by a belt of tickled trout.

On the Coalface of Clanger Insurance

Johnny's plans of an early exit from his Clanger leaving-do lay in bits as his excited team cheered Horner and Marilyn's pint-drinking race in a packed Cardiff bar. A few drinks had morphed into a barking-mad Clanger pub crawl after Marilyn had stitched up Johnny with the presentation of a long-service award.

Horner turned a dripping pint glass on to his head. 'It gets thirsty working on the coalface of Clanger Insurance all day.'

The defeated Marilyn staggered off to order another round at the five-deep bar.

'Less of that disrespectful "working on the coalface" piss-take,' said Johnny. 'Working in an office where the worst possible injuries are a paper cut or a twisted ankle from catching your flip-flop in a phone charger is no comparison to working underground.'

'I'm winding you up,' laughed Horner.

'Besides, without the mining industry there'd be no Clanger.'

'Joking,' said Mohammed.

'In the Nineties the Welsh Development Agency gave Clanger a million-pound start-up grant to attract them to Cardiff, a grant to economically regenerate south Wales following the demise of the mining industry. Therefore everyone in Clanger directly owes their jobs to mining and should show a little more respect when comparing their backside-numbing office work to that of working on a coalface.'

'I didn't know that,' said Horner.

'Clanger likes to take all the praise themselves,' said Johnny downing a whisky. 'But anyway Horner, you can drink better than any miner I know.'

'I just pour it straight down,' laughed Horner holding his Adam's apple. 'I've had plenty of exercise opening my throat.'

'Choking,' said Mohammed.

Horner gave Johnny a hug. 'We are going to miss you, butt.'

'I'll miss you lot of Clangers too,' he said, eyeing Joel who was showing phone filth to Lucy.

'That's disgusting,' gagged Lucy.

'Some more than others,' he added as Joel hid away his phone.

One of the girls put her hand up as if she were still in school. 'What was it like working down a coal mine, were there any toilets?'

'It was hard physical work.'

'I don't like the sound of that,' said Horner.

'But character-building, with great camaraderie and humour.'

'I like the sound of that,' said Horner. 'I'm camaraderie and humour all the way.'

'As to toilets, you'll have to use your imagination.'

'Bogging,' said Mohammed as the girls screwed up their faces.

Moses flexed his muscles. 'I heard miners were all hard.'

'Every weekend we had fighting inside and outside the Miners' Welfare club where someone had thrown a chair at the doorman or a door at the chairman. We got a daily adrenaline rush from rides up and down the shaft, or on coal-laden conveyor belts. And you know those Clanger emails that go around asking you to get involved in community projects and whatnot?'

'Delete,' said Mohammed.

'The community naturally grew out of the colliery. Libraries, welfare halls, institutes, snooker halls, sports and social clubs, and much more. We didn't need a begging email about it.'

'You didn't have email in the Stone Age,' scoffed Joel.

'But were the miners as brilliant as us?' said Horner.

'We looked out for each other, trusting the next man to watch your back. Is there anyone here you couldn't trust with your life?'

Joel shifted uncomfortably on his chair as all attention went his way. 'Why are you all looking at me?'

'And no miner I knew turned into a paranoid compliance-fearing jobsworth where every minute detail of work is scrutinised with threats of disciplinary and financial penalties until your job is nothing more than an arse-covering exercise.'

'You're cheering us up no fucking end by here,' said Horner.

'Sorry, you're right.' Johnny got up and made his way to the gents. 'And it's well past the time I went for a waz.'

When Johnny returned, the team were urging on Horner in his attempt to limbo under a table with a pint balanced on his head. Not wanting any long goodbyes, Johnny surreptitiously weaved through the packed bar to the door.

Living the Dream

Out in the street it seemed to be kicking off everywhere and Johnny soon had to negotiate his way around a screaming cat fight between half-a-dozen women rolling in the gutter with a disregard for sensible underwear. A ruck involving a stag night dressed as nuns in mini-skirts spilled out in front of him from a bar in Mill Lane, and at the St Mary Street road crossing he jumped for his life when a boy racer chased by a line of blue flashing lights ran the red light.

Once safely across the road, he navigated his way through a smorgasbord of street beggars and crack-heads on the Cardiff Central main drag. Johnny kept his eyes to the front and briskly walked past the array of tents, body bags and blankets. A cute Bichon Frisé yapped from the last grubby sleeping bag and caught his attention.

A down-and-out voice croaked from the depths of the bag. 'Spare some change, please?'

Johnny halted after a few paces, went back and presented his Clanger award to the street beggar. 'You only get one of these after twenty-five years of loyal service. Good luck.'

'Thank you,' he croaked, accepting the glass trophy. 'I'd like to thank this lovely dog for her help in you presenting me with this award. I'd also like to thank my parents, my sisters, my friends and everyone else who knows me. Thank you.'

Johnny resumed his journey, certain he had seen the street

beggar before. It sank in and he went back and gave him a prod with his toe. 'Slouch, what are you doing?'

Slouch poked his head tortoise-like out from the sleeping bag, 'Living the dream.'

Johnny crouched down, unzipped and opened the bag. It revealed Slouch and the dog cwtched together as if in a huge, quilted sardine can.

He wafted away the smell with his hand. 'Don't I pay you enough at the colliery?'

'I'm trying to earn a bit more. Fridays and Saturdays are the busiest times. The drunks give you loads of cash.'

'And a good kicking if you're not careful. If you wanted more money you only had to ask, I would've come up with something.'

'I didn't like to.'

'Why do you need more money?' Johnny had struck a nerve and Slouch zipped himself back into his bag. 'Sorry, it's none of my business.' He switched focus to the dog. 'Where'd you get the dog?'

'She's a stray,' said Slouch unconvincingly. 'The punters give more money if you've got a dog.'

'Made much?'

'Ninety-eight quid, two cheeseburgers, three coffees, a tin of Pedigree Chum, and a glass award. I like the award the best.'

'That's alright for a few hours lying down on the pavement on a Friday night. Good spot, is it?'

'It's the best spot for the train station. I had to scuffle with a load of crack-heads for it. They're all headshot down here.'

A gang of rowdy lads threw beer bottles at a wall as they passed by. Slouch burrowed deeper into his bag.

Johnny helped Slouch to his feet. 'C'mon or we'll miss the last train up the valley.'

'But I got a full day tomorrow. Saturdays are bumping.'

'Give it a rest. I need you fit first thing on Monday morning.'

'Can I still keep the award?'

On the train Johnny stood near a carriage door. Despite scarce seating space, Slouch sat wrapped in his sleeping bag on a four-seater ringed by empty seats. An outsider knowledgeable on eastern philosophy would think Slouch a Zen master projecting a protective occult aura around his being, but to those in close proximity, it was simply the smell. Johnny had a closer look at Slouch as he cwtched the Clanger award and buffed up the glass with a dirty sleeve. Straight scarecrow black hair poked out from under a teddy bear onesie, and thin bum fluff passing for a moustache gave Slouch the look of a messy toddler who had recently gorged a Marmite sandwich.

When they got to the van at Abercwmcoedmawr, there was a leaflet under the wiper. Johnny read it, rolled it into a ball, and threw it at Slouch. 'A stray? That's Mrs Jones Bottom Street's dog.'

Slouch cwtched up to the dog, 'Britney.'

'Because there's a £50 reward, half of Coed Mawr are out looking for Britney. Mrs Jones Bottom Street is worried shitless.'

Within minutes the van, with Slouch's sleeping bag hanging out the window for a good airing, pulled up outside the terraced house of Mrs Jones Bottom Street. All the lights were on when Johnny knocked the door.

'Who's there?' said Mrs Jones Bottom Street through the door.

Britney barked at the familiar voice, jumped from Slouch's grasp and scratched the door.

'Britney!' She unlocked the door and the dog jumped into her arms. 'Naughty girl, where've you been? I've been worried shitless.'

'This young man found her.'

'Thank you, I'll get the £50 reward,' she said while lip kissing Britney.

'Mrs Jones, I don't want the reward.'

'But you found my Britney.'

'It's reward enough to see you reunited,' said Johnny giving Slouch a pat on the back.

'But I'd be happy to walk Britney a few times a week if it's OK?'

'I can't get about as much as I used to,' she said, 'and Britney needs her exercise.'

Johnny ruffled Britney's ear. 'She won't run away again if she's getting plenty of exercise. He's already brought her back to you safe and sound. I'm sure he'll look after her.'

'I'm fed up of scooping her poop in the garden. It'd be better if Britney does her poop in the park where the dirty old pit used to be. My whites were black with dust coming off the washing line when that stinking place was working. I'm glad it's long gone.'

When Mrs Jones Bottom Street finished her rant against Coed Mawr Colliery, they finalised the dog walking plans and returned to the van.

'At least you won't get nicked for dog-napping. You know what, Slouch? I think you missed your vocation in life.'

'What's a vocation?'

'It's something you love doing, and you're good at, and you end up doing it for a living. Those who find their vocation in life never do a day's work in their lives again because they love what they do.'

145

'I'd look after people's dogs, groom them, take them for walks, talk to them and keep them happy. I'd do it for nothing.'

'Start by making a plan.'

'The Crew, they'd laugh at me.'

'They laugh at you anyway so there's no loss there.' He started the van. 'Where do you want to be dropped?'

'The park.'

'Looks like rain. You're not roughing it tonight?'

'I'll make a tent over the Old Wheel bench.'

'That injunction is a bit of a bastard, isn't it? What if I drop you at the allotment? You can bed down in the shed with a cup of tea. I'll bring you breakfast in the morning. Of course I trust you not to smoke any skunk in there or whatever.'

'I don't do that any more. Not since the pixies frightened me. They scratched and bit me because they know I did something really bad. But I'm trying to make good.' Slouch wiped his nose with the back of his hand. 'Can you do me a favour?'

A Favour for Slouch

The next morning Johnny drove to the terraced streets below the posh houses and parked in Rhymney Terrace. His back pain had flared up again and he needed the aid of the deputy stick to get out of the van. From the roof of a mid-terrace property, a roofer carelessly spun slates shattering into a skip. Marmite stubble and black straw hair betrayed the roofer to be Slouch's dad. The front door yawned open and a woman Johnny took to be Slouch's mum emptied a dustpan into the skip. Two girls, one of primary school age and another a little older, swept the pavement around her.

Johnny leaned against the skip. 'Hi, my name is Johnny

Morgan. I live on the other side of the village. It's about your son.'

'Sacha,' she shrieked as the girls froze to their brushes, 'is he alright?'

A voice whined from the roof. 'What's he fucking done now?'

'Simon, no need to shout,' she said. 'It's about Sacha.'

Johnny tucked the stick under an arm and raised his hands to placate them. 'There's nothing to worry about, your son is OK.'

'He's no son of mine, he nearly burned our house down and killed the fucking lot of us,' shouted Simon from above the eaves. 'Siân and the girls are still coughing their guts out all night. Their lungs might be damaged for the rest of their fucking lives.'

'That's enough of that language in front of the girls,' Siân shouted up at him. The elder of the girls coughed, followed by the younger as a show of support.

'Slouch, I mean Sacha, is sorry for what he did to the house, he's sorry for what he did to you and to his sisters. He knows he can never put it right but he's trying to make amends. He's done work for me and has worked weekends elsewhere. He's saved his money and wants you to have it. He's sorry.' He appealed to Siân as she had far more sense than Slouch's dad. 'He'd tell you himself but he can't because of the exclusion order, so he asked me to give you this.' He held up an envelope bulging with cash.

'Simon?'

'We don't want it,' said Simon, half-hanging over the eaves. 'It's probably money he got from selling drugs.'

'It's not drug money. It's from honest hard work.'

'Honest hard work,' laughed Simon. 'The headshot lazy good-for-nothing hasn't got it in him. What hard work is that then?'

'That's my business. It's also from his weekend work, whatever it is he does on the weekend. But whatever it is, I know it isn't easy.'

'Weekend work for fuck's sake,' said Simon as he spun another slate shattering in the skip.

Siân snatched a piece of broken slate from the skip and flung it up at Simon. 'I told you, that's enough of that language.'

'He shows willing,' said Johnny leaning back on his stick. 'Perhaps he deserves another chance.'

'He doesn't deserve another chance,' shouted Simon. 'We gave him chance after chance after fucking chance.'

'And he knows it. He's had months to think it over in the park sleeping rough on the Old Wheel bench. I imagine he'll be there today,' said Johnny to Siân and the girls. 'In fact he's doing some dog walking in the park at one o'clock.'

'Sacha has always been good with dogs,' said Siân holding back a tear. 'Even as a little boy, dogs seemed to like him. But Simon wouldn't have a dog in the house,' she said accusingly to the roof.

'I want to see Sacha,' whimpered the girls in harmony.

'He told me to let you know he misses you all.' Johnny threw the envelope into the skip near Siân. One of the girls picked it up and passed it to her.

'Don't take that,' ordered Simon, 'and get those girls indoors.'

'They'll stay where they are,' snapped Siân, taking the envelope.

'Get those girls in the house.'

'Perhaps it's better if you do go inside, girls,' she said shooing them in and shutting the door, 'before your stupid father falls off the stupid roof and breaks his stupid head on the stupid pavement.'

'We're not going to see him in the park,' shouted Simon. 'When he put the gas under the chip pan and passed out full of drugs face-down in the fucking butter dish, he shat in his own nest!'

Many a curtain twitched along the terrace. Several neighbours braved the doorstep to investigate the shouting.

'Some people blame the parents,' said Johnny up at Simon as the girls waved to him from the front window. 'Anyone in the valleys naming their son "Sacha" is asking for it.'

'Have you any idea what we've been through? We've been living in temporary accommodation since the Fire and Rescue Service axed their way through our front door, that's after the time we spent in hospital with smoke inhalation. Then the fucking house insurance wouldn't pay out because of a drink and drugs clause.'

'You should've been more careful with your choice of insurer.'

'What would you know about insurance?'

'I'm not up a ladder doing a botch roof job because the insurance wouldn't pay out.'

'There's nearly £1,000 here,' said Siân in disbelief.

'We don't want anything from him,' shouted Simon. 'Take it back.'

'That's not part of the favour I'm doing for your son.'

'Take the money back or I'm coming down there.'

'It's not mine to take back.'

'I'll come down there and I don't care how fucking old you are.'

'Simon,' said Siân.

'I'll check myself for fucks,' said Johnny searching his pockets.

'No Simon, I can't find a fuck anywhere. So I couldn't give a fuck.'

'I'm fucking coming down,' he said, stepping from the roof ladder onto the ladder.

As he put a foot on the top rung, Johnny pulled the ladder away and it clattered across the road.

Simon hung with one hand on the gutter and the other on a rung of the roof ladder, 'Bastard!'

'Sacha will be dog walking in the park at one o'clock,' Johnny reminded Siân as she looked at her dangling husband and held the envelope with uncertainty. The girls ran out of the house as Johnny walked back to the van.

'That's right, walk away, but I'll find you, you old bastard.'

'Watch your language,' shouted Siân, 'the girls are back out.'

'I'm easy to find, Simon. Best place is the allotments in the shed that looks like a coal mine. You can't miss it.'

The gutter started to come away as Simon struggled to swing his leg up onto the roof. 'Girls, get the ladder.'

'Leave it be,' screeched Siân. 'Your father can hang there until he comes to his senses.'

A car sped into the street and screeched to a halt in front of the ladder. The irate boy racer parped the horn and threw up questioning hands like a ham actor. More cars pulled up behind and soon Simon dangled from the gutter to a racket of car horns and bad language.

Johnny drove out of the street as it all kicked off behind him.

At one o'clock Johnny hid in the bushes near the Old Wheel and watched Slouch, with Britney on his lap, sitting quietly on the bench. The colliery washery once occupied Johnny's overgrown hiding place, and the longer he waited for Slouch's family to arrive, the more he experienced mining flashbacks. Dematerialised voices of washery workers echoed around him in the greenery and he heard the ghostly hum of conveyor belts.

Slouch's excited sisters brought Johnny out of his reverie as they raced along the path and jumped all over their big brother. Slouch's parents appeared behind the girls and he received a tearful hug from Siân while Simon scowled nearby. Mother and sisters sat with Slouch on the bench. They moved up, making space for Simon, and after a little deliberation he sat with them.

This touching moment called full-time on Johnny's spying mission and he left the ghostly washery behind with a good feeling. He had witnessed the true value of Julie's Colliery, and knew what he had always known: that there's far more to coal mining than what people see on the surface.

The Reunion

A minibus pulled into the Trewatkins Hotel car park and out stepped the colliery team.

Johnny had them gather around. 'I heard the talk in the back of the bus and I know some are having second thoughts so I'm not forcing you to go. But we've been invited and it'd be good to show our faces. Think of it as a team night out.'

'It's only a small affair,' said North-Eye in support, 'and there'll be drinks over the bar from Geronimo and the boys.'

Jayden and Charlie walked away.

'We've changed our minds,' said Jayden. 'It's not our thing.'

'Reunions are not my thing either,' pleaded Johnny.

'Jayden,' said Joanne. 'At least show some respect. People are expecting you to be there.'

'We've decided.'

'Well, be careful on your way home.'

'Aww shut up,' shouted Jayden. 'You're so embarrassing.'

'You're the one who's embarrassing.' Joanne nudged Johnny. 'Dad, I'm still not happy with those pair.'

Johnny did not want any of it. 'What about you, Spider?'

'I'm team captain. I couldn't get out of it if I tried.'

'Good man. And you, Lippo?'

'I'm not scared to go for a drink in Trewatkins,' shouted Lippo at Charlie and Jayden as they disappeared down the street. But for all his bravado he lurked behind Spider.

'Slouch?'

Slouch, gleaming in clean clothes and smelling of roses, rubbed his hands together. 'What are we hanging about for?'

Joanne took Spider's arm and tweaked Slouch's cheek as they walked to the entrance. 'Slouch, you scrub up well.'

'Only a handful bothers to turn up,' said North-Eye to Johnny. 'It starts off quiet but always ends in arguments and ruffled feathers.'

'It's come down to this, has it? The lifeblood of industrial south Wales squabbling in a pub corner like a bunch of forgotten old men.'

They stepped into the Trewatkins Hotel and the packed bar.

'Are we in the right place, North-Eye?'

'It's never this full. There must be something else going on.'

Geronimo, Banger and Billy Donkey stood at the bar.

'There they are,' announced Geronimo.

All heads turned towards the newcomers and they were applauded, back-slapped and fussed over, all the way to the bar.

North-Eye smiled, waved, and gave the thumbs-up to no end of old familiar faces. 'I haven't seen so many miners in bastard years.'

'I told them to keep it quiet,' fumed Johnny as they reached the bar, and he childishly imitated Geronimo from their last meeting. 'Who are we going to tell?'

'Stop worrying,' said Geronimo, passing around a few waiting pints from the bar. 'They're all on our side.'

'*Our* side, you've only helped us out with a job or two?'

'Listen, we've lined up a good thing for you and your boys. Everyone here is itching to get back underground, to see your miniature colliery and see your boys working a real coalface.'

'They're all happy to pay an entrance fee,' said Billy Donkey with his eyes sparkling. 'I saw to that.'

'That's a good idea,' said North-Eye. 'I can see that working.'

'There's too many know what we're up to already. I'm the one who'll be up shit creek.'

Geronimo nudged Billy Donkey. 'Of course, they'll need our help.'

'Too right, Geronimo, they'll need mining guides with years of experience taking visitors underground, like us, at Deep Mine Museum. They can't organise all those pit visits on their own.'

'Did you hear about Tom the Splicer?' interrupted Banger as Johnny was about to let rip on his old mining colleagues.

'Look out, Doom and Gloom is off,' said Billy Donkey, winking at Lippo as he took a drink. Lippo edged behind Spider.

'He's gone, heart attack, putting out his wheelie bin. I can't believe it,' continued Banger. 'He was only seventy-six, makes you wonder what it's all about.'

'Never mind Tom the Splicer, God rest him. You said there'd only be a handful at this reunion and look at it.'

'You're the talk of the valley,' said Billy Donkey.

'And it's you three that's been doing all the talking.'

Geronimo tapped a glass with a pen to get order. He took a karaoke microphone from a tattooed barmaid. 'I don't know about anyone else here, but it's been a long time since I felt a buzz like this about the old days.'

The miners agreed with a ripple of applause.

'Johnny the Cutter and North-Eye have brought it all back. Believe me, the boys they got working down there are as good as any of us were. Ask Billy Donkey and Banger, they'll tell you, because we've seen them at work. Anyway, I'd like to propose a toast.'

Glasses were raised as the miners stood. Geronimo took his pint from the bar, raised it and turned to face Johnny, North-Eye, Slouch and Lippo – 'Julie's Colliery.'

The toast echoed around the bar, the old miners necked back the beer and banged empties on the tables. Johnny, Slouch and Lippo did not know where to look. North-Eye had a tear in the corner of his eye and wiped his glasses. 'It's a bit bastard smoky in here.'

Johnny looked around for Spider and spied him further along the bar with Joanne. They were getting pretty cosy together but he did not have time to think about it.

'Ladies and gentlemen, Johnny the Cutter,' announced Geronimo as Billy Donkey whipped up a round of applause.

Johnny glared at his three smiling old workmates. 'It's stitch-up after stitch-up after stitch-up from ...' Geronimo thrust the microphone at Johnny, '... you fucking arseholes.'

Eyebrows were raised as the words reverberated out from the speakers with Jimi Hendrix feedback.

'Sorry, I meant these three at the bar. I asked them to keep it quiet and they beat the NUM lodge tom-toms. Seriously, thank you for the warm welcome, albeit in a pub bar as it only seems yesterday our miners' halls were full to bursting. You had to arrive early or you'd get turned away at the door, unless, you knew someone on the committee.'

Johnny got out of jail with a laugh.

'I can see a few familiar old faces. I didn't realise so many of you were still alive, particularly if you listen to Banger because according to him, he's already been to your funerals.'

Banger threw up his hands as the audience had a good laugh.

'Is that you, Elvis the Washery?'

'Aye, it's me,' said Elvis sat on a mobility scooter, preening a thin grey quiff, 'and it's brilliant to see you again, Johnny the Cutter.'

'I told you Elvis is still going,' said Banger.

'Banger makes it sound like he's running a sweep. Who else here is still alive? I've worked with Chief, Jack the Stent, Grabber and Bryn the Mole in a few districts. Good to see you again, fellas. I caught a whiff of Gullick oil when I came in and sure enough there's a flange of fitters, Greaser, Bob, and Wil Overalls. And lo and behold a table full of Banger's mates from the electric shop. I knew you were sparkies because you're all sitting down doing fuck-all.'

The rival tradesmen genially flashed the fingers at each other during another good laugh.

As Geronimo ordered a round of drinks, he caught sight of Minge Jenkins shouldering his way through the crowd on the far side of the bar followed by Minja, Pea-Brain, Dai Milk and Spanners. He nudged Billy Donkey. 'Well, well, it's mad Minge Jenkins.'

'This is my first reunion ...' said Johnny while curing the microphone of feedback.

'Where've you been then?' shouted a heckler.

'Working ... working in ... insurance.'

Johnny endured a wave of derision and guffaws.

'Alright, alright, it paid the bills. Reunions are not my thing. It's not out of disrespect. There's no one else I respect or admire more than the people in this room. Perhaps I've been worried I'll start going on about the Strike and end up talking bollocks all night. But I'll say one thing about it. We stood together all through that conflict one hundred per cent firm. No miner from the three collieries in this valley even thought of crossing a picket line. We all know how it ended. They broke the Strike. They broke the Union. You've only got to walk down the street to see how they broke our communities, but they never, ever, broke the miners of the Coed Mawr valley.'

As Johnny received a standing ovation, he handed the microphone back to the barmaid.

North-Eye passed Johnny his pint. 'Not bad for talking bollocks about the Strike.'

Johnny necked back a third of his pint, and as he wiped his top lip he saw Minge Jenkins eyeballing him across the bar.

'What's all this then?' shouted Minge for all to hear. 'A *Last of the Summer Wine* night out? Haven't you in-bred Coed Mawr hillbillies got any pubs left up there in the arsehole of the world?'

'Yeah, who do you think you are coming down here and drinking our beer,' said Minja. Minge gave his grandson a swift backhander for stepping on his toes.

All eyes were on Johnny but he kept his cool and turned his back on the old coal merchant.

'Geronimo,' shouted Minge across the bar, 'you wouldn't happen to know anything about a pikey bastard selling cheap house coal in the valley, would you?'

Dai Milk and Spanners sought safety by looking at their beer.

'No, can't say I do,' said Geronimo, passing pints around from the bar in the silence. 'Billy, have you heard of a pikey bastard selling cheap house coal in the valley?'

'I haven't heard anything like that going on around here, Geronimo,' said Billy Donkey. 'What about you, Banger? Have you heard of any illegitimate members of the travelling community selling inexpensive anthracite in the valley?'

'News to me,' said Banger. 'I thought scrap metal and block driveways were the specialities of our good travellers.'

'There's a pikey out there who's branched out into selling coal from the back of a van in my valley,' shouted Minge, 'and when I catch hold of him, I'll rip his lungs out.'

In the following pregnant pause the tension got to Slouch. He shivered like a spaniel taking a dump and drew all attention by emitting a short high-pitched fart. 'It wasn't me.'

Minge grunted and necked back his pint as laughter filled the bar.

Johnny clapped a hand on Slouch's shoulder. 'Man up, Slouch, everyone knows they're little girls in Trewatkins.'

With Johnny not rising to Minge's bait, the atmosphere lightened up in the Trewatkins Hotel for the remainder of the evening, to the disappointment of those who wished to witness a rematch of the legendary Seventies street fight between miner and coal merchant. Knowing he had a good thing going, the landlord shut his blackout curtains after closing time and kept the bar open for a late drink. Geronimo suffered from an outbreak of Tom Jones karaoke and it was well into the early hours before they wrested the microphone from his gnarled fingers.

The Extraordinary Pit Visit

Outside Clayton's polytunnel Clayton and Smithy stood over a pan of water looking for ripples of disturbance. Clayton seemed none the worse for his psychedelic experience but Smithy had taken to growing sideburns, carrying a rugby ball and wearing 1970s Welsh rugby kit.

Clayton cupped a hand to his ear. 'Screaming, I swear I heard a woman screaming for her life.'

'Ghostly and distant,' said Smithy.

'There.' Clayton pointed at the rippling water and they squatted down for a closer look.

Below ground in the colliery, former canteen manageress Big Bertha from Merthyr screamed her tits off in a fit of claustrophobia. The pit visits were off to a bad start when the old canteen lady panicked while wedging herself tight between two iron drainpipes supporting the roof. Her predicament held up, and terrified a long line of visitors in the workings.

Geronimo and Billy Donkey spent twenty minutes pulling, pushing and shoving Bertha's backside this way and that before she slipped free with the aid of WD40. They escorted her back to pit bottom where Johnny used all his strength in pedal power winding Big Bertha up the shaft.

'I've got ... I've got ... claustrophobia. I can't ... I can't ... breathe,' Bertha squealed on her way up from pit bottom. Her coal-smudged, ashen face lit up on sight of Johnny and she waddled out of the cage.

Out of breath, he could not dismount the bicycle before Bertha grabbed him and planted a big wet kiss on his lips. 'My hero,' she screeched. 'They deserve every penny working down there.'

After removing her mining kit, Bertha disappeared out through the shelf door where a long queue of old miners lined up along the blind side of the fence panels, through the secret way, the hidden gap in the leylandii hedge and up the potholed lane. The lane resembled an Everest base camp for miners burdened by health problems caused by the coal industry. Stick-bound or saddled up on mobility scooters, many of the old miners were accompanied by family keen to share the unique experience of visiting a small working colliery before the end of the Coal Age. Dai Milk's cows did not know what to make of it and viewed the aged snake-like queue with suspicion.

Banger supervised the visitors in and out through the chain link fence, continually hushing them and pointing at signs lining the way – KEEP IT QUIET! SILENCE!

Johnny oversaw the transition from shed down to the pit bottom while operating the bicycle winder. Joanne kitted out the visitors in helmets and overalls while North-Eye issued cap lamps and checks.

Geronimo and Billy Donkey took turns taking visitors to the coalface, oblivious to the second way in and out via a marijuana forest in Bouncer's shed.

The team were not enjoying the visitor experience. Lippo cracked first and jumped on the face Tannoy. *'Can these dickheads stop eyeballing us? We're not fucking goldfish.'*

'There's no need for that, mun,' said Billy Donkey on the pit bottom Tannoy.

Geronimo got on the workings Tannoy. *'We've heard you don't do much down here anyway, lead-arse.'*

'Will you lot behave, we've got visitors,' snapped Johnny on the shed Tannoy. Geronimo, Billy Donkey and Banger were getting their feet too far under the colliery table for Johnny's liking, and he wished for an end to it without breaking any old friendships. He left North-Eye in charge of the bicycle winding while he went out onto the allotment porch for a whiff.

All appeared normal as he surveyed the allotment and observed the tenants tending their pristine plots oblivious to the long line of visitors screened behind his fence panels. Vince watered Betty Bingo's climbing clematis, Hoss varnished his hitching post, and Team Singh kept busy around the Bollywood shed. Johnny thought to cast a precautionary eye over the ex-coppers. He crept up to and peeped around Bouncer's shed. Sure enough, Clayton, Smithy and Mrs M hovered above a pan of water in front of the polytunnel debating the ins and outs of divining.

'Johnny,' said Parvinder behind him. 'You look like a man in need of noise.'

'Noise?' said Johnny defensively. 'Why would I need noise?'

'To mask the sound of the coal mining operation you have going on under the allotment,' said Parvinder as he signalled to his eldest, Gaganjit, who blasted Bhangra from the Bollywood shed, frightening the bejesus out of Clayton, Smithy and Mrs M.

'Coal mining operation?'

'It didn't take much working out,' smiled Parvinder. 'There are more people in and out of your shed than a clown's car at a circus.'

'It's that obvious?'

'Only to your immediate neighbour, I believe.'

Hoss cranked up Frankie Laine to compete with the Bhangra and Vince the Hippy gave Hawkwind a good airing.

Clayton stubbed his toe kicking the water pan in frustration.

With one thing less to worry about now Parvinder knew of the colliery, Johnny cheered up. Parvinder wanted Team Singh to have the Welsh mining experience and they vanished from the allotment to take their places in the queue next to Dai Milk's cow field.

When it came to their turn Johnny insisted upon personally guiding them through the workings to the coalface.

Once underground, Parvinder infected Team Singh with small bursts of laughter as the shopkeeper comprehended the overview. He grasped the humour of it all, hiding the colliery in plain sight under the noses of two ex-coppers. Johnny had never heard Parvinder laugh so much. He thought that maybe the ventilation in Bouncer's shed had malfunctioned and was sending skunk fumes into the workings. Between bursts of laughter, Parvinder offered to take bags of coal for his shop and soon sobered when haggling over the mark-up.

They bumped into Geronimo on his way out with a group of visitors, including Elvis the Washery on a mobility scooter.

'Brilliant, brilliant, brilliant,' said Elvis tugging at Johnny's sleeve. 'Twenty years I worked underground until my hernia in '65, then they put me in the washery, and when Shanko the Washery retired and died in '71, he died a week after retiring. Lots of the old ones died soon after retiring, because they loved working and when they stopped, it took the life out of them. I saw it happen many times. They gave me the foreman job, and I worked there till closure in '93. I haven't been underground since '65 and this is one of the happiest days of my life. I'm so happy, thank you Johnny.'

'You're welcome, Elvis. I'm glad you and other senior miners could come along today. It makes it all worthwhile.'

Elvis wiped a tear from his eye and drove the mobility scooter to pit bottom, 'Brilliant, brilliant, brilliant.'

Johnny, Parvinder and Team Singh halted at the coalface and watched the young team, their cap lamps lasering through the dust as they worked the coal with shovels and a jackhammer.

'This is so real. Better than Deep Mine Museum. I'm so pleased my Team Singh can witness a genuine working Welsh colliery. Would it be OK if I invited my cousins from Cardiff?'

'We'll see how the remaining visits pan out.'

'It's great to see someone hands-on with these teenagers. The Community Council will be delighted and you're sure to be nominated for a community award.'

'I'd rather you didn't mention it. I'm still trying to keep it quiet.'

'Those boys were off the rails and up to all sorts – drinking, taking drugs, fighting, burning down houses and stealing from my shop, but you've turned them around and given them something to believe in.'

At the face, Lippo threw down his shovel. 'My head's gone.

162

This is a right shit show.' He turned around and shone his cap lamp on Team Singh. 'It's the Pakis from the Paki shop.' He shook his light at Gaganjit who seethed in anger while Parvinder held him back. 'I knows that's the Paki who shot me up the arse.'

Johnny flew at Lippo and bundled him squealing to the ground. 'My apologies but this one is still a bit of a wanker. We have a zero tolerance with racism at Julie's Colliery, particularly with useless tools like this.' Lippo squealed as Johnny dragged him to the toolbar. 'And there's only one thing to do with tools.'

'Get off. Get off me, Spider, bro, help!'

Jayden, Charlie and Slouch shone their lights on Spider as he dropped his shovel and took his spindly frame to the toolbar. 'You're out of order, dissing Team Singh.' He held him down while Johnny slipped the toolbar through Lippo's earplug and locked it.

'Spider, bro,' Lippo squealed, 'what are you doing? Charlie, Jayden, Slouch, help, get me off this thing.'

'Take a good look,' announced Johnny. 'The tool is on the bar.'

'Help, get me off this thing, Crew.'

Lippo could barely be heard over Team Singh's laughter as he struggled to get his ear free from the toolbar.

'We have our own form of justice underground, so if Gaganjit gets his air rifle, Team Singh can fill their boots with target practice.'

'I'm sorry,' said Lippo, 'I'm sorry.'

Geronimo's light hurried through the workings. He whispered in Johnny's ear. 'Sorry, Parvinder, but I'm urgently needed at pit bottom. Geronimo will guide you from here.'

He hurried off as Geronimo surveyed Lippo squirming on the toolbar.

'Well, well, look at that, a mouth on a stick.'

When Johnny got to pit bottom, he found Billy Donkey checking Elvis the Washery's pulse. 'I think Elvis is dead. He told me how happy he was when I strapped him in the cage and when I asked him if he was ready to go up, he didn't answer. He stared into space with a big smile on his face.' Billy listened to Elvis's chest. 'One second he's talking, then the next he's gone. He's definitely dead.'

Johnny pushed Billy aside and took Elvis's pulse. 'Fuck me hooray, it's one thing after another. The inconsiderate ... couldn't he have waited a couple of minutes?'

'He's gone but by the look of him he died happy.'

'He's not gone,' improvised Johnny, 'he's only passed out.'

'But his eyes are open, there's no pulse and he's not breathing.'

Johnny respectfully closed Elvis's eyes. 'We need to revive him out in the fresh air. We've got to get him up the shaft, out of the colliery and into the lane as quick as possible.'

'I'm telling you he's dead and he died of happiness because of the joy it gave him to see a working colliery again.'

'We're getting him the fuck out of here.' He got on the Tannoy, instructed North-Eye to wind and Elvis the Washery, happily smiling in death, sailed up the shaft.

Billy Donkey took off his helmet in respect, 'All because it was his first time underground since '65.'

'Billy, you are missing the point. There's no underground for him to die in, and no colliery, got it? If you haven't got it by now, the brown smelly stuff will hit the wind turbine big time.'

'Shunt my drams.'

They climbed the ladder, removed Elvis's overalls, helmet and cap lamp and carried the dead washery foreman out into the lane. Johnny reassured everyone in the queue Elvis had passed out and needed fresh air. He also apologised as the visits were suspended until further notice. Billy Donkey and Banger sat Elvis on his mobility scooter in front of Dai Milk's fascinated cows. Johnny dispersed the queue of visitors and the paramedics arrived as the last formation of wheeled rollators and walking frames disappeared down the potholed lane into the bottom streets.

Off the Cake List

As the Elvis crisis unfolded, North-Eye, Joanne and the old miners made surreptitious exits from the allotment while Team Singh remained underground with the colliery team. When Johnny gave the all-clear they disappeared into the ethers as only Team Singh could do. Johnny let the colliery team off the leash and they caught a train to Cardiff for a night on the razz.

It left Lippo stuck on the toolbar. Sitting alone underground with a steel bar threaded through his earlobe gave him time to reflect. When Johnny released him, he sulked and moped his way to the shower. For ten minutes not a sound came from him until he shouted through the door. 'My ear still fucking hurts.'

Stripped to the waist, Johnny looked closely into a shaving mirror on the sink. 'This could be the last opportunity you'll have to play with your cock in the shower. If this was Clanger Insurance you'd be sacked and up the road.' With his index finger he scooped a small amount of Vaseline from a nearby jar and rubbed it along a build-up of coal dust on his eyelids. 'You're lucky this colliery is rough around the edges and not full of HR services, compliance officers and jobs-worth managers who do nothing all day except wait for someone to step out of line so they can jump all over them.'

'I said my ear still fucking hurts, from when you put me on that bar thing.'

'I put you on that "bar thing" because you racially abused our visitors, and not just any old visitors, they are my fellow allotment tenants and my good friends. There's no place here for racism. Do you understand? You're lucky Parvinder can find an ounce of tolerance towards bigoted racist arseholes like you and he was satisfied with the natural justice I handed out by putting you on that "bar thing". When he came into this valley and opened his shop, he came in the hard way and had to endure mindless racism every day, but he's not going to hear it here. Understand?'

Johnny listened for an answer but only heard the running shower and a gurgling plughole.

'But they shot me up the arse.'

'Fuck me hooray, I'm dealing with the brain dead.'

'OK, I knows it. I won't call them that word again. I'm sorry.'

'It's no use saying sorry to me. I haven't been racially abused. Will you go to the shop and apologise?'

'Me, go to the Paki shop?'

Johnny thumped the shower door. 'Singh's Corner Shop! Parvinder is now our customer. You can come with me when I make a delivery and personally apologise and perhaps we can all move on.'

'I said sorry when they laughed at me.'

'You would've said anything to get off the toolbar.'

'The Crew have gone down Cardiff, and I'm stuck here because you put me on that bar thing.'

'They're enjoying the money they earn from working here, so as I said, you can apologise to Team Singh and perhaps we can all move on. If it's too much trouble, you could always find work elsewhere.'

Johnny listened for an answer but only heard the running shower and a gurgling plughole.

'OK.'

'Now that's sorted, stop sulking and hurry up out of the baths.'

'You're still an old twat.'

'Tell me something new.'

Lippo turned off the shower. 'Pass me my flip-flops.'

Johnny held up his flip-flops. 'Who'd have thought pit head baths footwear would become fashionable. How much did they cost?'

'Forty quid.'

'Forty quid for a pair of baths slippers, what's the world come to?'

Lippo exited the shower wrapped in a children's beach towel covered in cartoon dinosaurs with his eyes thick with coal dust. He snatched the flip-flops.

'You *are* taking this bad. If you can't take it, don't give it out.'

'You knows they're smashing it in Cardiff.'

'The bright lights of Cardiff, it's a step-up from hanging about the Old Wheel guzzling cheap cider and smoking bad weed.'

'Slouch sent me a wind-up selfie with the Crew on the train. They called me a big tool.'

'I'll drop you at the station for the next train.'

'Don't know if I want to go now.'

Johnny motioned Lippo closer. 'Come here, butt, you got eyes like Alice Cooper. Use this Vaseline to get the dust off.'

'Alice Cooper? What the fuck are you going on about?'

Johnny demonstrated. 'It's an old mining trick. You stick Vaseline on your eyelids. Then you wipe off the coal with the corner of a flannel like this.' He held out the Vaseline jar.

Lippo's dinosaur towel fell to his ankles when he reached for the Vaseline and at the precise moment he bent over to retrieve it, following a swift knock at the door, Mrs M entered the shed.

'Johnny, I wonder if you could help me with …'

Mrs M stopped in her tracks. From where she stood the view that greeted her was of a wet naked young man wearing odd-looking earrings bent over in front of Johnny, who held out a jar of Vaseline while stripped to the waist. Both men sported black mascara. Johnny smiled weakly as Mrs M backed out of the door. He hurried out and caught up with her on the gravel path.

'My apologies, I should've knocked and waited, but I assure you I won't be at your door again.'

'It's not what you think, Mrs M.'

Mrs M came to an abrupt halt and looked him in the eye. 'And what do I think?'

'You think, er, I'm, er, back-scuttling young men in my shed.'

'It's entirely your own business what you get up to in the privacy of your own shed. By the way, your mascara is smudged.'

'I can explain.'

Mrs M folded her arms around her clipboard. 'You can?'

'Yes, I can.'

'I'm all ears.'

'You see, under my, I've got, er … no, I can't.'

Mrs M stomped down the gravel path and Johnny followed. 'You can explain to the committee. Not that we've much of a committee since Mr Clayton and Mr Smithy resigned but there are signs they may resume their previous positions. I won't mention it this close to the championship. I wouldn't want to spoil our chances of a third consecutive win.'

'It's a good idea to keep it quiet,' said Johnny.

'However, once the championship is over, don't be surprised if your tenancy is revoked.'

'But the plot has been in the family for three generations. I wouldn't like that, Mrs M.'

Mrs M spun her clipboard away like a frisbee and screeched in his face. 'It's not Mrs M! It's Margaret!'

Johnny put his fingers in his ears. 'Not the M-word.'

'Margaret, Margaret, Margaret, Margaret … Margaret!'

Every shrill 'Margaret' hit cowering Johnny like an electric cattle prod.

Mrs M stormed off down the gravel path, entered the committee shed and slammed the door behind her. A hanging basket fell and smashed to bits from the aftershock.

When Johnny got back to his shed Lippo had dressed.

'That Mrs M, is she alright in the bean, like?'

'Aye, she's alright, mun.'

'She screamed like you'd shat in her handbag.'

'Mrs M is sound.'

'Slouch screamed like that when Jayden put stingies in his sleeping bag. He thought pixies were biting him.'

'I imagine it's quite common when you're shit-faced on drugs.'

'Still giving me a lift to the station?'

'Decided to go, then?'

'You knows it.'

'You've still got eyes like a panda.'

Lippo pouted at the shaving mirror. 'It looks really wicked.'

Johnny raised an eyebrow. 'Whatever flaps your flip-flop.'

A little later, when Johnny dropped Lippo off at the train station, he had a minor surprise.

'Thanks for the lift,' said Lippo getting out of the van.

'I'm honoured, you being so polite. Have a good night out with the boys.'

Lippo ran to the platform. 'You're still an old twat, Margaret!'

Johnny allowed himself a laugh but he knew his run-in with Margaret had put Julie's Colliery on borrowed time.

The Wake

Elvis the Washery's wake at Coed Mawr Rugby Club generated a good turnout. Johnny, North-Eye, Geronimo, Billy Donkey and Banger sat black-suited and booted around a table of drinks and buffet plates piled high. They agreed it had been a fine service, a particularly nice day for a planting on the hillside at Coed Mawr cemetery, and a very good spread at the club. Despite the musty damp-ridden clubhouse being full of botched jobs and appearing to be on its last taped-up legs, they agreed Elvis would have enjoyed it.

Banger blew his nose in a paper napkin from his ham roll. 'Ben the Box did such a good job. What a professional.'

'Banger, get a grip,' said Geronimo crunching a mouthful of crisps and giving him a friendly pat on the shoulder.

'I can't help it, I always cry at funerals. He was only ninety-seven.'

'That's miraculously good yardage for a miner, butt,' said Billy Donkey. 'Must've been all those years spent doing nothing in the washery except watching the coal on the shaking tables with his feet up next to the stove.'

'It's so sad he didn't make the full ton,' sniffed Banger.

'I didn't realise you knew him so well,' said North-Eye, scoffing a sausage roll and getting pastry crumbs down his black tie.

Banger wiped an eye. 'I didn't, but he was one of us.'

'See what I mean about Banger being all doom and gloom,' said Billy Donkey opening and examining a cheese and onion roll. 'He can turn the upcast shaft into the downcast in the twinkling of an eye.'

'Come on, Banger,' said North-Eye, brushing down his tie. 'We know he still had most of his marbles at ninety-seven but when you're incontinent, blind in one eye and can't get out and about without a mobility scooter, it's no surprise is it?'

'You're making Elvis sound like a cat needing to be put down,' said Geronimo.

'I wish I'd been there to see it,' said Banger. 'What a way to go.'

'What do you mean?' snapped Johnny. 'You were with me in the lane when he died. He died peacefully on his scooter in the lane next to Dai Milk's cow field on a sunny day without a care in the world, the way we'd all like to go. Get the story right now, Banger.'

'Johnny, everyone knows he died underground.'

'I thought you sparkies were supposed to be quick on the uptake. All that "I can do your job but you can't do mine" and I've got to draw you a picture.'

'Billy said he died of happiness because he was underground for the first time since '65.'

'Billy can keep his mortality opinions to himself. I'm not sure dying of happiness is a fully recognised cause of death and besides, he died of natural causes in the fucking lane, where he was fucking found by the fucking paramedics. Anyway, the visits are disrupting the team. They don't like being gawked at like they're weird animals in an underground zoo. I've decided there won't be any more visits.'

Geronimo snapped his cheese and pineapple cocktail stick. 'What? There's a backlog of visitors ready and waiting.'

'Then they'll have to wait.'

'Say something, North-Eye,' pleaded Billy Donkey.

'Sorry boys, I'm with Johnny on this one. It was a good idea at the time but it turned into a bastard nightmare.'

'And you three can cool it for a while and make yourselves scarce around the colliery.'

'What's he saying?' said Billy Donkey.

Geronimo selected another cheese and pineapple on a stick. 'He's shutting us out.'

'What?' said Billy Donkey, 'but we're already part-time at Deep Mine Museum. You're breaking our hearts by here, mun.'

'It got out of hand. I know you had good intentions but Julie's Colliery can't be any bigger than what it is. Thanks for all your help installing the Tannoy and the electric and everything else, but please leave us to get on with it.'

North-Eye pointed a ham roll at them. 'Comrades, it's

Johnny's plot, Johnny's shed and Johnny's colliery, he's the manager.'

'But we haven't done any harm,' said Geronimo.

'I don't know about that, Geronimo. You pair kept quiet about working a cosy little number in Deep Mine Museum, didn't you? You didn't let us in on it.'

A shadow of guilt crept over Geronimo and Billy Donkey.

'But you didn't keep quiet about our little colliery. You've done plenty of harm by spreading the word. One wrong word to the wrong person and you've put me up shit creek, but you pair won't be. And here's a thought for you, if you had kept it quiet, as I asked, then we wouldn't be sitting around this table and Elvis the Washery would still be going strong to reach his ton, instead of, according to you lot, dying of fucking happiness underground.'

'I didn't think of it that way,' said Banger taking the paper napkin from North-Eye's ham roll and blowing his nose. 'Elvis, it's our fault.'

'We'll let you know if we need anything else,' said Johnny as Geronimo and Billy Donkey stared guiltily at their beer. 'North-Eye intends to set up an emergency number.'

'An emergency number?' said Geronimo.

North-Eye downed the last of his pint. 'We'd like to have a highly skilled troubleshooting team of mining consultants, such as your good selves, waiting in the background, eager to assist us at the drop of a bastard helmet.'

Billy Donkey cheered up. 'Troubleshooting team of mining consultants, I like the sound of that.'

Johnny finished his pint and stood. 'Now we're all sorted, drink up, it's my round.'

Charlie's Secret

Johnny had a lie-in on the morning after Elvis's wake while he recovered from a right skinful. He left North-Eye, who quit the wake early, to supervise the team and prepare for a mine inspection.

In his recurring hippy dream of marigolds and canaries, the pit hooter sounded and with a backfiring snore, Johnny opened a bleary eye. Hung-over and half-asleep, he sat up on the edge of the bed.

'Gagging for a brew, I'll get the kettle on.' He reached behind across the bed for Julie, 'Cup of …?' Coming to his senses, he sighed and put his head in his hands.

A gigantic eye greeted Johnny when he quietly popped his head around the shelf door earlier than expected as North-Eye squinted through a magnifying glass at a dozen tiny-scale, model miners. With Johnny having a lie-in, the surveyor felt safe to indulge in his secret hobby as a scale modeller on the shed table. He carefully positioned the miners around a lump of coal.

'Second childhood, is it?'

North-Eye jumped with fright, scattering the tiny miners. 'Frighten the bastard life out of me, why don't you?'

Johnny picked up a Lilliputian figure. 'A little coal miner. Who'd have thought it?'

North-Eye retrieved the figure and placed it on the coal. 'What happened to your lie-in?'

'I'll go out of my head kicking around an empty house with a hangover.'

'I've heard you're off the cake list and on the sex offender list.'

'Mrs M and I go back a long way and I don't like the thought of her getting the wrong idea.'

'It might keep her away from the shed.'

'I wouldn't bank on that. Mrs M is getting thicker with Clayton and Smithy, and they are well on to us.'

Johnny looked at the line of checks on the check board. 'I see everyone's in again today.'

'They looked as if they'd had a night on the pop themselves so you're not the only one in a bit of a shape.'

Johnny plonked his helmet on. 'Let's get this inspection under way and find out what shape they are in.'

'I had hoped to get it done without you in my bastard face.'

Once kitted out, they thoroughly checked the bicycle winding apparatus, cable and trapdoor. They each put a check on the check board and climbed down the ladder to pit bottom. North-Eye had written a list and they followed it throughout the workings, checking and examining electric cables, ventilation and roof supports. They arrived near the coalface where the team were at work.

'Let's turn our lights off and find out what they really think about working here,' said Johnny turning off his lamp.

They crawled on all fours towards the workers and sat watching in the dark.

Spider gingerly dug at the coal with a pneumatic pick. 'This fucking seam has gone hard.'

'Yeah, I knows it,' agreed Lippo, half-asleep while leaning against a post. 'It used to fall away all easy like.'

'I've had it,' said Spider as he dropped the pick and collapsed into a heap. 'Whose idea was it to go on the vodka bombs?'

Slouch drove a mobility scooter trailing a line of shopping trolleys and parked up near the coalface. He jumped off and ran retching into the darkness. Jayden and Charlie kept working, oblivious to Johnny and North-Eye sat behind them in the dark.

'They're getting well stuck in,' whispered North-Eye.

'Look at Charlie go.'

Charlie shovelled loose coal into a bag held open by Jayden.

'You've got a soft spot for Charlie,' whispered North-Eye. 'He's always been a favourite of yours.'

'Charlie is the best miner we've got. Never complains, gets on with it quietly, head down and arse up.'

Charlie bent down to pick up a lump of coal in front of Johnny and he observed Charlie in a different light, particularly his shapely rear end. 'Have you noticed anything odd about Charlie?'

'Like a sinister Goth terrorist always in sunglasses and scarf?'

'Apart from that.'

'He doesn't use our pit head baths, so what his parents think of him coming home as black as the road, I don't bastard know.'

'Apart from that.'

'Apart from that, no, I can't say I have.'

'Well, something's odd.'

They sat in the dark and watched. After wiping away sweat, Charlie wriggled half out of the overalls, knotted the sleeves together at the hips and revealed a healthy female form in a sports bra.

The old miners spluttered out. 'Charlie's a girl!'

Alerted to their presence, Charlie slipped back into her overalls.

Johnny took his helmet off and wiped his brow. 'Thank fuck for that, I thought I was on the turn.'

Johnny called a meeting at pit bottom where Spider, Jayden

and Lippo were infected by mirth at his expense. Johnny and North-Eye remained stone-faced during the laughter. Charlie, in a world of her own, turned her face away and twanged a tune out of a splinter in a pallet shoring up the side.

Slouch returned from his bout of vomiting. 'Did I miss anything?' It signalled another burst of laughter from Spider, Jayden and Lippo.

Johnny got serious. 'You think this is funny?'

'Your face,' laughed Spider.

'The joke's on me?'

'From the beginning,' laughed Spider.

'Now it makes sense,' said Johnny as it dawned upon him, 'that's why you were always sniggering.'

Slouch caught on. 'Didn't Johnny know Charlie's a …?'

'He fucking knows now,' blurted Lippo as he dropped and rolled around on the floor in laughter.

'Very funny, isn't it?' Johnny threw a look at North-Eye as the old surveyor shook his head. 'Tell them.'

'Women have been banned from working underground since the Mines and Quarries Act of 1842.'

'Hear that? Since 1842, so if any more of you fuckers are women, you'd better own up now!'

'What do you mean banned?' said Jayden with half a chuckle.

'Banned, as in, banned,' said Johnny. 'Not allowed to work underground in coal mines, banned.'

Jayden sobered. 'It doesn't mean Charlie?'

'Yes, it means Charlie.'

'Charlie can't work with us any more?' said Spider.

Lippo got up from the floor. 'You knows she did all the training.'

'Charlie won't be taking out a lamp again,' said Johnny.

'C'mon Grandad, Charlie designed our logo and everything.'

'It's bad enough if one of you boys had a bump underground, but a young woman? None of us could live with it.'

'Charlie passed all the safety stuff,' said Spider.

'Spider,' said North-Eye, 'to you and the rest of you boys, it's naughty and a bit of a laugh moonlighting down here, but if you had to measure and draw up the accident plans that I've drawn up after an underground accident, there'd be no argument, because you wouldn't want to see it happen to Charlie.'

'And it's against the law,' said Johnny.

Spider punched a pallet. 'This is all against the fucking law.'

'Regarding the law, if we're caught operating this illegal coal mine, a multitude of jobsworths will rain on us from a great bastard height,' said North-Eye. 'Add a young woman to the equation and you can double the fines and prison time.'

Charlie focused her attention on the musical quality of the pallet splinter and twanged away as Johnny put a hand on her shoulder.

'Charlie, sorry, but I'll have to let you go.'

Charlie snapped the splinter in temper and screamed. 'Fuck off, fuck off, fuck off, fuck off, fuck … off.' She speed-climbed the ladder, leaving them basking under a cloud of guilt.

'Charlie,' shouted Jayden before ducking for cover as her helmet flew down the shaft.

Her boots, belt, cap lamp and battery flew down and they ducked for cover.

'*Fuck off, fuck off, fuck off, fuck off,*' screamed a tinny voice on the Tannoy. Castors rolled across the floorboards and the armchair hurtled down the shaft crashing into the cage.

'Hang about now, Charlie,' Johnny shouted up the shaft before ducking from the kettle and a shower of mugs.

'*Fuck ... off, fuck, fuck, fuck, fuck, fuck, fuck, fuck off, fuck ... off,*' echoed on the tinny Tannoy.

They looked up the shaft as she slipped out of her overalls, threw them down and ran off in skinny fit shorts and sports bra.

'Any doubt Charlie wasn't a girl just disappeared,' said North-Eye.

'*Fuck off, fuck off ... fucking fuck off,*' screeched over the Tannoy as half-a-dozen hoop-backed chairs tumbled down the shaft.

'She's upset,' said Jayden.

Johnny righted a chair and sat down, 'You don't miss a trick.'

'Charlie loves working here,' said Jayden.

'*I hate it here anyway, and I hate all of you so you can all go and fucking fuck ... off. Pig bastards ... pig ... bastards!*'

Johnny looked enquiringly at Jayden, 'Pig bastards?'

'She doesn't mean it. She's got a bit of a temper.'

'You knows she's mental,' said Lippo as the bicycle wheel winder contraption flew down and dangled precariously above them in a tangle of ropes.

Johnny jumped from the chair. 'I took ages building that.'

Charlie turned out the coal bags. Lumps of coal scattered across the floorboards and rained down the shaft.

Slouch cushioned his head with his sleeping bag. 'She's headshot.'

'They're terrified of her in Trewatkins,' said Spider.

North-Eye picked up a lump of coal and glanced up the shaft. 'We're terrified of her down here.'

'I get the feeling,' said Johnny to North-Eye as they cowered under a hail of shrapnel from terracotta pots shattering on the side of the shaft, 'the 1842 Mines and Quarries Act banned women from working underground to protect the men.'

Shed doors slammed and glass panes rattled.

'Fuck me hooray, she's gone out the front.' Johnny climbed the shaft ladder like a rat up a drainpipe.

The shed looked as if a magician had conjured up a tornado of coal. Through the window he saw Charlie storming down the gravel path in her underwear with a bundle of clothes under her arm. She stopped to hop around while slipping on her trainers.

Johnny scanned the allotment. Luckily no tenants were about. He removed his helmet and cap lamp and stepped out onto the porch.

'Charlie, sorry I upset you. Come back, we'll work it out.'

Charlie flashed the fingers. 'Fuck ... off.' She stormed down the path in a tantrum, dressing along the way.

'It's not my fault. You played me along and made me think you were a boy. I had no idea you were a girl.'

Johnny watched her go. He gave out a heavy sigh, leaned on a porch post and saw Mrs M standing not more than five yards away on Bouncer's plot. Mrs M held on to her clipboard with one hand and held an extended tape measure in the other. With a look of exasperation, she retracted her tape measure and put it into a pocket.

'I can explain ...' Johnny pleaded with a slight smile, 'it's not what you think.'

Mrs M bit her lip for a few moments before turning around and disappearing into the depths of the allotment.

The Strike

Back in the shed Johnny pressed the speaker button on the Tannoy.

'The damage is nothing we can't fix and it'll be all up and working by the morning. Charlie has run off. You all know I thought the world of Charlie. He was … she was the best of you by far and put you all to shame on the shovel. She never mouthed off like Lippo, or did stupid things like Slouch, and she'd stop a pig in a passage better than Spider. Charlie got on with the job quietly, with no trouble, and was a pleasure to work with.'

No answer came. *'Hello, anyone down there?'*

'We're on strike,' answered Jayden on the Tannoy.

'What do you mean on strike?'

'Like I said, we're on strike.'

North-Eye climbed up out of the shaft. 'It's a stay-down strike.'

'We're not working without Charlie,' said Spider on the Tannoy. *'We've had a vote and it was unanimous.'*

'They've had a democratic show of hands to take industrial action,' said North-Eye. 'That's more than we had in 1984.'

'We're staying down until you oldies grow some brain cells and let Charlie work with us,' said Lippo on the Tannoy. *'You knows it.'*

'Sorry Johnny,' apologised Slouch, *'I know you did me a favour but it's like what they said, and because it's not nice.'*

'North-Eye, what have we done?'

North-Eye got out of his overalls. 'I'm sure you can sort it out.'

'Where are you going?'

'For one, I'm pissed at Charlie for losing my model miners, and two, this is nothing to do with me. I might be the surveyor, ventilation officer, training officer, safety officer, cost clerk and mining inspector of Julie's Colliery, but I'm not the bastard manager.'

'You can't walk out now, I need you.'

'From the off we talked about one of them getting killed etcetera, but if I had known then that one of them was a teenage girl, well.'

Johnny watched North-Eye disappear out through the shelf door.

'*Any oldies still up there?*' said Lippo.

Johnny had had enough and pressed the Tannoy button. '*Stay down then. I'm off home for lunch. I think I'll have sausages, mash, peas and onion gravy. Then I'll put my feet up with a whisky or three and spend the afternoon watching a good Western.*'

Johnny scuffed his way through the coal spillage to the trapdoor. While lifting it, he glanced down at the team gathered on pit bottom and they looked up with open mouths like tits in a nesting box. 'I'll see you tomorrow. If I come in tomorrow, I might take the weekend off. You'll have plenty of time to come to your senses.'

Johnny slammed the trapdoor shut and dust particles rained upon them. He spoke on the Tannoy. '*You've pissed on your chips.*'

'What's a Western?' said Slouch.

Jayden took off his helmet. 'I didn't think this'd happen.'

Lippo settled down in the armchair.

'No problemo,' said Spider, pinching Lippo's earplug and lifting him from the armchair. 'Get your lead arse up the ladder and open the trapdoor.' Spider settled down in the armchair while Lippo rubbed his ear. They heard the draw of the trapdoor bolt.

'We've still got the electric,' said Spider.

The pit bottom lights went out.

'Fuck,' they said.

'How long will our cap lamps last?' worried Jayden.

'Like I paid attention in training?' said Spider.

Dust fell from the floorboards as Johnny stomped around. Shed doors slammed and glass panes rattled.

'We won't be able to get out,' said Jayden.

'Easy,' announced Spider, 'we'll get out from Bouncer's shed and have a smoke on the way.'

The team went through the workings to the green door. Lippo took the lead into the passageway and climbed the pallet ladder but when he tried the trapdoor, it would not budge.

A familiar tinny voice came over the Tannoy. *'Don't think about climbing out through Bouncer's shed because I've piled heavy pots and boxes of dirty books on the trapdoor. If you start digging now, you might get out before I'm back on Monday, tar-rah.'*

'He's gone,' said Jayden, 'we're trapped.'

'Scary,' said Spider leading the way back to pit bottom.

'Gone?' said Slouch shifting in his sleeping bag.

'He's gone and left us down here,' said Jayden.

'In the dark?' said Slouch nervously.

Lippo developed a withdrawal tic, 'Without our phones?'

'Fuck,' they said.

'And our contraband,' said Spider.

'Fuck,' they said.

When they got to pit bottom Lippo shone his light up at the trapdoor, 'What now, bro?'

'You could do some work for a change and dig us out,' said Spider, 'or we chill and wait for him to come back.'

'Old twat said he might take the weekend off,' moaned Lippo.

'Whose idea was this?' said Slouch, getting more worried.

'North-Eye knows we're here,' said Jayden.

'If both oldies get wasted under a steamroller or summat, you knows we'll be stuck then,' said Lippo.

'Stuck down here for ever,' added Spider.

'Charlie would know,' said Jayden.

'You knows Charlie won't care now,' said Lippo.

Slouch cwtched into his bag. 'I'm not sharing my sleeping bag.'

'Like we want to buzz of sick and piss?' said Lippo.

'My sleeping bag doesn't smell. It doesn't, does it, Spider?'

'Anyone got any grub?' said Spider. 'I'm starving.'

'It doesn't smell,' said Slouch a little louder, 'does it, Jayden?'

'Me too,' said Jayden. 'We should've used our heads and done this strike after grub time.'

Slouch sniffed a corner of his sleeping bag. Although he had cleaned up his act and lived back home, he remained attached to his old friend and kept it stashed safe in the colliery workings.

'We'll end up eating each other,' laughed Spider.

'Eating each other?' said Slouch, horrified.

'Or bits of each other,' added Spider giving the nod to Lippo and Jayden.

Lippo kicked Slouch in the backside. 'You knows we'll have to eat bits of Slouch first.'

Slouch rubbed his rump. 'You're not eating me.'

Spider bounced a piece of coal off Lippo's helmet. 'I says who gets eaten first.'

'Who then, bro? Who do you say gets eaten first?'

Spider shone his light on each of them in turn and sinisterly rubbed his hands, 'We'll eat Slouch first.'

'Why me, why not eat Jayden first? He's the headshot one.'

'Am I fuck, you're the headshot one.'

'You are,' shouted Slouch.

Jayden kicked Slouch up the backside. 'You are.'

'No, you are,' said Slouch returning the kick.

'No, you are.'

'Don't start, or I'll bang the pair of you out,' said Spider.

'I don't knows about you, bro, but this coal mining is negging me out,' said Lippo. 'I want to go back to being a waster.'

Tales from Paranormal Wales

Johnny left Bouncer's shed, taking care not to be seen by Clayton, as outside his polytunnel the two ex-police officers were cooking up mischief with Mrs M. With a headful of strike business, Johnny did not hang around to find out what they were up to. After delivering his Tannoy message to the team from his shed, he went out and sat on the porch bench to think it over.

On the other side of Bouncer's shed, Mrs M tried to ascertain if Clayton wished to return to the chair of the association.

'If we exercise a zero-tolerance policy towards the flaunting of our rules,' said Clayton holding the lapels of his gilet, 'I may consider returning to my former position as chairman.'

'Chairperson,' corrected Mrs M.

With his inflated ego suitably massaged, Clayton strutted around like the president of the pig pen. 'The upshot is we don't have a cat's chance of a third consecutive win in the allotment championships.'

Smithy fondled the rugby ball tucked under his arm. 'Not with all these funny things going on.'

Mrs M clutched her clipboard. 'What funny things?'

'You saw the vibrations in the pan of water,' said Clayton.

'I agree it was odd but it's hardly cause for concern regarding the championship.'

'Then there's noise pollution, Bollywood music from Mr Singh, country and western from Hoss, and psychedelic nonsense from Vince the Hippy. Once one starts – the others start, as if in a loud music competition with each other. It's near impossible to propagate leeks with noisy neighbours.'

Smithy spun his rugby ball. 'The Americans used music torture on the Viet Cong in the Vietnam War.'

'And your point is?'

'Look how they ended up.'

'How who ended up, the Americans, or the Viet Cong?'

'Both.'

Clayton entered his polytunnel and returned with a laptop. 'My CCTV has picked up alarming footage. Be prepared for a shock.' He played film of Spider, Lippo, Jayden and Slouch mooning and slapping their bare backsides at Clayton's CCTV camera.

'Neighbourhood Watch, my backside.'

'Neighbourhood Watch, their backsides,' said Mrs M raising her eyebrows. 'Unsavoury, I agree, but surely just exuberant teenagers having harmless fun. Let's not forget their volunteer work. I recall you were not so welcoming of their help.'

'Not so trusting would be more accurate,' corrected Clayton before searching through the footage.

'In this instance it may be where the problem lies,' said Mrs M. 'Teenagers being teenagers.'

'I don't trust that bonk-eyed North-Eye either,' said Smithy.

Clayton played film of Charlie. 'This is footage from not more than half an hour ago. A young girl running around scantily clad and hurling obscene gestures at Mr Morgan. What on earth is that about?'

'I've no idea,' said Mrs M struggling not to let slip she witnessed the scene at first-hand. 'But on the subject of bare backsides and running around scantily clad, when are you due in court for indecent exposure Mr Smithy?'

Smithy nervously adjusted the collar of his rugby shirt. 'I was drugged, that's all I'm legally allowed to say until the case is heard. It would be inappropriate to comment further.'

'Our tea was deliberately contaminated with Lysergic Acid Diethylamide more commonly known as LSD,' said Clayton. 'We don't know how, or when, or by whom, but we are determined to find and bring the perpetrator to justice.'

'Good Lord, drugs?' said Mrs M, quite shocked.

As Smithy played keepy-uppy with the rugby ball, Clayton happily ran his fingers through a wind chime and dropped his voice to a whisper. 'I've suffered no ill-effects but Mr Smithy hasn't been the same since. He sometimes thinks he's Gareth Edwards.'

Smithy hugged the ball. 'There are drugs in the allotment.'

'You know this for certain?'

Smithy stood pompously with Bouncer's shed behind him. 'As former police officers we have a nose for this kind of thing.'

Clayton produced a cork board from his polytunnel. 'We're still gathering evidence. This is a geographic profile and you can see ...'

'Really, Mr Clayton,' interrupted Mrs M while looking at

the photographs, coloured pins and line drawings all pointing at Johnny's shed, 'this is going to extremes.'

'Geographic profiling is a proven investigative tool used to identify the source of criminal activity.' Clayton smacked Johnny's shed in the centre of the board. 'The hotspot is right here.' He opened a cardboard box and showed her a drone. 'Once we've mastered the drone camera we should have enough on Mr Morgan and his gang to make a sound case.'

Mrs M looked at the drone in horror. 'I believe CCTV is a tool for crime prevention, not for spying on your neighbours.'

'It's the only way to catch him at it.'

'Catch him at what?'

'Whatever secretive criminal activity he's up to in that coal mine shed of his.'

'That's why you'll never find a coal mine in the Home Counties,' added Smithy in a scoffing plummy English accent.

'I'm not sure what "coal mines in the Home Counties" has to do with it but I know you are both secretive about your leek growing activities. Pot, kettle, black, don't you think?'

'The art of growing leeks is by nature a secretive affair with many secret propagation methods,' said Clayton condescendingly, as if after only two months engaged in the activity he was now the Monty Don and Alan Titchmarsh hybrid genius of leek growing. 'Have you witnessed anything suspicious in the vicinity of Mr Morgan's shed?'

Mrs M did not know what to say but she knew she did not want to throw faggots onto the fire of this witch hunt. 'No more than Betty Bingo, Vince, Hoss or Parvinder.'

'Ah, yes, Mr Singh. Now he and Mr Morgan are joined at the hip and enjoy flaunting our alcohol rules like naughty schoolboys around that smoky chiminea. Not environmentally friendly at all, which may be of interest to the Council's Enviro-Crime team.'

'Who can blame anyone having a quiet drink after a day in the allotment – it's hardly drunk and disorderly behaviour?'

'It's a thorough disrespect of our rules. It doesn't help matters that Community Councillor Singh continually backs up Mr Morgan when he should know better and whose shed is quite frankly, the most gaudy, cheap-looking thing I've ever seen in an allotment.'

'The Bollywood shed is adored by all and it's gone a long way to brighten and lift the spirit of the allotment.'

'The spirit of the allotment, where we've felt strange vibrations, endured noise pollution, been poisoned with hallucinogenic drugs and even had a suspicious death?'

'Natural causes at age ninety-seven is suspicious? It was nothing to do with us. He was found on his mobility scooter out in the lane with a big smile on his face.'

'Suspiciously close to the hotspot,' said Clayton pointing to his cork board. 'The allotment has rapidly gone downhill since I vacated the chair. It's no surprise there's been no suitable candidate to replace me. Since the shed painting episode, Mr Morgan has gone from bad to worse and if you want this disruptive influence to continue ...'

'Very well,' interrupted Mrs M, 'I will confront Mr Morgan and find out precisely what is going on.'

'That would be tipping him off while we're still gathering evidence,' Smithy reminded Clayton, 'and he'll make his dubious activities harder to detect.'

'Besides, we're still trying to make sense of it all,' said

Clayton searching his laptop footage and facing the screen to Mrs M. 'In addition to the vibrations we've got baffling CCTV evidence of paranormal activity.'

'Mr Clayton, you really are pushing the boundaries. What possible paranormal activity can be going on in the allotment? Are you certain the alleged LSD experience has left you unscathed?'

'My camera picked up this most unusual footage from the evening we were drugged, just look at the movements of this water barrel across my plot, ghostly or what?'

'That's not all,' said Smithy with a spin of his rugby ball. 'A few days ago we distinctly heard the prolonged ethereal screaming of a woman in considerable distress.'

'You make it sound so sinister,' said Mrs M becoming concerned about their mental health. 'Could it be – the voices in your head?'

Clayton snapped the laptop shut. 'We intend to get to the bottom of these incidents one way or another.'

On the other side of Bouncer's shed, Johnny paced around on his porch looking for something to take his racing mind off the stay-down strike. He looked up at the Welsh flag for inspiration as it fluttered in the breeze, and then spotted the familiar plastic flowerpot on the edge of Bouncer's plot. It invitingly leant back at an angle on a small mound of earth like a rugby ball begging for a good kick. He adopted a kicking stance, ran and kicked the pot. Luckily, he was wearing steel toe caps as, on connection, he perceived the pot was full to the brim with earth.

The pot cleared Bouncer's shed by a whisker, sank a foot deep into Clayton's polytunnel and sprang up in the air.

'I came for a rational conversation and all I get is paranoia about Mr Morgan and nonsense about paranormal activity,' said Mrs M.

The pot crashed down on Smithy's head rendering him unconscious before he landed spread-eagled in Clayton's rhubarb.

Clayton suspiciously looked up and scanned the clouds. 'Strange, it fell straight out of the sky.'

Marching in the Sun

Upbeat after converting the flowerpot over Bouncer's shed roof, Johnny happily stepped back into his shed. When he reached for the trapdoor, it thumped up and down as if alive. He drew back the bolt and it sprang open. Slouch jumped out of the shaft like a jack-in-a-box, wrapping his arms and legs around Johnny's leg.

'They're gonna eat me!'

Johnny struggled around the shed with Slouch attached to his leg like an amorous Yorkshire terrier, 'Get the fuck off.'

'Don't let them eat me.'

'No one is going to eat you.'

Slouch wept into Johnny's overalls. 'They said they'll, eat, me.'

Hearing Spider, Lippo and Jayden having a banging laugh on pit bottom, Johnny got to the Tannoy.

'*Will someone get this headshot retard off my leg?*'

'That's crossing a picket line?' shouted Spider.

'*Fuck the picket line.*'

'I haven't got to go up there, have I?' said Spider to Jayden. 'He's your grandad.'

Jayden went up the ladder and peeked over the trapdoor

rim. He snatched Slouch's sleeping bag and threw it down the shaft.

Slouch emitted a pathetic howl at the loss of his beloved sleeping bag and released Johnny's leg.

Jayden grabbed Slouch's ankle and dragged him to the shaft. He clung on by his fingernails, scraping lines in the floorboards before disappearing over the edge to crash down on pit bottom.

Johnny composed himself, stood at the trapdoor and looked down at them. 'I remembered I used to be a NUM lodge official. Do you know what the best part of the Miners' Strike was?'

Spider reclined in the armchair, 'Kicking fuck out of coppers?'

Johnny sat and dangled his legs like a schoolboy over the edge of the shaft. He studied a lump of coal plucked from the floorboards.

'It was when the Strike was over and we marched back to work behind our lodge banners and a brass band. The whole village came out to cheer us on and we were applauded in every street, from every window, and at every corner. My wife Julie walked with me every step of the way. Julie earned the right to march with us. She was our fundraising manager, personally collecting far more donations than anyone else; our food parcel distributor; ran the children's Christmas party; had duties too numerous to mention and was as active as any NUM member. I'd punch anyone's lights out who said otherwise.'

Johnny examined the coal in his hand. 'It was a cold, overcast late winter morning, and we were wrapped up in scarves and duffle coats, yet it seemed we were marching in the sun.'

He discarded the coal and it rattled across the floorboards. 'No one wins in a strike. Everyone loses. I propose Charlie is reinstated to work here.'

The team cheered but Johnny calmed them with a raised hand.

'But Charlie works on the surface with me and does not go underground until I say so, that should keep everyone happy including North-Eye. Give us oldies time to get used to the idea, and maybe Charlie can be integrated back underground. If you're all in favour, raise your hands.'

They raised hands and Johnny raised his hand with them.

'Grandad, what's Charlie gonna do?'

'I need help with sales. Our fire pit and chiminea customers are flying south for the winter. We must find new multi-fuel customers soon or we're finished.'

Johnny's Secret

When Charlie turned up for work the next morning, Johnny beamed with delight. While they loaded the van with bags of coal, North-Eye crawled around on the floorboards with a magnifying glass searching for his tiny 00-scale miners, scattered during Charlie's meltdown.

Johnny held the shelf door. 'We're off now.'

'I'll catch you later,' grunted North-Eye getting to his feet. He went to the Tannoy. *'Boys, has anyone seen any small figures about an inch high, like little people, down there?'*

'Little people, like, pixies?' gulped Slouch on the Tannoy.

'No, they are scale model miners. They're not bastard pixies.'

'I've seen loads of pixies,' said Lippo menacingly, *'they're crawling all over the roof, up the posts, on the face and they're all coming to bite the fuck out of headshot Slouch.'*

Johnny closed the shelf door on Slouch's screams and left North-Eye to sort it out.

Out in the van Johnny arranged the Lilliputian miners on top of the dashboard with Blu Tack. 'I thought they'd bring us luck with our coal sales,' explained Johnny, but Charlie sat in silence, hoodie up, hidden by scarf and shades. 'I'm sure North-Eye won't miss them.'

A storm raged on top of Coed Mawr tip but it did not seem to bother Charlie who stood firm against the elements while she watched Johnny emptying bags of muck onto the growing pyramid of spoil. Once back in the van, he offered Charlie a driving lesson but she sulked in silence. Without a word or grunt from Charlie all morning, Johnny wondered what he had let himself in for.

They made for Dai Milk's boot sale but on arrival discovered the field to be a muddy wash-out. Dai Milk's Farm Produce gave up on the day and, as the van crawled past the entrance, the farmer and his windswept family miserably squelched out from the field and chained the gate. Three generations of the myopic farming family ran the farm produce business; Dai Milk's father – Old Dai Milk; Dai Milk's son – Young Dai Milk, and Dai Milk's Thai bride and wife of twenty years – Mrs Thai Milk. The Dai Milks tended to reproduce identically. Not only did they look the same, they dressed the same, with wellies, raincoats and thick glasses. Even the diminutive Mrs Thai Milk had naturally assimilated the family characteristics.

Johnny sounded the horn at the soaked Dai Milks and they looked inquiringly at the van, simultaneously pushing jam-jar glasses higher up their noses.

'We closed,' said Mrs Thai Milk, 'You go away now. We open next week.'

'You can't have it all ways, Dai,' shouted Johnny as Dai stood at the gate with a face like misery. 'Think of the money you're making from the wind turbines.'

Johnny wound up the window as he drove away. 'Did you see the look on his face? Like a panda with a sore foreskin. If Dai Milk knew where our coal came from, he'd expect it for next to nothing. Don't be fooled by the rope holding up his trousers and a raincoat that first saw life in the Sixties, he's minted. They're a funny lot though, aren't they, Dai Milk, Mrs Thai Milk, Old Dai Milk and Young Dai Milk? There'll be a generational shift one day when Old Dai Milk dies and they'll all move up a notch. Dai Milk will become Old Dai Milk and Young Dai Milk would be promoted to Dai Milk and his son the next Young Dai Milk. I've seen it happen many times over the years. They must be cloning themselves in the cowshed.'

Johnny tried door-to-door sales around the valley streets when the weather brightened up, and throughout the day he talked half to himself and half to Charlie because she remained so deathly quiet.

'The van might be rusty, creaking and getting on a bit but it was brand-new and gleaming at one time. The first thing I did with my Coal Board redundancy money was buy this van. We've been mates ever since.' He patted the dashboard and one of the tiny miners fell over. 'Julie wasn't too happy, mind. She would've preferred a new car but I argued it would be handy for the allotment and whatever, and it has proved to be the case. Julie came around a bit when I surprised her with a Mediterranean cruise. It was the best holiday we ever had. Better than Miners' Fortnight in Trecco Bay, Costa del Hi-yah Butt, Porthcawl. What's the best holiday you've ever had, Charlie?'

He got no reaction. Johnny had a thought. He reached over and pulled the scarf from her ear. She slapped his hand.

'Sorry, just checking for headphones. You heard me then?'

The Coed Mawr terraces did not produce any new customers. The villages of Trewatkins and Abercwmcoedmawr were Minge Jenkins territory and Johnny did not need a run-in with the mad coal merchant. In Aberbargoed Charlie knocked door after door but she barely raised a curtain twitch. The doors that did open swiftly closed in her face following curt abuse. Johnny suggested she try without the scarf and shades. Charlie reluctantly made a go of it but covered up again after more of the same. It was the norm wherever they went and Charlie became disheartened at every turn.

'Don't take this all to heart,' he said when she got back in the van and slammed the door. 'People don't always mean what they say and they soon feel bad about it later.'

When the rain returned Johnny headed for home. Despite the rain, he knew the bigger picture, as sales in general were not going well. He looked at Charlie knowing a bad idea when he saw one. Driving around the streets with an old man trying to sell coal from the back of a van did not even make the bottom of the list of wise career moves for a teenage girl.

'We've had two types of luck today, bad luck and no luck,' he said breaking the silence as they approached Coed Mawr village. 'If we stepped in shit there'd be a nail in it.'

Charlie adjusted her sunglasses. Johnny glimpsed behind the mask and saw her tears.

'At least it's Friday. It'll be dry next week and we'll try our luck in another valley. Where do you want to be dropped?'

Charlie casually waved a finger. He understood this meant 'anywhere'.

As Johnny pulled over, Charlie opened the door and got out before the van stopped. He braced himself for an almighty slam but she hesitated as if having second thoughts and held the van door.

'Anyway Charlie,' he said after a few moments, 'you've been great company and it's been nice having someone to talk to.'

Charlie swung the door back and forth slowly on its hinges and the van creaked with rust and old age. 'What are you going to do with the bags of coal?'

'Apart from telling us all to fuck off yesterday, that's the most I've heard you say. Now don't worry about the coal.'

'If we're not selling the coal where's it all going?'

'It'll be alright, mun, I've got it sorted.'

Charlie leaned on the creaking door. 'It's got to be going somewhere. How much have you sold this week?'

'I don't hear a peep out of you all day and now you can't stop,' laughed Johnny as he reached and grabbed the door handle. 'You've got the rest of Friday off, have a great weekend and stop worrying.'

Charlie resisted his pull on the van door and they engaged in a small tug-of-war. 'But next week we'll have lots more to sell.'

'A minute ago you wanted to get out of the van.'

'What are you doing with it all?'

'Like I said, I've got it sorted.' Johnny wrenched the door from her and slammed it shut. He drove off and checked the mirror. Charlie stood with attitude in the centre of the road watching him go. 'I liked Charlie better when I couldn't get a word out of her.'

Johnny hammered the van up to the top streets and parked in front of his house. He took a bag of coal from the back of the van and put it on his doorstep as he unlocked the front door. The door barely opened. He gave it the shoulder and lumps of coal tumbled out onto the doorstep. He squeezed through the doorway into the hall.

One of the coal bags stacked in the hall had fallen over and blocked the front door. He moved the spillage with his foot, replaced the bag on the stack and surveyed the scene. Thankfully, just the one bag had fallen over and the coal bags stacked along the hall, up one side of the stairs and packed high on top of the landing, looked fine. Picking up the new bag from the doorway, he searched for storage space. Johnny stepped into an amphitheatre of coal bags in the lounge surrounding his TV, armchair and side table of drinks. Bags filled the kitchen apart for functional space in front of sink, fridge and cooker, and when he kicked open the downstairs toilet door the coal bags reached the ceiling. 'Where's the coal house when you need it?'

He looked through the kitchen window into the garden, 'Shed.'

He passed the jam-packed conservatory, opened the back door, walked down the path and booted the shed door open, 'Bingo.'

Johnny plonked the bag down, pleased at the ample room to stack the remaining new bags. To make space he moved an old fruit box full of junk and glanced inside. His face lit up as he picked out a shiny shovel, a shiny brush, a shiny poker, shiny tongs and a shiny stand. 'The companion set,' and with a broad smile he turned to the shed door. 'I've been looking everywhere for ...'

Charlie stood in the shed doorway holding a bag of coal.

Johnny put the companion set back in the fruit box. 'I didn't have the heart to tell you all,' he stuttered, 'you're such good workers and I can see you've started believing in yourselves and ...'

Charlie thrust the bag into his hands to shut him up. She went down the garden path and into the house. Johnny put the bag down and followed her. When he got to the front door Charlie pushed in past him with another coal bag from the van. Johnny's secret was out.

THREE

WEIRD SCENES INSIDE THE COAL MINE

BBC Wales News, July 1984

When Johnny finally forced the door shut on his packed garden shed, the heavens opened and heavy rain bounced six inches high on the patio. He ran into the house and found Charlie in the living room relaxing in a nest of coal bags and studying a framed photograph.

'How about I get the kettle on for a big cup of tea?'

Charlie held up a crystal glass of his Penderyn whisky he had failed to notice at her side. 'This is a lovely photograph of Julie.'

'Yes, it is.' He got himself a glass and poured a belter. 'You're not the first woman in Coed Mawr wanting to work underground. In fact ...' Johnny rummaged under the TV and put a disc in the CD player, 'this is a news item I converted from VHS to CD. It's filmed outside the colliery gates during the Miners' Strike.'

Charlie's eyes lit up. 'Awesome.'

'I'm outside the picket line of Co-Ed Maw-r Colliery in the upper Rhymney Valley on this beautiful summer evening and I'm speaking

to the community fundraising manager Mrs Julie Morgan and her very shy two-year-old daughter Joanne. Mrs Morgan ...'

Julie lifted Joanne into her arms and she shyly snuggled into her bosom. 'First things first, let's get the pronunciation right. It's not Co-Ed, it's Coed as in coy, and Mawr rhymes with hour.'

'My apologies. Mrs Morgan, there seems to be no end in sight to this conflict, do you think the ... coyed m-hour community can continue to bear the burden of this strike?'

'It's no burden. We'll do whatever it takes to protect the jobs in the Coed Mawr valley and protect the thousands of jobs in communities throughout the country by keeping one hundred per cent solid in our commitment to the strike. I'm in contact with similar community groups not just in south Wales but in Scotland, Yorkshire, Kent and the north-east of England, and our resolve remains strong.'

'I understand you were once an employee at the colliery ...'

'I was a timekeeper for several years until my daughter was born.'

'I take it that's an office-based position, but seriously would you work underground?'

'It's only unfair antiquated legislation preventing women from working underground, otherwise I'd work down there with my husband, and I know many women who feel the same. So the answer is, yes, seriously I would work underground.'

'And would you want to see your children and grandchildren working down the pit?'

'If it's good enough for us, it's good enough for them. That's why I raise funds, to preserve these jobs not just for here and now but for our children and grandchildren so they have an economic future in their own community.'

Joanne turned out from Julie's bosom and pointed a tiny finger at the camera. 'You swines.'

'Mrs Morgan, you mentioned your husband and I understand that he is a cutter driver in the colliery. Surely you don't want him to endure working in those atrocious dusty and dangerous conditions when it's apparent that deep mining is no longer economically viable in the United Kingdom in the long term?'

'Only to the Tory government bean counters, who juggle the figures whichever way they want. They import millions of tons of heavily-subsidised, substandard, open-cast brown coal where the environmental impact on those Third World countries is devastating and will be for decades to come. Yet they won't subsidise our own coal industry which produces deep mined coal of a higher standard, that burns with less environmental impact than these cheap imports. There's no sense to it unless you are a fat cat in the city reaping the profits from your overseas investments.'

'Mrs Morgan …'

'In the Seventies the National Coal Board estimated there are seven to eight hundred years of coal reserves left in the United Kingdom. In this small valley alone there are reserves for another sixty to seventy years and the three collieries here are among the most profitable in south Wales.'

'Mrs Morgan …'

'We won't stand aside when communities similar to ours throughout the United Kingdom dependant on the mining industry, are starved of investment, bullied by this Tory government and ravaged by pit closures when there are still ample coal reserves left untouched underground. Can you understand what would happen to this community and mining communities like ours if they closed the collieries? Of course you can't, you can't even pronounce Coed Mawr.'

Joanne pointed a tiny finger at the watching millions. 'Swines.'

'That's banging. Can I borrow it? I'll transfer it to my phone and send it to you, and Jayden, and Joanne. I promise to look after it.'

Johnny ejected the CD. 'There's also footage of four coppers dragging me to a police van outside Aberthaw power station, but it's only a couple of seconds and not near as interesting as Julie's item.' He handed the CD to Charlie. 'Fill your boots.'

Charlie took the CD with one hand and downed her whisky with the other. 'Is there any vodka?'

Blind Date in the Twilight Zone

The pit hooter sounded and Johnny awoke from a dream of marigolds and canaries with a backfiring snore. 'The pit hooter, I'm still waking up to the pit hooter.'

He sat up to get his bearings. Empty drink bottles littered the floor and he felt as if he had just arrived back on earth after a quick spin around the galaxy. Charlie, wrapped in towels, lay next to him on a makeshift bed of coal bags. Johnny glanced down in surprise at his similar attire of towels. He vaguely became aware of others in the room and squinted at Joanne and Jayden standing in the doorway, agape in shock.

'I know this looks creepy in a sort of sugar daddy way but it's all very innocent. It was a drinking game of Charlie's, I think she made it up as she went along, it involved drinking whisky, vodka and smoking Bouncer Williams' skunk. Then we couldn't stop laughing. Then we couldn't breathe for laughing so we went in the garden for fresh air. It was pouring with rain. We laughed and arsed about mud-surfing on the lawn until it turned into Glastonbury. The neighbours complained about the noise and I told them to ... oh ... I told the neighbours to fuck off. Then I grabbed a load of towels from the airing cupboard, when I managed to find the airing cupboard, and we stripped, not at the same time mind, I don't think, and put our wet clothes on the radiators.'

Jayden stayed rooted to the spot while Joanne slumped into the armchair before she fell down.

'Then in my dream, Julie laughed at me for making a tit of myself and said Jayden's lucky because Charlie's a lovely girl and they are going to be very happy together. It's all we ever want for our children and grandchildren, to be happy. There's no big secret to the universe other than to be happy. They are always the best of my dreams, when I'm with Julie and she talks to me.'

Jayden sat next to his mother on the arm of the armchair.

'Jayden, Charlie's a diamond and loves you to bits. Not only can she drink like a fish, she's a good laugh, good on a shovel and can throw a good punch. That makes her all right in my book. OK, she's moody and a few shovelfuls short of a full ton, but that's teenagers. I was one once, but you've got your gran's approval and mine, if you ever needed it, so look after her because if you don't …'

'It's Charlie who looks after me.'

'Why,' said Joanne, 'is the house full of coal?'

'You've noticed. It's a little surplus we have and there's nowhere to store it.' Johnny got up and marched around the room with a half-boner protruding in his towel.

Joanne covered her eyes, 'Dad!'

'Oops, a bit of morning glory, take no notice.' He stepped into the hall, hitched up the towel and donned a donkey jacket from the coat hooks. He returned to the lounge and moved a coal bag to look out of the window. 'Still raining then?'

Charlie turned over and snuggled down into the bags. 'If I'm a diamond, does it mean I can work underground with the boys?'

Johnny kicked a bag of coal. 'We're overproducing as it is. When we clear this surplus, I'll think about it.'

Spider, looking well-groomed, entered the lounge.

Johnny performed an elaborate welcoming bow. 'Come in, why don't you? Happened to be passing did you, butt?'

'Sort of,' said Spider with a guilty glance at Joanne not unnoticed by her father.

Jayden got up from the chair arm and sat next to Charlie, while Spider sheepishly sat on the vacated chair arm next to Joanne.

'I hardly recognised you, dazzling in new clothes and with a toy-boy haircut.'

'Grandad, I'm alright about it, why can't you be?'

'I didn't say I wasn't alright about it, did I? Poor Lippo must be beside himself with unrequited love at the end of his bromance.'

'He's found a new friend in Cardiff,' said Jayden as he got comfy on the bags with Charlie.

'Whatever tickles his pickle,' said Johnny, hitching up his towel. 'Joanne, you can talk, coming in here all shocked and accusing.'

'I didn't say a word.'

'You didn't have to. It makes sense why I've hardly heard a peep out of Spider lately. You've neutered him like a cat.'

Spider growled and Joanne held him with a calming hand. 'Don't lose your temper now, Adrian.'

'Adrian?' laughed Johnny.

'Dad, Adrian's a lovely young man and we get along just

fine but if you're around he gets on an aggressive guilt trip. So chill, because he's in a delicate mood at the moment.'

'Out of respect for Joanne I'm off the weed. Cold turkey,' said Spider. He examined the works of a joint in the ashtray where North-Eye's tiny mining figures appeared to be working on it. 'But I can see you've had a puff.'

'Seems like I'm last to know anything that goes on around here, yet everyone knows my business.' Johnny sniffed at a familiar smell. 'Slouch, is that you out there?'

Slouch entered the cramped lounge wrapped in a drenched sleeping bag and carrying Britney. She yelped and licked his face.

'Fuck me hooray, it's like *Blind Date* in the *Twilight Zone*. Come in and sit down, if you can find an unoccupied bag of coal. I'm opening my house to the public to claim a council tax reduction.'

'That's a banging idea isn't it, Britney? I wish I had a house to open to the public,' said Slouch looking around the lounge. 'Charlie's got her kit off again.'

'Shut up headshot,' snapped Jayden.

'I'm not headshot, it's you that's headshot.'

Johnny put an end to it before it started. 'Slouch, why do we have the honour of your presence this lovely damp morning?'

'The climate crisis.'

'You walked Britney all the way up here in the pouring rain to discuss global warming and our carbon footprint?'

'North-Eye asked me to. He said he couldn't get an answer on your bastard phone.'

'I had a skinful last night and put my phone down somewhere. It's probably in a mud puddle on what's left of my lawn, but what's the climate crisis to do with North-Eye?'

Slouch wiped Britney down with his sleeping bag. 'He said go up to Johnny's and tell him Julie's Colliery is full of bastard water.'

A Troubleshooting Team of Mining Consultants

A suction hose slithered like an anaconda through the ink-black water of the flooded mine. A cap lamp at each end of the hose illuminated the rippling surface.

'Who'd have thought it, Billy?' said Geronimo shouldering the hose at the lead. 'Fancy our mate Banger having a Sykes pump hanging around in his garage all these years since the colliery closed.'

'Geronimo, I'm gobsmacked,' said Billy at the rear. 'You can only wonder what other sparkling mining gems are hidden away in that magpie's nest of a garage to the chagrin of his beloved wife.'

'With these workings flooding as easily as they did, I don't know how Johnny the Cutter could manage without us.'

'He's lucky he had an emergency number to call out a troubleshooting team of mining consultants, like our good selves, at the drop of a bastard helmet.'

'Good workers they might be, Billy, but have those youngsters ever worked underground knee-deep in water and installed a Sykes pump? Have … they … bollocks.'

Billy Donkey readjusted the hose onto his other shoulder and took up the sag. 'And fancy that? All along one of them was a girl. I knew there was something funny about the chopsy one with staples and holes in his ears.'

'It wasn't the chopsy one with staples and holes in his ears.'

'The bow-legged one with a face like a chisel?'

'Not him, everyone knows he's sparking Johnny's daughter.'

'It's not his grandson. Don't tell me it was the smelly one?'

Geronimo stumbled like a drunk on an underwater hazard but regained his footing in time to avoid a soaking. 'It was the other one, the Goth one with sunglasses who looks like a bug-eyed insect.'

'There's a turn-up for the books, women working underground? Personally, I think it might be a good thing but I doubt Banger would like to see his missus down here.'

Geronimo clutched an iron drainpipe for support. 'Lads or lasses, it doesn't change the fact that they had to call us out to sort their problems, and you don't find many of us troubleshooting mining consultants around nowadays, do you Billy?'

'Right you are, Geronimo, we are quite a rarity indeed in this strange post-industrial world we find ourselves living in and ...'

'*Your voices are carrying all the way up here to the shed and we can hear every word crystal clear,*' said Johnny over the Tannoy. '*Do yourselves a favour. Give the gossip and gloating a rest, you sound like a pair of pigs on fucking holiday.*'

'Well, there's gratitude for you, Geronimo.'

'And there's us going out of our way for them on our day off from Deep Mine Museum when we could be sitting around the house enjoying the delights of daytime television.'

The flooding crisis had brought both age groups of miners together and Spider, Jayden, Charlie, Lippo and Slouch stood around the shaft, feeding the hose down to pit bottom to be pulled into the deepest part of the colliery by Geronimo and

Billy Donkey. Banger wired up the pump control panel hidden under the shed table.

'Banger, you're sure this isn't going to strain that old lamp post? When I run the pump overnight, I don't want the village streetlights going out and find myself in front of a National Grid firing squad.'

Banger reversed his rump out from under the shed table and waved a screwdriver at Johnny. 'Don't go thinking I don't know what I'm doing; while you've spent years down in Cardiff selling Clanger insurance policies to people who don't need them, I've been busy robbing the Grid.'

Johnny had struck a nerve. 'Fair enough, butt, and thanks for your expertise. And if you don't mind me saying, I thought North-Eye was the master when it came to kifing old colliery stuff ...'

'Steady on,' said North-Eye.

'But Banger, you've taken it to a far higher level. You'll be telling us next you've got the pit hooter.'

Banger downed his screwdriver, raised his eyebrows and smiled.

An hour later the team were climbing like lemurs over the shed roof as they attached the pit hooter to the flagpole on the headgear. Below them Mrs M, Team Singh and a host of tenants stood dotted around the allotment wondering what the Neighbourhood Watch volunteers were up to. Johnny noticed Clayton and Smithy spying from behind Bouncer's shed. They knew they'd been rumbled and retired to the polytunnel to resume surveillance on CCTV. Parvinder laughed at the sight of Johnny up to more colliery mischief and clapped his hands to get Team Singh back to work.

While shouting instructions up to the team, Johnny had

difficulty keeping the older miners inside the shed as they encroached out on the porch every time his back was turned. 'Keep your heads down. We're attracting enough attention as it is without anyone clocking your ugly mugs.'

'He's a worrier, isn't he, Geronimo?'

'He's far too cautious for my liking, Billy.'

With the hooter installed, Geronimo, Billy Donkey, Banger and the young team sat around the shed staring at the master switch on the wall above Johnny's head as he sat opposite them in his armchair.

'I intended to install it on my garage roof and give it a blast every New Year's Eve to see in the New Year, but the missus wasn't having any of it,' said Banger replacing a screwdriver into his tool pouch. 'For years the hooter lived on the garage floor next to the freezer. The missus always stubbed her toe on it when she went out for the frozen chips. Her screams used to frighten the life out of me.'

Johnny reached behind and patted the master switch. 'We're grateful for the loan and rest assured we'll take good care of it.'

'All you have to do is throw the master switch, yank on the pull-down handle and, thar she blows,' said the old electrician.

After a few moments of silence, Billy Donkey shifted on his hoop-backed chair. 'Well?'

'Well, what?'

'We've finished installing the pump,' said Geronimo expectantly. 'We're all here and the tools are on the bar.'

'And?'

'It's knocking-off time,' said Banger. 'How about sounding the hooter now we've gone to the trouble.'

Johnny reached behind and patted the master switch. 'I don't know about that.'

Lippo bounced his helmet off the floorboards. 'You knows we've been up on the roof all day like melons and now you won't push the button thing and pull the handle thing, so we won't knows what the fucking thing sounds like?' He appealed to Spider. 'C'mon bro, back me up, you knows we all want to hear it.'

'If Johnny doesn't want to sound the hooter, that's OK by me.'

'C'mon bro,' pleaded Lippo. 'You knows it. I knows it. Everyone knows it.'

Slouch fidgeted in his sleeping bag. 'What's a pit hooter?'

'What does it sound like, Grandad?'

Geronimo turned knowingly to Billy Donkey. 'Hear that, Billy? What does it sound like?'

Banger fondled his tool pouch. 'It's a deep bellowing sound, once heard never forgotten.'

Lippo could hardly contain his excitement, 'Coolio.'

'It woke us up for work in the morning and told us when it was time to go home,' said Geronimo. 'You didn't need a watch because everyone within earshot knew the time from the hooter blasting out the shift start and end times. Early shift, day shift, grub time, end of grub time, afternoon shift and night shift.'

'It could be heard for miles and miles around,' said Billy Donkey happily reminiscing.

'Push the button,' Lippo salivated, 'and pull the fucking handle.'

'I've got as itchy a trigger finger as you lot,' said Johnny. 'I'm dying to hear the hooter for real again because every day I hear it in my dreams before waking up. But we're gonna have to wait.'

'You're having a fucking giraffe,' said Lippo.

'Coppers are never off-duty even when retired, and I don't want any more attention from Clayton and Smithy who can make shit storms out of nothing. Banger's got the right idea. We'll give it a blast every New Year's Eve when there's no one about. No one will know where it's coming from apart from us miners.'

Banger tucked his tool pouch into his overalls. 'If I'd known that earlier I'd have left it in my garage. The way it's going some of us might not be around to hear it New Year's Eve.'

'You've set doom and gloom off again,' said Billy Donkey.

'You can always take the hooter back,' said Johnny. 'And the next time your missus stubs her toe on it going to the freezer for the frozen chips, she just might frighten the life out of you.'

Banger shuddered and looked down at his boots. 'I suppose it will be something to look forward to.'

'And can you secure this switch? I don't want any waster pushing the button for a fucking giraffe.'

'I've got a lockable casing. It's been ...'

'... hanging around in my garage ...' interrupted Geronimo.

'... for years since the colliery closed,' added Billy Donkey.

Following an inspection of the workings, North-Eye climbed the shaft with a grunt and squelched his waders across the floorboards to report to Johnny. 'Good news, everything's fine underground. There's no build-up of gas, mainly due to the amount of water in the workings. You can safely run the pump overnight and the team will be back in work tomorrow.'

North-Eye removed his helmet and looked around the packed shed. 'What are you lot bastard waiting around for?'

'New Year's Eve,' they said.

If it Keeps on Raining the Levee's Gonna Break

The pump worked perfectly every night and the workings were soon water-free but they flooded again when the next storm rolled in from the Atlantic. Coal production slowed to a stop-start trickle as the team spent time repairing flood damage. Johnny trusted Spider to take charge underground and he rose to the responsibility. It meant Johnny and Charlie had little to do but hang around in the shed waiting for the rain to ease.

Johnny sat in his armchair, staring at the rivulets running down the Georgian windows and listening to the gurgling of the overflowing water butt. He twirled an inch-high mining figure between his fingers.

Charlie sat on the bicycle winder. 'I'm fed up.'

'That's two of us in the Fed Up Club.'

'It's ages since I went underground.'

'What bit of "You can't go underground" don't you understand?'

'You said you'd think about it.'

'North-Eye still hasn't come around to the idea.'

'I could take turns working with Jayden.'

'Job sharing might be a good idea. I'll think about it.'

Charlie got off the bicycle and put a finger through the bars of the canary cage. 'That's two things you've got to think about.' She smiled and pursed her lips at the little yellow birds. 'I liked being a miner and I miss working underground.'

'Join the club, I've felt like that for about thirty years. With our inability to sell the coal surplus in my house and because the workings keep flooding, the I Miss Working Underground Club is about to increase in membership. We'll have to shut down altogether.'

Joanne chirped her way in through the shelf door with a large bag of workwear. 'It's nice to see a decent drop of rain for a change.'

'Wonderful,' said Johnny with mock enthusiasm. 'Good for the garden and good for the allotment.'

Joanne placed the workwear bag on the sink draining board. 'Mrs M will be pleased after this long dry spell.'

'She'll be delighted,' grumped Johnny.

Joanne picked up on the vibes. 'What a happy-looking pair.'

'Just another day in paradise, isn't it Charlie?'

'Hmmm,' agreed Charlie, far more interested in the birds.

'No work for you two today, then?'

'An old bloke in a robe with long grey hair did request our help in building his Ark but we didn't want to go out in this weather.'

'I've brought the lunches.' She cheerfully emptied a bag of labelled, packed lunches onto the draining board and fondly positioned the lunch marked Adrian Team Captain on top.

Johnny flicked the tiny mining figure away. It pinged off a window pane, hit the canary cage and dropped down the shaft with a plop into water. 'I'll take them down later. At the moment they are welly-deep in water repairing the flood damage.'

'Don't sound so happy about it, Dad.'

'It's not just the weather. We can't sell the coal. Charlie must've knocked every door in the valley last week without any luck.'

'They kept slamming the door in my face,' said Charlie without taking her eyes from the canary cage.

'The swines,' said Joanne.

'Now it's raining hard,' said Johnny, digging his fingers into the arm rest, 'and the workings keep flooding.'

'You make it sound like the end of the world. You can always go back to your allotment and they can go back to …'

'Self-harming, cheap cider and a balloon full of laughing gas?'

'Anyway, I'm not surprised you've had no new customers.'

'Why's that?'

'Look at the state of the pair of you.'

'What's wrong with us?' he said as Charlie self-consciously tidied her hair.

'Who's going to open the door to a tramp and a terrorist?'

Johnny pulled up his collar. 'There's nothing wrong with my threads.'

'Since Mum died and you've spent all your time with the coal mine, you've let yourself go. You'd win a worst-dressed man in an allotment competition hands down.'

'Oh come on, Vince the Hippy?'

Joanne closed in on Charlie, studying her like a blank canvas.

Charlie leaned away. 'Why are you looking at me like that?'

Joanne removed Charlie's sunglasses.

'What are you doing?' said Charlie.

Joanne swept back Charlie's hair. 'You're a pretty girl, you won't need much fixing. I wish I could say the same for you, Dad.'

He shifted in the armchair. 'You can go off people, you know.'

Joanne took Charlie by the hand and led her away. 'Dad, you might know about coal mining but you know nothing about running a business, or sales, or presentation.'

'I was top telesales agent for years in Clanger and they gave me lots of useless bits of glass with my name on to prove it.'

'Only because the customers couldn't see who was on the other end of the phone.'

Charlie resisted a little as Joanne led her by the hand through the shelf door and out into the rain. 'Where are we going?'

'Don't worry, it'll be good.'

Johnny got up out of his armchair. 'What are you up to, girl?'

'Haven't you got a coal mine to run or something?' Joanne led Charlie through the rain to the secret way. 'We'll be back later.'

'Tar-rah then.' Johnny shut the shelf door on the rain. 'I'll find something to do.'

A Visit from the Cost Clerk

Johnny spent the rest of the day muttering curses at Eighties Tories while perfecting a ratchet and cog system for the bicycle winder. Upon completion, he wheeled a shopping trolley laden with timber onto the cage platform and stood back to admire his handiwork. He winked at the canaries and threw the ratchet lever.

'Here goes, fellas.'

The cage slowly lowered under the weight of the trolley as the ratchet clicked and clacked on the teeth of a rotating cog wheel, while the flywheels on the shed wall spun like the interior of a steampunk pocket watch. Johnny believed the canaries to be as delighted as he. 'Saves my little legs reverse pedalling. If we can figure out a way to make it wind up the coal, we'll be laughing.'

North-Eye entered through the shelf door and shook out his umbrella. 'Mrs M will be pleased with this drop of rain.'

'You'll be playing the global warming trump card next.'

North-Eye produced a notebook from a pocket. 'I've been working on the figures and it doesn't make good reading.'

'I was cheering up.'

'Productivity was excellent until the flooding, but I don't understand these sales figures.'

'What's wrong with them?'

'There aren't any.'

'The boot sales went quiet, door-to-door sales even quieter, there's the weather, and valleys people want something for nothing.'

'Did you really think I wouldn't notice you've topped up the cash flow every week?'

'You're sacked as colliery cost clerk. I need a trustworthy cost clerk who can keep books in an entirely slipshod manner.'

North-Eye flicked through the notebook. 'Most people are happy to be on the take but bizarrely you're happy putting more in.'

'They show willing, and I haven't the heart to tell them it's not paying its way.'

'You could give them your money and cut out the mining bit, because either way you'll be bankrupt.'

'There's a change in them. They are taking pride in themselves and their work. We've zero absenteeism.'

'It's because they know the money's good, your money.'

'They don't go to the Old Wheel on the drugs like they used to. I heard them talking about going on holidays together to Shagaluf. Jayden is saving up for a car.'

'It would make more sense if you just bought him a bastard car.'

'They're wising up and it's all because of the mining work.'

'I'm beginning to wonder why I'm in this venture.'

'Because if they cut you in half, you'd be like a stick of rock with MINER written down the middle, just like me.'

North-Eye went to and spoke on the Tannoy. *Spider, put the tools on the bar and get everyone up here for a team meeting.*

'We'll be up by there now in a minute,' replied Spider.

'What did you do that for?'

'If they are wising up because of the work, they should be wise to the truth.'

The team, glad of the break, soon climbed up the shaft, took off their wellies and sat around the shed.

'Team,' said Johnny, 'I can't sell the coal. I've hardly sold a bag for about a month and I hate to say it, but we'll have to shut down.'

Spider kicked off a welly. 'Shut down?'

'For a short time,' said North-Eye, 'until we find new customers.'

'Where's the money been coming from?' asked Jayden.

'Johnny has been committing financial suicide raiding his savings to keep us afloat.'

'Shut up,' said Spider.

'I knew something was up,' said Jayden, 'all those bags of coal around your house.'

'That's what all those bags were about,' said Spider.

'It wasn't my entry for the fucking Turner Prize.'

North-Eye pointed his notebook at Johnny. 'Yes, your house must be stacked full of bags.'

'Every room is jam-packed, conservatory, kitchen, downstairs loo and garden shed.'

'We can all go back to being wasters,' said Lippo.

Slouch buried his face in his sleeping bag. 'I don't want to go back to being a waster.'

'You knows we can start dealing again, bro,' said Lippo.

Spider grabbed Lippo by the throat and squeezed until his eyes nearly popped out. 'One more word and you will have such a slap, you knows it, I knows it, everyone knows it, melon.'

Johnny tried to keep positive. 'Maybe something will turn up in the winter. It used to be a good time for coal.' They were not convinced and only canary chirps broke the silence. 'We can restart production next spring or summer, when there's more demand, like there was earlier this year.'

'I can't wait that long,' said Spider. 'We're doing the work. Get out and sell it.'

North-Eye tapped his notebook. 'Minge Jenkins has got the market cornered in this valley. If we don't find new customers outside of the valley we're as good as finished.'

Joanne bounded into the shed though the shelf door. 'Dad, I might have sorted your sales problems. I'd like to introduce you to your new sales manager.'

Joanne led a bashful young woman by the hand into the shed.

'Aww Joanne,' said Johnny, 'I've told you no end of times to keep it quiet. We don't need anyone else involved. We've got enough going on by here.'

'This is Charlotte, your new sales manager.'

The canaries fluttered and chirped through the silence as miners, young and old, gawked at the beautiful young woman, smartly and professionally attired in a pencil skirt suit, standing before them.

Jayden broke the spell. 'Charlie, you look banging.'

Charlie shyly held onto a clutch bag with the slight wobble of a stiletto. 'Thank you.'

'Shut up,' said Spider in disbelief. 'Charlie?'

Slouch looked around, 'Where?'

Lippo pointed an incredulous finger. 'That's Charlie?'

'And there's us all week,' said Johnny, 'wishing you were a bloke.'

The atmosphere lifted as the team made a right fuss over Charlie and she threw a few model poses for a laugh.

Johnny gave Joanne a hug. 'Girl, you can work wonders.'

'It was an easy make-over. Little bit of polishing up, and I've had too many pies to fit into that suit again. Look at her, she's got it all and doesn't even know it.'

'And she's good on the shovel.'

North-Eye wiped his glasses. 'It'd be a good idea to be out and about selling as soon as the weather turns.'

'No one will slam a door on that pretty face,' said Joanne.

Johnny thumped the table for attention. 'How about we have a celebratory drink, on me, in the Coed Mawr Hotel? It's re-opening tonight under new management.'

The Good, the Bad and the Ginger

When the weather brightened up the next day Johnny could not wait to get going and arrived early at the shed. He knew the team was already underground by the checks on the check board so he got under the sink to switch off the pump. The pump was off and he realised he'd forgotten to switch it on when they went out for a drink.

'*Team,*' said Johnny over the Tannoy, '*I'm sorry you've got to work in water again. It's my fault, I forgot to run the pump overnight.*'

'*The water's gone,*' answered Spider.

'*What do you mean gone?*'

'*G-O-N gone,*' said Slouch.

'*The water can't have gone, the pump hasn't been on.*'

'*Shut up! There's no water down here,*' said Spider.

Johnny changed and went down to inspect the workings and, sure enough, the floodwater had mysteriously disappeared. Pleased and half-relieved it had seeped away somewhere, he decided to leave the worrying about where it had gone to North-Eye.

He picked up Charlie and she looked professional and positively glowing. He drove to the same streets where they'd experienced such bad luck the previous week. The inhabitants were far friendlier, and even if they did not want any coal themselves they knew someone who did, and with every sale Charlie grew in confidence. Wherever they went sales and customer numbers picked up.

The following day they arrived at Dai Milk's boot sale and, as the van crawled into the field, they passed Dai Milk's Farm Produce manned by Old Dai Milk, Young Dai Milk and Mrs Thai Milk.

'You pay five pounds for boot,' said Mrs Thai Milk officiously.

Although the boot sale professed not to take any traders, among the pasting tables full of bric-a-brac, second-hand clothing and junk, the odd baker, fishmonger and butcher were easy to find, happily selling their wares from the back of a well-stocked van. Spanners had a stall of nut and bolt novelty items, Vince the Hippy operated a New Age stall with Betty Bingo's help, and a Team Singh stall sold household cleaning goods. Johnny picked a spot next to a freezer van with two smiling butchers in trilbies and striped aprons. They nudged each other while admiring Charlie's legs as she gracefully slipped out of the passenger side of the van.

It took Johnny less than a minute to set up his pasting table. His wares included a box of fossils, a box of mining photographs, two large lumps of anthracite, an oil lamp and several brass coal mining ornaments, none of which were for sale, as the items were merely used to lure in the customers for the hard sell of the coal from the back of the van. The butchers became fully paid-up members of the Charlie fan club and fell over themselves helping her open two collapsible chairs from the van. Johnny still had North-Eye's tiny miners and, oblivious to the interest Charlie had already created in the boot sale, he positioned them at work around the lumps of anthracite on the table. 'If this doesn't draw them in, I don't know what will.'

They became busy early on as a crowd, mostly of men, quickly gathered around the stall. Charlie took cash sales with a smile while Johnny burrowed deeper into the van for the bags. 'Amazing Charlie, it's never sold this fast.'

Johnny reached for a bag when a shout echoed inside the van.

'So, it's not a pikey selling house coal up and down the valley, it's none other than that hairy fairy from the arsehole of the world, Johnny the Cutter.'

Johnny looked out from the van and the crowd of customers parted like the Red Sea away from Minge Jenkins, Minja, Pea-Brain and a host of reduced gene pool Trewatkins Zulus. Minge removed his coat while Rocky growled at Minja's heel.

Johnny had let it go on their last meeting at the reunion but not this time. 'Fuck me hooray, it's Minge Jenkins, coal merchant skinhead from Trewatkins and yee-haw cowboy builder. Shouldn't you be up Coed Mawr mountain fly-tipping the rubbish you gut from terraced houses, you inbred, twisted-up piece of ginger shit?'

After fifty years the bell sounded for round two of the Minge Jenkins and Johnny the Cutter fight. The coal merchant flew over the pasting table at the miner like a Doberman at the throat of a burglar. They grappled and bounced around together in the back of the van like huge peas in a giant whistle before rolling out and crushing the pasting table flat.

Minja set Rocky on Johnny. 'Rocky, kill.'

Charlie snatched a string of sausages from the freezer van and sent them sailing past Minja's ear. Rocky disappeared after them with a yap. 'Fuck you, Rocky.'

A straight punch from Charlie put Minja on his arse and, as he sat there dazed, she stepped onto his calf with a stiletto heel.

In the far reaches of the adjoining field, Dai Milk thought he heard a little girl screaming over the noise of his tractor engine.

Charlie left the stiletto stuck in Minja's leg as she pursued the other Zulus. Minja took one look at the shoe and passed out.

Considering they were both in their sixties, Johnny and Minge went at each other like young bucks, and stall after stall collapsed before them. Grappling like sumo wrestlers, they waltzed into Spanners' table and the sweaty no-neck mechanic hopped away like a toad in a shower of nuts, bolts, washers and spark plugs. When they got out of their clinches, calloused fists flew between the two like a game of Battling Robots and their grunts and groans were picked up on Dai Milk's antenna in the adjoining field.

Minge cracked Johnny across the shoulders with a luxury camping chair. 'Who's supplying the fucking coal?'

Johnny returned the blow with a box of second-hand books. 'Mind your own fucking business.'

Charlie clanked Pea-Brain with a decorative chrome exhaust and he sailed backwards across pasting tables full of bric-a-brac.

Sellers jumped for safety into car boots as stalls fell like dominoes. Betty Bingo hugged Vince the Hippy as his table crashed in a shower of calming crystals, healing candles and dream catchers.

Dai Milk drove into the boot sale, pushed his jam-jar glasses higher up his nose and could hardly believe his eyes as Johnny and Minge rolled together on the gravel in a cloud of punches and kicks.

Mrs Thai Milk and Young Dai Milk hurried to move boxes of farm produce from the path of the fight, but the fighters crashed through the last few boxes of tomatoes, satsumas and strawberries.

Old Dai Milk climbed up to the tractor cab with Dai Milk, and father and son ducked, weaved and felt every blow.

'Go on, Johnny,' shouted Parvinder as he and Spanners shared an upturned crate for a better view.

Minge threw Johnny through a tower of award-winning Welsh cakes and he came to rest on a sack of flour in the back of the baker's van. Both combatants took a breather, dusted themselves down and checked for lost teeth.

'Minge, after all these years we're still hitting each other in the wrong places.'

'I knew it was you,' sputtered Minge, 'the night of the reunion in the Trewatkins Hotel.' He spat blood and checked the bridge of his nose. 'The lot of you smiling and laughing like you were still the big bollocks around here. Miners, what a bunch of losers! The family business went down the tubes because of you and your union ...'

Johnny shut him up by thrusting a large cream cake into his face, but he slipped on a chocolate éclair. Minge staggered back, wiped the cream from his eyes. With Johnny at his mercy flat on his back in the cake debris, Minge growled and moved in to attack. A frozen leg of lamb belted him across the side of the head and the coal merchant stiffened like a plank and fell. Charlie wobbled off balance from delivering the blow but still managed to throw the leg of lamb back to the smiling butchers. She helped Johnny to his feet.

'Charlie, you're a knockout.'

Broken applause broke out from the wrecked boot sale and Charlie felt pleased with herself. 'They're all little girls in Trewatkins.'

'What a fight,' said Old Dai Milk.

'What I saw of it,' griped Dai Milk.

Mrs Thai Milk scolded Johnny and Charlie with a broken stick of celery. 'You two nutty crazy, no come here no more, we ban you.'

Shirley Temple

'Brilliant,' said North-Eye when Johnny and Charlie returned to the shed. 'How can we sell a house full of coal without the boot sales?'

Johnny accepted a damp flannel from Charlie and dabbed his battered brow. 'It's not my fault Minge thought we were gypsies.'

'Now he knows who it is, he'll hunt you down. You know he's as mad as ten bastard bears.'

'Bring it on,' said Charlie.

North-Eye sighed and got out his phone. 'We'll have to do something outside the box if Julie's Colliery is going to survive.' He trawled through several numbers, settled on one and rang. Charlie looked enquiringly at Johnny but he shrugged in reply.

'Hello, Jenkins & Son Coal Merchants of Trewatkins?'

Johnny shot out of his chair. 'Are you out of your fucking mind? We were trying to kill each other five minutes ago.'

'Minge, how are you butt? It's North-Eye.'

Johnny listened to the faint acknowledgement. 'I didn't know you and Minge were an item. Put the ginger fuck on speakerphone.'

North-Eye refused with a hand signal. 'Are you still trading mining checks? Good, I've a couple you might be interested in.'

Johnny strained to hear Minge. 'You kokum bastard …'

North-Eye held up a hand to shut him up. 'Great, but I was

also wondering, Minge, and don't get me wrong here, but would you be interested in several tons of high grade Welsh anthracite, all ready-bagged, which I can acquire for you at a competitive price?'

It took tram loads of tact and frequent massages of Minge's ego before North-Eye set up a meeting with the volatile coal merchant to discuss supply. They agreed a wind turbine on top of Coed Mawr Mountain as a neutral meeting place with Dai Milk, as butty to both parties, acting as mediator.

When Johnny and North-Eye got to the turbine, Dai Milk had already arrived and sat in his tractor cab flanked by Mrs Thai Milk and Old Dai Milk, while Young Dai Milk stood on the trailer. Johnny's van slowed on the gravel track, parked next to the tractor and his tyres made the snap, crackle and pop sound of a bowl of Rice Krispies. Old Dai Milk sat hunched up in the tractor cab rubbing his hands in anticipation of round three between the two old combatants.

'Fucking vulture,' said Johnny.

The team followed behind, squeezed in Joanne the Cutter's Fiat 500 and it snapped, crackled and popped as it parked next to the van.

They waited for what seemed like an age for the coal merchant to appear, and Johnny stared at a scattering of fly-tipped rubbish around the turbine where the culprits had creatively arranged burnt dolls and cuddly toys in Kama Sutra poses.

'Fifty shades of shite.' He fidgeted in his seat. 'I'm beginning to wish I hadn't let you talk me into this.'

North-Eye scanned the mountain road with a small telescope. 'Our business is digging coal, his business is selling coal. He's got all the regular customers and we haven't. It's either this, or go home, count how many bags you've got piled up in the house and divide it by how many times you can stick your head up your arse.'

'You are aware the only words I've ever exchanged with Minge Jenkins have been immediately prior to a fight or during a fight?'

North-Eye closed the telescope. 'Tell me something. The fight you pair had in the Seventies everyone of our generation raves about, what was it all about?'

'Did it have to be about something? He's from Trewatkins and I'm from Coed Mawr, it's always been more than enough.'

'There must've been more to it?'

'I suppose it helped that he was a skinhead and I was a hairy with hair like Jim Morrison.'

North-Eye tapped his telescope on the dash. 'Shirley Temple.'

'Shirley Temple? I had hair like Jim Morrison. No one ever called me Shirley fucking Temple.'

'If anyone said Shirley Temple up in the survey department we all knew who we were talking about. Johnny the Cutter, the cutter driver who couldn't keep the cutter to the line of the coal who caused us no end of trouble doubling back with face surveys. Even your team mates underground called you Shirley Temple, it was Shirley Temple this, Shirley Temple that and if the bonus was wrong it was Shirley Temple's bastard fault.'

'No one ever said it to my face. Mind you, thinking back there was always someone singing 'On the Good Ship Lollipop' over the Tannoy, but I thought it was a bit of a laugh. I used to join in because I thought it was a team song or something ... the two-faced ...'

'It's taken a while to sink in, forty or so years, but now you know.'

'It was Marc Bolan's fault.'

'What was?'

'The fight in the Seventies. I was dancing with this lovely girl in the Trewatkins Hotel to T. Rex and we got chatting above the music. Her name was Rose. She took a fancy to my hair and stroked my curls. "You've got lovely hair, like Marc Bolan," she said, and within seconds Minge Jenkins had jumped on my back and was trying to scalp me with his bare hands. I didn't know it was his girlfriend. We fought on the dance floor but kept missing our punches because of the trippy light from the psychedelic oil projector. We punched each other over tables and chairs until the music stopped and the lights went on. When we burst out through the hotel doors everyone followed us into the street. We wrestled on the tarmac, rolled through the streets and downhill to Trewatkins Colliery. The fight went on for ages because we kept hitting each other in all the wrong places. When we got to the colliery gates we took a breather, then a panda car full of plod turned up and the fight was over. That night I left the skin from my elbows, knees and knuckles on the Trewatkins tarmac and the big ginger fuck did the same. But that's what you get up to when you're stupid kids.'

'From what you've said about the boot sale I get the inkling Minge hasn't fully grown out of violent tribal behaviour yet, so best leave all the talking to me.'

'Thinking back, perhaps Rose had a thing for me and Minge was a green-eyed monster. I heard they later married.'

In the distance the Jenkins & Son coal lorry crested a hill and a Volkswagen Golf travelled close behind. North-Eye raised his telescope and spied Rose sitting next to Minge in the lorry. 'Definitely leave all the bastard talking to me.'

Knife

As the vehicles approached along the meandering mountain road, Johnny and North-Eye got out of the van. The coal lorry parked next to Dai Milk's tractor and the Golf parked next to the lorry. Minge, wearing a head bandage, stepped down from the cab and went to the tractor trailer.

Minja got out of his keyed Volkswagen Golf with the aid of a crutch and limped to the trailer with Rocky at his heel. Pea-Brain, wearing crossed plasters on his head, got out of the passenger side and two other equally vacant and battered Trewatkins Zulus got out from the back seats. They took up a spot behind Minge.

Joanne and Spider stepped out of her car, along with Charlie who had suitably dressed down in scarf and shades for the occasion. Lippo and Jayden disentangled themselves from sets of curling tongs while Slouch wrapped his sleeping bag around his shoulders against the mountain breeze. They took up a spot behind Johnny and North-Eye. Dai Milk hitched up his rope belt, pushed his jam-jar glasses higher up his nose and stood between the two groups like a referee.

Minge spoke first. 'Let's see what you've got.'

The two sides screwed each other out either side of a nervous Dai Milk while North-Eye took a coal bag from the back of the van.

'Johnny the Cutter,' growled Minge scratching his bandage.

'Minge,' said Johnny.

North-Eye thumped the bag flat on Dai Milk's trailer.

Minge sneered at the bag and shouted over his shoulder. 'Rose.'

Rose, in a white lab coat, got down from the cab and walked around to the trailer. 'For twenty-five years my wife Rose was the best dust sampler in the coalfield. She still is.'

North-Eye tapped the bag with a finger. 'You don't need a dust sampler to see this is top-quality Welsh anthracite.'

'After all these years you'd deny my Rose the opportunity to use her sampling skills?'

Rose patted the coal bag. 'I need a knife.'

'Knife,' barked Minge at the skittish Zulus.

North-Eye searched himself. 'Has anyone got a knife?'

Lippo drew a long blade from behind his back and offered it to Rose point first. 'I've got a knife.' With the exception of Minge, the Trewatkins contingent took a concerned step back.

Johnny gripped Lippo's wrist until the boy gave a yelp, he removed the knife from his hand and presented it to Rose handle first.

'Rose,' he said politely.

'Thank you,' replied Rose politely and they seemed to share a moment.

The moment went on far too long for Minge's liking and he worried North-Eye with a low growl.

Rose took the knife and got set to open the coal bag. She paused and examined the blade. 'This is my Sabatier knife.'

'What?' said Minge, 'Are you sure?'

'I'd know it anywhere. There's a little dent in the handle. I did that making a beef bourguignon when I was a bit tiddled with Chianti and dropped it on the kitchen floor.'

Minge glared holes into Lippo. 'That's my wife's knife.'

'Minge,' warned Johnny. 'Don't be a twat, Minge.'

'Take it easy, Johnny,' said Dai Milk, pushing his jam-jar glasses higher up his nose as the atmosphere grew tense, 'You too, Minge.'

'There must be a logical explanation,' added North-Eye.

'I found it on the cycle path,' said Lippo in a sweat, 'near the Old Wheel. Isn't that right, bro?'

Spider lit a rollie. 'Someone accidently dropped it doing a Usain Bolt down the cycle path on his way back to Trewatkins.'

The tension grew under the spinning turbine and the breeze picked up. Joanne locked arms with Spider, Slouch shivered in his sleeping bag while Charlie oozed menace from mirrored shades.

'Minja,' shouted Minge. Minja left Rocky with Pea-Brain and cautiously limped towards his grandad. When he got into range, without taking his eyes from Lippo, he gave Minja a backhander. 'Go and sit in your car.'

Minja nursed his cheek and shuffled off to the Golf with his tail between his legs. Rocky whined as his master passed.

'Rose, proceed.'

All were fascinated as Rose expertly sliced through the paper bag as if gutting a big brown fish of its black innards. She held lumps of anthracite sparkling like diamonds to the light. She mixed a teaspoon of small coal into a flask of clear liquid and examined the mixture as it settled to the bottom of the glass. Rose dabbed a finger in the bag and tasted the coal dust. They eagerly awaited her conclusions and Rose made ready to speak.

'It good coal, it burn good in kitchen and good in old farm boiler,' shouted Mrs Thai Milk from the tractor cab.

Minge scowled at Dai Milk. 'You backstabbing, bonk-eyed ...'

232

The farmer quickly held up his hands in peace. 'Wait a minute, Minge, we were only testing it short term and as you've now heard,' he looked daggers at his wife, 'our opinion is it's good coal. We'll be your first customer and I can guarantee all the farms will follow.'

'Listen, Minge,' said North-Eye getting another bag out of the van, 'we're all on the same side by here. Take these free samples for your trouble and you'll see the quality for yourself.'

'We haven't had a coal fire in years,' said Rose with a spot of coal dust on her lip. 'Far too much potch. We've got a nice long electric one, built into the wall under our TV, with the glowing coal effect, or you can change it to wood or pebbles. It's beautiful.'

Johnny guffawed. 'The living room of Jenkins & Son Coal Merchants has an imitation coal fire?' Helpless with laughter he threw a bag of coal from the back of the van at Minge's feet. 'Like plastic grass, decaf coffee and alcohol-free beer, you're nothing but a sham. The hypocritical insanity of the world never ceases to amaze me.'

Johnny's laughter infected the team and as they roared Minge shrank as if exposed to a dose of ginger kryptonite. Rose put a comforting hand to his shoulder.

With tears of laughter, Johnny seized the initiative. 'Do what you like with the free samples but if we don't hear from you by tomorrow we'll go alone, or go elsewhere.'

Minge poked the bag with the toe of his shoe. 'I still don't know where the coal's coming from.'

Johnny got in his van and started the ignition. 'It's on the bag.'

The team retreated into Joanne's car and both vehicles

reversed in a cloud of dust from the snap, crackle and pop gravel track. The dust cloud briefly obscured the Dai Milks and the Trewatkins contingent before dispersing up in the spinning blades of the wind turbine.

Rose sliced off a piece of paper bag from the trailer and showed the stamp to Minge. She squinted and smiled at the Old Wheel design – Julie's Colliery.

Circling Sharks of Apprehension

North-Eye gave a sigh of relief when Minge Jenkins rang the next morning and agreed to take all the coal. Johnny and Charlie spent the day emptying the house of bags onto the Jenkins & Son coal lorry while North-Eye got the colliery back into full production. For the next few weeks, the colliery ran like clockwork while Johnny and Charlie transported the coal to their best customer at Coal Yard House, Trewatkins.

The allotment basked in the sunshine of an Indian summer and morale at the colliery soared along with the temperature as the flooding problems were long forgotten. Charlie appeared happy with the surface work and Johnny could not remember the last time she mentioned working underground. At the end of each shift, they made the journey up the mountain to Coed Mawr tip where the views were stunning from the tip's edge in the evening sunshine. The pyramid of muck grew to resemble a castle turret and using the empty bags to collect fly-tipping to pack the mine workings became second nature.

Jayden got in on the tip experience and squeezed into the van passenger seat with Charlie.

'Awesome,' said Jayden as he and Charlie sat atop the castle turret laughing and posing for selfies against the setting sun.

Observing them happy together, Johnny remembered how angry and hopeless he felt at the sight of Jayden's self-harming train tracks, but now the old miner's heart soared like a red kite.

'Julie, that's so good to see, Jayden and Charlie together. They've all come good. It's amazing what work on the shovel can do.'

Spider and Joanne got to hear of it and the next evening they followed the van in Joanne the Cutter's Fiat 500. Lippo invited himself along and Slouch took Britney to stretch her legs. The team kept Johnny busy with impromptu driving lessons across the tip. North-Eye arrived in his Volvo and set up a tripod and telescope on the edge of the tip. They took turns enjoying the sights across the Bristol Channel, and when the light faded the telescope turned on the first stars in the iron-blue dusk.

Julie's Colliery came to life as perfectly as old Coed Mawr Colliery in microcosm. As the bicycle winder wheels spun, vacuum cleaners hummed and the canaries happily chirped, the small colliery lived, breathed and sang its own sweet song of coal. Out in the allotment things were all good as Mrs M kept away from the shed. Even Clayton and Smithy were quiet, although Johnny did see them attempting to fly a drone until it crashed spectacularly into Clayton's polytunnel. Repairing the gaping hole kept the ex-coppers out of Johnny's face.

Everything appeared to be going along swimmingly, yet several apprehensive thoughts circled around Johnny's mind like sharks around a swimmer in distress, the shark fins surfacing now and again while he worked.

'It's too good to last,' he muttered while taking a bag from a trolley.

'Did you say something?' said Charlie on the bicycle winder.

Johnny answered without looking her way. 'It's nothing. Us oldies have a habit of talking to ourselves.' He absentmindedly put the bag back into the trolley.

'Are you alright, Johnny?'

'Yeah, I'm alright, mun,' he said, unable to look at her. 'I'm in a funny mood. Everything is going so well but I'm sure I've forgotten something important that'll put the kybosh on it.'

Another disconcerting shark fin on the horizon was the Indian summer. It made hot clammy work in the shed for Charlie operating the bicycle winder, and Johnny increasingly got hot under the collar as her damp vest top and gym shorts left little to the imagination. He found it difficult in the close confines of the shed to gentlemanly avert his eyes. Charlie drew his eye with every movement, bending over, leaning forward, forever fidgeting and wiping away sweat. Confronted with this worthy of a cold shower experience, he yearned for a return of Charlie's wrapped-up Goth terrorist look.

He looked for help at Julie's photograph on the wall and heard her voice clear as a bell. *'Oh, stop worrying and get on with it.'*

Charlie put the brakes on the bicycle winder. 'You must still love her very much.'

'I wish she could see this. She'd love it. You remind me of Julie when she was younger, she looked out for me the way you look out for Jayden, although she didn't go around smacking people across the head with frozen legs of lamb.'

Charlie smiled at the compliment.

Joanne, loaded up with workwear, cheerfully popped her head around the shelf door. 'Woo-hoo, it's only us.'

North-Eye stepped in behind her. 'Luckily I didn't take it

seriously when you sacked me as colliery cost clerk, because I've recently discovered we've broke even.'

Johnny dropped his bag of coal. 'Joking?'

North-Eye waved his notebook around like a geisha girl's fan, 'Am I bollocks, excuse the language.'

Johnny announced the news on the Tannoy and called the team up for a celebratory tea break.

As they sat around the shed drinking tea, a yelp came from Slouch's sleeping bag. 'It's Britney,' he said sheepishly to Johnny.

'Don't tell me you've had that dog underground with you?'

'She was missing me. The 1842 thing didn't say anything about dogs underground, did it North-Eye?'

'Not to my knowledge.'

Johnny looked out the window. 'From today, no dogs underground.' He sipped his tea and admired the allotment in full glory. Every plot looked pristine with not a soul about until Parvinder stepped out of the Bollywood shed and walked up the path.

Johnny wondered why his neighbour was so immaculately attired in a three-quarter length silk suit and shiny shoes. He stepped out onto the porch and leaned against a post.

'Going anywhere special, a wedding perhaps, or has your knighthood come through?'

'Going? I'm not going anywhere. I called up to wish you all the best for today and to see if you were ready.'

'Ready? Ready for …' Johnny gaped in mid-sentence as further down the path behind Parvinder, Mrs M waltzed out of her shed in a smart blue suit and matching handbag. 'Fuck me hooray, the allotment championship!'

He rushed past Parvinder for a better view down the

allotment and, sure enough, a small expectant crowd waited outside the gates while the tenants lined up opposite the committee shed. The tenants, as befitting, had discarded the scruffy mishmash of cowboy hats, jeans, overalls and wellies, and scrubbed up appropriately for the occasion.

When Johnny turned back to the shed, Clayton and Smithy stared at him across Bouncer's plot like a pair of buzzards. Clayton resembled an untrustworthy Conservative candidate in a blue suit and tie, while Smithy wore a black blazer and red tie as if going to a WRU meeting. They looked at Johnny as if finding something unpleasant on the bottom of their shoes.

Johnny panicked his way into the shed. 'I've got to smarten up pronto for the allotment championship. North-Eye, I need your shirt.'

As North-Eye stripped, Johnny opened a drawer and threw out odds and ends before finding a knotted black tie covered in sawdust, 'My emergency tie for funerals and special occasions.' He blew off the dust, threw away his cap and wore the tie like a headband until he got into North-Eye's shirt.

Joanne helped with the buttoning up. 'Dad, I said you'd win the worst-dressed man in an allotment.'

'And I need black trousers and black shoes.'

'I've black skinny jeans in my locker,' said Spider.

'Black Vans trainers?' said Lippo.

'I've a silk waistcoat,' said Parvinder, rushing off to his shed.

Johnny appeared half-presentable once they shoehorned him into Spider's skinny jeans and Parvinder had come up with an ornate purple silk waistcoat. Lippo's Vans trainers passed for black shoes. They were a size too small but Johnny got into them with a squeeze.

'Listen up, Spider, Jayden, Lippo and Slouch, you four get underground out of the way. Spider, make sure everyone behaves and keeps quiet. North-Eye will shut the trapdoor and leave with Joanne and Charlie through the shelf door once they've made the place look presentable. Charlie, will take Britney home to Mrs Jones Bottom Street? Happy days!'

'No, she's coming down with me,' whined Slouch, cwtching up to the little dog. 'I'll take her home later.'

'I haven't got time for this. Britney is not going underground.'

North-Eye wrenched Britney away from Slouch. 'Get back underground out the bastard way.' He gave Britney to Charlie.

Spider kicked Slouch in the backside. 'Let's go, headshot.'

'Right, we're all sorted. Let's go, Parvinder.'

Joanne, North-Eye, Charlie and Britney watched through the windows as Johnny and Parvinder set off down the gravel path.

Parvinder lent a helping hand to Johnny while he walked daintily in the Vans trainers. The tight black skinny jeans gave the appearance he had waded waist deep in sump oil and his family jewels required constant re-adjustment along the way.

'Thanks Parvinder, and if you don't win best plot this year, I'll eat my testicles, if I can find them.'

'I hope he's got the sense not to stand next to Parvinder,' said North-Eye. 'He'll stick out like a sore thumb.'

Joanne collected up the tea mugs. 'There's no hope for him wherever he stands.'

A Favourable Impression

First and last impressions were everything to Mrs M in the valley allotment championship. She believed the consecutive wins of the last two years were all down to a formal welcome at the gates followed by a tea and cake sending-off in the committee shed. This feel-good sandwich either side of assessing the plots created a favourable impression with the judging panel and, fingers crossed, hopefully did the trick a third time in a row.

Mrs M had one last heart-warming look along the line of tenants. Clayton and Smithy had assumed a prominent position at the front of the line as if still holding office. Hoss looked every inch Wyatt Earp in a Prince Albert frock coat, bootlace tie and shining cowboy boots. Vince the Hippy appeared to be auditioning for the next James Bond in a dinner jacket and bow tie. Betty Bingo looked ten years younger and twenty pounds slimmer in a tight-fitting pink suit. She smoothed Vince's ponytail and brushed imaginary pieces of fluff from his collar. Parvinder organised Team Singh in a smartly-dressed line of height and age difference.

Mrs M did a double-take while trying to identify who squatted behind Parvinder's youngest and smallest children. She stepped down the line for a clearer view and her heart sank upon locking eyes with Johnny peeping around a salwar kameez. He smiled weakly, pulled himself up to his full height and self-consciously altered his tie. Mrs M opened her mouth, but the car arrived with the horticultural judges and she returned to her position before speaking.

The two officials, clad in identical green blazers with matching green clipboards, were greeted at the allotment gates by Mrs M and introduced to the CMAA tenants. Johnny gave the familiar judges a once-over as they shook hands along the line. First to the handshakes came Mrs Jacques, the stout valley society president, followed by, with a face like a bull terrier chewing a wasp, the stern and ancient vice-president Miss James. Of these two, Johnny preferred Miss 'What You See Is What You Get' James, as he found Mrs Jacques to be as false as an imitation coal fire. After a team photograph outside the committee shed to record the false smiles for posterity, the tenants returned to their plots to await judgement.

Mrs M explained the committee had recently relaxed the rules regarding shed colours, allowing the tenants the freedom to theme their plots. Initially received as an iconoclast, the judging panel warmed to the idea when spotting the Bollywood shed. Betty Bingo's plot was first for evaluation and they were all over it and gone within a sparrow fart. They wanted a piece of Bollywood.

Johnny got back to his porch without a care for the competition but hoped Parvinder won best plot, and if not him, anyone other than Clayton. As he thought it, his ears burned and when he glanced across Bouncer's plot, Clayton and Smithy sneered at him in the distance. He got the feeling the ex-coppers still had a trick or two up their sleeves.

Weird Scenes inside the Coal Mine

With the shed tidied up, Joanne, North-Eye and Charlie, along with Britney, exited through the shelf door. As Joanne gave the shed a last once-over she noticed the open trapdoor.

'Oops, we forgot to shut the trapdoor,' said Joanne and, as she spoke, Britney yelped, jumped from Charlie's arms and scampered into the shed. They chased after the little Bichon Frisé but Britney evaded capture under the chairs and sink.

North-Eye cornered the dog but Britney scooted around him and went tail first over the edge of the open trapdoor with a whine.

'Britney,' shouted Joanne.

Charlie climbed down the shaft. 'I'll get her.'

'You're not to go underground,' said North-Eye. 'Leave the dog to Slouch.'

But Charlie had already climbed down. She switched on her phone torch and shouted up the shaft, 'I'll only be a minute.'

'Whoa,' shouted North-Eye looking down the shaft, 'turn that phone off.' He hurried into a cap lamp and helmet.

Joanne looked down the shaft. 'Isn't that dangerous?'

North-Eye switched on his cap lamp. 'Too right it is.'

None the worse for her fall, Britney scampered through the workings and became happily reunited with Slouch near the coalface. Slouch cwtched her into his sleeping bag.

Spider shone his cap lamp on the loving pair, 'How'd that dog get down here?'

Charlie made her way to the coalface with her phone torch.

'Charlie?' said Jayden.

'Charlie, what's happening?' said Spider as a cap lamp lasered erratically behind her in the darkness.

'Britney fell down the shaft.'

Slouch smothered the dog with kisses. 'Aww Britney, you fell down the naughty old shaft.'

Up on the surface Johnny wanted it over with as soon as possible, but the judges were so impressed by the Bollywood shed they were reluctant to leave. Mrs M politely reminded them the allocated time had passed.

When the entourage neared Johnny's plot he shivered under

Mrs M's cold glance. 'This is our corner tenant, Mr Johnny Morgan.'

Johnny gave them a swift John Wayne salute. 'How be.'

'It's a fine position you've got here, Mr Morgan,' said Mrs Jacques. 'Good sun. How long have you had the plot?'

'The plot has been in Mr Morgan's family for three generations,' said Mrs M.

'My grandson has recently taken an interest. I hope to hand the tenancy on to him when I finally hang up my shovel.'

'Very neat and tidy, straight lines everywhere, a solid pathway, a raised vegetable bed and good use of the ground,' said Miss James who nearly broke her face when she smiled without notice. 'Excellent spacing of marigolds to keep the pests away.'

'Thank you,' said Johnny, pleased his judgement of character had been fully endorsed.

'What a magnificent shed,' said Mrs Jacques. 'I thought the Bollywood shed was the Shangri-La of sheds but your mining shed is oozing with character, community ethos and credibility.'

'These cascading strawberry plants on the fence panels are a wonderful use of space, creating an illusion the fence is alive and perhaps has a hidden secret,' said Miss James. 'You must've worked hard to get it like this.'

'Oh yes, Mr Morgan has been hard at it all summer,' said Mrs M, raising an eyebrow, and Johnny winced at the insinuation.

Joanne ducked and hid below the window as Mrs Jacques looked through a pane. 'What a fascinating contraption of wheels – and are those real mining lamps?' She reached for the door handle. 'Do you mind if I look inside?'

Johnny put himself between the judge and the door. 'It's not a good idea at the moment.'

Mrs M gave Johnny a nudge. 'This isn't the time to be particular about who has access to your shed, Mr Morgan. Why can't we go in and see the wonderful tribute you have made to the mining industry?'

'I'd love to show you around, but, er, I've recently painted the inside. It'll ruin your blazers.'

Mrs Jacques stroked her lapel. 'Yes, it most certainly will.'

Miss James took a step backwards. 'They're brand-new.'

Mrs Jacques scoured a line across her clipboard. 'You've had ample time to paint the inside of your shed leading up to this day.'

Mrs M's patience wore thin, witnessing the dropped points. She extended her tape measure and offered it to Mrs Jacques. 'Shall we see how Mr Morgan's spring onions measure up?'

They commenced measuring but became distracted by a speaker system blasting out the Welsh national anthem from Clayton's plot, where Clayton and Smithy stood proudly to the music. As soon as he captured their attention, Clayton operated a remote and his polytunnel retracted like an accordion revealing a table angled up at sixty-five degrees and covered in a sheet, under which appeared to be the Frankenstein monster. Like a faithful magician's assistant, Smithy threw back the sheet, revealing a gigantic leek.

'My word, that is a big one,' said Mrs Jacques.

'It's certainly an eye-opener,' said Miss James.

'How embarrassing,' said Mrs M.

'What a pathetic pair,' sniggered Johnny as it clicked regarding Clayton's shed-painting tantrum. The jealous ex-copper did not want anything to take the shine off his giant leek and this was his attempt at sabotaging Johnny's chances at winning best plot. But the joke was on Clayton because Johnny could not care less.

Underground, North-Eye caught his breath as he got to the face. 'Charlie, that was irresponsible of you to come down here, and without a helmet and cap lamp.'

'Charlie's got her phone,' said Lippo. 'Take a photo of us with our shovels in front of the coal.'

'You know the rules,' said Spider. 'No phones underground.'

'Come on Charlie,' urged North-Eye, 'let's get back up on top.'

'Yeah, let's have a picture of us at the coalface,' said Jayden. 'It'll be like one of those oldie pictures of miners.'

'C'mon bro,' pleaded Lippo, 'you knows it's only one photo.'

'Johnny will go skitz,' said Spider, 'I'll leave it to North-Eye.'

'Right-o,' said North-Eye. 'One little picture, but only if I take it. Charlie, give me your phone and get in the middle with the boys.'

'*Is everything OK down there*,' said Joanne on the Tannoy.

'*Everything is fine, Joanne*,' answered North-Eye on the Tannoy. '*We'll be up in a mo with the bastard dog. Excuse the language.*'

'*It might be an idea to stay down there because the judges are outside with Dad.*'

Charlie gave North-Eye the phone and they posed expectantly with shovels but North-Eye put the phone in his pocket. 'You think I'm stupid and would risk us all getting bastard killed? Remember the gas training? If firedamp gets into the main body of air between five and fifteen per cent …'

'You can kiss your arse goodbye,' said Spider as the floor beneath them cracked open and crashed down into a gaping void.

Posts creaked, buckled and snapped all around as the roof collapsed in a cloud of dust. Cowering from the falling roof, the team jumped for their lives away from a yawning black hole sucking everything down below them.

North-Eye got cut off from the others. He shouted through the dust at their cap lamps. 'Spider, take everyone out through Bouncer's shed. I'll go out this way.'

The Fall

Mrs Jacques measured the distance between two spring onions on Johnny's plot but as she extended the tape, one by one, all along the row, the spring onions disappeared. 'What the ...?'

Miss James tore the page from her clipboard. 'Does this sort of thing normally go on here?'

'Johnny, something very strange is happening to your spring onions,' said Mrs M.

Miss James skipped back a step. 'And is the ground sinking?'

A small whirlpool hole appeared in the raised bed and to their astonishment the spring onions disappeared into it.

Joanne burst out through the shed doors followed by a plume of black coal dust.

Johnny immediately grasped the situation. 'Roof fall!' He rushed to the aid of his coughing and spluttering daughter.

Joanne panicked. 'Jayden's still down there.'

'He's OK,' coughed North-Eye inside the shed. 'They've all gone out through our second way.'

'He looks like a real miner,' said Mrs Jacques, as North-Eye staggered through the shed doors with his cap lamp shining. 'That's why Mr Morgan didn't want us to go into his shed. It must be part of the theme.'

'I'm not so sure,' said Mrs M.

'I think so and I don't approve,' cackled Miss James. 'The tenants are trying to outdo each other with this unprofessional shed theme nonsense.'

'It's very good though, isn't it?' said Mrs Jacques. 'It's like an historical re-enactment.'

The discussion abruptly ended as Bouncer's shed door got kicked from its hinges. Jayden, Spider, Lippo and Slouch ran coughing and spluttering across the plot, followed by a plume of black coal dust and a back-draught of cannabis leaves.

At first, Clayton and Smithy were taken aback at how Johnny had managed to piss on their parade, but they soon enjoyed a good laugh at the Neighbourhood Watch volunteers comically coughing their guts out.

Johnny counted everyone. 'Joanne's OK, and North-Eye, and there's Jayden, Spider, Lippo and Slouch. Thank God you all got out.'

'What on earth is going on with those Neighbourhood Watch volunteers?' laughed Clayton.

'Neighbourhood Watch!' scoffed Smithy. 'My bluebottle backside.'

They ceased laughing when Clayton's shed and polytunnel abruptly tilted up at an angle and started to go down like the *Titanic*, spilling leeks, compost, and propagation equipment on the adjoining plots.

'My leeks,' lisped Clayton, running to the rescue. Smithy held on to the polytunnel but the polythene stretched in his hand as the shed sank deeper. Clayton grabbed his giant leek as he and the shed sank further into the ground. When he disappeared down into the workings, Clayton saluted like the captain of a sinking ship. Smithy, loyally clutching the polythene, got sucked under behind him.

'Coppers falling into mine workings,' said Johnny. 'There is a God after all.'

Britney yelped at Johnny from Slouch's sleeping bag. 'How did you get hold of that dog? I told Charlie to ... Where's Charlie?'

'Charlie is still down there!' spluttered Jayden.

'What do you mean "still down there"? How did Charlie get down there in the first place?'

Joanne put a hand to her mouth in shock. 'Britney fell down the shaft and Charlie went after her.'

Jayden got to his feet. 'I'm going back down.'

Johnny peeled off his shirt and tie like Clark Kent and rushed to the shed. 'No you don't. You'll listen to me and do as you're told.'

'Grandad, I thought you had a bad back?'

'Dad, you can't!'

Lippo coughed and threw down his helmet. 'You knows only a nutter would go back down there.'

In the shed, Johnny kicked off Lippo's Vans trainers and got into a pair of overalls. 'North-Eye, take Spider and go down through Bouncer's shed while Jayden and I will go down this way.'

'Both of you?' shrieked Joanne.

'Joanne, it's important you keep a clear head, ring for an ambulance and the Mines' Rescue Service. Then ring our emergency number and call out Geronimo, Billy Donkey and Banger. Stay near the Tannoy for further instructions.'

'There's something you should know first,' said North-Eye

as he and Spider were on their way to Bouncer's shed. 'It's more than a roof fall. The floor gave way underneath us. There must be old workings below ours and that's why the flood water disappeared. We don't know how much gas is down there, we don't have any breathing equipment, and it could all collapse at any bastard moment.'

'We can't wait for breathing equipment. Every second counts if we're to find Charlie.' As Johnny got into his cap lamp and helmet, Mrs M and the judges hovered around outside the shed. 'Mrs M, please keep everyone well back from the colliery.'

'My goodness, it's real.' Mrs M understood and drove the judges away like geese.

'This is really happening?' protested Mrs Jacques.

Johnny tied his boots. 'Lippo, you can operate the bicycle winder.'

Lippo punched a fist into his hand. 'Coolio.'

Slouch hugged Britney. 'What shall I do?'

Johnny switched on his cap lamp. 'You can keep that fucking dog away from me.'

Diego Maradon-ah

Once they had climbed down the shaft ladder, Johnny and Jayden made their way through the creaking colliery, all the while calling out for Charlie. Dust and debris fell everywhere in the eerie workings, and when they saw rising water vapour they knew they had reached the void. On the other side of the black hole were the cap lamp beams of North-Eye and Spider.

'Spider,' shouted Johnny, 'you're team captain, where the fuck was you when Charlie came down here?'

'It was Slouch and that fucking dog,' snapped Spider.

'It happened too fast,' said North-Eye, 'it's no one's fault and this isn't the time for a bastard inquest.'

'We'll argue about it later,' said Johnny looking into the abyss. 'How do we get down there for a look?'

The four cap lamps beamed into the misty darkness illuminating a jumble of fallen pallets, posts, doors and pine kitchen units like a messy surreal game of Jenga.

'Charlie?' called Jayden.

A fall of dust from the roof answered his call.

Spider picked up a piece of coal. 'That looks like water.' He threw down the coal. It did not bode well when they heard the splash.

North-Eye squinted, 'Wait, what's floating there?'

'Charlie?' shouted Jayden.

The lights shone on a body floating in the water. They were speechless until North-Eye put a hand on Spider's shoulder for support. 'Bastard hell.'

Johnny got on his knees and looked closer. 'It's a leek ... Clayton's Frankenstein leek.'

The giant vegetable floated away under a pallet.

'We could use the suction hose from the Sykes pump, secure it to a post and drop it down the hole,' said North-Eye. 'It'll be risky but one of us could climb down and see if Charlie is down there.'

'Let's not think about it, let's do it,' said Johnny, and he and Jayden went back along the workings to dismantle the suction hose.

They were uncoupling the hose when a mound of rubble moved under a split wooden post.

'Jayden,' said a dry voice.

'Charlie?'

Johnny shook his lamp at the others. 'We've found her, or rather she found us. Best go back out your way and wait on the surface.'

'Thank God for that,' said North-Eye as he and Spider made their way out.

'It all fell on me,' said Charlie as Jayden dug at the rubble with his bare hands.

Johnny announced the news on the Tannoy, then helped Jayden dig Charlie out. 'Lucky girl.'

The split post gave way when they pulled Charlie out. Johnny put his shoulder to the roof and stood firm like a pit prop. 'There's a squeeze coming on. Get going.'

Charlie smarted when she put weight on her foot. 'I can't put my foot down.'

Jayden picked Charlie up with a fireman's lift. 'Then I'll have to carry you.'

'Shaming,' she said, fighting him off. 'I'll give you such a slap.'

'You can slap me as much as you like when we're on the surface. C'mon Grandad, let's go.'

'Will you both hurry up?'

Jayden moved off into the crumbling workings. 'We're in the clear now, Grandad. C'mon.'

Johnny grunted at the roof squeeze. 'You're *not* in the clear. If this goes, it all goes. Get going.'

'I'll be back for you now in a minute.'

Jayden carried Charlie through the workings as the colliery collapsed all around. In the swirls of dust, he lost his way.

'Put me down, you're going the wrong way.'

'I'm going the right way.'

Charlie pointed at the light on pit bottom. 'It's down there.'

Jayden changed direction. 'I knew that.'

'You didn't.'

Jayden stepped onto the cage at pit bottom and shouted up the shaft. 'Wind us up.'

Lippo pedalled like an Olympic cyclist on the bicycle winder and they came up to top pit.

Joanne got on the Tannoy. *'Dad, where are you?'*

Jayden panted, 'I'm going back for him now in a minute, Mum.'

Jayden carried Charlie out through the shed doors and into the bright sunshine. The crowd around the edge of the plot cheered at the rescue. Slouch nailed the moment on his phone.

Charlie irately held onto a porch post. 'Put me down.'

Jayden complied and wondered why Charlie had a bright red scarf covering her leg. He realised it was blood. 'If you're giving me a slap then be quick about it.'

Charlie held her hand to strike but threw it around Jayden's neck and gave him a passionate kiss to more applause from the onlookers.

Joanne and Lippo interrupted the kiss by running out of the shed followed by a cloud of dust heralding another collapse in the colliery.

Porch posts creaked and the crowd panicked as the whirlpool-like sinkhole grew in size at their feet. They retreated to the safety of the neighbouring plots.

'Dad,' said Joanne. 'Where's Dad?'

Johnny kept his shoulders wedged to the roof and his hands locked tightly to his thighs. At every creak and squeeze he puffed, panted and kept his spirits up. 'In future, be careful what you wish for.' A nearby post splintered and collapsed. 'Lead arse Lippo must've put that up.' He spat and grunted at the strain. 'You see, my buddy Mohammed and all you Clanger gym monkeys? No miner worth his salt needed gym membership, we were far too bollocksed to go to a gym.'

Debris rained around him as the roof creaked but he remained cheerful and sang his own version of 'Don't Cry for Me Argentina'.

'Don't fall on me Mid-Glamorgan, the truth is I never left you, all through my mad mining days, and Clanger Insurance, what a cheating fuck-ah, Diego Maradon-ah.'

Johnny spluttered. 'If there's anyone up there listening, I could do with the hand of God myself over by here, right now, please.'

A shaft of light appeared from above and beamed down as if a messiah had been born at his boots. Rubble mixed with marigolds and spring onions cascaded around as he squinted at the dazzling light.

On the surface a gasp circulated the crowd as the ground sank, forming a bowl-like crater. A pile of moving rubble appeared at the centre like an inverted nipple. As debris fell, the rubble gradually resembled Atlas bent over holding up the heavens, but only a small pile of stones crumbled on the figure's shoulders. The figure spluttered, and above a pair of blinking eyes a cap lamp beam cut through the dust. The beam lasered around the astonished faces on the crater rim, and they gaped as if witnessing an alien emerging from the wreckage of a crashed spaceship. The beam settled upon Mrs M.

'Mrs M,' spluttered Johnny as stones fell from his shoulders, 'I don't think I'll win the best plot category this year.'

Leaning over for a better look, Mrs Jacques lost her footing. 'Help!' She grabbed Miss James and they both tumbled headlong into the crater. Mrs Jacques gave everyone an eyeful of racy stocking and suspender underwear as she somersaulted down.

Slouch got lucky and nailed it on his phone.

Spider, Jayden and Lippo jumped into the crater. Mrs Jacques and Miss James held out expectant hands but they passed them by to pull Johnny from the rubble.

'How's Charlie?'

'She's fine,' said Jayden, 'a little bump on the leg.'

They got Johnny to Bouncer's plot before he pushed them away. 'I'm not an invalid. Go and help the judges.'

Joanne gave her father a big hug, 'Dad.'

Johnny winked at Jayden. 'Gerroff, you're making me look a right tit.'

Mrs M turned her back on the crater where the judges were being rescued and made her way to the committee shed. 'I think I need a cup of tea, a slice of cake and a good sit down.'

Geronimo, Billy Donkey and Banger arrived, kitted out in masks and breathing apparatus for a mining rescue. They pushed their way through the crowd to the crater rim.

'Make way please,' said Geronimo, 'this is an emergency,'

Betty Bingo stepped aside. 'Are you the paramedics?'

'No, madam,' said Billy Donkey lifting his face mask, 'we're a troubleshooting team of mining consultants.'

Banger hissed in his mask like Darth Vader. 'The paramedics are right behind us.'

North-Eye greeted the miners. 'Thanks for the quick

response, fellahs, but it looks like it's all over – and in more ways than one.'

'Well, Billy,' said Geronimo taking off his helmet, 'it looks like the last cage has gone up without us.'

'And we were like muck from a shovel getting here, Geronimo.'

'Mind you,' hissed Banger, 'Johnny doesn't look too clever on his feet over by there.'

With the weight removed from his shoulders, Johnny felt as light as a feather and walked around as if stepping on fluffy clouds. He clutched at a sudden pain in his chest and his legs gave way. Spider and Lippo ran to Johnny's assistance, releasing Mrs Jacques to roll back into the crater, knocking Miss James down like a skittle.

Slouch made a pillow of his sleeping bag and as they laid Johnny's head down, Britney whined and licked his dusty cheek.

When the paramedics arrived and administered oxygen, Johnny looked up at the circle of concerned familiar faces gathered around him. He floated off into a sunless azure sky, like a huge movie studio going on and on forever, populated by marigolds and canaries. Julie stood on the hillside waiting for him and a white light dazzled on the horizon.

FOUR

THE MINERS
STRIKE BACK

Think Happy Thoughts

Johnny awoke with a backfiring snore.

Joanne sat in a chair at his side and held his hand. 'Dad.'

He blinked at the intravenous drip in his arm and looked around the puke-coloured hospital room until he got his bearings. 'I saw your mother as clear as day.'

'Dad, don't be silly.'

'One minute we were walking through marigolds happy as can be, the next minute Thatch ... the T-word materialised in a puff of blue smoke in my runner beans. Old Twat and Handbags sent riot police, Trudi Anderson and her climate nutters, a load of Council officials, and a JCB to destroy my shed.'

'Er, that is ridiculous, Dad.'

'Your mother led me underground to escape. We sat together in Julie's Colliery until she walked away into the white light. Don't worry, it's something she always does, but this time it was different because I held her hand and went with her.'

'It's just a dream.'

'It was more than a dream. Julie told me not to be afraid,

you see, your mum knows deep down I'm really a gutless coward.'

'Don't be so daft.'

'Your mum said death is nothing to be scared of, it's part of life. It's no big deal. What do you think of that?'

'What medication are you on?'

'Dreams of your mother,' he laughed, 'and some funny stuff they've been giving me. I'm sure the team would love it.'

'It's official, doctor's orders, you've got to stop getting angry about things in the past you can't change. Stop going on about the M- and T-words and the Tories, they don't seem to be such swines as they used to be. Think happy thoughts.'

Johnny clenched his teeth. 'Think happy thoughts, think happy thoughts.'

'When you collapsed the paramedics were already there to give you CPR. They couldn't have arrived with better timing. Think of how lucky you are.'

'Lucky me.' Johnny lifted an inch of his chest bandage and examined a long centipede of stitches. 'They said I could go home in seven to ten days after heart surgery. What day is it now?'

'Day three, you'll be home next week.'

'Home, where I can spend the rest of my life looking out the window of an empty house thinking happy thoughts and how lucky I am. I miss your mother every minute of the day. You know that, don't you?'

Joanne wiped away a tear. 'Yes.'

'It would help if you stopped looking at me with eyes like Dai Milk's cows. If I have to think happy thoughts for the rest of my life, tell me, is there anything cheerful happening in the world?'

Joanne blew her nose in a tissue. 'The canaries are safe and sound. I took them home and keep them fed and watered.'

'Good news. Those working birds deserve all our respect for putting their lives on the line for us. I love canaries.'

'Mrs M sent you a card and a piece of walnut cake in a box.'

'More good news, I'm back on the cake list. Read it out for me.'

'"Get well soon, Johnny", and I don't know what this means but "I now understand the mascara and the naked young man thing!" Best wishes Mrs M. x"'

'I'm glad she clicked on. We go back a long way, to primary school, The Beatles and the old colliery. I haven't the heart to tell her I don't like walnut cake. Julie's fruit cake was the best.'

'Parvinder sat in with you for ages when you were out cold.'

'Joking. Wonders never cease, Parvinder taking time out from his shop to watch over me. Did he leave any Indian beer?'

'Here's a thank you card from Simon, Siân, Sacha and the girls, whoever they are?'

'Slouch's family, it's nice of them considering I pulled a ladder away from his dad and left him hanging from the roof guttering.'

The hospital door creaked. Jayden and Charlie peeped in.

'Here they are, two of the most irresponsible miners on the planet. How's the leg, Charlie?'

'Still sore, want to see the stitches?' She peeled open a bandage revealing a snakelike line of stitches down her calf muscle.

'I hope you rubbed coal dust in it. You'll have a lovely miner's blue scar and an interesting story to tell your grandchildren.'

'Don't listen to him Charlie, he's on funny drugs,' said Joanne getting to her feet with a smile. 'If it's all happy days, I'm off. I can't keep the old dears waiting. Jayden, look after Grandad, he needs complete rest and strictly no excitement. Remember what I said, you too Charlie.' She gave Johnny a kiss.

'Gerroff, make me feel a hundred years old, why don't you.'

'Don't be soft, Dad.'

Joanne reminded the teenagers as she went through the door. 'Don't forget, you pair, doctor's orders, strictly no excitement.'

The door creaked shut and the silence could be cut with a scalpel.

Johnny pulled himself up with the trapeze bar. 'What's she on about "strictly no excitement"? I've always been straight with you pair so be straight with me.'

They could not look him in the eye and instinctively covered their mouths like a pair of speak-no-evil monkeys. Charlie offered Jayden the fruit bowl and he ate a grape. 'We can't say anything to get you excited, Grandad.'

'If you won't say anything, I will. It was good while it lasted.'

'While what lasted, Grandad?'

'Julie's Colliery and all that.'

Charlie shared a look with Jayden. 'It's still happening.'

'What's still happening?'

'Julie's Colliery and all that. Grandad, you're a hero and the whole world knows,' said Jayden, relieved to let it all out.

'Shut up.'

'Serious, Grandad. Slouch filmed the rescue on his phone and it's been on the news, all over social media and everywhere.'

Charlie put her hand on Johnny's. 'Everyone in the world knows you held up the roof for us to get out.'

'Grandad, when you conked out everyone lost their shit. Police, firemen, paramedics and news crews swarmed all over the place.'

Charlie held up her phone. 'They can't stop talking about it on the telly.'

'Look there, Jayden's carrying you from the shed ... you giving him a big kiss ... there's me holding up a pile of rubble in the sinkhole. Slouch is not as headshot as he makes out. There's Mrs Jacques falling in the hole with Miss James. How many around the world got an eyeful of those knickers?'

'It's gone viral,' said Charlie. 'Maybe it's because Parvinder says Mrs Jacques is really high up in the Council.'

'It's the sort of thing Parvinder knows about, and means there's a lot of trouble coming this way.'

'Mrs M said the allotment has been expelled from the association,' said Charlie. 'But she wasn't upset, she seemed happy.'

'Good news and a weight from Mrs M's shoulders. No more measuring between spring onions and petty allotment politics. Speaking of which, what about Clayton and Smithy?'

'They seemed OK when the Mines' Rescue Service fished them out of the workings,' said Jayden, 'but next day they wore neck braces, slings and head bandages.'

'They're cooking up compensation claims.'

'Charlie's so clever. She gathered bits of our phone footage from the colliery and made a banging YouTube video. She even added Gran's telly interview in the Strike.'

'You did that for Julie? Thank you, Charlie.'

Charlie smiled. 'I've kept your CD safe. Our YouTube followers are growing in Germany, India, Canada, South Africa, Australia and America. I didn't know there were so many miners in the world. Someone set up a crowdfunding page to help keep our jobs and re-open Julie's Colliery. It's up to half a million pounds.'

'Serious?'

'Serious,' said Charlie. 'And we've an advertising deal with an American mining company.'

'And another deal in Chile, wherever that is,' shrugged Jayden.

'South America,' said Charlie.

'I thought it was in Spain. Are you OK, Grandad?'

Johnny stared into space. 'I told everyone to keep it quiet and now the whole world and his fucking dog knows.'

'North-Eye registered us as a company. Julie's Colliery Ltd is now legit and we're all on equal shares.'

Charlie sat on the bed. 'Not that we want any money. We want everything to be like it was because it's ours and we built it together.'

'Where's the rest of the team?'

'At the allotment,' said Jayden. 'The Council and the Coal Authority want to pump concrete into the colliery, but we won't let the JCB and the concrete wagons through the gates.'

'A JCB, like my dream, but they can't hold them off.'

'We've got help,' smiled Charlie.

'Geronimo, Billy Donkey and Banger,' said Jayden, 'along with all the old Coed Mawr valley miners.'

Charlie jumped off the bed. 'And it's been going off all day.'

'What has?'

'I've got it on the news.' Charlie put her phone on the bedside cupboard. 'Listen to this.'

There were several arrests today in the village of Coed Mawr in south Wales. Tension has been building for days in the former mining community between Council officials, climate protesters and a gathering of ex-miners, at a small illegal coal mine housed in the village allotments. Last week, following an incident at the colliery, there was a dramatic rescue of a young female miner who was injured while underground. In the same incident two former police officers had to be brought out of flooded mine workings by the Rescue Services and two other individuals suffered minor injuries on the surface. The colliery owner and manager, Mr Johnny Morgan, who collapsed shortly after the incident, is in a stable condition in hospital following heart surgery.

The coal mine, known as Julie's Colliery, which had a workforce of women, teenagers and veteran miners, was declared a mine hazard by the Coal Authority, and Council officials now intend to fill in and cap off the colliery with concrete. The announcement has generated anger in the community.

Many locals blame the lack of employment in the area and have welcomed Mr Morgan's initiative to provide work for the youth of the village, although there has also been widespread condemnation as to how women were allowed to work at the illegal mine and in such dangerous conditions. The following report contains flashing images.

Johnny squinted at the screen. 'That's Clayton in the bandages.'

It's a danger to the community and a hotbed of criminal activity. The sooner it's pumped full of concrete the better. It's a miracle Mr Smithy and my good self managed to escape with our lives from that death trap, albeit not entirely unscathed.

Smithy popped up behind Clayton.

That's why you'll never find a coal mine in the Home Counties.

Johnny pointed at the screen. 'That looks like a music festival.'

'There's hundreds of climate protesters wild camping in Dai Milk's cow field, Grandad.'

'Here's Trudi Anderson,' said Charlie.

Despite clear Welsh Government legislation, there is an illegal coal mine operating in this valley, and we of Action Xtinction fully support the Local Authority and the Coal Authority, and will assist them in any way possible. Our climate is at crisis point. All fossil fuel must be kept in the ground. Action Xtinction will not allow these climate criminals to take us retrograde into the dark ages of King Coal and global calamity. The world is watching what we do here.

Johnny snorted. 'Trudi Anderson, picking on little old us instead of the giant polluters of our planet. She'd happily take us into a Stone Age world of living in mud huts and eating lettuce. Even then it'll be the wrong mud and the wrong lettuce.'

'North-Eye had an answer for her,' said Charlie.

We used recycled materials reclaimed from street skips or fly-tipping black spots in the countryside. The workforce walked to and from work, packaged the coal in biodegradable paper sacks, and everything ran on clean electricity. Our operating carbon footprint was virtually zero CO2 emissions, yet we find a horde of ill-informed, baying climate activists camped on our doorstep, gloating at the end of the Coal Age, an end in which they played no part to bring about.

Much has been said of the young woman who was injured in the incident but she is as good as, if not better than, any man I've ever worked with underground.

Johnny nudged Charlie. 'I knew he'd come around to it.'

I can't speak more highly of our workforce. They were only teenagers on the wrong track, with no prospects, no jobs, no way out of the rut they found themselves in, yet they learned new old skills, worked hard, and turned themselves around. They started out as a social problem, and with Johnny the Cutter's help they are now valued members of their community.

'Wow,' said Johnny with a laugh as the correspondent tried to get a word in. 'They can't shut him up.'

Our small colliery incident had minimal media coverage, a soon-to-be-forgotten "and finally" news item, yet Trudi Anderson turned it into a media circus to promote her climate beliefs. There's a host of Scandinavian news crews hanging on to her every word. How much CO_2 did they burn into the upper atmosphere getting here? Action Xtinction have caused far more environmental damage than Julie's Colliery ever could have. The hypocritical insanity of the world never ceases to amaze me.

'He stole my line.'

I'm a miner, like the majority of these people standing behind me are miners and we miners stick together when times get tough. Now, if you'll excuse me, I've got a picket line to get back to.

The news correspondent eventually got a word in.

A police cordon has now been set up around the allotment and the situation is described as stable but another stand-off is expected in the morning when work is to resume.

Charlie picked up her phone. 'Everyone is in our face.'

'The coppers want to interview you when you're up to it, Grandad. They're always hanging about the reception desk.'

'Did you see that? All the old miners came to support us. Like I said, they never broke the NUM in the Coed Mawr valley.'

Johnny pulled himself up and sat on the edge of the bed. 'Charlie, are my clothes in that cupboard?'

'Grandad, you're supposed to have a complete rest.'

'You don't think I'm going to lie in bed when it's time to stand up and be counted? We've more chance of finding Elvis Presley playing Hide the Sausage with Marilyn Monroe on Mars than we've got of re-opening Julie's Colliery, but it doesn't mean we should go down without a fight.'

Charlie held up Johnny's helmet, deputy stick and a clean set of white overalls.

'Let's think of a way to smuggle me out of here tonight without the hospital staff, the police, and the media knowing about it.'

A Gathering of Jet Streams

Former miners throughout the Coed Mawr valley and from mining communities further afield, prepared for an early morning shift of mass picket duty outside the allotment. A small showing of pickets braved the night warming their hands around an oil drum fire opposite the allotment gates. With donkey jacket collars turned to the chill, they swapped tall tales of the Strike. Alternative entertainment came from taunting the two police officers, who looked of school age, staunchly guarding the blue incident tape crisscrossing the gates. An occasional police car looking in on their colleagues drew jeers and two-finger salutes from the old miners, but otherwise the night passed quietly.

A shepherd's warning bloodied a crisscross of jet streams above Coed Mawr Mountain as the Action Xtinction climate protesters celebrated the sunrise in Dai Milk's cow field. Face-painted activists drummed drums, rattled tambourines, blew whistles, meditated, and wailed at the rising sun. Green vegetable dye, garlands of flowers and slogans decorated Dai Milk's cows – I'M A VEGAN; LOVE COWS EAT PLANTS; and FORK OFF! Dai Milk's cows did not quite know what to make of it but were far from caring as they grazed completely off their udders on the first magic mushroom crop of the season.

At the centre of the field, Trudi Anderson's brown yurt dwarfed the surrounding multi-coloured canvases like an enormous cowpat. She leant upon the door frame, drinking in the festival-like atmosphere from the vibrant tent village she had created. Trudi initially reacted to the news of the illicit coal mine as if discovering a dog turd in her rucksack, but quickly realised it to be the opportunity she had long waited for. She congratulated herself on her decisive action to immediately decamp from the gates of the open-cast mine and relocate where the festering sore of King Coal had re-emerged, here on the arsehole of the world at Coed Mawr village.

The fiasco at Jenkins & Son Coal Merchants taught Trudi a valuable lesson and there would be no underestimating the opposition this time. Trudi had mobilised two groups of activists renowned for their violent methods. The Shock Troops of Gia, a feminist branch of vegan climate extremists, built like pro wrestlers who at the bat of an eye were capable of castrating a man with a spoon. Worse still were the PAM, Punish Animal Murder, a covert troop of animal rights activists and anti-vivisectionists – black-hooded thugs with no peaceful intentions at this or any demo.

Trudi proudly looked on as the Action Xtinction procession formed in a hustle and bustle of activity as protesters made ready and took their places. At the head of the procession half a dozen mime artists held a coffin marked KING COAL. They were flanked by dinosaurs, stilts walkers, jugglers, students and grim-faced pensioners with banners reading PLANET NOT PROFIT and END COAL NOW and XTINCTION FOR COAL.

Trudi wailed a salute from her yurt and the Action Xtinction procession wailed back in reply. Trudi waved the procession on and, to the sound of shaman drums, the protesters moved forwards in a swirl of bubbles, balloons and pink smoke.

On the M4 westbound a black Jaguar sped like a bullet towards south Wales. An immaculately-dressed elderly gentleman with an aura of an East End villain checked his watch in the back seat. 'Roger, get a move on.'

'Yes sir, Mr Rosser,' said Roger the chauffeur.

'I want to get there this morning not next week.'

'Yes sir, Mr Rosser,' repeated Roger the chauffeur as he put his foot down.

'We don't want to get nicked for something as trivial as speeding, Grandad,' said an identically immaculately-dressed younger version of Mr Rosser sitting next to him in the back seats.

'Or draw any unwanted attention from the filth,' said another identically immaculately-dressed younger version of Mr Rosser who craned his neck around from the passenger seat.

Mr Rosser took a sip of medication from a small bottle. 'You'll shut your cakeholes and do as you are told. Today you're going to learn a lesson, a big lesson about loyalty and mates and how mates look out for each other, even if they haven't seen each other in years.'

In the Coal Yard, Trewatkins, Minja lined up Pea-Brain and

every other equally gormless Zulu he could muster and, with Rocky at heel, he stood next to the Jenkins & Son coal lorry awaiting inspection by his grandfather. Minge soon came out of the house with a face like thunder. He walked the line examining each Zulu with a great deal of muttering and head shaking like a tinpot general inspecting a ragtag assembly of raw recruits. When Minge cast an evil eye at Minja, Rocky whined.

Rose came out of the kitchen carrying an item resembling a Batman cowl. 'You forgot the Jenkins & Son Coal Merchants hood. It shouldn't be in a stuffy glass case on a day like today.'

'Thank you, Rose,' he said, taking the relic from her tiny hands.

Rose made her way back to the kitchen, 'Cottage pie for tea?'

Minge kept his eyes on the hood, 'Lovely.'

'With gravy?' said Minja.

'Shut up,' said Minge as he donned the hood and laced up the shoulder flaps.

The Zulus had never seen a coal merchant hood before but they understood Minge meant business when he put it on. To them he looked like a villain in a superhero movie.

Minja thought his grandfather resembled a medieval torturer clocking on for the dayshift. 'Awesome.'

'I never thought I'd see the day again when there'd be genuine Welsh house coal on the Jenkins & Son lorry. You have no idea what it means to me.'

Minge was right. They had no idea. And when Minge bowed his head and rubbed his eyes, several Zulus thought they heard him sob.

The coal merchant regained his composure and walked the line of terrified Zulus like a drill sergeant, scowling at each in turn from under his hood. 'If anyone here thinks it's OK for these big-headed, tree-shagging, foreign climate Nazis to invade our little valley and tell us what we can and can't do with our coal, you'd better get the fuck out of the coal yard now.'

No one dared move.

'OK … let's go.'

The Great Escape to Victory

The nightshift nursing staff congregated at the ward reception desk where the early hours were spent in a ritual of gossip and fits of hysterics. To the nursing staff, the nightshift was a scream. To the ward patients who were not drugged senseless, the nightshift was an NHS witching hour every hour of the night.

Jayden and Charlie, posing as decorators in their white colliery overalls, wandered into the party. Jayden carried a stepladder kifed from a maintenance room and Charlie, reprising her Goth terrorist look, held an empty paint tub she acquired from a skip.

'Way-hey, fancy dress is it?' said the charge nurse. 'Don't tell me … Ghostbusters?' The pride of nurses burst into hysterics and a rendition of the theme tune, 'Da-da-deh-da-deh-da, da-da-da-da-deh-da-Ghostbusters!' Patient alarms buzzed behind the reception desk like a swarm of bees.

Following the plan, Jayden put the stepladder aside and entertained the nurses by unbuttoning his overalls with a sexy twerk. Jayden's twerk rendered Charlie invisible and she easily got into the observation room where Johnny sat waiting in a wheelchair, suited and booted. When they slipped stealthily out into the corridor, a blast of music and a collective 'Whooooooo!' came from the reception desk.

Two nurses had Jayden pinned against a wall and twerked booty against him like a Chippendale cornered on a hen night. Clocking Johnny's wheelchair heading towards the lifts, the terrified teenager drew the nurses' attention away in the opposite direction by legging it down the corridor.

'Hey handsome,' laughed the charge nurse, 'you forgot your stepladder.'

The taxi driver happened to be a bigot who loved the sound of his own voice. He did not stop talking all the way over the mountain to Coed Mawr while Jayden, Johnny and Charlie sat quietly in the back seats wishing he would shut up.

'Fancy dress in the hospital, is it? Don't tell me … Ghostbusters?' He winked at them in the mirror and burst into the theme tune, 'Da-da-deh-da-deh-da, da-da-da-da-deh-da-Ghostbusters!'

Distracted with one eye on his unreceptive audience in the mirror, he suddenly swerved off-road to avoid a rogue sheep. 'Fuck!'

After a short bumpy ride along a dirt track, he screeched back onto the road. 'Sheep! The only reason God created the fucking things is so there'd be a creature on earth stupider than a woman.'

Johnny gave Charlie a calming hand as she growled with anger.

Oblivious to his lucky escape, the driver yakked about his long night of adventures driving around Merthyr with vomiting drunks, fare dodgers and rutting couples. He fished for a good tip. 'You're my last fare,' he said with an exaggerated yawn, 'lucky for you I was late going home when I got the call because you won't get a taxi at this time of the morning.'

'Lucky us,' said Johnny, feeling unsure about his next step as they neared Coed Mawr.

Johnny gave the driver directions when they got to the centre of the village, but upon turning into the allotment road he knew he had made a big mistake. The way ahead thronged with people and the pavements were clogged with vehicles. He whispered to Jayden. 'We should've gone down the potholed lane and through the secret way.'

The Action Xtinction procession marched towards the allotment gates in a swirl of pink smoke, bubbles and balloons. Ahead of the King Coal coffin marched Trudi with a nine-foot length of Norwegian pine over her shoulder. Sharpened at one end, flattened at the other and covered in aluminium foil, it resembled a gigantic flat head nail. A brown cardboard label dangled and read: THE FINAL NAIL.

The hundreds of villagers and miners on the grass verge of the bottom streets did not have the pizzazz of the protesters but they made up for it in grit, determination and grim looks. To rival the trivial rags of the outsiders, the miners proudly unsheathed the dusty Coed Mawr Colliery NUM lodge banner and it caught the wind like the mainsail of a ship.

A large police presence filled the space in front of the allotment gates and lined the fencing. Sporting neck braces and bandages like medals of honour, Clayton and Smithy appeared to be acting as advisors to the young officers.

Jayden pointed at a charm of Council workmen, kitted out in new white helmets and dazzling day-glow orange, 'Dickhead orange.'

'Oh yeah,' said the taxi driver, 'this is where a big bell-end nearly killed a bunch of kids and some old coppers down a coal mine. Now everyone's playing up. Fuck the coppers, but those poor kids? I'd bury the big bell-end down there.'

'The big bell-end deserves it,' agreed Johnny.

They edged through the crowd and a handful of old miners recognising Johnny pressed up against the taxi windows for a gawk.

'Fucking hell, the living dead are attacking my taxi.'

The taxi crawled towards a news crew gauging opinion from the allotment tenants. Hoss wore a ten-gallon hat, a fringed buckskin jacket and a pair of cowboy boots itching for a good kicking. Betty Bingo, joyless as if beaten to a full house, tied a red headband on Vince the Hippy; his Donovan-like countenance visibly soured to that of Charles Manson. Standing next to Mrs Jones Bottom Street and her dog Britney, Mrs M appeared forlorn with worry. Parvinder looked at ease giving an interview in front of the camera.

The driver manoeuvred through a flock of Action Xtinction canaries flapping wings in a swirl of yellow feathers. 'Look at this shower of arse-bandits. What the fuck do they look like?'

Johnny turned to Jayden. 'I don't know who to punch first, the bigot driving, or a climate coward dissing our canaries.'

Jayden wound down his window, leant out and snatched a beak mask off the head of a passing canary. By the time the protester turned around, Jayden had ducked back inside the taxi. 'Wear this or you might get recognised and arrested.'

A shot-putter of a policewoman stepped into the path of the taxi and signalled the driver to stop.

Johnny donned the canary mask. 'Driver, wait here for us, if you've got the nerve.'

Flying Pickets

Charlie helped Johnny out of the taxi. Aware of Clayton and Smithy's suspicious gaze from the allotment gates, Johnny pulled the canary mask down over his face. He made his way to the miners standing around the oil drum where Geronimo poked the burning timber with a pallet slat.

Johnny banged on the oil drum with his deputy stick and squawked like a parrot, 'Death to coal … Keep it in the ground.'

Banger reacted first. 'If you know what's good for you bird brain, you'll fly the fuck off from here a bit sharpish.'

Johnny briefly lifted his mask. 'It's me, you bacon heads.'

Geronimo pointed a smouldering pallet slat at him. 'Well, well, look Billy – Johnny the Cutter disguised as a canary.'

'Shunt my drams, Geronimo, wonders never cease. The last we heard of the charismatic owner and manager of our wonderful little colliery he was going the way of Elvis the Washery.'

'We thought we'd seen the last of you,' said Banger.

'You vultures will have to wait a bit longer for a plate of quiche at my funeral buffet.' Johnny jerked his beak at the crowd. 'It's a good turnout. You'd swear it was 1984 except we're older and the coppers are younger. One half look as if they should be doing their homework, while the others look like they're missing netball practice. Hardly any fit their uniforms.'

'It's not like the old days when we had those big bastards from the Met jumping on us,' said Banger.

'And soldiers in police uniform,' said Geronimo throwing the pallet slat into the fire. 'It's only been a bit of push and shove so far but now word has got around, these climate-

273

gloaters, Council arseholes and kiddie coppers will soon find out what we're all about.'

'I've a plan to charge them in two waves,' said Billy Donkey. 'I count to three and give the signal for the first wave to charge in. Thirty seconds later I'll signal a second wave charging in behind the first. They won't know what's hit them.'

'Has anyone seen the colliery team?' said Johnny, unimpressed.

'We haven't seen them all morning,' said Banger.

'Where are they?'

Horner pushed his way through the crowd. 'Is that you in the birdie mask, my old miner buttie?'

'Horner, what are you doing here?'

'Supporting an old Clanger workmate and looking out for my new boyfriend.'

'He and Lippo are, you know ...' explained Jayden.

Horner waggled his eyebrows. 'He said he was a miner and I thought, I haven't had one of those before, and the rest is history. Of course, I had to bring him out but it didn't take much. Johnny, you should've told me it's Tinkerbell central up here in Coed Mawr.'

'Poor Lippo,' said Johnny to Jayden, 'he doesn't know what he's let himself in for.'

'How's retirement treating you, my old Clanger buttie?'

'It's a bit too quiet for my liking.'

'Let's liven it up.' Horner waved over the Clanger team. 'I've found him. He's here with his lovely coal miner mates.'

'Sound,' said Mohammed, touching a huge ham fist with Johnny and nodding to Geronimo, Billy Donkey, Banger and the oil drum miners. Lucy and the girls took turns giving Johnny hugs while Moses shadow-boxed and showed off his high kicks.

Joel dawdled behind them. 'I didn't want to come, they made me, but I am a qualified first aider so I might be useful.'

'No "anything goes" pervy stuff if you're administering first aid.'

Joel rolled his eyes. 'You haven't changed a bit, still moany.'

Marilyn appeared, towering above him in a lace-up black leather jump suit and purple Doc Martens. 'Now I get it. When you said about opening a coal mine under your shed, you were serious.'

'Marilyn and my old Clangers, it means a lot to me you've all turned up today when it really matters. I've misjudged you.'

'I told you they think a lot of you,' said Marilyn.

Geronimo looked suspiciously at Joel. 'Are they all on our side?'

Parvinder arrived followed by Team Singh and the allotment tenants. 'Johnny, is that you under the mask?'

Johnny turned to Jayden. 'Great disguise, this.'

'Are you OK? The last time I saw you, you were unconscious in a hospital bed muttering about Margaret Thatcher.'

The miners grumbled and collectively spat into the oil drum fire.

'Parvinder, it's good to see you. But you'll give us all a fit saying the M- and T-words together out loud.'

Parvinder put a hand to his lips, 'Gentlemen, my sincere apologies.'

'Anyway,' said Johnny, 'thanks to you all for turning up today and supporting us and our small colliery …'

'And our allotment plots,' said Hoss from under his ten-gallon hat. 'They want to bulldoze the whole allotment.'

'What?'

Vince adjusted his bandana and swept back his hair. 'See

those suits in hard hats waving clipboards at the lorry drivers? They're 'elf and safety dudes, and they've declared the whole allotment unsafe.'

'It doesn't make sense,' shrieked Betty Bingo.

'How they can arrive at that conclusion just by looking at it, without any thorough investigation, or survey and without engaging in dialogue with the tenants is beyond me,' added Parvinder. 'It's moving far too quickly for my liking.'

'It's because film of Councillor Jacques falling into the sinkhole went viral,' said Johnny. 'I knew those knickers would come back to haunt us.'

Hoss clicked his knuckles. 'If anyone goes near my saloon they'll get a fight like the O.K. Corral.'

'Listen fellas, I'm really sorry for all the …'

'Don't have a downer,' said Vince serenely, 'we appreciate the wisdom behind what you did for the kids. It's good karma by the bucket-load for you from now on.' He placed a marigold into Johnny's overall pocket.

'Thank you, Vince.'

'And if these sons-of-bitches think they can drive JCBs over our allotment plots,' he assumed a cat stance, uttered a Bruce Lee chicken noise and kicked a hole in a pallet, 'they can eat shit and fucking die!'

'This reminds me of the solidarity we had in the Eighties. Everyone standing up to be counted, when it counts, and I thank you all for being here, but I've got to love you and leave you.'

'What,' said Horner, 'you've only just got here?'

'I was stupid to think I could be useful outside these gates. If I show my face I'll be first on the arrest sheet and I'm not wearing a mask all day.' He put a hand on Jayden for support.

'I'm going up to the colliery with my grandson and Charlie to see what can be done.'

'You can't go up there,' warned Billy Donkey. 'If this lot have their way they'll be pumping it full of concrete in five minutes.'

'I have to do something, anything, even if we are on a loser.'

Geronimo kicked the oil drum and a pulse of orange cinders twisted up into the air. 'We're used to being on the losing side but that doesn't mean we have to put up with these arrogant outsiders gloating in our faces about the death of coal. Who the fuck do they think they are? They're having it today.'

'As long as you can hold them off until I get up there. For those who don't know, Billy Donkey has a plan and any plan is better than no plan at all. He'll be glad to tell you all about it, tar-rah.'

Jayden helped Johnny back to the taxi. Charlie opened the cab door.

'Understandable, considering he has recently had a myocardial infarction,' said Banger, 'and has two prolapsed discs.'

Before getting into the taxi, Johnny pointed at the hi-vis Council officials and shouted back to his friends. 'The Council incinerator plant is pumping thousands of tons of CO_2 into the atmosphere while burning our recycling. These arseholes do far more damage to the climate than if we were still burning coal.'

Geronimo raised a chant at the hard hats, 'Scabs, scabs, scabs, scabs ...'

The chant grew throughout the crowd. They pointed

fingers at the gaggle of Council officials in hi-vis dickhead orange who did not want to be visible any more.

Johnny, Charlie and Jayden got into the taxi and it reversed back along the crowded allotment road.

At the allotment gates Clayton went on point like a gundog.

'There he is,' said Clayton to the Police Superintendent. 'That's Johnny the Cutter. He got into that taxi.'

Supt Abara looked at her watch and stood firm.

Clayton harboured doubts about the female Superintendent. 'Aren't you going to arrest him?'

'I saw someone in a canary mask. It's true we intend to interview Mr Morgan but I believe he's currently in hospital following heart surgery. Even if it was Mr Morgan I'd not inflame this situation any further. I've the safety of my officers to consider.'

'It is him, he incited the crowd and now he's getting away.'

'Mr Clayton, I thank you for your invaluable advice and local knowledge in this matter, but if you'll now please move along and let us deal with policing this incident.'

Supt Abara nodded to a Sergeant.

'Yes, Ma'am,' said the Sergeant ushering Clayton and Smithy away from the allotment gates and into the crowd. 'Stand clear please, gentlemen.'

Smithy stroked his rugby ball as he moved along. 'Policing has gone downhill since my day. We all looked after each other back then. We'd get stuck in, do anything we liked and got away with it. All you had to do was tell lies in court.'

Clayton resisted the Sergeant. 'You don't know who you are dealing with. They may look old and decrepit but they are hardened militant trade unionists. If it wasn't for the likes of us they would've brought this country to its knees.'

The taxi carefully reversed through the middle of the reformed Abercwmcoedmawr Colliery Brass Band led by wheelchair-bound Dai One-Stick. He tapped the baton on his portable oxygen tank and started the band with the rousing 'Men of Harlech'. Behind the band marched miners under the tasselled lodge banners of Trewatkins and Abercwmcoedmawr. Behind the banners, bagpipes shrilly wailed and a contingent of Scottish miners drove in on a fleet of mobility scooters. Behind the Scots flew banners from Barnsley and Durham, along with flags from Kentucky, Canada, Germany, France, Australia and Chile.

The brass band drowned out the Action Xtinction cacophony of whistles, drums and wails. Trudi Anderson had to do something quick. She swapped the Final Nail for a shaman drum and beat it above her head and ululated to rally her troops.

Flying the Flag

The taxi driver bitched at every bump on the chassis as he negotiated the potholed lane.

When they reached the leylandii hedge Johnny ripped away his canary mask. 'By here will do.'

Charlie helped Johnny out of the taxi while 'Men of Harlech' still competed with the Action Xtinction cacophony down at the gates. Jayden disappeared through the gap in the hedge.

'You live in a hedge? It gets madder and madder. What next,' the taxi driver looked in Dai Milk's cow field, 'green cows?'

Johnny threw cash at the driver. 'What green cows?'

He left the driver questioning his sanity and with Charlie's help went through the leylandii hedge. Jayden held the fence curtain open and they made their way behind the fence panels to the shelf door. Charlie opened the door and a sleeping bag jumped out like a ghost.

'Boo!' said Slouch.

'Give me another heart attack, why don't you.'

'Sorry Johnny, my bad.'

'You will be sorry if you do that again.'

Spider jerked Slouch out the way and helped Johnny through the shelf door. 'How are you feeling?'

Johnny scanned the shed. He noticed the bicycle winder appeared intact while outlines in the fine layer of dust betrayed where North-Eye had salvaged his memorabilia. 'I've had better days. What are you wasters up to?'

'Thought you was banged up in hospital, you oldie git?'

'Lippo, congratulations, my Clanger colleague Horner tells me the word "closet" has had a funeral and you've wised up on your outdated racist views.'

Lippo blushed. 'Don't start.'

Spider pointed out the window. 'No copper, Council dickhead or climate clown is coming up here. We didn't fuck up the climate. The climate was already fucked up and will be just as fucked up, with or without our colliery.'

'We'll slap 'em senseless won't we, bro? You all knows it.'

'And no Juh-Cah-Bah,' said Slouch.

'Juh-Cah-Bah?' said Jayden.

'The big yellow thing with flashing lights down by the gates.'

'Jay Cee Bee headshot!' said Jayden

'You're the one that's headshot.'

Johnny got tired of hearing it. 'Stop arsing about and listen up. Your team captain is speaking.'

Slouch mouthed 'You are' at Jayden.

'We built this ourselves, it's mine, Joanne's, Lippo's, Charlie's, Jayden's, Slouch's, North-Eye's and more than anyone, it's yours Johnny. Are you gonna stand there and give up without a fight?'

Johnny sighed and looked out the window across the crater crisscrossed with police incident tape. The Council had overcooked the crater with yellow and black health and safety tape and a large vinyl sign declared the area a secured site by the Coal Authority. He cast his eyes at the police vehicles, concrete wagons, JCB and the multitude outside the gates.

'Well, Johnny?'

'I knew you'd all come good. You gave Julie's Colliery life, were its heart and soul, and made it into a living and breathing thing. It's so good to see you standing up for yourselves, your place of work and your community, against overwhelming odds, like we did back in the day. But it's time to face up to the fact that it's over.'

Slouch's bottom lip wobbled.

'I thought I'd be of use up here but there's not a full shift left in me. I'll pick up a few things that mean the world to me, my oil lamp, these photographs, old Coed Mawr Colliery, our team, and Julie ...'

'I've been meaning to ask you about that picture,' said Lippo. 'If that's your wife Julie, who's the other bitch?'

'That's me, with my long Jim Morrison hair, you fuck-wit.'

'Shut up.'

'Everyone had long hair in the Seventies, apart from skinheads like Minge Jenkins.'

'Who's Long Jim Morrison?' said Slouch to Charlie but no response came from the scarf and shades.

'I hope you'll keep feeling good about yourselves and walk tall whatever you do from now on. Always remember we achieved something special here which in all likelihood will never be repeated.'

Diesel engines revved and alarms bleeped as the JCB and concrete wagons got set to roll.

Slouch panicked, 'Juh-Cah-Bah!'

Johnny looked to the gates. 'There are lunatics outside our gates who believe anyone caught in possession of coal with intent to supply should be sent down for twenty-five years to life.'

Spider joined Johnny at the window. 'Bring it on. I'm going to be handing out free slaps to anyone who comes in.'

Lippo stood behind Spider. 'I'm with you, bro. You knows it.'

Charlie reached for the door handle. 'They won't expect us to be inside the allotment.'

Jayden stood beside Charlie. 'Nothing you say will stop us, Grandad.'

'I won't say anything then,' sighed Johnny, frustrated at his inability to get involved and wondering what his next step would be.

'Grandad, you won't be safe here. Now you've got your stuff we'll take you back out into the lane.'

'There's no need, I'll manage on my stick.' Johnny ran a finger along the windowsill and rubbed the coal dust between his thumb and fingertip as they left. He looked at the rising exhaust fumes from the heavy vehicles outside the perimeter fence and saw the waving Action Xtinction flags. 'Hold your horses.'

'Grandad?'

'These climate cowards think a lot of themselves, don't they? Showing off and wanting to be seen as heroes saving the world.' Johnny removed a square of folded nylon from the table drawer. 'That's why they wear fancy dress and wave flags.' He unfurled the colliery flag. 'Let's fly our flag so they know who we are.'

Spider reached for the flag, 'Banging idea.'

'Coolio,' said Lippo punching the palm of his hand.

Johnny gave Spider the flag. 'Hoisting the flag for the first and last time will be a symbol of our resistance to the end.'

Jayden lowered the Welsh flag from the pole and Charlie attached the colliery flag to the rope. They joined Spider and Lippo at the crater edge while Slouch filmed Johnny raising the flag. It hung disappointingly limp, but a sudden breath of morning air cleared the leylandii windbreak and the flag flew straight out with a snap like the crack of a whip. They gave it a swift John Wayne salute.

On the allotment road, a cheer went up from the miners as the flag flew above the colliery.

When Spider heard the cheers, he headed down the path. 'Now they know who we are, let's go fuck them up.'

'Keep away from the JCB. I don't want any of you getting hurt.'

'Don't worry about us, you oldie git.'

'Get going Lippo before I put my boot up your arse, and say hello to Horner from me.'

Spider, Lippo, Jayden and Charlie marched down the gravel path. Slouch put his phone away, caught up and skipped into step with them. The white overalls dazzled in the morning light contrasting with the black leather helmets and steel-toe-capped boots.

Jayden waved Johnny away from the shed. 'Get going, Grandad.'

Johnny returned the wave with his deputy stick. 'I'm having a whiff. I'll go out through the fence now in a minute.'

As Johnny watched the team walk five abreast to the gates, Julie's voice sang in his mind. *'Don't worry about them, they'll be fine. It'll be alright, mun.'*

The solution came to him. He felt as if all the weight of the world had lifted from his shoulders and he wondered why he had not thought of it before. 'Yeah, it'll be alright, mun.'

Geronimo

The revving diesel engines ratcheted up the tension while the miners gave the dickhead orange Council officials a renewed rendition of – 'Scabs, scabs, scabs, scabs, scabs.' Supt Abara gauged the mood of the crowd, concerned that one small incident could spark a full-scale riot. Clayton and Smithy took up a position near the nervous Council officials.

'There's not enough old heads among those officers,' said Clayton.

'They're nowhere near up to it,' agreed Smithy, 'too many girls.'

In response to the chanting miners, Trudi Anderson instructed her mimes to hold the KING COAL coffin upright. She surmounted the coffin and a stilts-walker handed her the Final Nail. She held it aloft to rouse her eco-warriors but all eyes turned to a clown in giant red shoes who pushed his way through the crowd.

'They're destroying our tent village!'

A mess of mangled tents lay across Dai Milk's cow field as the Dai Milks drove a formation of tractors armed with a bale fork, hedge trimmer, and cultivator through the Action Xtinction tents.

The Dai Milks gave no quarter to the trespassers and the tractors wrought havoc upon igloos, awnings, gazebos and teepees. Old Dai Milk took great pleasure shredding the tents with the hedge trimmer while Mrs Thai Milk and young Dai Milk sliced up every piece of tent fabric under the cultivator. Dai Milk pushed his jam-jar glasses higher up the bridge of his nose and aimed his bale fork at Trudi Anderson's big brown yurt. The tractor crashed through the support posts and drove around the field skirted in brown fabric like an enormous chocolate blancmange, crushing the remaining tents and leaving a wake of destroyed sleeping bags, airbeds and guy lines.

Costumed protesters returned to the campsite and attempted to halt the tractors. They soon turned tail and ran for their lives as the Dai Milks pursued them across the cow field.

'You've been worrying my cows,' shouted Dai Milk as he skewered a T. Rex with a bale fork prong and raised him by the tail.

Behind the tractors came the Jenkins & Son coal lorry like a Mardi Gras float, full of Trewatkins Zulus armed with Dai Milk's paintball guns. At the wheel, Minge Jenkins barked in his coal merchant's hood, 'Fucking climate Nazis!'

The eco-warriors running to rescue their property ran into a stinging hail of paintballs. On the flat-back lorry, the no-neck mechanic Spanners proved an excellent paintball shot from the hip, blasting Action Xtinction buttocks with great precision. Minja unleashed Rocky and the one-eyed pitbull cross terrified protesters into a hasty retreat. Like Border

Collies at a sheepdog trial, Minge and the Dai Milks drove the remaining activists out of the field and onto the allotment road where they rejoined the throng in front of the allotment gates. Atop the coffin Trudi Anderson becalmed her rattled followers with a sweep of the Final Nail.

Billy Donkey's moment had come. Calling everyone into a huddle, he organised his two waves of attack. 'On my signal, the first wave will charge. Thirty seconds later the second wave will charge. The protesters and kiddie coppers won't know what's hit them.' Miners, Clangers and tenants opened the huddle and stood ready. 'After three ... one ... two ...'

Geronimo cupped hands to mouth, bent over backwards and barked out an almighty shout, 'Ger-on-imo!' He ran as fast as his hip replacement could take him, clotheslined a Velociraptor and dived head first into the startled police cordon.

'The big fucking show-off,' said Billy Donkey. 'He did that to me in Sheffield during the Strike. Fuck it ... three, everyone charge!'

Geronimo emerged from the police cordon with a young policewoman on his back and a young policeman around an ankle.

'Well, well, kiddie police? Do your parents know you're mitching off fucking school?'

'Watch your language,' said the young policewoman.

'You're under arrest,' said the young policeman.

Geronimo shook them off into the melee, grabbed a canary by the feathers and pulled him to.

'Wait,' said a voice behind the mask as the bird held up his wings to protect his beak, 'this is a peaceful protest.'

Geronimo punched him into the crowd, 'Wrong fucking protest.'

Supt Abara noticed the smug 'I told you so' look on Clayton's face and got on her phone. 'Deploy the back-up to Coed Mawr. It's getting out of hand.'

Looking every inch East End villains, three tall, menacing, smartly-attired gentlemen stepped out of a black Jaguar.

The eldest stopped and leaned on a gold-tipped cane. 'Hear that?' he said, delivering a lesson in life to his younger companions, 'that's passion for you.'

He hobbled over to Parvinder who was enthralled by the fighting. 'Hello, my name is Rosser. Do you know where I can find a gentleman by the name of Mr Smithy?'

'Certainly Mr Rosser, Mr Smithy is the gentleman in the neck brace, bandages and Welsh rugby jersey.'

'Neck brace and bandages,' said Rosser looking over the crowd.

Unaware of Rosser's observation, Smithy put a hand under the neck brace and had a good scratch.

'We believe it's an insurance scam.'

'I see, thank you, Mr ...?'

'Singh, Parvinder Singh.'

'Thank you, Mr Singh.'

'You're welcome, Mr Rosser.'

Rosser hobbled on his cane towards Smithy through the chaos of the road, protected on both sides by his two grandsons.

'They're not from around here,' Parvinder said to Gaganjit.

Smithy noticed Rosser at the last moment.

'Mr Smithy?'

'Yes?'

'The Mr Smithy who has a penchant for saying "You'll never find a coal mine in the Home Counties"?'

'Er, I have done, yes? And you never will.'

'My name is Rosser.' He handed his cane to one grandson then removed and passed his coat to the other grandson. Rosser turned and kicked Smithy full on between the legs. Smithy's eyes nearly popped out of his head as he doubled up. Rosser attempted to clench a fist but arthritis prevented closure of his fingers. A grandson stepped forward, clicked his fingers into a fist and stepped aside.

'Compliments of the Kent miners, that's Kent, as you'll find in the Home Counties.' He wound up an uppercut and chinned Smithy out.

'Respect,' said the grandsons.

The fighting intensified and Dai One-Stick, conductor of the Abercwmcoedmawr Colliery Brass Band decided the time had come for the 'William Tell Overture'.

Sentry Duty

Johnny struggled up on to a hoop-backed chair in the shed. The rope of the bicycle winder had lost the groove of the ceiling pulley and he took up the slack to fix it.

North-Eye entered through the shelf door, saw Johnny on the chair with the rope and grabbed his ankles, 'Don't bastard do it.'

'Fuck me hooray, another one frightening the life out of me.'

'What are you doing?'

Johnny wobbled on the chair, 'Fixing the pulley.'

'But it won't be here in five minutes? Hang about. You're supposed to be in hospital.'

'I got fed up of hospital food. I thought you'd be out front.'

'I came for my leather helmets.'

'You've just missed them. They've gone down to the gates on the heads of the team to give out a few slaps.'

North-Eye pined at the empty helmet rail. 'That's them out the bastard window.'

'The team walking down there five abreast was something to see.'

'Good for them. My Volvo's out in the lane if you need a quick getaway. You could escape justice to the Costa Del Crime.'

Johnny got down from the chair. 'What's all this registering us as a company, advertising and half a million pounds crowdfunding?'

'And there's a film company nagging to make a documentary. Luckily the team's got unseen film footage which will keep the story rolling and should be worth a few quid. I don't want any of it, I'd rather have my helmets back in one piece.'

'It's a good job we didn't keep it quiet. At least they'll have a leg-up when it's all over.'

'I had another look in the Glamorgan Archives and the old workings under ours were known as Mountain Road Works.'

'Now you tell me. If you had found that the first time none of this might have happened.'

'I had another look because Parvinder knew about Mountain Road Works from the Historical Society and he told you about them over a beer. Why didn't you bastard tell me?'

Johnny thought back. 'Parvinder did say something. No wonder it went tits up. My head was so far up my arse with the colliery.'

North-Eye collected a rogue model miner from the floor. 'We both knew what we were getting in to. As far as I'm concerned it's been a great adventure and no one is to blame.'

Johnny slapped a mining check on to the table.

Looking over his thick glasses, North-Eye picked up the check and ran his thumb over a detailed relief of colliery headgear. 'A Coed Mawr Colliery shot-firing sentry check, it's extremely rare and in perfect condition.'

'I acted as sentry when Dai Shot-Wire fired the road for the last time in the B.104 district. It's lived in my cutlery drawer since the colliery closed but it'll make a fitting centrepiece to your collection. You've been surveyor, ventilation officer, training officer, safety officer, mining inspector, cost clerk and you've been there for the team every step of the way; with all the duties you've performed, you deserve it.'

A tear appeared in his eye. 'Thank you, I think I bastard do.'

'There's one more duty I'd like you to perform. It's what it says on the check.'

'Sentry duty? You're not shot-firing?'

'Take up a sentry position near the Bollywood shed. Make sure no one, especially the team, passes for the next five minutes or so.'

'That's a big ask. What are you up to?'

'A surprise worth waiting for. I'll do what I have to do and be sat on the bonnet of your Volvo in no time.'

Unconvinced, North-Eye looked Johnny in the eye as they listened to the 'Scabs' chant at the gates.

'We've got a lot of friends out there,' said North-Eye. 'Miners have answered the call from America, Germany, Canada, Australia and more. Thank God for social media.'

'It's hard to believe.'

'Comrades we met during the Strike, from Yorkshire, Durham and Scotland. Rosser even turned up from Kent.'

'Smithy must've had a shock discovering you *can* find a coal mine in the Home Counties.'

The rumble from the crowd notched up as fighting intensified across the allotment road. Sirens wailed as police reinforcements arrived in riot gear and lined up behind a shield wall. The officers announced their presence by beating shields in unison.

'Get going before the Gwent Constabulary, JCB, concrete wagons, and all those climate lunatics roll this way.'

North-Eye squeezed his fist around the sentry check and exited onto the porch. Johnny followed him out. 'Do you like the flag?'

North-Eye squinted up and gave a swift John Wayne salute, 'Bastard brilliant.'

'When I lower the flag you'll know I'm on my way out to your car. Then we can both escape justice to the Costa Del Crime while that JCB chews my shed.'

North-Eye gave the thumbs up, 'Got it.'

Johnny looked up at a police helicopter banking sharply above them as it circled the allotment. 'The sooner you're in position the sooner we're out of here.'

Back in the shed, Johnny opened the sink drawer and removed a ball of string. He dug out the silver Zippo and put it in a pocket. Deep in the drawer he retrieved a snuff tin. Once opened, he picked out a small key and unlocked the master switch casing of the pit hooter.

Yippee-ki-yay

The police cordon began to fracture as the riot gathered momentum.

The allotment gates bulged inwards from the crush and the padlock jumped erect on its chain. With all police eyes diverted to the front, the colliery team strolled to the gates undetected. Spider signalled the team to scatter. They spread out and hid behind the sheds, tooling up with anything they could get their hands on.

The riot police shield wall advanced along the allotment road and the miners and their allies withdrew from the gates to the grass verge above the bottom streets. Regaining control, Supt Abara halted the shield wall and reorganised the police at the cordon. She directed snatch squads to clear the road of belligerent stragglers and sent a police line to back off the climate protesters.

Abara's decisive policing left a solitary clown lying, red shoes up, in the placard-strewn road and a flotsam of mimes and canaries receiving paramedic attention. Smithy left the battlefield on a stretcher with a rugby ball tucked under an arm. The away-day pensioners who thought making a nuisance at a climate protest would be better than hanging around the house all day had received an eye-opener. Nursing black eyes, broken bones, and searching the road for missing teeth, they discovered face paint and tambourines offered little protection against agitated militant ex-miners.

Trudi Anderson regrouped her bedraggled Action Xtinction force safe in the knowledge the experienced Gia and PAM factions had bloodied many a miner in the ruck.

With the situation under control, Supt Abara gave the nod to the Council officials. They waved the JCB and concrete wagons forwards in a cancerous-to-the-climate cumulus of blue-grey diesel fumes.

Geronimo seethed. Cupping hands to mouth he bent over backwards and barked his almighty shout, 'Ger-on-imo!'

The miners charged the cordon en masse, surprising the police who backed up against the gates.

The gates bulged inwards from the crush. The padlock jumped erect on its chain, a link snapped, and the gates flew wide open. Police officers fell backwards into the allotment under a wave of miners and writhed on the gravel like fish caught in a trawl. As the JCB swung around to enter the allotment, the driver braked hard to allow the path to be cleared.

Spider saw his chance. He climbed up to the cab as if with eight legs and grabbed the driver by the throat. While fending off Spider's attack, the driver put his foot down and the JCB accelerated forwards. Police and miners jumped for their lives as the machine hurtled into the committee shed like a wrecking ball. Spider threw the driver from the cab head first into a compost heap and the digger came to rest in the splintered debris.

Trudi Anderson sent in the PAM militants. The black-clad protesters skirted around the fracas at the gates in a buffalo-horn formation and entered the allotment. Jayden and Charlie ran from behind Betty Bingo's shed into their left flank. Using shovel handles, they cracked black hoodies and balaclavas until they stiffened and fell like planks of wood. The two young miners kept up the initiative across the allotment to Hoss's Wild West Saloon.

'Yippee-ki-yay,' said Hoss touching his ten-gallon hat as he stepped in front of the young miners. He entered the batwing doors.

'Yippee-ki-what?' said Jayden.

An activist defenestrated, with pike, from a side window into Hoss's runner beans followed by another out the front window onto the porch. Charlie and Jayden jumped clear as Hoss punched two black hoodies through the batwing doors to drape unconscious over his hitching post. Hoss stepped onto the porch rubbing his knuckles.

'Yippee-ki-yay,' said Charlie.

The PAM activists who stumbled on to Vince the Hippy's plot endured a flurry of blows from a variety of Kung Fu animal fighting styles accompanied by Bruce Lee chicken noises. Betty Bingo administered the coup de grâce to any dazed invaders with a swift clank of a tin watering can.

Slouch sheathed an activist with his sleeping bag. The bag whirled around blindly until Slouch punched where he judged the chin to be. He jumped onto the back of another AX protester, rode him piggy-back and bit his ear. While dismounting his screaming victim, six police officers sacked Slouch like an NFL quarterback.

The Clangers found themselves in the thick of it out on the road. Mohammed bear-hugged his way through the crowd while Moses spun in a blur of roundhouse kicks. Marilyn thoroughly enjoyed swinging an eco-warrior around by the braids.

Lippo, pinned down by the giant arse of a Gia Shock Trooper, squealed for help.

A hand lifted the trooper by the Mohican and slapped her away. Horner helped Lippo to his feet and draped an arm around him. 'I like your white overalls. Can you get me a pair?'

'Johnny said you was out here, bro.'

'He's my hero. I was being bullied and managed out of my job until Johnny came to the rescue and forced Clanger to manage out the bullying manager. Without him I'd be selling my arse for a living and I'm not getting any younger, or prettier.'

'I didn't knows you were handy giving out the slaps, bro.'

'Growing up mixed race and gay in the Rhondda does that for you, and now, butt …' he head-butted a canary, 'I like it.'

'Awesome, bro, now I knows you're hard.'

Horner hugged Lippo tight. 'You'd better believe it, bro. C'mon, let's get arrested and spend a night together in the cells.'

North-Eye witnessed the police regain control at the gates from his hiding place behind Parvinder's water barrel. He anxiously looked at the sentry check in his hand and back at Johnny's shed. 'What's he doing? Something's not bastard right by here.'

In the shed, Johnny hooked his oil lamp onto his belt and switched on an LED head torch. He stepped on the cage platform and threw the ratchet lever of the bicycle winder. The ratchet clicked and clacked, and while disappearing down the shaft he gave the spinning flywheels a swift John Wayne salute. Earlier he had threaded string through the ceiling pulley and, as he descended, the ball unwound and danced in the palm of his hand.

Johnny made his way through the collapsed workings threading the string over the cable grips on the split and broken posts.

He found a suitable place to sit near a Tannoy box, pulled up a board and leaned it against the coal seam. Exhausted, he puffed and panted while hanging his oil lamp on a crosspiece. He sat down and leaned back in relief against the board.

Something caught his eye on the floor. He leant over and picked up a tiny miner of North-Eye's. He blew dust from the figure. 'How are you, butt? My apologies for flicking you down the shaft a while back but the rain pissed me off big time. You can keep me company.' He placed the tiny figure on the Tannoy box. 'You'll have a grandstand view from there.' He gathered up the ball of string. 'You see this string? It's connected to … I'll show you.' He took up the slack, wound it tight around his hand and pulled. The string twanged and tightened along the cable grips, along the collapsed roadway, up the shaft, over the ceiling pulley, around the bicycle winder and yanked on the pull-down handle of the pit hooter.

Hear that Lonesome Whistle Blow

A magic spell fell across the land. The riot ceased as combatants stood like Antony Gormley sculptures staring at the source of the noise; below the flag on the headgear of Julie's Colliery, where the pit hooter sounded a long deep bellowing note.

The pilot of the circling police helicopter worried the noise came from his engines and ran a hasty instrument check.

Geronimo looked up from the canary he held by the scruff.

North-Eye stood as if to the National Anthem.

Minge Jenkins removed his hood in respect.

Tears came to Banger's eyes.

'Mint,' said Mohammed.

Billy Donkey discarded the clown he throttled, caught the eye of Lippo and gave him a wink.

'Awesome, coolio,' said Lippo with a floss dance.

Horner joined in with the floss dance and sang. 'I'll be there, I'll be there, with my little pick and shovel I'll be there, when the coal comes from the Rhondda, when the coal comes from the Rhondda, I'll be there.'

The long bellowing note resonated up and down the small valley. In the park the hooter startled a banditry of coal tits from the rim of the Old Wheel, and Rose heard it clearly while pegging out her washing in Trewatkins. On Coed Mawr Mountain the noise scattered sheep and wild ponies across the hillside.

The hooter fell silent.

A volley of paintballs splattering into riot shields renewed the hostilities. The riot police charged into the paintballs with raised batons and dragged Minge, Minja, Spanners and the Zulus from the coal lorry and to the police vans but not without bragging rights in the Trewatkins Hotel for years to come.

Supt Abara ordered her officers to clear the gates and the police chased the old miners through the allotment plots. The miners were off on a geriatric steeplechase through the prize-winning foliage as they negotiated cloches, cold frames and raised beds as best they could on replacement hips, knees and mobility scooters.

With the gates clear, Trudi Anderson urged her battered force forwards with a swing of the giant nail and they hobbled into the allotment.

'Follow me,' Trudi shouted at the JCB driver as he wiped compost from his overalls. She shouldered the nail and led Action Xtinction up the gravel path towards Julie's Colliery.

Clayton slithered among the Council officials as they gathered behind Supt Abara and her officers. They marched into the allotment in the wake of the protesters but got held up by the JCB as it reversed out of the committee shed debris.

Clayton rejoiced at the sight of Lippo, Horner and Slouch subdued in a crowd of police. Lippo and Horner went quietly, while Slouch ploughed lines in the gravel with his fingers as officers dragged him from the allotment by his ankles.

'Sacha!' screeched Siân and the girls.

Slouch's dad Simon threw off his coat and waded in among the arresting officers. 'Get your hands off my son!'

Half-a-dozen police officers manhandled Spider to a riot van and he resisted arrest with flailing arms and legs.

'There go those most splendid Neighbourhood Watch volunteers,' sneered Clayton with his lateral lisp.

Action Xtinction neared the Bollywood shed and North-Eye apprehensively glanced at the colliery. 'What are you playing at? You sounded the pit hooter, now get out. Don't tell me you've gone underground? You can't have, you've no reason to?' North-Eye stared at the sentry check in his hand and a penny dropped. He jumped out onto the path and brought Trudi down with a rugby tackle.

'Get off!' shouted Trudi. 'I'll have you arrested for assault.'

'You don't bastard understand,' pleaded North-Eye. 'You can't pass a shot-firing sentry. Look at my sentry check.'

'Are you some kind of pervert?'

'I'm not a pervert.'

A Gia Shock Trooper the size of a pro wrestler tore North-Eye away from her beloved leader and hurled him like a rag doll behind the Bollywood shed. 'All men are perverts.' She retrieved the nine-foot nail and with a click of her heels, handed it to Trudi as the Action Xtinction founder got to her feet.

Trudi waved her supporters on. She ran up the path and around the crater rim, wailing like a Valkyrie and brandishing the Final Nail like a spear. She stopped for a breather on the shed porch and waited for the protesters, and media circus, to catch up.

Action Xtinction ripped away the police incident tape and edged around the crater rim. Beaten up Gia Shock Troopers and PAM took up positions either side of their leader on the porch. The dishevelled mimes arrived with the King Coal coffin. Bloodied students and pensioners blew whistles, drummed, rattled tambourines and wailed as best they could through missing teeth. A wretched student held a KEEP IT IN THE GROUND placard upside down until righted by a helpful passing dinosaur. Clowns, canaries and monkeys danced away their aches and pains in a gloating victory jig. A news drone hovered above the shed and higher still the police helicopter circled overhead.

With the JCB revving back into position and the way ahead clear, Supt Abara moved her officers forwards. The hard-hat Council officials followed behind the police and waved the concrete wagons into the allotment.

Clayton's faith in policing had been fully restored. Impressed at how the new generation of officers had handled the miners, he loosened his neck brace, puffed out his chest and grew an inch or two. He laughed at North-Eye sitting dazed with wonky glasses at the Bollywood shed. 'This is more like it.'

North-Eye came to his senses as the JCB thundered up the path. He cringed as a thick black tyre crushed a black leather helmet flat, 'No, not one of my antique bastard helmets.'

The Final Nail

Johnny chatted to his tiny comrade on the Tannoy box while removing the three photographs from his overalls, and arranging them around where they could be seen. 'This is my wife Julie, and my good self, in our younger days. This is Coed Mawr Colliery in its heyday. And this is the team of Julie's Colliery.' He pulled the silver Zippo from a pocket and placed it next to the tiny miner. 'And this is Spider's Zippo I've taken a fancy to. Look after it. It's contraband.'

Satisfied all media eyes were upon her, Trudi Anderson stood on the shed porch and held the Final Nail above her head. Her eyes lit demonically as she raised a chant – 'Death to coal, death to coal, death to coal.' The chant reverberated around the crater.

Like Johnny, Trudi saw Julie's Colliery as a living thing; a living and breathing thing, and she had to kill this climate evil stone dead, like the heroic slaying of a dragon before it spread throughout the world.

Cheers rang out as the Gia Shock Troopers and PAM ripped the Georgian doors from their hinges and hurled them into the crater.

'We stand together today of one mind, to end man's rape of our beautiful planet. The evil pursuit of coal must be eradicated from our good earth and the message must be clear to coal mining criminals the globe over. If you dare open a coal mine anywhere in the world, we Action Xtinction will hunt you down and destroy you.'

Trudi took time out to milk the broken and subdued cheers from her injured supporters. She held the nine-foot length of Norwegian pine with both hands above her head. 'This is the final nail in the coffin of Welsh coal mining, the final nail of that raping capitalist King Coal. Coal mining in Wales is dead, dead, dead!'

Supt Abara stepped onto the porch with Trudi and addressed her Action Xtinction supporters. 'You have broken through an inner police cordon set up to protect the public and you are all committing an offence, namely obstructing police officers from their duty, under section 89 of the Police Act of 1996. I instruct you to immediately and peaceably vacate this allotment.'

A battered pensioner put his fingers in his ears and ululated. The wailing grew in volume as other protesters likewise, with fingers in ears, joined in. Unimpressed, Supt Abara turned to Trudi Anderson. 'I want you and your protesters out of this allotment immediately or you're all under arrest. Tell them to leave peaceably now or you will be the first arrested.'

Underground in Julie's Colliery Johnny switched off his cap lamp and held the oil lamp at eye level. He adjusted the wick to get a testing flame and examined the blue hue appearing above the small arc of orange yellow. 'What do you think, butt, about ten per cent methane? North-Eye said Julie's Colliery is gassy.' He turned up the flame and returned the lamp to the crosspiece.

Johnny picked up Julie's photograph, kissed the tips of his fingers and placed them to her lips. He put the photograph in his overalls over his heart and picked up the silver Zippo from the box Tannoy. He flipped the Zippo open and flipped it shut. He looked at the tiny miner on the box Tannoy. 'Are you up for it, butt?'

Charlie, Jayden, Hoss, Betty Bingo and Vince the Hippy came out of hiding in Hoss's Wild West Saloon and made their way up the gravel path. North-Eye stepped in front of them.

Jayden attempted to push past, 'I'm not letting them …'

North-Eye held out his sentry check. 'Johnny gave me strict instructions. You can't pass a sentry. Get behind the shed and that means the lot of you.'

As he steered them behind Bollywood, along came Team Singh and Parvinder. North-Eye grabbed hold of him. 'You too, Parvinder, and Team Singh, everyone get behind the shed.'

'But what for?' protested Parvinder.

'Just listen to me and bastard duck.'

On the shed porch a cruel smile curled in the corner of Trudi Anderson's mouth as the wailing grew in volume.

Supt Abara lost patience. She stepped from the porch and strode purposefully down the path, 'Sergeant.'

'Yes, Ma'am.' The Sergeant, accompanied by a number of officers, hurried at the double towards the shed.

Clayton could hardly contain his excitement as he anticipated the coming arrest.

Trudi had other ideas and she leapt into the shed, drew back the Final Nail with both hands, and shouted at the top of her lungs, 'Death … to … coal!' With all her Scandinavian might she hurled the nail down the shaft. Elated and orgasmic, Trudi turned to her supporters and the watching media.

As she stepped out onto the porch with hands raised in victory, a tinny voice sounded on the Tannoy behind her.

'*Fire!*'

Johnny released the Tannoy talk button, flipped open the Zippo and rolled the flint wheel down the post.

It sparked.

Johnny and the tiny miner disappeared in a flash of blinding white light.

Julie took Johnny's hand. They were young and as alike as two hippy peas in a pod. A foot deep in marigolds, they walked together, under a sunless azure sky, and into a white light on the horizon.

The explosion flashed through the collapsed workings and up the shaft like the inside of a gun barrel. Roof, headgear and shed panels blew out in all directions. The bicycle winding contraption, shower unit, vacuum cleaners, sink, armchair, hoop-back chairs and tools hurtled through the air. Johnny's shovel spun upwards, sliced through a news drone and caused the helicopter pilot to take evasive action.

Every stitch of Clayton's clothes blew away as he got blasted off his feet and into the King Coal coffin.

Out on the allotment road, the miners and their allies ducked for cover from the blast. Police officers bundling Spider into a riot van released him and hid behind the vehicle. Spider looked back at the explosion in bewilderment.

The report echoed throughout the valley's three villages and further afield in the lower Rhymney Valley where it turned the heads of passengers boarding a train near Brad Pit. A knot of cyclists collided and piled up near the Old Wheel.

Tenants, miners, police officers and Council officials stood up like stoned meerkats to observe the growing mushroom plume above the allotment. The police helicopter beat a hasty retreat from the swirl.

Climate activists shaking in terror wandered aimlessly in smouldering rags while others were set into the leylandii hedge windbreak like scorched Christmas decorations.

The digger driver jumped from his cab as the ground below the JCB gave way and the machine keeled over into the sinkhole like a dinosaur in its death throes.

Behind the Bollywood shed, Team Singh, Hoss, Betty Bingo, Vince the Hippy, North-Eye, Jayden and Charlie emerged from under a covering of baubles blasted loose by the explosion.

Jayden made a move to go to what remained of Johnny's shed but North-Eye held him back and looked him in the eye. Jayden understood. Charlie gave him a hug.

When the smoke lifted, they found Trudi Anderson among the tent detritus in Dai Milk's cow field, impaled like a sausage on a stick upon the Final Nail with a big look of *'I'm so bastard stupid'* on her face. Dai Milk's green cows did not know what to make of it.

For the rest of the day, the remaining pubs and clubs in the three villages of the small valley saw unprecedented business. Generally agreed to be the best time anyone had enjoyed in the valley since the Miners' Strike, glasses were raised to Johnny the Cutter, and Julie's Colliery.

In the next ten days, as Trudi Anderson hovered between life and death, extensive candlelit vigils were held throughout Scandinavia in her honour. The thought of personally contributing to global warming via her injuries significantly aided Trudi Anderson's recovery.

It's a Working Man I Am

One year to the day, North-Eye waited patiently outside the cemetery.

Fresh from a talk show tour of the United States, where the team had kept the story of Julie's Colliery rolling, he toyed with two miniature figures in his hand. The years had rolled back for the old surveyor with a Joanne the Cutter make-over of designer glasses, designer stubble and a lacquered quiff to his thin grey hair. He looked up when two black Audis arrived at the cemetery gates.

Jayden stepped out of the driver's side of the leading Audi and a shapely leg with an unusual blue scar slipped out of the passenger door. Jayden opened a rear door for his mum and she got out of the car with a wreath of African and French marigolds.

Spider checked the knot of his tie before getting out of the driver's side of the second Audi. Lippo and Horner, attired in twin three-quarter length jackets and with matching multi-piercings, got out of the back, and adjusted one another's tiepins.

A familiar old white van drew up alongside. Slouch, just as immaculately suited and booted as the others, albeit with his top shirt button undone and tie the worse for wear, jumped out of the van – which had had a make-over re-spray of wrap-around decals – 'Sacha's Dog Grooming and Walking Service'. Slouch released Britney from the back of the van and savoured a moment to fondly stroke his old sleeping bag, now the van dog blanket.

North-Eye filled with pride as the smartly-dressed team approached the cemetery gates. They entered the cemetery together and met others along the way who got into step behind them: Geronimo, Billy Donkey, Banger, the Dai Milks, Spanners, Minge, Rose, Minja, Pea-Brain and a line of gormless Trewatkins Zulus. Mrs M, Parvinder, Team Singh, Hoss, Vince the Hippy and Betty Bingo and other allotment tenants joined the impromptu cortège, and they were joined by a full headcount of the Clanger team.

They gathered at the graveside and stood before a large object covered in a white sheet.

Jayden stepped forward. 'Thank you all for coming. As you know we never did find my grandad but he told me there was something he really wanted to do in the cemetery which he never got around to doing, so the team got together and ...' he pulled on a tasselled rope, '... he told me he wanted something more elaborate.'

The white sheet dropped away and revealed a monument topped with a marble cutter drum. The centre of the cutter housed a relief of Julie and Johnny modelled from the shed photograph.

Lippo started a round of applause. 'We all knows that's coolio.'

'Fuck me hooray, Johnny would love this,' agreed Horner.

Jayden and Joanne laid the marigold wreath at the monument base and they stepped back to see the big picture. 'Do you think they would like it, Mum? Of course, he's not in there with Gran but you know what I mean.'

Joanne wiped away a tear and Spider locked arms with her.

North-Eye positioned miniature figures of Julie and Johnny on the monument.

Slouch stepped forwards with Johnny's long-service award and placed the glass trophy next to the miniature figures. Marilyn and the Clanger team gave a round of applause.

'Awesome,' said Mohammed.

Slouch gave the Clanger team a smile and a bow.

'They're not clapping at you,' said Lippo, 'they're clapping because it's a Clanger award, headshot.'

Geronimo handed Banger a tissue to wipe his tears and blow his nose. 'Can't we find a little colliery of our own, Billy? We've more time now we've had the push from Deep Mine Museum.'

'It's our own fault,' said Billy Donkey, 'recommending these youngsters for our jobs. Our tools are on the bar for the last time.'

'Johnny and North-Eye trained them well. Jayden, Spider, Lippo and Charlie, they've got a job for life in Deep Mine Museum.'

'If they can stop jet-setting around the world earning big bucks telling the story to everyone and his dog,' sniffed Banger.

'Talking of dogs, pity about the smelly one who gets on so well with man's best friend,' said Billy. 'We could've had a full house.'

The gathering relocated to the revamped Coed Mawr allotments. Mrs M ceremoniously declared the allotments open with a snip of shears to a bowed ribbon. A joy to behold to all, and painted with yellow and navy NCB colours, the new committee shed's first function – to host Johnny's belated wake.

Parvinder had secured the future of the allotments by taking out an injunction against the Council regarding their heavy-handed handling of the whole affair. In the media spotlight, the

Council swiftly did a U-turn with an out-of-court agreement. Senior Council official Mrs Jacques took early retirement and resigned her post as president of the Allotment Association. The Coed Mawr allotments were deemed safe following an accurate safety survey and only the damaged plots belonging to Johnny, Bouncer and Clayton were lost and pumped with concrete.

Clayton and Smithy recovered from their injuries, although Clayton's lateral lisp now lisped from the opposite side of his mouth and Smithy spoke an octave higher. They made a series of personal injury claims but were exposed by undercover Clanger fraudulent claims investigators. By then they had long finished with the CMAA and were on the waiting list of a rival allotment in the valley.

At the inquest, affairs at the colliery were surprisingly found to be well above board since North-Eye kept precise notes on training, inspections, gas readings, ventilation, roof supports, water volume, pumping, electrical supply, materials, tools, production and had a detailed plan of the underground workings tied in to Ordinance Survey. North-Eye also produced evidence of his searches for old workings in the vicinity. When it came to safety, everything that could have been done in the mine had been done more than adequately; there had even been a second way out.

The colliery team were gobsmacked at this evidence; they thought North-Eye played with model miners all day.

When Police Superintendent Abara gave her version of events the focus shifted onto Action Xtinction for causing the explosion, as when they broke through the inner cordon, Trudi Anderson defied police instructions to leave and threw a length of Norwegian pine covered in aluminium foil down the shaft. Seconds after her irresponsible act, the colliery exploded, and a friction spark from the foil was suspected to be the probable source of ignition.

No references were made to anyone being underground at the time of the explosion and those in the know kept it quiet, the way Johnny the Cutter would have liked it. Johnny Morgan, whereabouts unknown, last seen miles away in a hospital bed recovering from heart surgery; his mysterious disappearance a problem for the local health board. Rumours regarding his whereabouts added to the mystery as over the years there were unconfirmed sightings at mining operations in Australia, Canada and South America.

North-Eye received a hefty fine he considered nothing more than a smack on the wrist. He explained to the team, 'A fair outcome, after all, I might have been the surveyor, ventilation officer, training officer, safety officer, cost clerk and mining inspector but I wasn't the bastard manager.'

The Local Authority landscaped the three lost plots and revamped the allotment. The team donated the crowdfunding to mining heritage groups throughout the country as they earned more than enough from selling the story.

Johnny the Cutter's wake got into full swing and the tenants and colliery team laughed with the Clangers as Horner attempted to limbo under a table. Spider and Gaganjit roared laughing while re-enacting last year's riotous exploits with Minja and Pea-Brain.

Minge Jenkins, Rose, the Dai Milks and Spanners had bagged a table and tucked into the ample spread. Sitting at the opposite table were North-Eye, Geronimo, Billy Donkey and Banger. They stuffed themselves stupid with sausage rolls, sandwiches, quiche, and washed the lot down with bottles of Cobra beer from Singh's Corner Shop.

When the old miners had had their fill and reclined back bloated, Geronimo grabbed the karaoke microphone and gave his version of 'It's a Working Man I Am'.

North-Eye got up and brushed the crumbs from his tie. He searched out Spider and whispered in his ear. Spider rounded up the team and they slipped away from the wake, following North-Eye up the gravel path as Geronimo gave it his all.

Mrs M had already stolen away from the good send-off and busied herself by planting marigolds around the upright stones of the landscaped rockery on Johnny's plot. She ceased work and watched perplexed as North-Eye and Julie's Colliery team, after exchanging brief pleasantries, passed by and went out through the secret way, through the gap in the leylandii windbreak and into the potholed lane.

North-Eye leaned on a fence post and looked across Dai Milk's cow field while toying with his Coed Mawr shot-firing sentry check. The team lined up along the fence and looked across the field although they did not know what they were supposed to be looking at. Dai Milk's cows paid them little attention. They had seen it all before.

'It's funny how things work out,' said North-Eye. 'When they grilled me in the inquest trying to catch me out with this and bastard that, luckily enough I had the answers and covered our arses with my records, plans and evidence of my mining searches.'

Lippo played with his nose ring. 'Is this a long story?'

Joanne held back Spider's raised hand.

North-Eye put away his sentry check and unfolded a photocopy of a map. 'Anyway, as evidence they produced a copy of a page from an old journal which I found interesting. It proves the Mountain Road Works closed in the early 1860s when the miners left for the higher paid jobs in the new Coed Mawr Colliery. In other words, the old workings only went as far as this potholed lane.'

'There must be a seam of coal just below the surface across Dai Milk's cow field,' said Spider like a terrier on a rat.

North-Eye fanned himself with the photocopy, 'Untouched and waiting millions of years for someone to come along and dig it out.'

'If we find somewhere to sink a shaft,' said Jayden, 'digging down and shoring up the sides ...'

'Of course,' said North-Eye, 'any mining activity would be highly dangerous, highly against the law and highly bastard unpopular with everyone jumping on the climate bandwagon.'

Charlie gave Jayden a hug. 'Then we'll have to keep it quiet, and as long as women can work underground.'

'You'll need someone to sort the workwear and make regular lunch deliveries,' said Joanne.

Slouch scratched his head. 'Where's all this happening to?'

Shh-wing ... the sound of an arsehole vaulting over a wire fence shivered up the lane as Lippo jumped into the field. 'Keep it in the ground? You knows they can all fuck off.'

Acknowledgements

As an ex-miner, mostly spent as a surveyor's assistant at Deep Navigation Colliery, Treharris, south Wales, 1974–88, I still enjoy a good shift on the shovel. While digging a vegetable patch in my garden I came across a few rogue lumps of coal. I buffed up a lump with my sleeve, stared at it for a short while, and saw the premise for *The Miners Strike Back* – What if an ex-coal miner discovered a seam of coal and opened a small clandestine colliery?

A switch marked mining that had been turned off for many years in my mind suddenly switched on. I saw comedy in the story and a quirkiness that might appeal to readers. As an authentic voice, perhaps I could capture a little of the miners' humour before it disappeared for good.

The further I drove a heading into this story the deeper a sense of injustice arose within me. I saw injustices everywhere and they demanded to be heard at every opportunity in the dialogue.

Before I'm accused of climate denial for my depiction of Action Xtinction, I should point out that my house is fully insulated and covered in solar panels. I recycle everything and have done so since childhood in the Sixties, I compost and grow my own veg, I don't drive and I've never owned a car. My carbon footprint is way down there with my dress sense, as my clothes literally fall off before I buy new. I have a Greenpeace vest older than most climate protestors from when I was a paid-up member of the organisation in the Eighties.

Back in the day, Greenpeace were my heroes for putting their lives on the line out where it really happens in the big bad world. I have no such admiration for this current generation of climate protestors who played no part in the demise of coal mining in this country, yet gloat and delight at kicking an industry that's already down and out – it's as honourable as beating up a corpse. I see this as injustice and make no apology for sending a few bullets back.

In this final showdown at the end of the coal age, coal is rarely out of the news. There are good and bad sides to the old industry but with the damage to the climate attributed to burning fossil fuels, the good side is largely overlooked and coal is portrayed as the villain of the piece in a black hat. I found this an injustice and disrespectful to those former miners who are still knocking around and are well aware of the good side. Coal mining should at least be portrayed in a grey hat.

I've still got my NUM union card and I treasure it along with my Greenpeace vest, but the switch marked 'Mining' that suddenly turned on in my mind when I started writing *The Miners Strike Back* can't ever be turned off.

First, a big thank you to my wife Sally who has been on this writing journey every step of the way. Sally is a voracious reader and her honest critique drove the work forwards and improved it no end.

A big thank you to my beta readers: Leanne Dicks, Owen Edmonds, Alex Ham, and Joseph Dicks. Thanks also to the eccentric Jeremy Swattridge, and to Gareth Willis. The outrageous Ross Jones also deserves a shout-out, as does Paul Young.

I'd also like to thank all my former mining colleagues at Deep Navigation Colliery for their humour, with a special mention for fitter Robert Brain MBE, and Huw 'Chunky' Williams. At Deep Navigation Survey Department: Unit Surveyor the late Peter Evans, Steve Picton, and the late Robin Withey for Johnny the Cutter's catchphrase.

Thanks to all the team at Y Lolfa, particularly Lefi Gruffudd and my editor Eifion Jenkins, Carolyn Hodges and Eirian Jones.

I found YouTubers Alyssa Matesic, Abbie Emmons, Harry Bingham and Natalia Leigh all helpful sources during rewrites.

Also by the author:

A refreshing look at a sport devoid of modern commercialism, this is a
lively story full of colourful characters, and is a revealing glimpse into
social history and the passions of the working man, as well as a fascinating
insight into what can fairly be claimed as Wales' first national sport.
£14.99

Also from Y Lolfa:

£9.99

£9.99

Ask for a print quote!
www.ylolfa.com